stributed by Beverly Content LLC

ver design by Sheila Parr
ok design and composition by Sheila Parr
ver images © Barbol / Shutterstock, Nerijus Juras / Shutterstock,
vid Papazian / Shutterstock

taloging-in-Publication data is available.

nt ISBN: 978-0-9987657-0-9

nted in the United States of America

st Edition

Jennifer Farrell Vreo

The

RELUCTAN

ROBBER

JENNIFER FARRELL

For Elaine and John Farrell
and Bill Voss

CHAPTER ONE

Stephanie was standing in front of her freezer, trying to choose between a microwavable meal and a dish of Blue Bell ice cream, when she got the call. She knew right away this was not routine. At least it wasn't routine for her, and it definitely wasn't routine for Forsyth.

Tom, her boss at the *Bee*, said something had come over the scanner, a possible robbery or homicide. He was giving her the heads-up because of her latest story. Maybe this was another in the recent series of break-ins. Maybe they had even caught the guy. If that happened, it would be a big story for her. She shut the freezer door and headed for 902 Magnolia Lane. Lucky for her she knew her way around Forsyth very well.

Stephanie rounded the corner, slowing her car as she approached the police lights. She parked, turned off the ignition, and sat, just getting her bearings. She could see five people, two in police uniforms, all clustered in a yard inside a crime scene bordered in yellow tape. One was wearing a white coat, then there was a photographer who was so young he looked like he needed his mother's permission to be there, and Michael McKay—Mick. For Forsyth, that was just about the entire law enforcement community.

She opened her car door and walked toward a small knot of people. Stephanie stood next to a man in shirtsleeves, his tie loosened. He was talking to an older woman with a silver ponytail. Stephanie decided on the direct approach.

"What happened?"

"Not sure, but it looks like somebody shot Edie Spence and the pizza delivery guy," the ponytailed lady said.

"I can't believe it. In Forsyth? It doesn't make any sense," the man responded.

Stephanie had a feeling that the man would be more likely to talk to her, so she shifted her focus to him smiling sweetly. Sure enough, he told her that they were standing in front of Edie Spence's house. She was a nurse, his neighbor, and this was a real quiet neighborhood. He didn't know who called 911, but it might have been the man sitting sideways in the open police car with his dog resting on the grass in front of him. Meanwhile the ponytailed lady only nodded. Stephanie was good at picking the right man at least some of the time, she thought.

The man repeated that he couldn't believe it. It was obvious to Stephanie that, believe it or not, something bad had happened here. And it really was unbelievable. Forsyth was the kind of place where everybody followed the high school football team, where there were concerts in the park in the spring. The house she was standing in front of was a perfect example, with its green paint and crisp, white trim. Even the signs at the town's entrances announcing "Forsyth: The Safety City, Population Twenty-Three Thousand" were dust- and dirt-free.

She knew it wasn't perfect. After all, she'd grown up here. Now she reported on stolen laptops at the high school, the occasional domestic disturbance, and the latest robbery. But still, a double murder? If this actually was a double murder as the neighbor had guessed, it would be a huge deal for her and the paper.

In Forsyth, the paper hung onto readers by reporting on all the local news: sports at the high school, church events, weddings, funerals, car accidents, and stories about the city council. The news in the *Bee* wasn't going to be found on the Internet. Like the story about Frank Lamby having one too many and veering off the road into the Lone Star Chevrolet lot, sideswiping not one, not two, but an unbelievable fourteen cars before coming to a stop and hopping out wearing nothing but sunglasses and a hat. You had to get the *Bee* to read that story. That Stephanie still had a job was due to a mixture of skill, marketing, and just plain luck. At least she had an in with the Forsyth police.

Forsyth was lucky to have Michael McKay heading the department. She had talked to Mick about enough DUI's, car crashes, and scuffles at the high school to get to know him, and, for that matter, respect him. One of the first times she had met him, when she was still married, they had talked about the reluctance of domestic abuse victims to come forward because their names would appear in the *Bee*: everyone would know. She'd run into him at the hospital while doing a story on the importance of early detection in breast cancer.

Mick was at the hospital checking on a woman who had fallen off her ladder for the second time in two weeks. She had a black eye and two cracked ribs. Her husband had brought her in. Again. The doctor called Mick about his suspicions, but the woman hadn't wanted to change her story. Mick had pressed her, but she didn't want the whole town reading in the *Bee* what really happened at her house on Friday nights. Mick expressed his frustration about the situation to Stephanie. She could see his point. She ran it by Tom, explaining why privacy in certain matters was better for the community. So, the *Bee* had dropped domestic disturbance calls from "Police Beat."

That was the beginning of their collaboration. Any reporter knows you have to get along with the police, but she had real respect for Mick. He seemed to respect her, too. She ran the information he wanted to get out, like the problems he was having with kids driving too fast on Fifth Street. Stephanie had done an exposé of sorts about the high school kids racing on Fifth. Parents who read the articles proposed posting groups of volunteers along the first four blocks past the high school to patrol the area. That slowed them down.

Of course Mick had not been too pleased with the latest story she had been running, but they weren't supposed to be completely buddy-buddy. The very nature of their jobs shaped their perspective. Even though they were both doing the same thing—trying to find out what happened—they came at it differently. He was skeptical and, despite her training as an investigative journalist, she tended to take a warmer view of human nature.

Finally she saw Mick glance her way. She held up her hands like she was praying, tilting her head to the side. He held up a finger indicating just a minute, and she nodded. He was wearing his usual uniform of tan khakis, a blue button-down shirt, and topsiders. She imagined walking into his closet and seeing rows of blue shirts hanging next to rows of khakis. He probably slept in them. His hair was trimmed, reddish-brown, always neat. When he turned his serious green eyes on her it always made her feel like he was suspicious of whatever she was saying. If she had told him she had a grilled cheese for lunch, she was sure he would look at her with doubt and chew on his perpetually chapped lips and think she had the tuna salad.

CHAPTER TWO

Mick looked up to see Stephanie Gallagher standing behind the yellow crime-scene tape.

He usually made an effort to get along with the press. And Stephanie had been reasonable. She reminded him of the woman who did the weather reports on Channel Five, who was always nicely dressed and conservative, but that woman's chest went all the way to New Mexico when she turned to point on the weather map. Stephanie had the same kind of hair as the weather lady, too. Kind of flippy on the ends, like it was smiling. Yes, he supposed it was better to talk to her than to the reporters who would come streaming in from Dallas.

The coroner was checking the bodies, and the photographer was taking every picture imaginable. The funny thing about a crime scene was that it looked so ordinary. Not the epitome of evil or a sight to take your breath away, like you think it's going to be. It was like those magazines in the dentist's office when he was a kid. Find the things that don't belong in the picture: the mitten in the tree branches fluttering with the leaves, the spoon growing along a row of daisies. And yet, it was the mitten and the spoon that you couldn't stop seeing once you'd spotted them.

The pizza delivery guy looked like he was taking a nap on the grass after a touch football game, his hand reaching toward the pizza box. The woman looked like she was testing a mattress, lying on her back with her purse straps still around her shoulder. Ordinary, except that part of his head was missing and her hair looked like it had been dyed red.

Mick shouted over at Mason to take the temperature of the pizza the kid had been delivering.

Mason said, "What do we need to know that for?"

"Just take the temperature! Let's get as much information as we can! Do you want to sit in court and have some smart-ass lawyer say it couldn't be his guy because the pizza was already cold?

"Don't let anybody walk on the grass until the photographer is done—and make sure we get pictures of everything!" he added.

It wasn't like he had never worked a big crime scene before, but it had been a while, and he hadn't been in charge then. He had to fumble around in the trunk of his car to find the yellow crime-scene tape. When he located it under a bag of sand, it had been covered in a fine dust. Now he felt the weight of responsibility pressing down on his shoulders like that sack of sand.

And he really was responsible. He immediately recognized the gun that the dog walker witness had given Mason. It was the gun stolen from one of the victims of the recent break-ins. Mick had good reason to pay special attention to a stolen firearm, but he never expected it to turn up this way, as a murder weapon. Why was his burglary suspect carrying the damn gun? Really, the thief had never even broken in before, just committed crimes of opportunity.

Mick didn't need a forensic team to tell him the guy was a good shot who knew what he was doing. Hitting two people with shots to the chest and head when you are under pressure is not as easy as it might seem. But, that didn't really narrow things down here. There were a lot of hunters in Forsyth.

Maybe that explained the dog walker, too. Mick glanced over at the man with his head in his hands, still holding his dog's leather leash. The dog was a huge black Lab. That probably explained it. He was a hunter out with his hunting companion; he stumbles on something like this, sees the gun on the ground, picks it up, and fires. He would have to take the man down to the office just to get his statement on tape.

Mick could see Mason taking the temperature of the pizza. The pizza box looked like the kid had just set it down and opened it as if he were serving someone. He could see that a couple of the triangles were missing. That must be the big Lab's handiwork. The man had said he thought his dog ate some. Pieces of pineapple glistened in the box like shiny fake jewels on the velvety tomato sauce.

It was from the same pizza place they ordered from at the station, although he didn't think he'd ever seen this delivery guy. Not that that made it any better, but Mick hated to think the dead kid was somebody he had crossed paths with, like that made it even more his job to keep the guy alive.

Looking back over his shoulder at the bodies on the ground made him feel determined to catch the bad guy. In a way it was a shame the man with the dog hadn't tried to shoot the killer instead of just shooting in the air. But wait; what was he thinking? That would be all they needed, citizens taking justice into their own hands.

Mick wanted to get back to the office to talk to his only witness in private: the man still had his head down, like he might witness another terrible scene if he looked up. Mick asked one of the men with a squad car to let Mason use the car to drive the dog walker to the office. Maybe he could get enough from the dog walker for an ID.

Mick stepped over the yellow tape, started toward his car, and motioned for Stephanie to walk with him. She had been standing with her hands folded like she was praying, pleading for a chance to talk to him. With her head bent sideways, he pictured her with a halo sliding off. The little crowd of neighbors parted to let him pass. Not until he opened his mouth to talk did he realize he was angry with Stephanie.

"OK, so I know how you love alliteration. Well, your poor Reluctant Robber just turned into a murderer! I guess that makes you a Reckless Reporter and me a Determined Detective. You practically told the bum he had every right to steal in these hard economic times. I guess he just took it to the next level! And now two innocent people are dead."

He could tell from her intake of breath that he had hit his target, but the first thing she said was, "How could you possibly know it was the same guy? How could you know it was the Reluctant Robber?"

Once a reporter always, a reporter, he thought. Right now, he didn't want to give her any more facts than he already had. To be honest, he didn't even want to talk to her at all. "The gun . . . you must have found the stolen gun," she said.

"Double homicide, still under investigation," he said in a flat tone.

He slid into his car, but, as he started to close the door, he felt deflated, a little guilty about tearing into her.

He turned before closing the door and said, "I'll fill you in on some more of the details when I can. We'll probably have some kind of statement for the press in a couple of hours. And Stephanie, do me a favor and keep the Reluctant Robber stuff on hold til I make a statement. We need to find this guy. For what it's worth, I agree with you, the guy is probably some kind of desperate amateur, but that only makes him more dangerous now."

Mick sighed. Poor timing for a temper tantrum. At least he hadn't yelled what he'd been thinking since he read her article: *Wrong, wrong! He's a burglar, not a robber.* You'd think a reporter would know the difference.

He closed the door and started his car as she held her hand in a wave. He put his car in drive and started down the road without so much as a glance back at her or the crime scene, otherwise known as somebody's home. He usually drove pretty fast. After all the years of driving a squad car, he was used to people giving him the right of way, getting out of his way. No one ever passed a cop. Tonight he drove slowly through town.

He loved Forsyth. He had a "Forsyth: Love or Leave It" bumper sticker on the back of his truck. Funny to think that if his life had gone according to plan, he would have seen the world but missed Forsyth. He'd always dreamed of flying. But it hadn't worked out. He had thought he had perfect vision; his nickname was Hawk Eye. But it turned out he was color-blind, just enough to keep him from his dream.

He turned north on Beldon and watched the people in the Safeway parking lot pushing carts and loading bags into their trunks. They hadn't yet heard what had happened. They would soon enough.

CHAPTER THREE

Mick could see Mason and the dog walker pulling up next to him in the station lot. Mason parked a couple of spaces over and left his car door open. The dog walker got out of the front seat and turned to open the back door for his dog.

The dog was spinning around and around on the seat, first to Mason's side and then back to the witness's side, trying to find the best way out. Finally, the man grabbed the leash and yanked. The dog landed at his feet with a thump, made a noise that sounded like "chuff," and looked up at his master with a "Now what?" expression.

While the guy was pulling the dog to him, Mason (holding his nose) left all the car doors open to air it out and then turned to Mick.

"Sorry about that," the walker said, although Mick was pretty sure he hadn't seen Mason's gesture. "I should have thrown these away before I got in the car. I just wasn't thinking."

As he was talking he was untying a couple of plastic bags from the leash. It was a big dog, and Mick thought, *I'd rather have a Chihuahua than have to pick up that much shit.*

Mason gestured to the trash container at the side of the building, and the guy trotted over and tossed in the two sacks. The three men and the dog walked up the ramp and into the building. When Mick turned to point the way to the conference room, he got his first real look at the guy. First impression was that he was pretty shook up. He was in his late forties or early fifties and in pretty good shape, maybe a little over six feet and one-ninety. He was wearing sweat pants with longhorns on the bottom and a gray, long-sleeve Nike shirt with the sleeves pushed up. He wore a plain wedding band and his watch was nice, a Rolex. He looked familiar to Mick, but that made sense.

Forsyth was a small town, and Mick had probably run into him at some point.

The man was petting his dog and murmuring, "It's OK, it's OK." Mick wondered if he was trying to reassure the dog or himself.

"Let's sit in here," Mick said as he opened the door.

The room had one long rectangular table and five chairs covered in navy blue fabric with gray dots. The guy sat down heavily, like he had just finished a marathon. Maybe the Lab sensed something, because he put his big head on the guy's lap and looked up at him. Mason slid into the chair across from him. Mick sighed as he pulled up his gaze from the dog to the man.

"Can I call my wife and tell her I'm OK and to come and pick up Rex?"

"Sure," Mick said. He gave Mason a nod and said, "We'll have someone call her right away. Write down the number, and while we're waiting for her to get the dog, let's just run through your story real quick. Hey, you know the dog was a witness, too." He tried for a light touch, but Mason and the man just looked at him. Joke or not, it was true. The dog was at the crime scene. "Get a fur sample from the dog before he leaves," Mick said, hoping he sounded in control and like he knew what he was doing.

He passed Jackson a pad of paper and pen. Time to get started. Mick said, "OK, name?"

"I'm Jack Jackson." As soon as Jackson said his name, Mick recognized him. Jackson ran the biggest business in town, although these days that wasn't saying too much. Mick had a flash of the signs coming into Forsyth: "Welcome to Forsyth, The Safety City." Safety meaning the seat belts made at Jackson's plant.

Mick had just been out there. At the Colby house, home of one of the Reluctant Robber victims, they had found one of those laminated calendars, about the size of a playing card, from National Safety Inc. It wasn't Colby's, so it seemed likely the thief had dropped it.

Jackson kept his hand on his dog. Maybe that calmed him down, because he seemed to be getting over the shock.

"My vet told me my dog is a little overweight, so I've been walking him whenever I have the chance. Tonight I thought I'd get in a good walk before dinner. I probably had been walking about twenty minutes when Rex pulled on the leash. I wasn't paying attention, and he nearly pulled me over. At first I thought he was chasing a cat or a squirrel; he does that sometimes.

"He lunged forward, and that's when I saw the pizza box on the ground. Rex grabbed a slice and wolfed it down. I was afraid he was eating someone's dinner. I started trying to pull him away from the food, and then I saw the kid on the ground. I was pretty sure he was dead. Shit, you could see half his head was gone.

"I spotted the gun while I was pulling the dog back. It was just lying next to the kid. I bent over to check on the kid. Out of the corner of my eye I thought I saw movement. The adrenaline kicked in, and I grabbed the gun, thinking I had to protect myself or something. I don't know. Then I saw a guy running away, and I yelled, 'Stop! Stop!' a couple of times. When he didn't stop, I shot the gun in the air. Twice, I think.

"He didn't stop. I turned back toward the kid, and that's when I saw the woman by the porch. I knelt down to check her, but she was dead, too. I got out my phone and called 911, told them I found two people dead and where I was. I walked back to the sidewalk to wait. I knew enough not to touch anything else. I was just getting ready to call my wife when the police car rolled up. I told the officer what I saw, and he opened the back of the car so I could sit down. I guess I was pretty shook up."

Before Mick could ask his questions, there was the sound of knuckles rapping on the door. Mason opened the door and partially entered the room. He turned to the witness and said, "Your wife's here to pick up the dog."

Mick stood up as Mrs. Jackson followed Mason into the room. She was wearing some kind of tennis outfit. Fitness seemed to be a theme in their family. She was slender, but you could see the muscles in her arms when she took the dog's leash. *Country club cute*, Mick thought.

Jackson reassured her that he was all right and said he'd be home soon, with a glance at Mick for confirmation. Mrs. Jackson—Anne, she had told Mick and Mason to call her—slid her eyes over to Mick.

"Oh, yeah; we have a few questions and want to do a few tests, but it won't take long. We'll bring him home in a while." Mick glanced at the yellow legal pad in front of him. Just a few questions.

CHAPTER FOUR

Stephanie watched Mick drive away. For a second it looked like he wasn't moving at all, like he couldn't get his car to go. Even after it started moving he drove slowly, like he was reluctant to leave.

Stephanie shuddered. She would be happy to get out of here, but first she had to get a few facts. She wrote down the address of the sweet, green house, the license number of the delivery car, and the phone number of Antonio's Pizza, written in red and green letters next to a map of Italy on the side of the car. Enough to start.

She climbed in her car and, unlike Mick, drove away just over the speed limit. Her car was an extension of her office. She spent almost as much time in it as she did in her office out by the high school. Her car had empty pretzel bags, a few balls of silver wrapping with old gum in them, and a bottle of water. She reached for it to take a drink and noticed the newspaper on the seat under her purse. She was proud of her piece on the robberies, but was Mick right? Could she have contributed to this crime by sympathizing with the robber? She eased her car into her parking space and picked up the paper.

Reluctant Robber Returns Stolen Items
by Stephanie Gallagher

When Martin Colby was robbed last week he expressed gratitude to the perpetrator for at least leaving him some cash. Now Mr. Colby is again grateful.

Colby reported someone entered his home on March 6 between 8:30 and 9:30 p.m. and stole his wallet after taking out forty dollars and leaving it for him. Some other items of value were also missing, but Mr. Colby was most distressed about his driver's license.

"I am eighty-six years old, and I hate that I have to go get a new one," Mr. Colby said. After the story appeared in the March 7 edition of the Forsyth Bee, *Mr. Colby's license was mysteriously returned to him.*

"I went out to get the paper, and when I picked it up, I found my driver's license lying underneath it. If I would have known the thief was going to return it I would have asked for my little pistol and my eighty-five dollars, too," Mr. Colby joked.

The robbery is similar to four other break-ins in the last two months, where small amounts of money were left at the scene. Forsyth's largest employer, National Safety, has been laying off workers. Difficult economic times seem to be forcing the perpetrator to resort to crime, however reluctantly.

OK, maybe she had sounded a little sympathetic to the thief. It was just a story angle. And it was a crazy story about the old guy getting his license back. It proved something, too: at least one person had been paying attention to her stories. The thief had to have read her first story to know about the old guy and his license.

The *Bee's* offices were full of activity this evening. She put her head down and walked quickly toward Tom's office. He was on the phone behind his desk.

He was checking his watch while he talked on the phone. She could tell from his end of the conversation that he was talking about the news conference the Forsyth police would be having. She wanted to get the details and start preparing for it, but first she wanted absolution from him for Mick's theory about her Reluctant Robber article. She felt like a little kid running home to tell about the bully picking on her.

She waited till he hung up the phone and then told him what Mick had said about the Reluctant Robber being emboldened by her sympathetic treatment of him. Tom, ever the newspaperman, ignored that and asked how the police could know so quickly that it was the Robber. After all, they hadn't been able to get a lead on who the guy was or even exactly how he operated, so how did they know this was the same guy? Stephanie handed him the copy of the paper with her story about the returned license.

"The gun," she said. "Whoever did this must have used Colby's gun."

"Yeah," Tom said, "that could explain it, but how could they have figured that out already?"

She thought. "Well, what if they found the gun at the scene?"

"Could be," Tom said, "like in *The Godfather*, leave the gun and, in this case, the pizza, too. Well, we'll know after the police give their statement. It'll take some time to notify the families, so you have a while to get over there."

"Alright, I'll head over, but I have an idea." She was feeling the sting of Mick's rebuke. "I don't want to write about the murderer. Everyone will be covering this story. I think I can add the most by covering the two victims. After all, they lived here, and we'll have the inside track to that part of the story. Honoring them and not the murderer. What do you think?"

Tom stared off into space, probably reading the headlines in different papers before he nodded and said, "That could work. Try, and let's see what you get. You have some time 'til the official statement. Go."

CHAPTER FIVE

Mick waited for Mason to shut the door behind Anne Jackson and then checked his legal pad, looking at the questions and hoping for answers. "Did you hear any shots as you got close to the house?" he asked.

"No" Jackson said, "I was listening to my iPod, and I didn't hear anything except Garth Brooks."

"Well how about your dog? Would he have heard the shots? Was there anything you noticed?"

Jackson said, "No, no; he's a gun dog, in his day a really good one, and gunfire wouldn't faze him."

"OK, let's concentrate on the man you saw," Mick said.

Jackson interrupted, "That's just it. I really didn't see him, exactly. It was more like I sensed his presence or something. Just kind of a shape."

"OK, that's good. Think about the shape. What size was it? Where exactly was he when you first saw or, I'm sorry, sensed him?"

"I couldn't say for sure about size. I guess medium. He was by the bushes just past the porch steps."

"Could you tell anything about what he was wearing?"

Mick noticed a slight hesitation before Jackson spoke. "No, like I said, I didn't really see him. Just kind of an outline of him."

"Alright, could you tell if he was wearing a cap?"

"I'm not sure."

Mick pressed him. "You could tell something about his clothes, though." He wasn't asking a question, he was making a statement.

Jackson hesitated for another second before answering. "I'm not positive about this, and I kind of hate to say it, but I think for an instant I saw the National Safety logo on the guy's back. Like he was wearing one of our jackets. Lots of people in town have those jackets. I see the logo all the time. But I thought I glimpsed it for a second. I could be wrong."

Mick gave Mason a look. Jackson had definitely seen the National jacket. Between the calendar and now the jacket, it was looking more and more likely they would be back out at National. Maybe Stephanie was right, and it was some poor, laid-off bastard trying to hold it together. If that were true, how to explain the shootings? And not just shooting wild and running, but actually dropping those two.

"Jackson, we need to take your clothes and shoes. We'll give you something else to wear."

"Why do you need my clothes?"

"Well, we need to make sure we have them, since you were at the crime scene, just to exclude you. We need to make sure, if we find fibers, that they didn't come from you. We'll do a test on your hands, a gunshot residue test, too, even though we know you shot the gun, and then we'll take you home. We'll be in touch. You let us know if you remember anything else."

"I will. I want to help as much as I can," he added sincerely.

Mick left him with Mason, but he did not want to do what he had to do next: track down the next of kin.

Before he could get started, Rainy, the district attorney, called to say he wanted Mick to stand next to him when they gave their official statement to the press.

Mick put on a navy sports coat, grabbed the emergency tie he kept in his desk, and went out to meet Rainy in front of the building to say a few words to the press. To his surprise, there was a decent-sized crowd. How the hell had they all gotten here so fast?

He noticed Stephanie Gallagher standing in the crush of people. She was looking at him calmly, seemingly forgiving him for his outburst at the scene. She wasn't so bad. Without her help, Candy Watkins would still be getting beat up once a week. But all he wanted now was to get back to the scene. He wanted to fix this unfixable event.

Mick gave his brief statement. Two people had been found dead, apparently of gunshot wounds. He listened to Rainy give his very brief statement, expressing confidence that the perpetrator would be apprehended soon. Then he headed back inside, ignoring the questions shouted at Rainy and him.

He could see Stephanie Gallagher, but she did not ask about the stolen gun. No one else there understood the significance of that. Not yet.

He walked through the building to the back doors and out to the parking lot, intent on heading back to the Spence house. The ambulances with the bodies were pulling out as he drove up. Sad to see them going with no flashing lights, no sirens. No need. A couple of news trucks were parked on the block. He felt like saying, "Move along, nothing to see here."

But, surprisingly, they ignored him as he stepped back over the yellow tape. He thought of a phrase they all said when he was in school: a world of hurt. That was where he was going. A world of hurt.

There was still a team working inside, including the photographer. The flashes from his camera looked like lightning striking inside the house. Mick walked up the back porch steps and into the kitchen.

The first thing he noticed was the smell of food. A cookbook in a plastic holder, turned to a turkey chili recipe, was placed in front of a simmering crockpot. It made Mick realize he was hungry, which made him feel ashamed of thinking of food at a time like this. He wanted to check and see if the team had found anything inside that suggested the murderer had been in there. So far, it looked like everything had happened outside.

At first glance, the house looked incredibly tidy, everything in its place. They would know more after the husband checked it over to see if anything was missing. The woman's purse had been next to her body, and the kid had cash in his pockets. Maybe Jackson and his dog had scared the guy, maybe he was searching for their cash and that's why he had dropped the gun.

The report Mick got from the team going over the house made him wonder again if the murderer even made it inside. No forced entry, but the Reluctant Robber hadn't ever broken in, so that didn't mean anything. Mick walked to the front of the house and looked out the window. He opened the front door: no deadbolt. Jackson had seen the guy. Maybe someone else had, too.

Mick turned to see the photographer zipping his camera back in its case.

"Why didn't he just run out the front door?" Mick asked, more to himself than the photographer.

The photographer must be from the county, too. Matt—according to the plastic-encased nametag around his neck—said, "Maybe he didn't know they were out there. He sneaks out the door and he runs right into them, panics, and shoots."

It sounded plausible, in a horrible way. Mick could see a framed picture of a happy family sitting on the counter, a father and mother smiling with their arms around a pretty teenaged girl and a slightly older boy. The shooter had erased this happy family, just like that.

Mick turned back to Matt, who was looking at him through the camera lens, and said, "Get the pictures to me as fast as you can."

CHAPTER SIX

Stephanie decided to start with Antonio's, everybody's favorite pizza place. For one thing, she was starving and she could grab something to eat while she chatted with the delivery boy's coworkers.

She looked down at her laptop. It had a yellow Post-it note on it with the victims' names. She used her laptop for most things, but she always had pens and paper on hand, too: an old habit. This would be a delicate operation. The names of the victims had only just been officially released. Adam Moore, poor kid.

She turned into the tiny parking lot in front of the restaurant and went inside. A chubby girl in an Antonio's T-shirt with dark, curly hair yearning to be free from a headband, her head nestled in her elbows on the table like she was just trying to catch a quick nap, sat at one of the tables. Her shoulders were shaking. She was crying. Stephanie could see she was holding in her hand—the one with rings on three fingers—a card from the Forsyth police.

The boy behind the counter stepped to the register. He didn't bother with the smile. Not tonight.

"Pick-up?" he asked.

Stephanie considered. "No, no. I want to order a cheese and mushroom pizza," she said. He waved his hand behind him and she could see the incrementally bigger boxes mounted on the wall: personal, small, medium, large, and jumbo.

"Personal," she said.

She sat down next to the girl and decided to take out her press credentials.

"You must be upset about Adam," she said after the introductions.

THE RELUCTANT ROBBER 21

The girl, Jessica, sniffed a few times and nodded. Her long eyelashes were wet with tears.

"The police just left," she volunteered.

"What did they ask you?" Stephanie said. The counter kid called her number, twelve, even though she was the only customer in the restaurant.

The phone rang and he turned to answer it while she sat back down with her pizza and looked expectantly at the girl.

"They wanted to know about Adam: like how long he worked here and what his hours were, how much cash he carried . . . just stuff."

"Hmm," Stephanie nodded.

"You know what really gets me? I was so happy when the order came in. Tuesdays are usually slow. I thought Adam was going to be really down tonight, because this guy he's been delivering to for like about a year just died. Adam always booked an extra half hour and stopped to visit with this old man. Uncle Tony didn't mind, because the old guy was a regular, and anyway, like I said, Tuesdays are slow.

"When the old man died, Adam was really bummed. He was even going to go to the funeral and all. When I took that order, I was glad Adam would have something to take his mind off that old man."

Stephanie listened, absorbing the girl's shock at a world turned upside down. Old people were supposed to die; she expected that. But not boys she knew. They were supposed to come back and maybe flirt a little.

After she had finished her pizza and talking to Jessica, Stephanie drove back to her office to go over her notes.

Jessica's uncle Tony, the owner, had agreed to hire Adam Moore as a favor to someone from the high school. Adam had been working at Antonio's for three years, on and off. It sounded like a lot of offs, but about six or seven months ago Adam had begun to be a better employee and, according to Jessica, a better person. Tuesdays were usually slow nights, so Adam had been helping make up the boxes between deliveries. He didn't used to help out, but it was part of his new attitude.

He left with the Tuesday night Hawaiian Special. It was the only order he had right then, so Adam had hopped in his car with the pizza all tucked in its warming case. Stephanie thought that if only somebody else had had a craving for pizza, that kid would still be alive. Random.

The story about the old man who had just passed away, the one Adam visited on Tuesdays, piqued Stephanie's curiosity. She checked back through the obituary section of the paper. Usually the *Bee* just printed whatever the family submitted, but, if someone important died, she would write up something.

Stephanie had done a write-up about an executive who helped to found the trucking company in town, which was still in business. After National Safety, it was one of Forsyth's biggest employers. Before that, he'd been the football coach at Forsyth High. She rustled through the *Bee* and found the obit she had written. This had to be the old guy Jessica had been talking about: Harlan Tucker.

Stephanie put the article aside and started in on what would be the front-page headline story of the *Bee* tomorrow. Now Tom was scouting for pictures of the victims. In a small town like Forsyth, that wasn't that difficult.

She finished the article and checked her watch while Tom read over her story about the murders.

"What about adding at least a hint that the Reluctant Robber might be involved? I don't think that would strain our ethics. People are going to put two and two together anyway," Tom said.

"Well, I think you're right; they will add things up. But we'll have more facts in the morning. I think the story stands on its own without that detail," she said.

"Okay, then that's how we'll run it," Tom agreed.

That was the good thing about Tom as the editor: he didn't edit too much.

CHAPTER SEVEN

Mick headed back toward the office. On the way he rolled into the drive-through at McDonald's and ordered a cheeseburger and, just to be on the healthy side, a chicken sandwich. He could wash it down with a cup of coffee while he worked.

What they were doing now was putting together the little pieces of information they had all collected. Most of the information would be incomplete. One way to try and get a more complete picture was to check and see if there were any other witnesses.

Nine times out of ten with a murder, it was going to be a relative or someone else the victim knew well. If this case was going to be in that category, it would either have to be someone they both knew or an O. J. Simpson deal, where the waiter returns the sunglasses at just the wrong moment.

The woman's husband had been out of town—actually, on a plane—at the time of the shootings. That didn't necessarily rule him out, and it could be the woman was the one who was in the wrong place at the wrong time. Maybe someone wanted the pizza delivery kid dead. Or maybe this murder was one of the rare ones, done by a stranger.

Mick had checked the serial number on the gun, although he knew the moment he saw it that it was Martin Colby's stolen gun.

The funny thing about the pizza delivery kid was that they were looking at delivery guys, or guys pretending to be delivery guys, as suspects for the string of burglaries. He had thought the thief was a kid, not some poor guy stealing a loaf of bread for his family like Stephanie Gallagher had hinted in her article. It had to be someone who could go up to a house unnoticed. Someone who might have an idea about people's schedules. They would know more after they talked to all the potential witnesses, or in other words, people who were neighbors just a few hours ago.

Mick unwrapped his food and thought about how much he missed his wife. He checked his watch and calculated her time. He couldn't call now. In a town like Forsyth, if he ever went to the bar out on the highway it would be in the *Bee* before morning. Of course he could drive to Dallas where no one would know him, but he didn't want to.

That was the thing; he didn't want to. When he was younger and out on patrol waiting for speeders he was shocked at the offers he got. Like once, when he stopped a girl, maybe twenty-five and cute as can be, she rolled down the window and said how grateful she would be if he let her off with a warning and that she'd be glad to show him just how grateful—in her car or his. She mentioned specifics. He was never sure if he handled those situations right. The cute girl he let go with a warning, partly because he was so embarrassed, he just wanted to get away from her as fast as possible.

He'd always wondered if that had been the right call, if letting her go without consequences had convinced her that kind of behavior worked. Where had she ended up? Nowhere good. And why the hell was he thinking of that now? Like he needed to add a little sadness to this day?

He sat at his desk and looked over his notes on the break-ins. How could he have known it would turn into a murder investigation? The crowd had thinned out in the office. All of the Forsyth police department, some of the people from county, and a few state guys had been and gone. Might as well go home, catch a couple of hours of sleep, and start fresh in the morning. He checked his watch. It was morning.

CHAPTER EIGHT

In the morning, Stephanie found Forsyth transformed. The front page of the *Bee* had transfixed the town.

When she stopped into the Quick-Mart for a doughnut and a Dr. Pepper, the stand that held the *Bee* was empty. The television news ran a brief story about the murders. The rest of the world had other news stories to follow. In Forsyth, there was only one story. This story. Her story.

Stephanie started out her day with Edie Spence's coworker and friend, Pat. She wanted to shadow Pat for the morning, get a better idea of who Edie was and what it meant to work in hospice. When Stephanie had asked to meet her where she and Edie worked, Pat laughed.

"Well, you can drive around with me. Hospice isn't in a place. We go wherever the patients are."

Hopping into Pat's car, Stephanie said, "Wow, your car is as messy as mine."

"Yeah, you can see I have a lot of junk in here. You know how you hear those stories on the news about someone driving off the road and being trapped in their car? Well, I could survive for a month in mine. And if you think I'm bad, you should see Edie's car! She really might have a kitchen sink in there. Oh, I still can't quite believe it," Pat said, tears suddenly appearing. She reached for a Kleenex and wiped her eyes. Then she squirted some disinfectant on her hands. "We deal with death and dying all the time. In fact, Edie was supposed to go to a funeral today . . . and now this . . ."

"Whose funeral was she going to?" Stephanie asked.

"A patient she had for a long time. A man who used to run Forsyth Fleet."

"Harlan Tucker? I did an obit on him. How long was he her patient?"

"Oh, maybe two years."

"Really? I thought hospice was for when you were dying."

"Well, it is, but we don't have a time limit for how long it takes."

Pat pulled into the parking lot of a two-story building that looked like a cross between a dormitory and an office building. She parked in the slot farthest from the building. "Because we can walk," she said.

She gathered up her bag and Stephanie followed her into the building. The lobby was brightly lit with a desk off to one side of the door and a little sitting area with a couple of couches and chairs arranged in groups on the other side of the entrance.

There was a bulletin board on the wall next to the receptionist's desk. The schedule for the day's activities was listed, along with the menus for the day. There was musical entertainment at 10:00 a.m., seated exercise at 11:00 a.m., bingo at 2:00 p.m., a movie and root beer floats in the great room at 3:00 p.m., a red hat tea party at 4:00 p.m. Their social life was more active than hers. *Well, it's my own fault*, Stephanie thought with a sigh.

Pat must have noticed the sigh, because she glanced back at Stephanie from the desk where she was organizing the paperwork required to have Stephanie tag along. Patient privacy laws were complicated, and Pat was doing her a favor. Of course Pat wanted to get Edie's story out, to talk about her friend. She'd made that clear. *I hope she doesn't think I was sighing because of the paperwork*, Steph thought. Not a good way to start an interview and gain trust.

Paperwork filed, Pat led her down the hall and knocked lightly on the door. A mere formality it seemed, because she didn't hesitate but walked right in.

A frail-looking woman sat upright in a blue upholstered chair. Pat introduced her to Stephanie as Miriam. She was a tiny woman, drowning in what used to be called a housedress, a cross between a bathrobe and a real dress. She had nice tennis shoes on her tiny feet, although she was certainly not going to play tennis today. Her hair was pure white, like she was topped by a snowdrift.

Miriam was working a crossword puzzle, and she peered at Stephanie over her glasses and asked, "What's a seven-letter word for appease that starts with an M?"

"Mmmm, I'll have to think about that," Stephanie said. And, for the life of her, she could not think what the word was.

Pat went on checking, listening to the old lady's heart with a stethoscope. Tests and checks done, she sat back to chat with Miriam. First, questions about her health, and then more general things like "How was bingo?" Miriam told about a visit from her grandson: what a handsome boy he was and how very, very big he was. *Must have got that from the other side of the family*, Stephanie thought. It was amazing, really, how much these patients shared with Pat. It must have been the same with Edie.

Stephanie watched Pat checking a bruise on the old lady's arm and started to pack up her bag. Miriam snapped her tiny, bony fingers and said, "I've got it! 'Mollify!'" Stephanie was impressed.

Pat walked briskly to the next room on her list. The TV was blaring so loud Stephanie could hear it before they even rounded the corner into the room. An old episode of *Bonanza* was on the screen.

Pat lowered the volume before she began to check the woman's feet, which were wrapped in giant, quilted oval slippers with Velcro straps coming over the tops. The woman had steel-gray hair in tight curls, kind of like the Brillo pads you use to clean a grill. But she had big brown eyes and she seemed really happy to see them. Pat asked her how she was, and she said she was feeling a little tired since she'd been up late, studying.

"I've got a big test and I need to study. I'm not sure if I can pass it and so I told the others to go on without me. I just have to pass this test!"

Pat carefully checked the foot that had a wound on it. Stephanie thought, *Note to self: take care of your feet.* Pat, all efficiency, changed the bandage, washed her hands again, and patted the old lady on the hand.

"Get some rest," she told the old woman, but then Pat turned the TV back up to blaring.

Pat had a couple of visits that she hadn't been able to get permission for Stephanie to observe—HIPAA laws—so Stephanie walked back to the lobby to wait for her.

In the lobby there was a wall with a floor-to-ceiling birdcage. Stephanie sat down to watch the birds fly from branch to branch. Little nests had been constructed and were hanging from the branches. They looked more like hornet nests, but the birds seemed to like them and went in and out somewhat pointlessly, Stephanie thought. Although it wasn't like her life didn't seem a little pointless, too.

Her life now was like the stories she had read about people who lost an arm or a leg and yet they still felt like it itched or hurt. Her whole life had changed, and still at odd moments she forgot. *Oh yeah, he left me*, she had to remind herself. She had changed her name back, right away. That was one good thing, at least; she didn't have to be Mrs. Popkins anymore. When people called her Steph Popkins it sounded like a disease. *Oh my God, you have Steph Popkins.* What a ridiculous name that was! She was smiling about that small victory when Pat walked back to the lobby to get her.

"I've got to do a few things before I go over to the funeral," she said as Stephanie stood.

Pat had explained that she wanted to represent Edie at Harlan Tucker's funeral. *And really*, Stephanie thought, *I'm already in the proper mood for a funeral.*

CHAPTER NINE

Mick opened his eyes after what felt like just a few minutes and checked his watch on the nightstand. Six o'clock. Time to get up and face the nightmare of last night.

First, though, he'd call his girls. When he and his wife, Julie, had first talked about this great opportunity for their daughter, Colly, he had thought, *How bad could it be? It was just a little more than two months.* It was funny to feel homesick when you were the one at home. This was a good time to call. They'd be having lunch right about now.

Julie picked up on the first ring. He could hear people talking in the background, traffic noises.

"Can you hear me?" he asked.

"Yes, I can hear you. Are you OK? We heard that two people were killed in Forsyth. Is it true?" she asked.

"How'd you find out about it already?" he asked, thinking *bad news travels fast.*

"One of Colly's friends texted her, so we saw the news when we got up. I've been waiting for you to call. Do you want us to come home? Do you need me to be there?"

Of all the excuses he'd daydreamed of as ways to have them come home early, he had to admit this was not one that had ever occurred to him. "No, there's no point in your coming home. For one thing, I'll be pretty busy."

"Who did it?" Julie asked. She had a lot of faith in him, and she was a detective's wife.

"I don't know. It could be the burglar who has been on a spree for the last few months. You remember."

"Oh my gosh, Mick, why would he kill two people over the petty cash amounts he was taking?"

He could hear Colly in the background asking to talk with him. "Just a minute," Julie said.

"I don't know, Jules. Maybe he felt cornered. Anyway, I want to hear about my girls."

"Okay, love you. Here Colly, it's your turn."

Mick waited for the phone handoff.

"Hi, Daddy! Are you okay? I can't believe something like that could happen in Forsyth. All the kids are talking about it. Did you catch him yet?"

Another vote of confidence. "Of course, we'll get the guy. How's the singing going?"

"Great. Did mom tell you we played at a concert and we got to meet some of the royal family? We were invited to a tea party afterward. It was really fun. Today we're going to do a concert at Oxford. Hey, Daddy, they're calling us to get on the bus. I miss you. I wish you could be here."

"I miss you, too, but I sure am proud of you. You listen to your mom, and I'll talk to you tomorrow. Good luck at Oxford."

Good luck at Oxford. Not words he ever imagined himself saying to his daughter. Mick realized he was still smiling when he went in to shave. He was pretty sure the smile wouldn't last, though. He was in for a rough day, starting with another talk with his only witness.

The National Safety office building was long and low with truck bays on the back and the offices in front. Mick walked up the concrete walk, lined with azaleas in bloom, to the front door. In the lobby there was a sort of museum with information about the company in display cases for him to enjoy while he waited for Mr. Jackson. Jackson came up behind him to peer at what he was looking at.

"That's how my great-grandfather started the company, making woven goods. Then we segued into the seat belt market. It was a good run."

"Was?" Mick said.

"Well, we're tied to Detroit, so when they have problems, we have problems. Come on back to my office. You want some coffee?" Jackson gestured to a corner of the museum where a table was set up with a coffee machine and cookies on a plate. Mick walked over to pour himself a cup and noticed a box with a cardboard display saying "It Is Good to Be Safe." Inside were calendars just like the one they thought the Reluctant Robber had dropped. Mick picked one up and put it in his pocket.

Jackson's office was nice—a lot nicer than Mick's—but not lavish. There was a big desk and a leather chair on wheels, sitting on a plastic square for easier maneuverability.

Behind the desk was a credenza with pictures of golf outings, fishing trips, and team pictures of the Forsyth High Falcons from a variety of years. There were a few football trophies amid pictures of the Falcons. There was a picture of Jackson standing with the governor. *Pretty impressive*, Mick thought as he settled into his immovable chair.

Jackson slid his chair back and sat down. Today he was dressed in a suit and tie, but somehow he looked smaller than he had the night before in his sweats.

"I'm still feeling a little shaky from last night. I had a hard time getting to sleep, playing the 'what-if' game . . . What if I'd gotten there a minute earlier? Maybe I could have stopped what happened . . . or maybe I would have wound up dead, too. I don't know."

"There was nothing you could have done to save those people, but maybe you'll be able to help us find the guy who did it and get justice for them."

"I wish I could remember more details about what I saw, but it was so fast . . . you were right last night when you said my dog was a witness. If he could talk, we'd probably know a hell of a lot more. I'm not sure what more I can add to what I said last night."

"Well, the one thing you said last night about thinking you saw your logo on the jacket . . ." Mick let his words trickle down to nothing.

"I said I had an impression of that, but you know, I see that logo a thousand times a day. I have several of those jackets myself. It could be I saw a jacket and just thought it had the logo on it. It all happened so fast. Do you think that it's important? I mean, there are lots of those jackets floating around this town."

"I know; we're just trying to get as much information as quickly as we can. Some detail you might remember could turn out to be important. I'd like to talk to you about personnel here, too."

Jackson rolled his chair back a few inches and blew air out of his mouth; *whew.*

Mick held up his hands in a wait, wait signal. "I'm not asking for any personal information or anything you feel uncomfortable giving. I just want you to tell me if you know of anyone who is having trouble here because of the slowdowns. Anyone who might have sprung to mind when you realized what had happened."

"Everybody here is having trouble because of the slowdowns, starting with me. But I'm not going to throw names out. Surely you can see how wrong that would be?"

Mick said, "OK, I understand your position. If you think of anything that you can say about your employees, let me know. Just a couple more questions and I'll let you get back to your day. I know you said you didn't get a look at the guy, but you were on the street cleaning up after your dog. That had to take at least a minute or two, right? Is it possible that the guy saw you? Maybe even recognized you?"

He saw Jackson absorb the information in the question. A little shadow crossed his face and he stopped rolling his chair. *Gotcha!* Mick thought. Could be that Jackson wouldn't be quite so reluctant to talk if he thought he might be in danger. *See, buddy, my problem is your problem*, Mick thought.

Mick sat there, waiting. Jackson seemed to be about to say something else, but he hesitated. Finally, he spoke. "He could have recognized me, but I doubt it. I was facing the street and couldn't see into the backyard until my dog pulled me, so I don't think he could see me either. I think he was already running away before I got there. Anyway, I don't think he ran because of me, and he sure as hell didn't slow down and look back when I shot the gun in the air."

Mick wrapped up the interview, thanked Jackson for his time, and put his now-empty coffee cup on the desk. He had gotten what he could out of the meeting. Despite Jackson's assurances that he hadn't been seen, Mick knew he would play out what had happened. The evidence was pointing to a National Safety employee: the calendar, the jacket, the slowdowns.

He wished for the hundredth time that he had spent more time on the Reluctant Robber robberies. Previously, it had seemed like kid stuff—really kid stuff, as in, he thought it would turn out to be some high school kid. He had thought they would eventually find someone who saw something or he thought someone would come home in the middle of a robbery, and they'd catch him that way. Well, he'd been right about someone being home. He'd just never expected the Reluctant Robber to turn violent.

To protect and serve. Mick hadn't done too much protecting, so he'd better serve, and find out who had done this.

CHAPTER TEN

Mick checked his watch as he slid into the car. He had an appointment in twenty minutes at the hotel where Edie's husband was staying with his children. What a shock that must have been, to get on an airplane with your happy life intact and then get off and find out your whole world had exploded—your wife was dead.

Mick was dreading this meeting. Dr. Spence was on the plane at the time of the killings, but that didn't mean anything. He could have hired someone to hurt Edie. He could even have arranged the robberies. But what hitman was going to count on finding a gun to steal and then take the chance of returning the old man's driver's license without being seen? That just didn't make sense. Mick usually favored putting the husband at the top of the suspect list, but he couldn't work Dr. Spence into it. That meant the guy was just some poor slob of a victim of the randomness of life.

Mason had said the husband had been distraught on the walk-through. As far as he could tell, there was nothing taken. Everything was just where it was when he left except, of course, his wife. If nothing was taken, did that mean the murderer never made it into the house? If that was true, why shoot two people? He could have just abandoned his plan and run.

Mick pulled up to the hotel parking lot. The hotel was supposed to look like a Swiss chalet with a sharp, peaked roof. This was not Switzerland.

He walked over to the front desk. Two employees were eyeing

him, both wearing white shirts with striped ties. He asked for the room number of the new widower and they immediately got suspicious. He pulled out his badge. That usually made people tense, but in this case, it was like letting air out of a balloon. They relaxed, and the male employee said, "One-twenty-three," without having to look it up.

"We're trying to keep reporters out. You know, trying to make sure the family gets their privacy," the female employee explained.

"You're doing a good job," Mick said, as he stuck his badge back in his pocket.

Mick knocked on the door of room one-twenty-three and waited. The door was opened by a man in his late thirties wearing hospital scrubs, probably another volunteer from Edie's hospice work. Mick pulled out his badge as the man stuck out his hand. A little awkwardly, Mick shifted his badge to his left hand and shook the man's hand as the man showed him inside, motioning to the other room.

Mick walked past him into a room with two beds and a round table with four chairs around it. A kid who looked to be about Colly's age was sitting with his face in his hands. Next to him was a girl, a little younger, a box of Kleenex in front of her.

Sean Spence pushed back his chair, unfolding from his seated position. He was tall, with clipped blond hair. He patted the two kids on the back and ushered Mick into the other room.

It took only one look at Dr. Spence to know that the man was devastated. So much for Mick's hired-gun killer theory. He stuck out his hand, unsure of the appropriateness of the gesture under the circumstances.

"I'm so sorry for your loss," Mick began. "I know this is hard, but we want to find who did this to your wife. You already helped by meeting at your house and going through it with Sergeant Mason. I just want to ask you again, now that you've had a little time, did anything seem out of the ordinary at your house?"

"No, no, I didn't see that there was anything missing. We keep some money for emergencies in the kitchen drawer and, as far as I can tell, none of that was missing. Edie's jewelry was all sitting on her dresser or in her jewelry box. No electronics were missing. I keep some drugs and syringes at my house: you know, antibiotics, animal tranquilizers, that sort of thing, but nothing was missing there. The kids didn't see anything missing from their rooms either."

"I wanted to ask you about the kids and then maybe talk to them, too, if that's alright. What time did they get home last night?"

"Well, my son goes to SMU, so he doesn't live at home. My daughter drove to Dallas to pick me up at DFW, and then we were going to drive back together."

"That's right; you were out of town on business. What kind of business?"

"Well, Edie always says monkey business," he said with a smile, and then, just like a shadow passing over his face, it was gone. "I guess I should say 'always said,' but you know, I still can't believe it. Before you got here, the kids and I were talking, and my daughter said maybe we should call and check on Adam Moore's family. And I thought about what a great kid she is. Then I thought, 'I'll have to tell Edie, she'll be proud of her,' and then I remembered . . ." Sean had to stop and compose himself. "But you asked about my trip."

"That's OK, take your time."

"My old college roommate has a ranch in Montana, and I go up to see him every year, maybe help with breeding. It's usually a fun trip. Oh, my God! I just realized I didn't call him to let him know. Hold on a minute."

Sean went over to the other room and Mick heard him ask his friend to make the call for him. Then he came back and sat down again.

"The funeral director is coming over in a little while so we can make the arrangements. My wife's friends have been great. She was a hospice nurse, so they kind of know the ropes. I'm sorry; you were asking me about the trip. I go every year and spend three or four days. Some years Edie and the kids go, too. God, I wish had taken them with me!"

Mick said the only thing you can say in this situation. "You can't blame yourself. I have just a couple more questions for you. I know this may sound strange, but I have to ask: did you or your wife have any enemies, anyone who would want to hurt you? Maybe someone who was upset with her because of her nursing, a bad outcome? Or someone you owed money to, anything like that. This is the time to tell me."

Dr. Spence looked confused. "Why would anything like that matter? I thought this had some connection to the break-ins. You mean . . . you don't think this was a botched burglary?"

"I think it probably was just that, but I have to ask, just in case there is something else. I'm just trying to eliminate other possibilities." Botched burglary, Reluctant Robber . . . was the whole world communicating in alliteration?

"No, Edie's patients were in hospice care, which means they were already dying when she first got involved. Her job was to make sure they died with dignity and without pain. So there couldn't be a bad outcome there. She's a great nurse. And, as for me, I'm a vet. I just take care of animals. I don't owe anyone money, I don't gamble. I can't think of anyone who would want to hurt us."

"OK, like I said, I had to ask, just to make sure we eliminated other possibilities. Can I just ask your kids a few questions?"

"Sure, sure. We want to find the person who did this. You can ask anything you want."

Mick walked over to the other room with Sean. He would have preferred to talk to the kids alone, one at a time, but Sean just didn't feel like they could do that right now.

In the adjoining room, Mick sat down at the table with the kids. He introduced himself and reached over to shake the boy's hand. Dr. Spence watched silently from the doorway.

"Mick McKay," he said, and the kid said, "Steven Spence, and this is my sister, Beth Anne."

"I know this is hard, but I need to ask a few things to help with the investigation. Beth Anne, when did you last see your mother?"

"I took Daddy's car to school so I could leave right after and go pick him up, so I left a little early because sometimes the parking lot fills up and you can't get a space. It was about seven-thirty, I guess, when I left home."

"OK, was there anything unusual?"

"No, Mom was already dressed for work. She was going to finish putting some chili in the Crock-Pot and leave right after me. She told me to drive carefully and not to let my dad stop at McDonald's, because she was making his favorite for dinner."

"What about you, Steven? When was the last time you talked to your mom?" It was a hard question to ask, and, as soon as Mick said it, he wished he'd said it better. He could see the kid thinking, *Yeah you're right, I'll never talk to my mom again*, but he answered calmly.

"I called her the night before."

"Did you talk about anything special?"

Steven looked over at his sister before answering. "My sister's birthday is coming up, and I called my mom to tell her I got her this initial necklace that all the girls at school were wearing. My mom was happy I remembered, and she wanted to know which girl had picked it out with me. My mom knows a lot of my friends."

Mick looked down at the tabletop. "Did any of you know Adam Moore, the guy who was killed with your mother?"

Sean shook his head but Steven said, "He was a few years ahead of me in school. Dad, you remember, he was the really good soccer player. The *Dallas Morning News* came down and did a story about him. He was that good. I can't remember exactly, but I think he was injured or in an accident or something."

"I kind of remember that," Sean said, nodding his head.

"I remember him, too. I knew that name was familiar," Beth Anne said. "He came to talk to our soccer team when I was little. You know, give us some tips. He seemed like a nice guy."

"Well, do you think your mom knew him?"

"I don't think so. I wasn't that good at soccer. I only played for a couple of years. When I was finished with soccer, my mom was finished, too."

"OK. I want to ask you and your dad if anything unusual happened at your house in the last week or so. Did anyone come up and ask for directions? Did anyone come to the door selling magazines or candy or anything you can think of? We're trying to see if the robbery victims had anything in common or if they were being watched. Anything at all that you can think of will help."

Mick could tell they were eager to help. Beth Anne plucked another Kleenex out of the box and twisted it around while she considered. She added the damp Kleenex she had been holding to a little pile next to her.

"I'm not home that much during the day, but I can't think of anything unusual." Sean paused. "You think what happened to Edie has something to do with the story in the paper, the Reluctant Robber? I thought he was just a guy down on his luck who was stealing to feed his family or something. Why would he shoot people?"

Mick could feel the tops of his ears go red. Stephanie's stories in the paper made it sound like people should take up a collection for the guy instead of throw his ass in jail. He was not one of those black-and-white cops. He could see some gray areas, but stealing was wrong, and this guy was bad. He guessed that she was regretting her angle now.

"You know, sometimes criminals escalate. They get away with one thing so they feel emboldened to try something else. We do think there is a connection, so call me if you think of anything else." There was no point in telling them any more.

CHAPTER ELEVEN

One down, one to go. Mick headed out to talk to Adam Moore's family.

Adam had lived with his sister in an apartment building behind the Brookshire's grocery store. Mick could see the trash containers behind the store as he searched for unit 12A.

The apartment door had a wooden sign that spelled out WEL-COME in different colors, but the colors were faded: maybe the sentiment, too. Mick could hear a TV laugh track as he pushed the doorbell. A young woman answered.

If he had been playing that game where you said the first word that popped into your head, he would have blurted out *scrawny*. She wasn't old, but she looked dried up. She looked sad and defeated, like her brother's murder was just one more bad thing in a long line of bad events.

Mick took out his badge to show her, even though he had an appointment and she was expecting him.

"Tiffany Hudson?" he said, and she nodded. He wanted to tell her to be careful in the future, not to just open the door to anyone, but this was not the right time for that conversation. He stuck his badge back in his pocket.

The furniture in 12A looked like it had come from garage sales: an old brown and orange couch, a beige chair in some kind of velvety fabric with worn places on the arms and a worn patch where your head would rest. Still, everything looked clean and neat. He saw her wince slightly when he sat in the old chair, probably where her brother usually sat.

"I am so sorry for your loss," Mick said, to start out. "I just want to ask a few questions, and I want you to know that we are going to do everything we can to find the person who did this to your brother."

She nodded.

"So, your brother lived here with you?" Another nod.

"Just the two of you?"

"Yes."

"What about your parents?"

"Well, both of our dads were pretty much no-shows. I don't even remember mine, and Adam's dad was just around for a few years. Not the most pleasant years either. Our mother has been in out of the picture for a long time.

"I got a job at Shady Oaks while I was in high school, and I just kept working there after I graduated. By the time Adam was in high school, our mother had found the love of her life again, so Adam just kind of started staying here with me." She shook her head. "Just so you know how long gone our mother is, I can't find her to tell her Adam is dead."

"Maybe I can help with that. When we're done here, you can give me her last known address and phone number and I'll see what we can do. This is a lot for you to go through alone." Mick felt sorry for her. Not like he hadn't seen bad parents before, but he couldn't help but compare the Spence family to this nonexistent one.

"Was your brother worried about anything lately? Was anybody bothering him, anything unusual going on with him?"

"No, why? I mean it was just a robbery gone wrong, right?"

"Yeah, that's what we think, but part of my job is to look at everything, just to make sure we aren't overlooking anything. So I have to ask you some questions that might not make sense but could be important. I know we both want to find the person who did this." He thought he sounded reasonable and he could see her tilt her head to the side to consider before she answered.

"If you are asking was my brother was into drugs or something, I can tell you straight up, no. He was even thinking of going to college again. You can ask Tony, his boss at the pizza place, or the manager here at the complex. They'll tell you Adam was a good worker."

Mick could tell this was not her first rodeo. She probably had spent her whole life taking care of her brother, and she wasn't going to let Mick push him around, especially after he was dead.

"OK, so, no drugs, no trouble. Tell me about your day yesterday."

"Adam drove me to work because he wanted to take the car in the afternoon before work. He does odd jobs around the complex for the manager, and yesterday he was planning to clean out the laundry room. You can ask the manager the specifics, if it's important. He keeps track. We get a reduction in our rent based on how much Adam does."

"Do you know why Adam needed the car?"

Tiffany looked down and picked up a piece of her skirt.

"It's why I'm dressed like this. I'm going to a funeral. Yesterday was the wake. It's some old guy who was a regular customer of Adam's, Harlan Tucker. Adam would talk to him and sometimes have pizza with him, you know, visit with him. The guy was nice to Adam and helped him. Mr. Tucker talked him into trying for college again and helped him do all his applications and what not. It made a big difference to Adam. So, yesterday he went to the wake and today we were going to the funeral together. Now, I'm going by myself."

Well, Mick thought, *now I know why the kid was at the wake.*

He said, "Hmm," but the girl didn't add anything else, so he asked, "Can I see his room?" Maybe the kid had some love letters, clues about the robber, something. Mick could only hope.

The girl pressed her lips together into a thin straight line and said, "This *is* his room. The couch pulls out to a bed. I have the bedroom. But he keeps some of his stuff in the dresser over there."

She pointed to a dresser painted a dark green. He walked over to check it out under Tiffany's watchful gaze. On the top was a trophy from Adam's soccer days with a couple of medals and ribbons draped over it; a framed picture of the team with Adam in the middle, smiling; a shot glass in the shape of a cowboy boot; and a menu for the pizza place.

Mick couldn't help but compare the kid's meager possessions to what Colly had in her room. Her room was jammed full of pictures from dances, pictures of her singing in different places that Julie had framed, old corsages, her TV, laptop, books, magazines stacked around her frilly pink bedspread. Mick had to shake his head to stop himself. Tiffany was eyeing him now, and he didn't want her to read what he was thinking.

He opened up the drawers and looked in each one. Just the usual. The bottom drawer had some papers in it, college applications and letters neatly placed back in their envelopes. Too bad Adam wasn't ever going to get the chance to get out of here. Sometimes things are what they seem and this seemed to be a simple burglary gone bad, a tragic case of being in the wrong place at the wrong time.

Mick turned back to the girl. "If you can give me what you have on your mother, I'll see what I can do to find her," he said, and even he could hear the sad resignation in his voice.

Mick headed back to the office to add to the file what he'd gotten in the last interviews. He could see Mason sitting on his desk talking to the new guy, Austin Tyler—or was it Tyler Austin? Mick could never remember. He was never sure if he was calling him by his first name or his last name.

They had the *Bee* spread in front of them. Mick had checked earlier and he knew Stephanie had kept her word. There was a lot about the victims, but no mention of the Reluctant Robber or the stolen gun.

"What's up?" Mick said, walking around the desk to see the paper right side up.

"Austin says he saw the victims together yesterday."

"Really? Where?" Mick asked, a little surprised by the revelation. What were the odds?

"I was working yesterday, directing traffic for a wake at Coad's Funeral Home. You know how those things go; a bunch of cars come at once and block Sixth Street, so I was just getting them into the lot. After a while it quieted down, so I went in to get a cup of coffee. Mrs. Spence was standing there talking to the kid. She motioned me over.

"When I walked up, she asked me about the route we were taking to the cemetery after the service, which is today. I told her we'd start out on Sixth and turn on to Clay Street and take that all the way out. Then, she said, 'I know you're busy now, we'll see you tomorrow.' And I went back outside. I was the first responding last night, but I didn't recognize them until I saw their pictures in the paper today. They were together at the wake. Kinda weird."

Mick considered. He knew the kid had been at a wake. The sister had told him that, but not that he had been there with the other victim. This was odd.

"Did you see if they left in the same car?" he asked.

"No, but they could have and I probably wouldn't have noticed. I was outside just another half hour or so. By then, the arriving cars had slowed down to a trickle, so I left."

Mick glanced at Mason to see if he was having the same reaction. Mick couldn't quite believe that there was something going on with those two in the romance department, but it wouldn't be the first time an unlikely couple had gotten together.

"Who was the wake for?" Mason asked.

"Harlan Tucker, from the trucking company, so there were a lot of people there. Half the town."

It was Mick's turn. "Hmm, a lot of people. Did you see either of them talking to anyone else?"

"No, but like I said, I just got my coffee and left. I was only inside for a few minutes."

Mick looked down at the paper again. But he couldn't see any answer in the pictures. "She's old enough to be his mother, for Christ's sake!"

"Maybe a MILF," Austin said, and Mason nodded.

"What the hell is a MILF?" Mick asked irritably. Mason and Austin looked at each other, waiting to see who was going to tell. Austin's face had turned pink. What the hell could this kid know that he didn't? Mick turned to Mason and said, "So?"

"Well, a MILF is short for a mother I'd like to . . . well, you can guess what the 'F' stands for."

"Sort of like Mrs. Robinson in that movie," Austin offered, to help with the explanation.

Great, Mick thought, *he must be throwing in an old movie as a generational helper for me.*

"Well, even if he was delivering more than pizza to her, what difference does it make? Although it could be the answer to something I've been wondering about. She was making dinner for her husband, we saw that. So why order a pizza? But, remember, the robber is our primary suspect. We've got the gun. We've got to find the guy who stole it." Mick paused for a moment. "I just don't see any way this is anything but a robbery gone bad. Even if she was screwing the mailman, the UPS man, *and* the pizza delivery guy."

Mason shrugged. "No, kind of fishy, though."

"Good job, Austin, thanks for bringing this up," Mick said. *Thanks for adding more confusion*, he thought.

CHAPTER TWELVE

Mick waited till late afternoon to start knocking on doors, closer to the time of the murders. He could see Mason down at the other end the block. He was hoping that someone would remember seeing something that seemed out of place.

He already had his badge out before he hit the doorbell. People were bound to be feeling jumpy after a couple of homicides on their block.

The first house he tried was directly across the street from the Spence house. A young girl maybe nine or ten answered the door and looked him up and down before calling to her mother. So much for the extra caution he'd anticipated. It was like watching a scary movie where you want to scream at the characters, "No! No! Don't split up!" But they do, only to get picked off by the guy in the hockey mask or the nut with the chainsaw. He sighed and waited while the mother appeared, dragging a little boy by the hand.

"Mallory, you are supposed to wait for me to open the door. Remember?" Mallory was still looking at Mick. Evidently she didn't remember. Mick started in on his spiel, and the harried mother waved him into her toy-strewn living room. The little boy and girl were now drawing large crayon pictures on a plastic desk.

"Were you home last night?" he began again.

"Yes, we were here," she replied.

"Did you see anything unusual, hear anything unusual?" he asked.

"Well, we heard the shots. Of course, at the time, I had no idea that they were shots. I was just starting dinner and I heard the popping noises. I thought it was one of those nailers the construction workers were using earlier, you know, to put nails in really fast. The Terrells are redoing their front porch. It's been kind of noisy." Mick nodded. A lot of people had heard the shots. Not many of them had recognized them as shots.

"And you were home all evening?"

"I had to run out for a prescription at around 6:00 p.m. and we got back at about 6:30 p.m."

"Did you see anyone on the street when you got home?" he asked.

"Let's see. We saw someone walking a dog. I remember because Mallory"—and here she raised her voice to send a message to the little girl—"Mallory wants a dog, but of course she has to prove she can be responsible." The little girl had just been about to smack her tiny brother with a crayon; she stopped.

That didn't seem right, Mick thought. Jackson wouldn't have been there yet, so either it was a different dog, or the time was off. Nine-year-old witnesses were not the most reliable. On to the next neighbor.

The next house looked just like the other houses on the block: immaculate. He pushed the doorbell and could hear the ding-dong sound of the bell, then running footsteps. When the door opened a crack, a little furry dog barreled out and raced through his legs.

A man wearing glasses and holding the paper called back into the house. "Connie, get the leash. Buster got out!" Connie came running with the leash and handed it to the man, who after a quick nod to Mick took off down the steps after Buster. Evidently Buster did this a lot.

"Don't worry. Ken knows how to get him back. It's not your fault. He just runs sometimes."

Good thing she wasn't the detective, Mick thought. She was wrong on both counts. He wasn't worried about Buster, and he didn't feel guilty about his escape.

After one more look at her husband trying to corral Buster, Connie turned to him with a curious look. He held up his badge and told her why he was here. Had she been home? Did she notice anything? Did she hear the shots?

"I didn't get home till about 6:45 p.m. I let Buster out and he started barking. He's little, but he can be loud. I called him in so he wouldn't disturb the neighbors, and he ran to the front door and barked some more, so I didn't hear a thing except for him barking."

By the time she finished, Buster came back, trotting and happy with his master. So Mick repeated the questions. But Buster's master, Mr. Lotz, hadn't come home till after the police cars were on the scene, and he hadn't noticed anything unusual that day.

"I feel terrible about what happened. Sean Spence is our vet and he's always been so good to Buster. I just can't believe something like that could happen here," he said, shaking his head. Buster, exhausted by his game of chase, sank down and put his head on his paws.

Done with the Lotzs, Mick scanned the block for Mason. Still inside.

He wasn't sure what he hoped to get from this exercise. He was considering asking if anyone had seen someone wearing a National Safety jacket. But if he mentioned it, there would be someone who would want so much to help that they would remember what he suggested. He didn't want to muddy the water. He'd been around long enough to see how easily people could be manipulated.

He spotted Mason walking out of the house next door to Buster's and they met on the sidewalk in front of the car. Mason looked at him expectantly, and Mick knew he had the same expression on his face. Like falling soufflés, their faces dropped at the same time. They hadn't learned anything they didn't already know.

CHAPTER THIRTEEN

When they got back in Pat's car, Stephanie thought of something her mother used to say to her: "What happened to you? You look like you just lost your best friend." That's exactly how Pat looked, and it was true; she had just lost her best friend.

"You were really good with those ladies. I can tell they trust you. Do you think they know who you are?"

"Oh, I don't know. Sometimes yes, sometimes no. It's hard to say what anybody is thinking, let alone people who are thinking across time."

"What do you mean, thinking across time?" Stephanie asked as she jammed her seat belt into the buckle.

"Well, it's kind of like time travel. You never know where you are going to find them. Not like Mrs. Ramsey; she's living in the present. But take one of my patients, Mrs. Fane, for instance. Sometimes she is worried about her mother escaping, and that's just as real to her as you sitting in the room, maybe more real. You can't tell her not to worry, her mother is long gone. I could go back and see her tomorrow and she might be in the present, just like Mrs. Eldridge. Sometimes she'll talk about playing bingo or a terrible car crash she saw on TV, and I'm not sure if that happened fifteen minutes ago or fifty years ago.

"It's a lot like being able to travel through time, only I'm not sure where I'll be. Or for that matter who I'll be! Trust me, there are times when I want to say, 'Hey, I'm a visitor from the future.' Like with Mrs. Eldridge, I'd love to tell her, 'Don't worry, you are going to pass the test!' Of course she wouldn't believe me. She was a lawyer for the county back in the day before there were very many lady lawyers. I think she was studying to pass the bar today. Poor old girl, I sure would like to tell her, 'Not to worry, you made it!' But like I said, she wouldn't believe me, and anyway, that's part of my job: to go where they are, where they need to go."

Pat maneuvered past the "Doctors Only" parking signs. "And, believe me, it is not all grim. Some people just love to tell stories from their past, and I enjoy hearing them. There are days that people just want to repeat. Their memory takes them back to those days. And not the days you think would be important, like graduation or your wedding day.

"One story I like is about a girl walking home from school. She already has a job lined up at the mill. When she gets to her house, her mother is hanging out clothes to dry in the backyard. The girl puts down her books to help, and her mother takes a clothespin out of her mouth and says, 'Me and your dad figured it out so you can go ahead and go to college in the fall. I guess you'll have to work pretty hard this summer, though.'

"I bet I've heard that woman tell that story fifty times. Now when I hear it, I can smell that clean laundry smell and feel the damp cotton sheet blowing against my face. I feel the slow happiness she must have felt, realizing that her life just changed. I hear a lot of stories." Pat turned left into her parking lot and turned to Stephanie. "I just hope the days I remember will be good ones." She said it with a chuckle.

But, to Stephanie, it sounded serious. *When I'm old*, she thought, *I hope I don't have to come back to the last two years*. Anywhere but. It occurred to her that her mother had stopped saying, "You look like you just lost your best friend." Maybe when Pete left her, it all sounded too true to her mother who, like everyone else, was being careful around her these days. But really, she hadn't lost her best friend. It sometimes surprised her that she could honestly say she didn't miss him.

What really hurt her was not his absence but his betrayal and the fact that she hadn't been smart enough to see it. Duped: that was the word for it. She'd been duped. When she'd met him in her last year of college she thought she was the luckiest girl in the world. Pete was serious, sensitive, and into her. "I'm going to make you happy every day of your life," he told her.

She had searched through her past for signs of coming trouble, but, even in hindsight, she couldn't see a single one. They were so excited when he got into dental school. Back then, she could look into the future and see a shining road ahead of them: the beautiful wedding, Hawaiian honeymoon, dental school. And they were happy. She was glad to support him while he was going to school. They took walks together for fun and counted their pennies for a dinner out. The scrounging hadn't mattered because they were on their way to their bright and happy future.

Besides, everyone they knew was in the same boat: young and starting out. Their best friends, Warren and Sara, were even poorer than Stephanie and Pete because they were both in dental school. They'd take turns having each other over to watch football games. She spent lots of time with Sara: window-shopping trips, doing each other's nails. And Warren was just like a big, happy teddy bear, always hugging everyone. The other nice thing was that they were just as much in love as Steph and Pete.

The four of them had talked endlessly about where and how to set up their practices. Pete had an offer to go in with a dentist who was looking for an orthodontist to join him. They weighed the pros and cons of each situation. It had been so exciting, so daring, when they decided to set up their own practice. Parker, Parker, and Popkins—it even sounded like a fun place. Pete loved the idea of working with friends who he could trust. Of course they all knew it might take a little longer to get down that golden road, but they would be in control of their own destiny.

It had worked. They started to make money. Pete got her emerald earrings for their fifth anniversary, and they were getting ready for the next big step on their shining road; they started talking about having a baby. Warren had teased her, saying, "Isn't it getting to be time for a Popkins to pop in?" She had answered, "I'm waiting for a Parker to park." Ha, ha. The joke had been on her, alright.

Then, one night, Pete came home and said, "Let's go for a walk, I have something I need to talk to you about." She thought he wanted to tell her that he thought they had enough money that they should try for the baby they both wanted. She couldn't believe it when he started telling her about Warren and his questionable accounting practices with the insurance companies.

She kept saying, "Not Warren!" and "Are you sure?" Pete assured her that it was Warren and that he was sure. "I talked to him as soon as I discovered what was going on. He told me I was being over-honest. But the guy is definitely cheating."

"Does Sara know? Does Sara condone this?" Stephanie had asked. Yes, Sara knew but she couldn't do anything about it and she was going along with it. She felt powerless to stop it. Her poor friend Sara.

"Oh my God, I can't believe it. We'll have to report him, friends or not. I'll call Sara. She'll understand. I just can't believe either one of them would do this."

Pete stopped walking and turned to face her. He held both of her hands. That was the thing, he explained; he couldn't prove he hadn't been involved. It would be their word against Warren's. He had fool-ishly signed things he should have looked at more carefully.

Stephanie still didn't see how they were trapped. If Pete reported it to the insurance investigators, they would believe him. He was reporting it to them, not trying to hide what had happened. But he'd already thought of that, and just being under investigation would be devastating for him. She thought he might cry, all the hard work he had put into the practice . . .

She squeezed his hands and they turned to keep walking. He explained he just wanted to walk away. It was the best thing to do under the circumstances. He could leave with his reputation. He hated to do this to her, but things would be OK once he started in a new place. It was just a setback.

"Well, sure, you have a lot of patients who will go with you. You'll get more, and everything will be alright."

"That's where Warren really screwed me, Steph. Do you remember that lawyer who helped us set up the practice? I signed a non-compete agreement. I can leave the practice, but I can't set up a new one within a one hundred–mile radius."

She had argued that under the circumstances Warren wouldn't dare enforce that contract, but Pete was equally sure it would be dangerous to go against it. They went home from that fateful walk and got out a map. Pete drew a circle around the office and Forsyth was just outside the circle.

She had never considered going back to her hometown: too small, she thought. But Pete convinced her. They could go back for a year, make the best of it, and then return and start over here. She had wanted to call Sara and Warren, just to say goodbye or, maybe, good riddance, but Pete persuaded her it would be the wrong thing to do. Better to make a clean break and stay clear of them. She had boomeranged back to Forsyth.

So here she was. Stephanie shook her head, trying to clear out the old but painful memories. Pat didn't seem to have noticed her lapse; she had more important things on her mind. She thanked Pat for taking her around and helping her to understand more about who Edie was, what she did. They made plans for their next meeting at Harlan Tucker's funeral later that morning, and Stephanie set off to find out what she could about Adam Moore—and to stop thinking about that damned Dr. Peter Popkins.

CHAPTER FOURTEEN

Mick had seen a lot of sadness connected with this murder, and now he was on his way to what he expected to be an even sadder place. He was going over to meet with Edie Spence's coworkers at hospice, not a place he wanted to be. He checked the address and headed out.

He expected some kind of group home for dying people, but he found himself in front of a nondescript two-story office building. Past a reception desk where a large lady sat talking on the phone, he could see the office was divided into the ever-present cubicles. He had expected it to look more like a hospital than the accounting office it resembled.

The large lady, wearing a colorful smock with puppies and kittens on it, smiled up at him. He waited while she wrapped up her call and asked how she could direct him. *You could direct me to the murderer,* he thought, but instead he said, "I'm Officer McKay, here to see Pat Loomis."

The receptionist beamed at him, pushed a button on her phone and said his name. A short, dark-haired woman wearing another colorful smock, this one with smiling stars on it, appeared from around the cubicle wall. She was holding out her hand to him. He shook it and followed her back to the inside of another cubicle in the maze.

"I am sorry for your loss. I know it's hard to lose a coworker," he said to her.

And of course he did know. One of the guys he had started out with, Gary Raymond, had pulled over a speeder, just routine. He was stepping out to talk to the driver when a pickup truck veered into him: no malice, just carelessness. He hated to admit it, but there was carelessness on both sides. It was a bad place to pull over, right after a curve. Gary was impossible to see until you were right there.

With the entire force, Mick had gone to the hospital to see him; talk about a wall of blue. His family was in a big waiting room, surrounded. Gary died the next day.

Mick was in a dangerous profession where coworkers might be killed. And Edie Spence was in a profession where people were dying all the time. There were some similarities. You expect to help people in car crashes, not be in the car crash. The people at hospice expect to help dying people, not to become one. He could only imagine how hard it was for the ones who saw Edie Spence every day.

"Where are the sick people?" Mick asked, trying to get an idea about the layout.

Pat smiled. She reminded him of a kind kindergarten teacher, patient with his questions. "Oh, we go wherever they are," she explained. "Sometimes they are in their homes, or with a relative, or in a nursing home. Most of the time our patients have exhausted all possible therapies. They aren't going to get better. Our goal is to make sure their final days are as pain-free and comfortable as possible. We want them to have their dignity."

Mick nodded, "That's admirable. Do you ever have problems with families? What I mean is, could one of Edie Spence's patients have been dissatisfied, even angry with her?"

Mick watched as the kindly teacher turned into one who could whack your fingers with her ruler. "No, and I'm not sure what that question even has to with anything. Edie was killed by someone she surprised robbing her house. You don't think one of her patients got, quite literally, off their death bed and went out to shoot her and that poor boy, do you?"

She made a good point.

"I'm just checking out all angles. This is the beginning of the investigation, and I would be remiss if I didn't gather all the information I could about the victims."

His reply softened her a little, but not all the way back to kindly kindergarten teacher. "No, Edie didn't have any angry patients. She was a wonderful nurse and a caring person. People sensed that in her. Besides, we work on teams. It wasn't Edie alone out there. She worked with a doctor, a social worker, a chaplain, a nurse's aide. She wasn't solely responsible for anyone."

Mick wanted to check on Edie's relationship with her husband. He had planned on asking her coworkers if they knew about any problems. But he felt he was still in trouble with Pat. He'd have to be less direct.

"Well, aside from patients, was there anyone Edie ever mentioned having a problem with? Family, friend, coworker, anyone?"

But Pat was already shaking her head. "No, she got along with everyone. I know people say this a lot, but she was really just an exceptional person. Everyone liked her. She was kind, considerate, and funny. She was my friend."

She started to cry, and Mick felt like calling out to someone for help. But all he could do was reach over and pat her hand.

Mick got Edie Spence's schedule for the day of the murder. No names, because of the HIPAA laws. But Harlan Tucker's wake was included in her sign-out sheet, so it didn't seem she was hiding anything.

"I appreciate your help. I'll keep in touch, and you can call me if anything occurs to you that you think I might need to know. Call me directly, not 911." He was trying for a little lightness.

But she looked at him and said seriously, "We never call 911."

CHAPTER FIFTEEN

tephanie glanced at her watch. Right on time. She checked her notes: Tiffany Hudson. So, she and Adam didn't have the same last name.

Before she could knock, the door opened and Jessica and the cook from Antonio's Pizza walked out. Jessica was still crying, and the cook was still scowling. They were followed by a man who looked like a bearded snowman. Round face, round body. Must be Tony.

Stephanie introduced herself, patted Jessica on the back, and walked in past them to meet Adam's sister. She looked like she was one of those movie special effects where the person just fades away. She was halfway gone, just fading and wispy. Unlike Jessica, she wasn't crying. She looked too dried up for that. Tearless Tiffany.

Stephanie started out by saying, "I am so sorry for your loss. I want to do a story for the *Bee* about your brother so people will know what a great guy he was, and I wanted to find out more about Adam from you."

Tiffany looked toward the door. "The people who just left, Tony and Jessica and Brad, they're going to help with the funeral. It's going to be at their church with lunch afterward. Can you put that in the *Bee*? I want Adam's friends to come. It's really generous of Tony to do all that. I wouldn't know how to do a funeral, the planning and everything."

"Yes, of course, we can put all the details in the *Bee*. We'll put it in his obituary, and I'll make sure it goes into my article about him, too. Why don't you tell me about your brother, to get me started?"

Tiffany sighed, gave a *what difference does it make* kind of shrug, and began. "I want the obituary to say positive things, nice things.

Adam, he didn't have it easy. He sure didn't come out a winner in the parental department. My mom got pregnant with me when she was seventeen. She probably did her best. Her parents were pretty mad about it—about me, I guess. We lived with them. They were less happy a couple of years later when she fell in love again and took off, leaving me with them. I didn't see her for a few years.

"She thought it was all going to be different after that, when she married Adam's dad. Third time's the charm, and all that. We were going to be one big happy family, with money; that was important to her, too. Unfortunately, it turned out he was better at talking about money than actually making it.

"By the time Adam got here, she was pretty much supporting everybody. That didn't last long. She found another guy who looked like a better bet to her, but he wasn't all that interested in kids, at least not hers. So we went back to Gran and Pop's place. She didn't tell us she was leaving us there. Told us we were going on a vacation in the summertime. I was old enough to know the drill, but Adam believed she was coming back for us before school started. He was brokenhearted when she didn't show. It took her two years to come back for us.

"The next man she found was really crazy, like just out of a mental hospital, and they had knock-down, drag-out fights. One night she got mad at him for something. I can't remember what now. She went outside with Adam's baseball bat and started smashing up her boyfriend's car. She'd pretty much finished with all the headlights and taillights and was starting in on the windshield when our neighbor came running out. Oops, wrong car. The police came, and off we went to foster care. But you get the picture."

Stephanie did get the picture. Not happy stuff. She tried for a different topic. "I heard Adam was a really great soccer player in high school. Is that right?"

"Oh yeah, he *was* good at soccer. When he was little, my mom figured out that she could sign him up for soccer, and someone else would watch him for a few hours. The coach and the other mothers took pity on him and started to pick him up for practices. If he noticed he was the only kid whose mom never brought the snacks or came to his games, he never said anything. I couldn't help him much then. I was working and trying to make sure I got out of school.

"I've always thought he got to be such a good player to show his gratitude to the people who helped him. But it could be it was just all he had to do, so he played hard. If there had been a football camp or a ballet class where she could have dumped him, he probably would have been good at that."

"Jessica said they even had a special cheer for him at Travis." Stephanie wanted to have something positive about him and for his sad sister.

"Yeah, when he scored, all the kids would sing 'that's-a-Moore-ray' because of his name on his jersey. He was a great player, but, like I said, if it weren't for bad luck he'd have no luck at all. He was all set to go to college with a scholarship, first one in our family to go to college. Right before he was supposed to graduate, he got into an accident on a friend's motorcycle. He broke his leg in three places. He'd already signed with State, and they would have let him come anyway, which I thought was decent of them. But he knew he wouldn't be able to play again. He just kind of went wild, and that was the end of that."

"What a shame. I know it hasn't been easy for you, and now this." Tiffany hung her head, her wispy hair drifting forward.

"Do you think I could see Adam's room?" Stephanie asked.

Tiffany's head snapped up and she said, "He doesn't have a room, OK? This is it. Don't you get it? We were just getting by."

Whoa, whoa, thought Stephanie, *what did I say?* Somehow that was the wrong question. Try again. "My first apartment, I had one of those beds that came out of the wall. I'd pull it down at night and put it back up in the morning. You know how people are always saying they love breakfast in bed? To this day I still can't stand it."

Tiffany was nodding at her. Better. Then she pulled herself out of her chair and opened a closet. Not so snappish now.

"These are Adam's papers and pictures, stuff he saved. You're welcome to take a look at them. I have to go down to see the manager. I'll be back in a couple of minutes. OK?"

"OK, thanks, I'll be here," Stephanie said.

After Tiffany left, Stephanie opened a thirty-by-thirty packing box from U-Haul. Wow, poor kid; his whole life in this box. She took out a school picture: Adam with freckles and smoothed-down hair in a striped T-shirt. There was a note in big, loopy handwriting from a girl named Carrie, a big stack of college applications, some papers from school, an old essay from one of his English classes. The students must have been instructed to write about their first day of school.

Stephanie sat down cross-legged in front of the box to read Adam's essay. It was sweet, all about his mom crying more than he did and how he told her it was the best day of his life and she replied, "You are going to have a life full of happy days! I'm going home to make some cupcakes for when you get home. Love you." And he had to tell her, "It's OK, don't cry, I'll be home soon."

The kid wasn't a bad writer, and his mother must have cared for him some of the time. Maybe Tiffany had been exaggerating about her tough childhood.

Stephanie had no more than thought the name Tiffany when in she walked as if summoned for questioning. Steph decided to come at her from an angle.

"You were right. It looks like Adam was very serious about college. I saw his applications. I can see he wanted to end up at Southern. Where did he start out? Do you remember where he went to kindergarten, for instance?"

"We both went to Crockett for elementary school."

"Do you remember his first day of school? I might include something like in his story."

"Poor little guy. I wish I could have done more for him, but I was just a freshman in high school and I had my own worries. I did try, though, I tried. I got all his clothes out the night before and I left a note for my mom. She must have been between boyfriends then because she was going out a lot. Anyway I left her a note to remind her she had to take Adam for his first day. He was excited, too. You know how little kids are."

Stephanie thought, *Yes, but not from personal experience.*

"So, about four o'clock in the morning I hear her come stumbling in. She must have found the note and then she starts swearing. She comes lurching into my room and saying I'd have to take Adam, because she brought a friend home. I knew enough not to argue with her when she was smashed, so I just agreed. High school started a whole hour before the kindergarten, but what could I do?" Tiffany held out her hands like she was waiting for an answer to fall into them from the sky.

"You were doing your best."

"Yeah, I was doing my best. But I had to get to school, and this is the part I hate. I had my boyfriend pick me and Adam up. We drove to the school and we just opened the car door and left him. He had to sit there for an hour all by himself. I wish I had at least gotten out of the car with him.

"When I got home, there he was, sitting on the porch. He'd walked all the way back. I was amazed that he could even find his way. Our mom's friend was still there, and she told him to sit outside. That was his first day of kindergarten and my first day of high school. I don't think it makes a very pretty story for the *Bee*, though."

Stephanie wished it could have been the way he wrote it, not the way he lived it.

"Could you give me a list of Adam's friends? I'd like to include some comments from them in his obituary, too." She waited while Tiffany wrote down some names.

"I don't know all their phone numbers," she said apologetically. "He'd been seeing a girl, Carrie. You can try her. You might also want to talk to Lacey Thomas; she really stood by him during his accident, no matter how I felt about her influence on him. She's kind of a wild card. Sorry I can't be more helpful."

"That's OK. Don't worry about it. I'll be able to track them down."

And she had. One of the names on the list was Jason Dent. He was on his way home from college to go to Adam's funeral. Stephanie met him at the Round the Clock. He was a big, square-shouldered, nice-looking kid with hair so blond and silky, he could have been in a shampoo commercial. He ordered chili fries and a milkshake. Stephanie stuck to iced tea.

"Adam and me, we were friends when we were real little," he began. "The thing was, we both loved to play soccer so we spent a lot of time together. His mom was kind of not around, so he came over to my house a lot. Then he had his accident and I went to see him in the hospital. But once he got out, we kind of stopped hanging out as much."

He paused to suck half of his milkshake through his straw. When he came up for air, Stephanie asked, "So what changed? Was it because he couldn't play soccer anymore?"

Jason scooped up some of his fries but hesitated. "No, it wasn't that, really. But I went away to school, and when I came home he was just hanging with different people and into different stuff than me."

He shoved a handful of fries into his mouth while Stephanie formulated her next question. "What kind of stuff was he into?"

"I don't know, just stuff I didn't want to do."

"Look, I am not going to write anything bad about him in the paper. I just want to try and understand what kind of person he was, what kind of challenges he had, right?"

Jason shook his head. "Just you know . . . stuff I wasn't into. So we didn't hang out that much." Jason looked at his watch and Stephanie got the message.

She asked one more question. "What's your favorite soccer memory of Adam?"

"Oh, wow. We had some great games in high school. We went down to State three years in a row and Adam was the reason. Those were some fun games and we were like heroes when we got back to school on Monday. Sometimes when I'm playing with my college friends I think, 'If Adam were here, we'd be playing better.'"

Stephanie decided to check in with the first girl on Tiffany's list. When the girl answered the door, her blonde ponytail—long, thick, and with the kind of highlights you couldn't get out of a bottle—Stephanie thought, *Shoot, did all of Adam's friends have perfect hair?*

There were painted Adirondack chairs in the front yard. Carrie Wasbaugh asked if Stephanie wanted to sit outside, and she did. They settled into the chairs and Stephanie asked her how she had known Adam.

"We met in grade school. We played soccer together, and he was in some of my classes in high school. We got to be friends."

"Were you dating?" she asked.

The girl looked at her with sympathy, like she was thinking, *You poor thing, you just don't know anything do you? And you can't even sit in your chair.* But she was patient. She sighed and tried to explain the world to Stephanie.

"People in high school don't go on dates. You go out with a bunch of people, like for a bonfire down by the river or to the games, but not on dates." When she said the word "dates" she made quotation marks with her fingers. "But Adam and I, we were pretty close in high school, then he was in that accident and we kind of lost touch for a while. And then recently . . . he was going to try and go to Southern with me in the fall," she said, brushing a tear from her cheek. "He was so happy and excited about everything. It makes it seem even more unfair that someone killed him. I mean it's *so* unfair. If he had to get killed, why couldn't it have been right after the accident, when he was miserable? Why now, when we were happy?"

Stephanie didn't have an answer for that. "Tell me about a special memory you have of Adam."

"I just can't stop thinking of the last time I saw him. We went on a picnic to celebrate the future. He was so excited about going away. We went down to River's Edge Park, and he pushed me on the swing. It was like we were both little kids again, just happy in that little kid way. I keep thinking of how happy he was." Now the tears were flowing down both cheeks and Stephanie felt her eyes start to well up, too.

"I know what you mean. It doesn't seem fair," she said.

When she sat down at her desk that night, she vowed to give justice to Adam Moore the only way she could. She would write him the obituary he deserved. Bless his heart, Tony had come through and set up the rush funeral arrangements for Adam so that the funeral could be held Wednesday, before Edie's. Just the thought of how busy the funeral home was this week made Stephanie sad. But Tony's gesture renewed her faith in mankind . . . and made her determined to eat more pizza. A win-win.

CHAPTER SIXTEEN

Mick decided to drive back to the office and see if he could get any kind of line on the pizza delivery kid's mother. He had heard that the funeral was going to be held ASAP to accommodate the church's sadly busy schedule, so best to get started now. Not quite sure how much help that would be to Tiffany, but at least it was something.

Poor girl. Alone. It was something he secretly worried about for Colly. As an only child, she'd be by herself after he and Julie were gone. He knew it was a crazy thing to worry about. Still, it wasn't the way he and Julie had planned it. They had wanted a big family, at least three or four kids.

After Colly, he and Julie had tried and tried. But in the end, after all the treatments, there were no more babies. So they concentrated on what they had instead of what they didn't. As his mother said, "You take what you get and don't throw a fit." And they were so lucky to have Colly. He and Julie had carefully selected names for a baby girl or a baby boy. They picked Colleen for a girl, vowing no nick-names. That all changed when his mother started calling the baby Colly-Dolly-Doo. From then on, she was Colly.

And she was the darling girl, especially when she sang. She was such a tiny girl, but when she opened her mouth to sing, she sounded like one of those very big, very fat opera singers. Man, that girl could sing—what a voice! Once, when Mick was starting out, he was first on the scene when some guy had forgotten to get his baby out of the car. He'd been distracted, but the temperature was in the nineties. The baby didn't make it. When Colly came along, Mick put a Post-it note on the car handle with "Colly" written on it, but right from the start she made enough noise that there was no forgetting her. Julie kept the note, though, and put it in Colly's baby book.

Her first grade music teacher had called and asked them to come in for a conference. He and Julie knew Colly could sing. The music teacher told them Colly had perfect pitch, something Julie already knew. They didn't push her, though. He and Julie always told her they only wanted her to be happy when she grew up.

But then, this chance to sing on the tour in Europe had come up. He and Julie had debated about whether it was a good thing to have her concentrate so much on her music, but her voice coach had said she might get a scholarship. If they had had more kids like they had planned, Julie wouldn't have been able to be a chaperone on the tour, and without her along they wouldn't have let Colly go.

So, in a way it was like Mick's old dream of going into the Air Force. Sometimes if your dreams don't come true, you find new and better dreams—or maybe help someone you love reach their dreams. Mason appeared and cut short his trip down memory lane.

"What's up, Mason? Anything come in yet?"

"Yeah, we got a preliminary report from the coroner. Nothing we don't already know there. Both victims shot in the chest and the head at pretty close range. Shooter must have been holding the gun between ten to twelve inches from them when he did the chest shots, held it to their heads when he shot them there."

Mick looked down at his hands. He was holding them like he was praying. "Well, he must have shot them both once while they were standing and then turned around and shot them in the head when they were on the ground. The guy had to be fast or the second victim would have turned to run is the way I figure it."

To shoot two people at such close range, that quickly, would take nerves of steel. It was difficult to imagine the shooter being flustered by the appearance of the pizza delivery boy and the nurse and then composing himself to shoot them in such a precise, cold way.

Mason nodded. "Yeah, that makes sense. One other thing. The coroner said there would have been a lot of blood. With the killer so close, he would have to have gotten some blood on him. What do you think about releasing the information that the killer was wearing a National Safety jacket? Then all we have to do is wait for someone to call about seeing someone in a bloody jacket."

"I think it's too early. I think Jackson saw that jacket, and you think Jackson saw that jacket, but we have to wait till he says he saw that jacket. Let's hold off on that. Anything else?"

"We combed the yard for fibers. We didn't find much. And nothing on the victims. We checked Jackson's clothes. Nothing from him on them, or vice versa. The witness had gun residue on his hands, and we did find a few dog hairs on Adam Moore, most likely from when the dog was eating the pizza. What we didn't find was any of Edie Spence's hairs or fibers on Moore or his hairs or fibers on her. So that's about it so far. We should be hearing about the bullets soon. What'd you find out in the interviews? Austin and I are taking bets on whether the victims were more than friends."

Mick felt a little dirty and disrespectful talking about the two murdered people that way. Maybe because he had talked to the families and to him they were real people. Maybe because he wanted to believe that it wasn't true.

Still, he was curious. "So who's betting which way?"

"Austin is betting yes and I'm betting no."

Well, that was interesting, but the thing Mick couldn't get away from was, what difference did it make? He knew when the ballistics report came in it would verify that the bullets fired were from the gun stolen from Martin Colby. What he really needed to do was solve the burglaries; that would solve the murders.

Mick gestured with his thumb—Out—and Mason slid off the corner of the desk and left Mick alone. He opened the burglary file and started reading. Again.

CHAPTER SEVENTEEN

Stephanie pulled up to Parkland United Methodist Church. A Forsyth policeman wearing a florescent green vest held up his hand to stop her and let a line of cars coming from the other side pull into the parking lot. She looked down at her notes from the obituary, always prepared.

When she looked up again the policeman was frantically waving his hand at her. *Sorry, sorry*, she thought as she pulled into the lot.

People dressed in dark, subdued colors were getting out of cars all around her and heading for the church entrance in little groups of two and three. Stephanie turned, pushed the key to lock her car, and joined the procession.

The pews were filling up when she got inside. She was looking for Edie Spence's coworker Pat, but off to the left she saw two familiar heads and moved toward them. She slid into the pew and smiled at her mother and father. Her mother's mouth made a little "O."

"Working," Stephanie said before she was asked. "How about you?"

Her dad reached across her mother's lap and squeezed her hand. "Daddy used to do some business with Harlan Tucker. Of course, he retired a while back. But here we are. So sad about the nurse and the kid getting killed. I thought you'd be working on that story today."

"I am. The nurse who was killed? Edie Spence. She worked with Mr. Tucker, and I'm doing a story on her."

Stephanie could feel her mother checking her out as she talked, like when she was little and she could tell by putting a hand on her forehead if she was sick. Now she was checking for signs of a broken heart, apparently just as easy for her mother to spot. Another thing to hate about Peter; he made her parents worry about her.

Now Stephanie tried to give them both the "see, I'm happy" smile she knew they were searching her face for. They seemed satisfied. Stephanie turned past them so she could check out the church. One row back she spotted Tiffany Hudson. She was looking at her lap, like one breath might knock her right over. Poor thing.

Stephanie tried to catch her eye, but Tiffany was intent on her lap. She saw Pat from hospice come in with a group of people and take a seat in a pew a couple of rows ahead of her. There weren't many empty spaces.

Two middle-aged women started up the aisle, followed by a small knot of people. Must be the family. The women were crying and clinging to each other like Dorothy and her friends approaching the Wizard of Oz. Only instead of a Wizard, there was a coffin on wheels, covered with a cross of white roses. The minister came out and the congregation stood to sing "I Will Raise You Up on the Last Day."

Stephanie picked up the hymnal and sang along. While she was singing she thought about Adam Moore and Edie Spence. They had both planned to be here today.

She let her mind wander as the minister talked about, Tucker and his willingness to help others.

CHAPTER EIGHTEEN

Mick tried to look at the robbery file with fresh eyes and keep out the murders. Well, that was impossible. He read his notes about his plan to check in at the high school. Mick couldn't shake his hunch that it had been a kid.

They had checked out National Safety because of the calendar, but anyone could have dropped that. Hell, it could have belonged to Mr. Colby. He was an old man. He might have forgotten that he picked one up.

If Adam Moore and Edie Spence were alive today, he would be over at the high school checking to see if any of the guidance counselors had noticed a student with more money than usual. Maybe there were rumors. A kid might brag to his friends about the burglaries. If the burglar was a student, he had now become a murderer. Mick leaned back in his chair and peered out the office door.

"Hey, Mason!"

Mason always reminded Mick of Mr. Potato Head. He had a big nose, ears that stuck out on the side, and that big, happy mouth. Julie thought he was adorable. Despite his Potato Head, he had to fight off women. They loved him: from the old waitresses with teased-up hair and wrinkles around their mouths from smoking and hard living to Colly's silly, giggling, young girlfriends. He'd never understood the expression "she threw herself at him" until he'd gone out for a drink with Mason.

Mason came jogging down the hall.

"What's up?"

"OK, I have some hypothetical questions to ask you. Suppose our burglar was a kid, like we considered before."

"Alright."

"OK, now suppose he somehow messes up and winds up shooting two people. Do you think he would be able to just show up at
school like nothing happened?"

Mason nodded. Mr. Potato Head was in agreement.

"Maybe we should head out to the high school and check to see
who didn't show today. It can't hurt, might help. What do you think?"

"I think you're right, Mick. If it is a student, if . . . But I just don't
see some kid who just got his driver's license putting two kill shots in
those people. Do you?"

"I can't picture anybody but a stone-cold killer, no matter how
old, taking the time to do the head shots after the victims are down.
And that's what's got me so worried about finding him before he gets
his hands on another gun, kid or not."

Forsyth High was like some kind of gigantic beehive with kids going
in and out, in and out, tossing balls back and forth out on the front
lawn, running around the track on the field. People everywhere, and
all of them moving.

Mick and Mason fell in behind a group of kids pushing through
the big double doors into the high school. The school had the smell
of old gym socks mixed with some vague fried foods. They walked
down the shiny linoleum squares toward the principal's office. The
movement around them seemed to be intensifying, like the cre-
scendo of a piano piece Colly used to play. Then the bell rang, and
he and Mason were suddenly alone in the hall.

The principal's office had windows on both sides of the door so
you could look in and see the high desk where a blue-haired lady
sat who looked like she was hired just to remind everyone, hey, not
all people are young. Doris Kingly, the sign over her desk read.
Mick pulled out his badge, even though he was pretty sure the lady
remembered him from other, less tragic high school visits.

"Hi, we're here to see Mr. Lavelle. From the Forsyth police," he
added, just in case she didn't catch the badge.

"Oh, Mr. McKay, it's terrible what happened with those two

people. I just can't believe it. Mr. Lavelle is in the cafeteria. He is setting up for the grief counselors. Adam Moore went to school here, and of course Beth Anne Spence is a student here now, so Mr. Lavelle thought some of the students might need something like this. You all can walk down the hall to the cafeteria or I can have him paged. There's coffee in the cafeteria."

"Thanks, we'll go on down and find him." Mick nodded his thanks.

Mr. Lavelle was carrying a couple of bright blue plastic chairs over to a table where two women were setting out leaflets and a sign-up sheet. Lavelle did his best to wave with the two chairs in his hands and moved toward Mick and Mason.

"Right with you," he said.

He set the chairs down at the table and said something to the women that caused them to look up at them. Lavelle took off his glasses and started polishing them with a Kleenex from his pocket. "Hi, Mick. What a tragedy, huh? Something like this is supposed to happen in big cities, not in a place like Forsyth."

"Yes, it is a tragedy." Mick didn't add that bad people could be found anywhere. Why did everyone assume that all bad things happened in big cities?

"Has anyone come in to see the grief counselors?" Mick flicked a look at Mason. He wondered if Mason was thinking the same thing. If you just shot a couple of people, maybe you could use a little grief counseling.

"No, not yet. We're still getting everything set up. But I'm glad we have the resource. I don't think I'd know what to say to the kids. Come on back to my office and we can talk. Grab a cup of coffee if you want. It's Starbucks." He gestured toward a table where coffee urns were sitting on an out-of-place-looking checked tablecloth.

Settled in chairs in front of Lavelle's desk, Mick wasted no time in coming to the point. "We want to see which kids are absent today. If one of your students was involved in this, we think they may have skipped school." Mick thought that by throwing in the "your" in front of the word "students" he could push Lavelle a little.

"You know I can't just hand out information like that, Mr. McKay, and besides, you can't really think one of our students is responsible."

Mick noticed that the students were not only Lavelle's now but his, too, with the "our." And he was Mr. McKay.

"We don't know who is responsible, but we are not ruling out the possibility that it could have been a student here at Forsyth High. I'm not asking you to do anything out of the ordinary here today. All I want you to do is take a look at the list of absent students and tell me if there are any names on the list we need to check to see if they are truant. That's all. Truancy."

Lavelle leaned back and took off his glasses. He started cleaning them again. Mick thought, *how dirty could they be?* He knew the principal was stalling, considering his options. Finally he put his glasses back on, tugged at the sleeves of his too-short jacket, and picked up the phone on his desk.

"Doris, would you bring me the absentee list for today, please. OK, thanks." He put the phone down and peered through his spotless glasses at them.

Mason leaned forward in his chair and put his hands on his knees. "Did you know the Moore kid?"

"Yes, he was a so-so student. Not a lot of support at home, as I remember. Great soccer player, though."

Doris walked in, gave Mick and Mason a sharp look, and set the paper on the principal's desk. Lavelle ran his finger down the names on the list.

"Just anything out of the ordinary, anything unusual," Mick prompted.

"No, the only unusual thing is that we have some kids out for Coach Tucker's funeral. Other than that, it looks pretty ordinary. I don't see any names on the list that I would think of as possible killers. That's for sure."

"OK, OK, just let us know if anything catches your attention today, anybody acting in a strange or inappropriate way. Keep the list. We may come back for it," Mick said, rising from his chair.

"I'll keep it and I'll let the guidance counselors know, too, but I think you are making a mistake. I've seen a lot of stuff go on, but I just can't picture any of my students killing two people." Mick noticed they were back to being his—when they weren't murderers.

The halls were still empty when Mick and Mason walked out.

"Well, that was worthless," Mason said as they pushed out through the big, heavy double doors.

"I don't know. We got some people thinking, and that might lead us somewhere. Plus, a lot of students saw us. Never underestimate the importance of police presence. There'll be talk, and if the wretch who did this goes to that school, he'll hear about us, might think we know more than we do, and that is *not* worthless. Eighty percent of success is showing up."

Mick paused, turned, and pointed to the school motto carved in stone above the doors. He pointed up and Mason read out loud, "Ye shall know the truth, and the truth shall set ye free."

Mason added, "Yeah, yeah, well I'm hoping the truth is going to wind up making somebody not so free."

When Mick turned back around, he spotted Jack Jackson coming up the winding path toward them, dressed in a dark suit and tie.

"Hey, Mr. Jackson. I didn't expect to see you again today."

Jackson looked up, startled. "Oh, Mr. McKay. We're just getting back from the funeral I was telling you about this morning. I have to go in and sign my son back in. Rules."

Mick hadn't noticed the kid trailing behind Jackson, or maybe he had and hadn't connected them. The kid was undoing his tie and tugging it off his neck as if his father might turn around and use that to pull him into the school.

Jackson turned back to him and seemed annoyed to find him so far behind. He waited till the kid got closer and then introduced them to his son, Charles. The boy shook hands with Mick and Mason, but that small act seemed to sap all his energy and afterward he just stood gazing at the ground. Mick saw Mason watching the kid as well, noting his strange behavior.

"Well, we better head in. Chip hates to miss class."

Wow, really, Mick thought, *how the hell could you tell?* The kid showed no emotion at all. Of course he had just come from a funeral, and kids don't like to be reminded that people aren't immortal.

Mick called over his shoulder. "Remember, if you think of anything, let me know." Jackson nodded and waved as he pushed open the door and waited for his son to catch up to him. Chip turned back to see if they were still watching him, and Mick waved to him as the heavy door slowly closed.

"I think we made him nervous," Mason said.

"Occupational hazard," Mick answered.

It was, too. Even some of Colly's friends were nervous around him. Maybe they thought he could tell who had sneaked a beer out of somebody's garage refrigerator. It went both ways, though. People he and Julie knew from church or the neighborhood considered him a friend, but he took his job seriously and there had been a couple of uncomfortable situations.

One time he had caught a kid smoking marijuana down on River Road: Matt Lockman. Mick knew his family from church. Matt's father had been furious with him for filing charges, even though it was not the first time Mick had caught him. Apparently it cost Matt his spot on the football team. No amount of pleading could make Mick change his mind. His parents soon stopped speaking to the McKays at church.

Matt Lockman had gotten his revenge later, though. He was in choir with Colly. Every practice started with prayers for community members who were sick or dying. Matt read through the list of sick members and then said, "Let's say a prayer for Julie and Michael McKay, who passed away today." Colly was little enough at the time to be very upset. She was beside herself, still in tears, when Julie came to pick her up. Some kind of clerical error was what they said at the church. But Mick knew.

Eventually Matt went off to college and immediately fell back into his drug habit. His parents brought him home and also relented on their icy treatment of Mick and Julie. Of course, if they'd cut off everyone Matt had had run-ins with, they might not have had any friends left. The plain truth was it was hard to be friends with people you might have to arrest for drugs or drunk driving or spousal abuse. And you never knew who that might turn out to be.

CHAPTER NINETEEN

With her parents, Stephanie headed for the church hall, "Amazing Grace" still echoing in her head, the closing hymn for Harlan Tucker. Feeling a little dizzy, Stephanie gave her parents air kisses and stepped into the large hall where a lunch was being provided. She wanted to catch up to the hospice nurses and whoever else might have known Edie and Adam. After all, they had both known Harlan Tucker, so his family and friends might have known them, too. Besides, she was hungry, and the Methodist ladies were known for their pies.

She crossed into the room already set with long tables and food on a counter, buffet-style. She picked up a plate and put some fried chicken and potato salad on it. She saw Pat and some of the other hospice nurses, and she went to sit with them.

One woman, Dee, was tall and thin and wore bright red lipstick. The other woman, Lynn, was what her father would call plump and then some, with bright red hair. They kind of looked like they matched in some funny way, maybe red and red.

Stephanie said to them, "I really admire y'all. I don't know if I could do what you do."

The conversation naturally turned to hospice and their experiences.

Dee said, "When I first started doing hospice, one of the nurses I trained with asked me how I could deal with people who are going to die. I said, 'Honey, if the people you are working with aren't ever going to die, I sure don't want to meet them. We're none of us getting out of here alive.'"

"Patients deserve comfort and care throughout their lives, even at the very end," Lynn said.

Stephanie agreed. That's exactly why it was her important for her to get these articles on Adam and Edie right, to give them the dignity they had not been given at the end.

Finished with her food, Stephanie headed over to pay her condolences to Harlan Tucker's daughters, who she'd already mentally nicknamed the sob sisters. They hadn't stopped crying once. *Try and have a little compassion,* she scolded herself. You'd think sitting with Pat and her friends would rub off on her a little.

"I am so sorry for your loss. I know your father was a great man," Stephanie began. Mary Sue squeezed Kay Kay's hand.

"Yes, he was such a great man," Mary Sue said while Kay Kay nodded.

"He was the kind of man you could count on," Kay Kay added.

Once Stephanie had explained that she worked for the *Bee* and in fact had written the obituary for Harlan, the sisters cozied up to her and decided to tell her a few stories about their beloved daddy.

Stephanie asked if it was hard growing up with a father who was so interested in sports.

"You mean, was Daddy disappointed that he wound up with two daughters and no sons to play football?" Kay Kay asked, exchanging a meaningful glance with her sister. "No. Matter of fact, Daddy always said how happy he was to have daughters. I think for some reason he was glad not to have football players. He always said he had enough of coaching boys to last a life time.

"Oh, and he took all the things we did seriously, too. He went to every one of our dance recitals. Well, almost . . . Mary Sue, you remember when you were so sick. I think it was before you got your tonsils out?"

Mary Sue nodded. "Oh, I do remember. You cried and cried because of the big dance recital over at the high school. You were afraid you couldn't be in it because I was sick."

"Yes, and Daddy said he would flip a coin to see who would stay home and take care of you and who would get to go to the recital. Well, sure enough he flipped the coin and told Mama to call it and she yelled 'tails.' It landed heads. I saw it just as plain as I am seeing you now, but Daddy said, 'tails it is,' and off you and Mama went. He couldn't stand to see us cry."

Wow, Stephanie thought, *he would be having a hard time today.*

"Did you know Edie Spence, your dad's nurse?" she asked.

"Yes, she came out when we first decided to put Daddy in hospice. She was one of the reasons we put him in St. Paul's Hospice," Mary Sue said, and pointed to her sister.

Kay Kay must have gotten the signal, because she continued the story. "It was my idea to sign Daddy up for hospice. Mary Sue and some of the rest of the family didn't want to do it at first. They thought it was like giving up on him. You know, just letting him die because we wouldn't be trying any more treatments. Of course, the doctors had already told us the cure would kill him a lot faster than the disease."

Like a tennis match where Stephanie couldn't see the ball, it had somehow wound up back in Mary Sue's court.

She continued, "And Kay Kay was so right! We could rest easy that Daddy was never in pain. And that was such a blessing for us. That, plus the nursing care they had: someone who would come over and give baths or bring meals, provide spiritual counseling. And it wasn't a death sentence. Edie told us Daddy could stay in hospice care as long as he needed to. Hospice was truly a blessing for us."

She looked at her sister when she said "us" and Kay Kay resumed. "We saw Edie lots of times, and she'd call to let us know how things were going with Daddy or, if we were worried about something, we'd call her. In fact we talked to her right before Daddy died. She called to let us know how he was doing. She knew we were worried about going off to the wedding. And then afterward, well, Edie was so kind to us.

"I think going to Daddy's wake was one of the last things she ever did. We considered trying to change the funeral when we heard the news about her, but we had family coming from out of town and people who took the day off and might not get to come if we rescheduled.

"So here we are. Edie was just the nicest lady. We just can't believe someone would hurt her. When Daddy first got sick we had tried taking turns to stay with him, but it was hard, especially for me, because I babysit. When we decided on hospice for him, it was a relief to know he was okay.

"Then one of the boys from Daddy's last team—his family owns National Safety—well, he arranged to have the wife of one of his employees come and stay with Daddy, you know, as a housekeeper. He told us we'd be doing him a favor, because he was trying to find extra work for the employee, and this would be good for everyone.

"And it was. Rosa Morales was with Daddy for two years. We were doubly blessed to have the hospice nurse and Rosa, doubly blessed. Rosa was there on that last day, too."

Kay Kay started to cry again at the mention of the last day.

In an effort at diversion, Stephanie tried to refocus the conversation. "Did you know that Adam Moore, the boy killed with Edie, visited your father?"

The sisters exchanged another glance. Mary Sue's turn this time. "Well, what happened there is, we were worried about Daddy losing weight. We brought him food and it would just sit. So we landed on the idea of having some food delivered, a pizza, once a week.

"Turned out that Daddy liked to visit with the delivery guy. I don't think he ever mentioned his name. I know Daddy was encouraging him to go on to college. In a way, I'm glad he's not here to see two people he cared for killed like that."

"I agree," Kay Kay said. "He would have been so upset. At least he was spared that. I remember him talking about pushing the boy to go on to college, too. Daddy always believed that education was the most important thing, and, for some boys, sports could be a good way to get an education."

Now Stephanie was going to tread lightly and carefully around the next question. "I know there were some not so happy times in your father's life, too, when he was coaching."

"I imagine you are talking about poor Charlie Atkins. Nobody suspected that boy was suicidal. Nobody. Who can explain something like that? Charlie had a loving family, lots of friends. He had everything to live for. People blamed Daddy because he bawled him out after the game. Charlie addressed the note he left to him, but I still don't get why anyone would blame our father. That poor boy must have had some other problems that didn't have a thing to do with football or our father.

"Daddy told us about it later and said he was sad, but I can tell you for a fact he did not blame himself for what happened. His conscience was clear on that. Whenever he talked about it, and that was rarely, he said his job was to take care of his players, and that is what he'd done. I know from time to time people whispered about it, but I learned from my class at the Mental Health Center, you should not blame yourself for not stopping someone.

"Why, if Daddy had been there in time to keep that boy from jumping off that balcony, he would have just tried something else another time. That's what happens a lot. They keep trying till they get it right. And, you know, he might have taken someone else out with him. Now that would have been a real tragedy."

CHAPTER TWENTY

Stephanie checked her notes and her watch. Edie Spence's family was staying at the fake chalet hotel on Route 21. It was on the outskirts of town, and Stephanie always imagined it looking around town at all the square limestone buildings and running to the edge of town to hide, like a girl dressed wrong for a party.

Stephanie knocked on the door where Dr. Spence and his kids were staying. She didn't blame them. It would be hard to be home right now. Edie would be missing from every room.

Dr. Spence opened the door and invited her into the room.

"Thank you so much for meeting with me, Dr. Spence. I am so sorry about your wife. I can tell just from the little bit of research I've done on her that she was an amazing woman."

"Yes, she was. Please call me Sean; when someone calls me Dr. Spence I automatically look behind them for a dog or a cat," he said, pointing to a chair for her.

"I heard you were a vet. That must be a very rewarding job, helping animals."

"Well, I actually started out to be a doctor, but I became a vet because of Edie."

"Oh, she liked animals?"

"Yes, she did, but that's not why. I met Edie when we were in college. Almost the first day I got there, actually. It didn't take long to decide she was the girl for me.

"One day we were hanging out outside my fraternity house, a whole bunch of people, and I overheard her say she could never marry a doctor because she was in the school of nursing. It was too much of a cliché for her. I was planning on medical school. My father was a doctor, and I just always imagined that's what I would be, too.

"But right then I decided to become a veterinarian. Now Edie always laughs when I tell that story. She thinks I changed my mind because of a great biology professor I had who pushed me in that direction, and I'm just saying that to be romantic. She never believes that story is the pure truth, but it is. Even at nineteen I knew I could be happy doing a lot of things, but I'd never be happy without her." He looked at Stephanie and repeated, "I'd never be happy without her."

Stephanie listened and thought about the kind of love she wanted in her life. She thought once that was the kind of love she had. What was worse: having this kind of love and losing it, or thinking you had it and realizing you had been deceived? Stephanie took in Sean Spence's haggard face and felt her heart constrict. A question for another day.

She cleared her throat and said, "Well, I know from my other interviews that Edie was special. Personally, I think anyone who works in hospice is a saint."

Sean looked up from staring at the floor and right into her eyes. She thought he was going to tell her more about the saintliness of his beloved Edie. But he laughed.

"You're getting the wrong picture of her if you are seeing her walking around with a halo doing good deeds all day. Yes, she was compassionate and caring, but I mean to tell you, that girl was fun—and funny."

It was nice to see him smile as he talked. He just looked like the kind of man who was meant to be happy. He was handsome in a rugged, casual kind of way. What was she thinking? Handsome? The poor guy just lost his wife, and she was sizing him up like he was on Match.com. How far down had she sunk?

"Still, it must take a special person to work in hospice," she prodded.

"I'll tell you how Edie got into hospice," Sean said, swiveling his knees toward her and leaning forward in a you-don't-want-to-miss-this pose.

"When we were first married, we were both working crazy hours. I was trying to set up a practice and doing some work for the university, and she was working maternity at the university hospital. One of her first patients was a young woman who came in, had her baby, and then had some kind of complication, something minor, I don't remember what.

"But, anyway, Edie took care of her. The woman was anxious to go home because this was her second baby, and she wanted to go home and see her older child. Whatever the complication was, they thought it was all worked out and she was scheduled to go home. Edie went into her room to say goodbye when she started her shift in the morning, and the woman had died during the night. Some freak thing, a blood clot, or something. Edie took it hard. Of course, there was nothing she or anyone else could have done to prevent it, but she took it hard.

"A couple of months later she signed up to do hospice nursing. I was worried about her. I said, 'But honey, you were so upset by that woman's death, do you think you should be doing hospice where *all* your patients are going to die?' And she explained to me that it wasn't so much the dying as the being so unprepared for it. She wanted to help people feel as good as they could in their last days. She could accept that. What she couldn't take was the suddenness and unexpectedness of death.

"So she joined hospice, and she always said she started her nursing career at the beginning of life but it was the end of life care that came to be where she felt most useful."

"I know what a difference she made in people's lives. I just came from the funeral of one of her patients, Harlan Tucker. His daughters were telling me how important Edie was to their father, how much they appreciated her help and support."

"That's one of the things I just can't stop thinking about: Edie comforting people, how determined she was that no one die alone, scared, or in pain. But that's how she died. All alone, in pain, and she must have been so scared. Why wasn't I there? I just hope she didn't know the kid was going to die, too. I keep imagining how much anguish she would have felt over knowing he was suffering and she couldn't help him."

A woman dressed in a hospice uniform like Pat's came from the other room, carrying a phone. "Sorry to interrupt, Sean, but I think you need to take this."

Sean said, "Stephanie, excuse me for a minute." And he walked back into the next room toward the table where his children sat.

The kids, a teenage girl and boy, switched places with their father. He sat down at the table and they got up and headed toward Stephanie.

"Stephanie Gallagher with the Forsyth *Bee*. I'm so sorry about your mother."

"Thank you. I'm Steven Spence and this is my sister, Beth Anne."

"I'm sorry to be meeting you under these circumstances. I was just telling your father, I know what a wonderful person your mother was. I'm doing a story about her, to honor her." Stephanie did not add, "Because I feel like I screwed up with my stories about the robberies." So far, Mick was the only person who had suggested that she was at fault, but when a little time passed she wondered if the families would blame her.

Now there was just pain and confusion. The girl seemed very shook up. Poor thing! What a shock, to have your mother killed at your house: the person who keeps you safe and the place you feel safe, both gone at once.

"So are you students at the high school?" Stephanie asked, just to get the ball rolling.

"No, I was, but I graduated last year. My sister is a sophomore there," Steven Spence answered.

Stephanie knew she wouldn't get anything with the "tell me about your mother" line. Maybe because of her earlier talk with Tiffany, the idea to ask about the first day of school popped into her head.

She said, "I went all through school in Forsyth, too. I loved a lot of it. I started at Travis Elementary. Did you go there, too?" When Beth Anne nodded yes, Stephanie asked her about her first day of school.

"My mom made a real big deal about it. I remember we had cupcakes and she had balloons taped up in the kitchen. She helped me pick out my outfit, which will live on in infamy because of all the pictures she took that day. She made me feel like I was special and going off on some grand adventure."

She pushed a Kleenex into her eyes and her brother reached over and gave her shoulder a tap.

"Mom let us pick what we wanted for dinner the night before school started every year," Steven said. "This fall, when I was getting ready to go back to school, she asked me and I told her, 'You don't have to keep doing that; I'm in college.' But she made meatloaf and an ice cream pie. She was just like that."

Stephanie felt all that the Reluctant Robber had stolen from this family.

CHAPTER TWENTY-ONE

Mick and Mason headed back to the office.

Austin was just getting back, too, from directing traffic at Harlan Tucker's funeral. Mason stayed in the hall for a minute to check in with him and then came back into Mick's office.

"Hey, Austin and I are going out to Bucko Burgers tonight. I know you're still on your own. You want to come with us?"

When Mick watched police shows on TV, he could give entire lectures on what was wrong with the shows. The thing that really got him about police shows, the one that bugged him the most, was that they always had these great partners. They went everywhere with each other, always together. Who had the money to send out two people?

But if he were going to have a partner, it would be Mason. He was younger and less experienced, but he was smart, with good instincts. It would make this whole Reluctant Robber–double murder fiasco much easier to handle, having another person to share the responsibility. So far he was pretty much going it alone. The thing was, though, he wasn't Mason's partner; he was Mason's boss, and now he had to draw the line.

"Gee, thanks. A burger and a beer does sound good and all, but we can't go out tonight, no matter what time we get off. Think about it. There will be people at Bucko's who'll say hi to us and not all—but a lot of them—will be thinking, 'What the hell are the police doing out having a beer and some fun while two murders go unsolved in Forsyth?' And worse, there might be press people. Even people from Dallas can find good burgers. We don't want to be sitting with a beer in front of us, looking like we aren't doing anything. We also don't want to be talking about our investigation to the press or anybody else, at this point—in a bar over a beer."

He could see Mason mulling over the wisdom of his remarks. He thought, *He's getting it.*

But Mason nodded his assent, and then blurted out what Mick did not want to think about. "What if we never solve this?"

So much for understanding. "Just lay low for a week or two. I actually believe we are going to find this guy, but even if we don't, attention will die down after a while."

"OK, you're right, Mick. I'll tell Tyler we can do it some other time."

As a peace offering, Mick threw in, "We'll all go out and really celebrate when we solve this."

Mick knew the press would be all over town. He imagined the out-of-town reporters driving around until they found someone with missing teeth and overalls. "There, stop! That's the one we want to interview. He looks to us like a good representative of what we think we're going to find when we come down here." And of course they expected Mick to be like the cop on the *Dukes of Hazzard.*

Mason headed down the hall to give the update to Tyler Austin— or Austin Tyler—and left Mick to contemplate what he was going to have for dinner. Going out was out. He couldn't stand the thought of ordering a pizza; he'd be thinking of Adam Moore. That left drive-through at McDonald's or peanut butter, neither that appealing.

He decided to postpone the decision and take another look at his file on the burglaries. He had the feeling that there was a page missing, and if he could only find that page it would all fall into place and he could figure out who the robber was and why this time things had gone so terribly wrong.

He had Stephanie Gallagher's news story. The article was light and fluffy, the robber returning old man Colby's license. Ha-ha. The good-hearted thief and all that bullshit about hard times drove him crazy. It was easy to feel sorry for the poor criminal suffering from low self-esteem—easy until the criminal held a knife to your throat. Then people came to a different understanding. They weren't so interested in the criminal's self-esteem issues or his crappy childhood. Then, they wanted protection. Do-gooders.

When he started out, working nights, sometimes he used to run into a group in Dallas. They went out at night to give sandwiches to homeless people. The police, meaning him, were trying to get the homeless folks to go into the shelters for the night: safer for them and safer for the other people walking around at night.

People in the sandwich group used to tell him how bad they felt that there were so many people lining up to get a sandwich in this country, the richest country in the world. He told them, "If you took those free sandwiches down to the precinct building, I guarantee you'd have police officers outside, lining up for a free sandwich." And not because they were hungry; free is free.

So he was on the streets trying to protect the homeless from each other and anyone else who might prey on them, and the sandwich people were trying to protect the homeless from him. It was not a win-win.

Mick turned his attention back to the file. Adam Moore sure hadn't had a happy childhood, but he didn't go out and knife people. Or did he? Time to think about him. Maybe the paper he was missing was the report he should have but didn't on the items returned. They had just made a note of the return.

What if old Mr. Colby noticed something that day? He'd been out walking his dog when he was robbed, but what about when the thief gave him back his license? It was worth checking back with him. Mick looked at his watch; not too late. He decided this time he would take Mason with him.

Martin Colby's house was on a quiet, tree-lined street. Mick rang the bell and it was instant bedlam: a dog barking, a man shouting, and heavy footsteps. When the door opened a crack, Mr. Colby leaned out, with his feet planted together to corral a little furry dog with great big ears.

"Sammy, no!" Colby said firmly, but if Sammy heard, he didn't show it. Mick got out his badge and Colby held up his finger, just a minute. He shut the door and Mick and Mason exchanged a look. When the door reopened Sammy was on a leash. He showed a lot of interest in Mason, sniffing his shoes, running from one foot to the other foot, but at least he stopped barking. Mick couldn't remember seeing the dog when he came out to talk about the burglary. Some detective he was if he had missed this yapper.

"Sorry about that. Sammy is so excited to see new people. These men are policemen, so you better be a good girl!"

That explains it, Mick thought. Samantha. No wonder she went for Mason, just like all the girls. Mick sighed and started off with a little small talk.

"That sure is a cute dog, what kind is she?"

"Samantha is a papillon. That's French for *butterfly*. See how her ears kind of look like butterflies?"

And now that it was pointed out to him, Mick could see. They did look like butterfly wings. Martin Colby gestured to some chairs and picked up the newspapers that were layered over them. Mick and Mason sat down. Sammy rested her head on Mason's shoes. He leaned down and rubbed her furry ears.

"That's funny. It usually takes her a while to warm up to people. I guess she likes you," Colby said. Mason smiled.

Mick pulled out a photo of the gun and showed it to Martin Colby, who confirmed what they knew. It was his gun, the gun that was stolen from his house.

"Well, I guess you're here to talk more about the robbery. I sure am sad to think it was my gun that killed those poor folks. I can't tell y'all how bad I feel about that. But I don't know what all I can add to what I've already told you."

"That gun being stolen sure wasn't your fault. I know you have been helpful to us about the robbery, but we wanted to ask you if you noticed anything odd or anybody not where they should be the day your driver's license was returned."

"I didn't see anyone around. It was just under the paper when Sammy and I went out to get it." At the mention of her name the little dog's ears twitched, flying butterflies.

"What time did you go out to get the paper? Do you always go at the same time?"

"Let's see . . . we get up and Sammy goes out in back and then I feed her and put the coffee on. I always put her leash on when I take her in the front. This isn't a busy street, but the kids use it to get to school, so I worry about cars. The lady across the street, her Pekingese ran out in the street, chasing a squirrel, and got hit by a car. I had to help her carry him to the vet. That was a sad day, for sure. The boy who hit him was real shook up and sorry. Sad.

"So, just to be safe, I leash Sammy up to walk down to end of the driveway for the paper. Then we come back in and I have my coffee, fry an egg and some bacon for breakfast. I'm too old to worry about cholesterol. Then, I make my bed and read the paper."

That was a lot of daily detail but not what Mick needed to know. Mr. Colby clearly enjoyed having someone besides Sammy to talk to.

He tried again. "So, about what time is it when you walk out to get the paper?"

"Well, I get up about 6:15 a.m. I don't set an alarm clock any more. Don't have to. When I was working I always thought how nice it would be to just sleep till I woke up, not have to pop up with the alarm. But now I can't sleep past 6:30 a.m. anyway. So there I am, up at 6:30 a.m., no matter what."

"Yeah, I know how you feel about alarm clocks. So what time do you think it is when you go out to get the paper?"

If Martin Colby noticed Mick was repeating the same question, he didn't appear too concerned about it.

"Like I was saying, it's after I let Sammy out and put on the coffee, so I guess it's around 6:45 a.m. or 7:00 a.m. Depends on how long it takes Samantha in the backyard. Right, girl?"

"Hmm. Do you know what time the paper is delivered here?"

"Not exactly. I just know it's always there when we go out to get it. Isn't it, Sammy?"

The little dog raised her head off Mason's shoes and looked at her owner. She stayed where she was, though. Maybe she enjoyed having company, too.

"OK, and when you picked up the paper that day, you found your license lying on the sidewalk?"

"That's right, only it wasn't lying on the sidewalk. It was right under the paper. I looked down the street but I didn't see anybody. There were some kids heading to the high school. I think maybe the track team. They were running.

"I remember at the time I considered calling out to them, but like I said, they must have been on the track team. They were running pretty fast, so by the time I saw the license and noticed them, they were out of earshot. Even the one who was limping and being helped by his friends was going fast."

So someone had to have come after the paper was delivered and before Colby walked down the driveway. Mick wanted to determine what time the paper came. It might be worth checking with the high school to see what group was running by that morning. It was possible that one of them noticed someone outside Colby's house.

Mick wondered if the thief had time to sell the gun and trade it for drugs or even just toss it out the window of his car. That would explain the change in modus operandi. Stephanie liked the alliteration, which is why she called the thief the Reluctant Robber. But, technically, he was a burglar until the night he confronted the victims, and then he turned into a robber.

Could it mean there were two people committing the crimes? A burglar and then a robber? Some kid breaks in a few places, steals a gun, and that gun winds up with the wrong guy. That seemed unlikely. Usually the simplest explanation was the right one.

Besides, there weren't that many places in Forsyth where you could go for a transaction like that, and it didn't make any sense for the sale or trade of the gun to be anywhere but Forsyth. If the kid took it somewhere else to sell, how did it get back here? How much time between the break-in at Colby's and the murder? Enough to somehow transfer the gun? Unlikely.

He was looking for only one person. That was the simplest and best explanation. But now he couldn't shake the feeling he should be looking for two. He sighed when he thought of telling Rainy. Rainy hated the idea there was one criminal in Forsyth. He would really hate the idea that there might be two.

"One more thing, Mr. Colby. Do you recall if the gun was loaded?"

"Of course. What's the point of having a gun that isn't loaded? Right, Samantha?"

Mick nodded, but he was thinking, *What's the point of having a gun like that anyway?* He'd never seen a gun used to prevent a crime, but he had seen plenty of accidental shootings. But he wasn't here to have a debate about the NRA, and he was pretty sure Samantha didn't have an opinion about anything except kibble.

"Well, we'd like you to come down and be fingerprinted. We may get some prints or partial prints from the gun, and it'd help if we had yours on file. I can have someone drive you if you like, or you can just come by the station. We'd like to get them as soon as possible."

"Sure, just let me put Samantha in her crate and I'll drive right down there. I got my license back, you know." He scooped up the little mop of a dog and said, "They're going to fingerprint me. We sure are having some excitement around here, aren't we, Sammy girl?" Mick watched as Martin Colby coaxed the little dog into a wire cage with a pink cushion.

"I don't remember seeing Samantha the first time I came out," Mick mused.

"Let's see, I think that was the day she was having her teeth cleaned. They have to put her under for that, so she stays overnight. We don't want to take any chances do we, Sammy girl?"

"Who's your vet?" Mick asked.

Martin Colby was bent over, pushing some kind of little bone through the cage door. "Why, poor Dr. Spence is our vet. He's the best."

When he straightened up to face Mick and Mason he said, "I feel terrible that it was my gun, just terrible."

CHAPTER TWENTY-TWO

Stephanie walked back through the lobby and out to her car. *What a shame*, she thought, *such a nice family*. It would be a shame no matter what kind of family.

It was terrible to even think this, but Sean Spence seemed like the perfect man. He'd be remarried in a jiffy. All the single women and some not-so-single women would be over there with casseroles and cakes. Well, he was a dream.

Of course that's what she'd thought about Pete, too, and he had turned out to be a nightmare. She could remember the end like it was yesterday. So much for all that Dr. Phil and getting on with your life stuff. She could see Pete dressed in his running clothes. She had told him she was heading over to her parents' house to pick up a platter to use for a party they were having at their house that night.

"OK, I'll just take a shower and then I'm all yours. Let me know what I can do to help." He had actually uttered those words, "I'm all yours," when in fact he wasn't hers at all.

She was in her car when she remembered a book she was going to bring for her mother. She pulled back in the driveway and opened the kitchen door. Still sweaty from his run, his back to her, she had thought about sneaking up on him and giving him a hug.

But what she heard stopped her dead in her tracks, like the game she and her sister had played where they would run and jump and one would yell "freeze!" and the other would have to stop in whatever position she was in. It was like someone yelled "freeze!" And Stephanie froze with one foot on the ground and one in the air.

He was holding the phone, saying, "Honey, honey, you know it has to be like this. It's only for a little while longer and then we can be together out in the open for the rest of our lives. Trust me; I am going to make you happy every day of your life. I promise." Stephanie still didn't know what made him turn around. She didn't cry. She didn't scream.

When he saw her all she said was, "I guess I won't need that platter after all."

That was the beginning of the end. No wonder Sean Spence looked good to her.

Stephanie wanted to go to the high school and see what else she could find out about Adam Moore.

As she got closer it was like a scene from the movie *Godzilla*. All the students pouring out the doors of the school and tearing out of the parking lots, trying to get away from there as fast as they could. *Just wait*, she wanted to tell them, *what you are running toward might not be so great*. Oh gosh, did she sound bitter? Bitter and old. Her parents were right; she was letting the divorce change her.

When she first told her parents about Pete and how stupid she felt for being so trusting, her mother had said, "There's nothing wrong with being a loving, trusting person. You just loved and trusted someone who wasn't worthy of your trust. Shame on him for deceiving you! You can hold your head up and be proud of the way you acted."

Well, she wasn't feeling so proud now. Maybe a return to high school, a time when she thought she couldn't make any mistakes with her life, would make her feel better. *But I doubt it,* she thought wryly, as she pushed through the familiar, heavy door.

Mark Lavelle greeted her warmly. There was something so boyish about him, almost as though through osmosis he absorbed youthfulness from being around high school kids all day.

He had some old *Flyers* on his desk. "I rounded up some information after you called, Stephanie. These are some of the articles about Adam Moore. I talked to his guidance counselor, and of course I can't give you any confidential information. But I can tell you that she liked him and that he was the kind of kid you didn't mind going that extra mile for because he was so appreciative of any help. I thought you might like to talk to his soccer coach, Andy Gilbert. He's teaching driver's ed and his last carload gets back about now. He'll be here in a few minutes."

Andy Gilbert, another blast from her past.

"Sure, I know Andy from high school. I'll wait here for him."

"Is there anything else I can do for you?" he asked.

"No, no thanks for gathering all the papers. I just need a chance to look through them."

"Well, why don't you just stay and use my office? Andy'll be along soon, and y'all can just talk in here. I've got to go and check on the grief counseling center we've set up. When you're finished with Andy, let me know, and we can get a cup of coffee in the cafeteria."

Stephanie glanced up at him with her eyebrows raised and he immediately said, "Hey, the coffee here is good."

Stephanie didn't need to check his ring finger. She knew he was single. That was life in a small town. You know things. This was the closest she'd come to a date since her divorce. She managed a smile and said, "Thanks, a cup of coffee sounds good."

For some reason this small gesture lifted her spirits.

Stephanie picked through the old copies of the *Flyer* on the desk while she waited for Andy. She found a few good articles about Adam and a picture of him after a goal, looking heartbreakingly happy. Really, for a high school paper the *Flyer* was excellent. Forsyth High might be known for great football teams, but there was a lot of support for other activities. And it showed.

She was shuffling the papers she didn't need into a neat pile when she noticed that the *Flyer* she was holding had an article about Coach Tucker. The article was just a note about his passing and the fact that he had coached teams to five state championships. It made her stop and wonder about the small world factor.

When she came up with the idea to do a series on the murder victims, she had planned to illustrate how two such different people crossed paths and died together. But maybe they weren't crossing paths for the first time. Maybe they already knew each other. Edie Spence and Adam Moore had both spent time with Harlan Tucker, and now all three were gone. She wondered if Mick knew or if she should call and tell him.

Maybe the Robber knew about Harlan Tucker's wake, knew that Edie Spence would be there, and thought he could rob her unoccupied house. Did that make sense? Maybe, maybe not, but it would give her a reason to talk to Mick. She might learn something from him. Right now she just wanted to finish up her meeting with Andy and go practice a little flirting over a cup of coffee with the principal.

Andy walked in the room with a big smile on his face. He hadn't changed at all, literally. He appeared to be wearing the same clothes that he had worn in high school, right down to his sneakers.

"Hey, Miss Stephanie! Lori and I were just talking about you! She was just saying how we need to invite you over for dinner. I think she's getting tired of talking baby talk."

Stephanie felt a twinge of jealousy. Talking to a baby with your sweet, supportive husband coming home at night didn't sound so bad. She put on a big smile and said, "I'd love to! It would be so much fun to catch up."

Andy seemed pleased with himself. "Mark said you wanted to know about Adam Moore."

She nodded and waited.

"I can tell you this; he was the best soccer player I ever saw. He was fast, agile, and strong. I've never seen such a natural athlete. He was a good kid, too. The boys on the team liked him, looked up to him. I liked him, too. He got a bad deal. His sister just about raised him, as far as I could tell. It was a great time for me when he was playing. The whole town was excited about watching soccer games. In a football town like this, that's saying something. We had scouts from big schools coming down to take a look at him. He got a good deal at Tech. Full ride.

"But then he had the accident. I tried to talk him into going to Tech anyway, but he was discouraged. And who can blame him? The kid started out with a bad deal and turned everything around only to have it all snatched away from him. I guess he kind of gave up, got into some trouble. I went to bat for him. But you know how it is. He didn't have an outraged father running in to say his son was innocent. So he's the guy who gets sidelined."

Stephanie thought that must be one of the drawbacks to being a coach; all Andy's expressions seemed to be sports related. He probably asked his wife if he could go to first base with her.

"What did he get in trouble for? Why did you have to"—and here she cringed a little; it just didn't sound right coming out of her mouth—"go to bat for him?"

Andy didn't seem to think it sounded strange. She was speaking his language. "Oh, just kid stuff. He was in the cafeteria, and Alyssa Kenner asked him to watch her stuff while she went to pick up some ice cream. At the end of the day she checked her bag and couldn't find her phone. She accused him and the girl he was sitting with, Lacey Thomas, of taking it. They denied it. It could have been taken by anybody; she didn't check her bag until the end of the day.

But her parents came in and demanded that we call the police and probably the FBI. Mark told Alyssa's dad that he would do an internal investigation. He talked to every kid at the lunch table. Didn't get much, so he gave Adam and Lacey a one-day suspension. I talked him down to community service hours. That satisfied Mr. Kenner." Andy paused, looking uncharacteristically regretful. "I've got some great pictures of Adam playing. You're welcome to those."

"OK, thanks Andy. I've got some pictures on file at the *Bee*, but I'll let you know. I appreciate your time, and you tell Lori to call me and we can set something up."

Andy saluted her and left the room. Now she was ready for that cup of coffee with Mark Lavelle.

CHAPTER TWENTY-THREE

Mick had an easier time than he expected finding Adam Moore's mother—just in the nick of time, too. Everybody thinks you can find out so much about people on the Internet and sometimes you can, but it's a lot harder to find someone who doesn't want to be found, or someone who changed her name like Linda Kane Hudson Moore Murkowski Sheffield did. How did that woman get all those men to marry her?

Mick finally tracked her down, in jail in Arkansas for writing bad checks. She wasn't the type to use her Social Security card. He had found her through her arrest record. He'd make a call and see what he could do. Or should he? Would it help Tiffany to have her mother there wearing an ankle bracelet?

Once again he wished he had Julie to talk to. He missed her, and Colly. He was going to go with the idea that a bad mother might be better than no mother in this situation and see what he could do. Probably call Rainy and pass to him the job of getting Mrs. Sheffield out of jail for her son's funeral. Time was of the essence here. Adam's funeral had been scheduled for Wednesday, since the funeral home was double-booked. Unexpectedly busy—what a sad thought.

Mick went over his notes and decided on his next moves. He would head back out to the high school and check out the group of athletes that had run by Martin Colby's house. Second on his list was a call to the Spences. By now, they might have noticed something missing or something amiss if they had gone back to the house. The evidence techs would be all done.

That would be another thing he could do tomorrow: check in on them. This thought inspired another rant in his head. On TV, there was always the same team, week after week, solving the crimes together. In reality, he didn't know the techs. They were probably in the same group as the young photo guy. He often worked with complete strangers. It wasn't like the same four people teaming up each episode, joking with each other and knowing each other's families. So much for all that buddy-buddy stuff.

Well, he and Rainy certainly knew each other and, in a funny way, they were buddies. Rainy could be a little pompous, sure, but he had to get elected from time to time. He needed the stage presence.

Mick hated to call him. Rainy would see his caller ID and think there was a break in the case. He'd be all excited, and there was nothing to be excited about. Yet.

Rainy picked up on the first ring, breathless, like a girl waiting for her boyfriend to call.

"Nothing new," Mick said instead of saying hello. "I need some help getting the Moore kid's mother out for the funeral." He explained the details.

He could almost see Rainy's droopy face sighing in resignation.

CHAPTER TWENTY-FOUR

Stephanie had to admit, it was a pleasant change to have coffee with Mark Lavelle, even if it was right back at Forsyth High.

Of course, he, like everyone else in town, had heard the saga about her failed marriage. The empty dental office still had Peter Popkins, DDS, painted in shadowed letters on the door next to the frozen yogurt shop. She'd probably saved a bunch of calories by avoiding that location. If Mark Lavelle stopped for the chocolate vanilla twist, he would have seen it, too, but they hadn't talked about it, which was a part of the pleasant change for her.

People were forever asking her if she was alright or trying to get the dirty details about what had happened, what went wrong. Now she was coming to believe that even the word she always applied to her marriage—failed—didn't mean she was a failure.

For one thing, she was pleased with the shape her article was taking. Her work was good. She was thinking it might turn into more of a magazine piece, bigger than she had thought at first. She knew Tom loved her first article. Adam Moore and Edie Spence had crossed paths more than once, and she thought that added interest to the story. Casual acquaintances meet and then die together. Soon Mick would confirm what they both already knew; the murder weapon was stolen by the Reluctant Robber.

When that news broke it would push the story like a west Texas oil gusher, and she would be on the top of it. Stephanie wanted to be ready when that happened.

She was heading over to Harlan Tucker's house to talk some more to his daughters before they closed up the house and headed back to their lives. She knew from talking to them at the funeral that they were planning to start cleaning out his house, with the help of his aide. She wanted to find out if Adam and Edie had ever met at Harlan's. It gave her a sudden chill to think of the three of them, all alive last week and now all three dead.

Stephanie wondered if it meant anything even if she did find out that Edie and Adam had met here at Harlan's. She admitted to herself that calling Mick and giving him something he might be able to use in solving these murders would make her feel better. And maybe the small dose of male attention she had gotten from Mark Lavelle made her want more, made her want to talk with Mick, a man she respected.

She felt like a person recovering from a bad hangover. You saw a plate of spaghetti when you were sick like that and it made you gag. But her hangover was wearing off, and now not only could she stand the sight of that spaghetti, she might be ready to try some. Not that she would ever think of Mick exactly like that. Why did he even pop into her head now?

When Pete took up with Sara, Stephanie's sister had suggested she give Warren a call and give old Pete and Sara a little taste of their own medicine. She had been just desperate enough to do it. Warren cried when she called him to talk about their mutual marital breakups, but he must not have been crying all that much because he had already fallen in love with the hygienist in their office. He told Stephanie how Mandy could sense his unhappiness and offered him support and sympathy. Of course Mandy knew what was happening with Pete and Sara, knew about the affair. Apparently, Stephanie was the only one who hadn't known.

Anyway, according to Warren, one day Mandy was showing him a possible cavity in the mouth of a terrified teenager and their hands brushed together. He told Stephanie that even through the latex of the gloves he felt a spark. They had looked at each other and fallen in love. Really? Through latex? So Warren had Mandy to help him get over the pain of losing Sara.

After that conversation, Stephanie couldn't help but feel that that office must have been a little Sodom and Gomorrah. It was a wonder they had any time to remove plaque buildup, with all the hanky-panky going on. Perhaps she should have gone in for more checkups. She might have spiced up her love life and whitened her teeth at the same time.

But Warren had been kind and told her that there was going to be life after Pete, and a happy life, too. Warren moved on. He and Mandy set up a practice in Nashville. In the end, Warren had decided to let Sara and Pete have the practice. Stephanie wondered if Pete had known all along that was the way it would work out; he would get the original practice, he would get Sara. It was a good plan. That was why he had duped her into helping him get a job one hundred miles away and comply with the non-compete: when his time was up he could return to the practice that Sara had been building for them and their future.

She sometimes wanted to ask Warren when he first suspected and if he thought their moving to Forsyth was the dirty trick that she had come to believe it was. But just last week she had gotten a save-the-date card from Warren and Mandy. He didn't want to dwell in the past. Did she? And who knew? Maybe she'd go to Warren and Mandy's wedding, maybe even with a date. Nashville might be fun. She liked country music.

Harlan's house was in a neighborhood of older homes, not too far from where Stephanie had lived growing up. There was a big tree out in front with roots pushing up through cracks in the sidewalk. It looked like it was telling the sidewalk, "I was here first." The house was red brick with white shutters. Stephanie could see a few cars parked in the driveway.

She parked on the street and walked up the buckled sidewalk through the shade to the front door. Kay Kay, holding a bottle of Windex, opened the door to let her in.

She called out to her sister, "Mary Sue, the reporter is here." Mary Sue came through a swinging door and behind her was a short Hispanic woman with a long dark braid down her back: Rosa, the aide who had been taking care of Harlan, living with him for the last few months. Stephanie wanted to talk to her, too. She was the one who would know if Edie and Adam had ever met here. Stephanie asked the sisters if she could speak with Rosa.

"You can try, but she's not comfortable in English. She and Daddy communicated just fine. Of course, he got along with everyone, and I don't think they were talking about nuclear disarmament or anything like that. I'm not sure what she can tell you, but you are welcome to talk with her. Would you like some iced tea?"

"Love some, thanks."

Now, Stephanie looked into the waiting eyes of Miss Rosa and tried to gather her thoughts in Spanish.

She asked Rosa about Harlan's last days and last visitors. Rosa replied in rapid Spanish, so Stephanie had to concentrate to pick up the words. She got most of it, though.

The Mister had only a few visitors in the last couple of weeks. He was very tired, hardly getting out of bed, too tired to see people, and he often slept through visits, even when people came.

Stephanie asked, "Who came?" And Rosa was off again with Stephanie trying to take notes but realizing she needed to look at Rosa in order to catch everything she was saying. A long parade of family members had come, but it had quieted down when they were all traveling to the cousin's wedding.

Stephanie asked about Adam Moore bringing a pizza, and Rosa nodded, "Sí, sí, he is bringing the pizza just like before, but the Mister he is not eating it."

"How about Miss Edie? Did she ever eat pizza with the Mister and Adam?"

"No, Miss Edie, she is coming in the daytime, and the pizza, it is coming at night."

"What did the Mister and the pizza man talk about? Did you ever hear what they were saying?"

Rosa was already shaking her head. "No, my English is not so good."

Stephanie thought, *My Spanish isn't great, either.*

Well, that was that. Edie and Adam might have both been here, but not at the same time: no intersecting. "Did the Mister ever talk to you about Edie or Adam? Ever say anything about them to you?"

"Sí, he says he wants to show pizza man the paper. He tells me wake him when pizza man comes. Very important he shows him the paper."

"He wanted to show Adam the paper?"

"Sí, the letter from the mail. The Mister is very excited about this. He wants to talk to Miss Edie and pizza man. "

"Gracias, Rosa."

Stephanie brought her sweating iced tea glass out to the kitchen where Kay Kay and Mary Sue were sorting through drawers with utensils in them, placing things in one of three piles: keep, give away, or throw away, they explained.

Stephanie rinsed out her glass and asked them if they knew anything about the letter that had so excited their father.

"It was the strangest thing. We were just talking about it. It was funny that he didn't mention it to either of us. We called to check in on him often. Of course, we never would have gone to the wedding in the first place if we'd known the end was so close. But it was hard to talk to him on the phone."

"You mean it was hard for him to hear on the phone. I'm sure he was waiting for us to come home to tell us about it. He'd rather talk in person," corrected her sister.

Kay Kay nodded her agreement with her sister.

Stephanie asked, "Do you know what the letter was about?"

"Oh yes, we found the letter. It was on Daddy's nightstand. We always knew there was something about Daddy's college football days that was, I don't know, off limits or something. He just never talked about it. And then we found the letter that explains it."

Mary Sue added, "I don't think we didn't talk about it because Daddy was still upset about it, but more like it was behind him. But you know, if you'd like to see the letter—or, I should say, letters; there are two of them—I don't see any harm in showing them to you. Would you like to see them? They don't have anything to do with your story, of course."

"I'd like to see the letters. Y'all make it sound kind of mysterious."

"In a way I guess it is mysterious, but more like a mystery solved. I'll get them for you. Are they still on the stand, Kay Kay?"

"I guess so, I didn't move them."

Mary Sue left to get the papers and Kay Kay wiped a tear out of her eye as she went through dish towels that should have been consigned to the rag pile. "I just wish we were here with him at the end, is all."

Mary Sue returned and, seeing her sister in distress, gave her a pat on the back with her free hand as she offered the papers from Harlan Tucker's nightstand.

Stephanie took the letters from Mary Sue and read them through once. Then she sat down and read them again. Mary Sue was right; they didn't have anything to do with her story of the murders, but what a story these would make! She read through them one more time. Meanwhile, the sisters came to the same conclusion as she had: all the dish towels were raggedy.

Dear Mr. Tucker,

I found this letter in one of my father's books. He had obviously been planning to send it to you but he had a stroke and was sick for a few years. By the time I got around to going through all his things after his death the letter was five years old. I am not sure if you are still with us, but since it was my father's wish to send the letter I am going to comply with his wishes. I did not know about the facts in the letter. I do know my father was a good man. I doubt that after all this time, this letter will have much of an effect on Mr. Tucker's life or, if he is gone, his family, but I do want to let you know that my father intended to right the wrong he had done. The letter is in the envelope my father had started to address. If you have any questions you can contact me at the following number, although I don't know if there is anything I can add to what I have told you.

Sincerely,
Daniel Connelly

To Whom It May Concern:

This letter is to set straight an injustice that was done to Harlan Tucker by me. I once foolishly placed a bet on our football team, the Hobart Wild Cats. When the National Collegiate Athletic Association investigated, I became frightened that an inquiry would point to me and I would be expelled from the college. I had plans to go to medical school and I knew that an expulsion would end my career aspirations. In order to avoid suspicion when the investigator came, I put the name of the man I had placed the bet with and some of the money I had won in Harlan's locker. Just for the record, I bet on the Wild Cats, not against them, not that that excuses anything. At any rate, despite Harlan's protests about his innocence, he was suspended for two games. I know now that I should have admitted my mistake. I came to realize that Harlan had been offered a slot on a professional team and that that offer was rescinded due to the betting scandal. I believe Harlan knew it was me who placed the evidence in his locker, and yet he never turned me in. I did go to medical school and served as a medic in the army before setting up my practice. I have tried to live a worthy life, and though I know there can be no justification for what I did, I pray that Harlan can use this information now to clear his name with the National Collegiate Athletic Association, and I pray he can forgive me.

Sincerely,
Wendell Connelly

Stephanie knew this was a great story: her kind of great story. She was already thinking of titles . . . "Forgiveness from the Past" . . . "Death Bed Declarations" . . . She bit her lip as she put the pages back in the envelope.

She glanced up at the sisters, still busy looking at the sea of possessions that they would have to wade through. They agreed to let her have the letters and write about Harlan's vindication in the *Bee*.

CHAPTER TWENTY-FIVE

Stephanie walked out carrying Harlan Tucker's letter from Mr. Connelly like it was a rare and historic document, which in a way it was. She carefully put it in a folder and set it on the backseat of her car. It was cleaner back there than the front seat.

What a story, she thought again as she pulled her sunglasses down from her head. She was already going over her introduction to the story. "Forgiven Fifty Years Too Late." She wasn't really sure about the fifty years part, but it did sound good . . . Or maybe it sounded a little tabloidish.

She was confident that when she showed the story to Tom, the two of them could come up with the perfect angle on this story. She was sorry it didn't come to light earlier. Harlan Tucker might have liked to see the story in print. Although maybe what the rest of the world thought hadn't been important to him anymore. Maybe it was just part of his past.

Stephanie wanted to think that you get over things; you recover completely and move on, that things from the past are just that—past. From what Miss Rosa had said, though, it appeared Harlan was pretty excited about the note, excited enough to tell his two usual visitors about it. Stephanie had a picture of the three of them—Edie, Adam, and Harlan—laughing and celebrating around Harlan's kitchen table.

She shook her head, and her sunglasses wobbled a bit. It was odd that she was imagining them that way. The three of them were never there together, but it did make a nice picture and it would have made a good story. Still, Harlan Tucker did tell them his good news. They might have had a pizza party together if they had all lived.

Stephanie felt a chill. She wasn't sure why, but thinking about the three of them all being dead made the hairs on the back of her neck stand up. *Some hard-boiled reporter*, she sighed and shivered.

Tom was sitting at his desk eating a granola bar, the crumbs falling on the cheap veneer of his desk.

"I just heard the most amazing story. I'm not sure if it is a companion piece for my articles or a stand-alone," Stephanie said as she eased into the chair in front of Tom's desk. "But wait till you hear it."

"Imagine that, a reporter with a story." Tom brushed the crumbs off his desk and into his hand. He checked for the wastebasket. Too far. He rubbed his hands together and the crumbs fell roughly back where they started. "OK, so what's the story?" Tom tilted back in his chair and waited.

"Well, you know the obit we ran on Harlan Tucker?" Stephanie waited for his nod and then went on. "So, he was the high school football coach." Tom rocked a little in his chair. Stephanie knew that he was the keeper of all Forsyth facts. If they were ever included in a Trivial Pursuit game, Tom would certainly win. "And you know he played some college ball."

Tom rocked back down. "Not only that, he was being considered by a professional team. I can't remember which one, but I know the paper ran some stories on him."

Stephanie nodded, "Yeah, yeah, so old Harlan gets a letter last week from someone he went to college with, and what do think the guy says?" Tom shrugged and Stephanie plunged ahead. "I'll tell you. He confesses to gambling and to letting Harlan take the fall for it. Says he's led a good life, with only that one regret. Did he really make up for his sin? Anyway, he's on his way out, and he wants to make amends.

"So what does he do? He sends a letter to Harlan or his family, if Harlan's gone. The letter details his misdeeds. Harlan receives the letter only days before he himself dies. And he is jubilant. He can finally put to rest the old rumors about him. He wants to tell everyone. He can let people know the truth without hurting anyone. Of course, at this point most of the original players are gone, as is our late confessor. Still, it brings joy to the old guy. Vindication at last. What do you think? Isn't that a great story?"

Tom responded with a question. "Do you know the last time Forsyth had a double murder?"

"No, but I'm sure you do."

Tom nodded. "It's kind of a trick question, because Forsyth has never had a double homicide until Tuesday. Do you get what I'm saying? This is a big story, Stephanie. I like the idea of in-depth stories of the victims. I'm not sure if the timing on the coach story is right. Who is going to want to read about something that happened a long time ago to somebody who's dead when we have this big story right here in front of us?"

Stephanie had to agree that Tom's comments made sense. But there was something about this story, some pull she couldn't explain. She was trying to formulate an answer that would satisfy Tom. He must have sensed her difficulty.

He sighed and said, "If you want to write it and you feel like you can keep up with the murders, go ahead. I'm just here to advise and edit you, not to tell you what to write. You do what you think is best. Just consider what I'm saying, OK?"

CHAPTER TWENTY-SIX

Mick rolled over in his bed and flung his arm to the other pillow. During the moments between sleeping and dreaming, he forgot he was alone. Then his eyes started to open and he remembered. He was alone. Alone. He gave himself the little pep talk he had been giving himself for the last couple of weeks. *It's good for Colly, Julie had to be with her or they'd both be worried sick about her, it wasn't for that long.*

That was the idea that he told himself to remember as he climbed out of bed and started his day. He had actually started crossing the days off the calendar from Brownie's Auto Parts hanging in his garage. How silly was that? But he had to admit he felt lighter, happier, every time he put those lines on the calendar, as if he were drawing his girls closer to him. He made his mark for the day and opened the garage door.

His plan for the day was to talk to the high school kids who had been running past Martin Colby's house, see if the Spences had anything to add, call the lab team, and, finally, follow up with Jack Jackson to see if he remembered anything else about the person he'd seen running away. Or if he had an idea about who was in such desperate straits that they might—reluctantly, he thought, using Stephanie's word—resort to robbing houses.

In the car he checked his messages, something he was constantly telling Colly and all her friends never to do. He had a message from the county, and he knew the autopsies were done, so they had run the ballistics test. He made a U-turn, another thing he told Colly not to do (cops only) and headed down to the office to find out what he already knew. He'd check in at the high school later.

Rainy was waiting in his office to talk to him.

He didn't smile when Mick walked in. He wasn't a glad-hander kind of politician. There was a reason for the expression "sober as a judge," and Rainy knew it.

Mick told Rainy briefly about Adam Moore's mother and asked if Rainy could get her out in time for the rush funeral. Rainy said he would try. The county guys had sent over the ballistics test. There was no doubt about the weapon.

That made it hard for both of them. It would have been much easier to have the killer be a stranger just passing through. But it was someone who was here long enough to commit five burglaries and then the murders. It also meant there was no rounding up the usual suspects.

When the burglaries had first started, Mick and Mason had checked on the local drug dealers and a couple of the other likely suspects. Earl Merrick was known to walk in uninvited and help himself if he found a garage or house unlocked when he needed a little extra cash. They had checked him out as their most likely, but he was in a Dallas jail for exposing himself.

And it was very unlikely that there were two burglars with the same MO. Mick gave Rainy the information he considered noteworthy: the high school track team might have seen something in their run by Martin Colby's house and the fact that the victims knew each other. Rainy picked up on the "knew each other."

"Do you mean 'knew each other' as in the biblical sense?" he asked, his sad face drooping down and his eyebrows going up.

"No, I don't believe that, but I can't prove there wasn't something there."

Rainy chewed on that fact for a second before jumping to the obvious. "If they were fooling around, could it have been the husband?"

"All bets are off on that, because we know the murder gun was stolen from Martin Colby. I can't see Dr. Spence staking out the house, stealing the gun, and murdering his wife and her lover with it. Too many holes. How would he know he would find a gun? And besides, we know he was on a plane at the time of the murders. So

I think what we are talking here is small world; they just met a few times and both wound up in the wrong place at the wrong time."

"Well, what about some crazy, love-sick teenage girl? You know women get jealous, too."

"Again, we got the Reluctant Robber thing. Same deal."

"Shit. A random killing makes everyone nervous. Feeling like the killer could strike anywhere next. I like it a whole lot better when it's a family member murder; so much neater and easier for people to understand. Everybody has occasional thoughts of killing a husband or wife."

Even here in Forsyth, he'd had to advise women to get restraining orders on exes. One guy—nice, good-looking, with a good job—just could not stop following his ex-girlfriend around. Mick started out having a talk with him, just to explain that he couldn't keep doing it. The funny thing was, other women were giving him the eye. He could have just started something new, but no, he kept telling Mick he couldn't live without his ex-girlfriend. He was sure that she would soon come to the same conclusion about him. Mick made a point to be outside the church when the ex married someone else, having never reached that conclusion.

And, sure enough, the lovesick guy showed up. Mick stepped out of his car, just to let the guy see him, and that was enough. The guy drove away without causing a scene. It all sounded cute when Garth Brooks sang about showing up at his ex's wedding, but in real life, it wasn't so cute.

Mick got the call the next morning. Highway patrol had spotted the car on the side of the road and gone to check it out. The guy had shot himself in the head. Mick never told anyone. But he always believed he saved the woman's life that day. And maybe some others, too.

Truth be told, he couldn't have done it without Stephanie Gallagher. The *Bee* published the police calls for the week in Friday's paper, in the "Police Beat" column, but he knew it was called "the Beatings." Oh, most of it was harmless; somebody locked out of their car or a mailbox knocked down, kids picked up for drinking (and sometimes more) in the park.

But they also published the domestic disturbance calls. He knew, just like everybody else who had ever watched a made-for-TV movie, that domestic abuse didn't just happen in some trailer park. It could happen anywhere. If the news that your husband took a swing at you because dinner was late was going to hit your neighbor's porch on Friday, you might think twice on Thursday about calling the police for help—help that might be really needed. So, a woman could wind up battered by her husband, then beaten by "Police Beat."

When Stephanie started at the *Bee*, one of the very first times Mick met her, they'd been talking about the paper and police relationship, and he mentioned how much he hated the *Bee* "Police Beat." Sometimes it seemed more like gossip, and the worst kind of gossip, the kind that really hurts. Stephanie was already a prize-winning journalist. She listened to what Mick said, and "Police Beat" stopped printing identifying information.

He wasn't sure how she got Tom to drop the idea. Maybe by publishing it the way they did, now people had a chance to guess who was beating up who. They might sell more papers that way. Who knew? The one thing he did know was that it saved women and kids from getting the shit beat out of them, just like he knew he had saved that woman's life on her wedding day. He wished he had thought a little more about that when he went off on Stephanie about her Reluctant Robber story.

Mick turned back to Rainy. "Look, I'm not ruling anything out yet. At least we have the ballistics report. We can throw that out to the press. I'm afraid it's going to be like pouring gasoline on a fire. They'll really be riled up after they know the connection between Stephanie Gallagher's Reluctant Robber and the murders." Mick cleared his throat and looked down. He wasn't sure how Rainy would take giving the *Bee* the story first. "I'm going to let Stephanie have the story today."

Rainy was too preoccupied with his own necessary encounters with the press to object to Mick's idea. Or maybe he agreed with Mick about giving the story to the local press first. After all, Rainy had to get elected here by the people who read the *Bee*, not by the folks who read *USA Today*. And Rainy would still get his chance to look concerned and determined on the six o'clock news.

"Let me know if you find out anything; I want to look like I'm on top of this."

"Will do. I should be getting something back from state on the fingerprints real soon."

Mick gathered up his things, heard the phone ringing on his desk, and made a grab for it. Stephanie Gallagher. He told her that it was the gun stolen by the Reluctant Robber that was used to kill Edie Spence and Adam Moore. He was telling her what she already knew. What they both wanted to know was who the Reluctant Robber was.

CHAPTER TWENTY-SEVEN

At the high school, Mark Lavelle saw Mick come into the office, peeked around the door before Doris could do anything official, and called Mick into his office.

"Some of your student athletes may have seen something when they were out running early the morning of April 8—something having to do with the robbery at Martin Colby's house. Can you tell me which group would be training at about 6:30 in the morning?"

The principal tugged his shirtsleeves out from the protection of his jacket and looked up at the ceiling. Mick glanced up quickly, too, just to check and see if the answer was written up there.

"That would be our early optional P.E. class," he said. "We let the students who are doing a sport have a P.E. class before school so they can fit it into their schedule. During the season, their sport practices count toward their P.E. credit, but when they aren't playing their sport, we give them credit for the training time. Most of them take it pretty seriously, too. It isn't goof-off time."

Mick nodded to show he didn't for a minute think Forsyth's finest high school athletes would even think of goofing off. "Could I talk to them? Just see if any of them saw anything?"

Before he even got the last words out of his mouth, Mark was shaking his head, sadly. "No, Mick, you know there is no way I could let you talk to any student without permission from the parents." Which, Mick knew, was not technically correct.

There were circumstances where he could interview a student without parental consent. This did not seem like the time to argue, though. Mick tilted his head and tried another approach. "OK, how about if you ask them and I just come along and listen? Look Mark,

I'm not down here to see who skipped class or who was drinking under the bleachers. I'm talking about two brutal murders, in *this* community. I know you want me to catch the killer, and I know I want to catch the killer, and I'd bet money the parents of these kids want to have this killer caught. This is not going to be an interrogation. I just want to know if they saw anyone on the street that morning.

"My job is to keep them safe, just like it's your job to keep them safe. Let's work together on this. Imagine if the killer strikes again and we could have prevented it. Do you think that would be in the best interest of your students, of Forsyth? Help me do my job."

Mark tugged at his sleeves again, pulled off his glasses, and rubbed them with a Kleenex. Now he could see clearly. "It will take a few minutes to get the whole group down here. But what does the robbery have to do with the murders?"

He waited for Mick's reply. Mick's turn to look at his cuffs—frayed.

"We think there is a connection between the break-ins and the murders," he said as he pushed his chair back. "And let's meet in the gym, instead of here," Mick advised. "We don't want them to feel like they did anything wrong. I think the principal's office might make them nervous, which they obviously have no reason to be."

Mark pressed the button on his intercom. "Doris, could you please send notes to the classes of the early P.E. students? Maybe better wait till the bell rings, so we don't catch them between periods."

What if this was not just a random robbery gone bad but the beginning of a crime spree? Mick had been around long enough to know that criminals often started with small crimes and then escalated. He knew if he could just find one string to grasp he could unravel the whole thing. And with a crime like this there were bound to be loose ends.

The bell rang, giving Mark and Mick the signal to head down to the gym to meet the group that had been summoned. It was quite possible that one of those kids might have seen someone early that morning almost three weeks ago.

That was a problem. Three weeks was a long time for a kid. But Mick held his head up and tried to be positive.

All his positive feelings drained away like dirty dishwater down the drain when he looked over the assembled group. Just kids. Jostling each other and moving restlessly on the bleachers. They looked like Colly's kindergarten class getting ready to settle down on their cots. Why did he think he could get something useful from them?

He scanned the group of about twenty and recognized a few of them, mostly from watching high school football games. And that was a good thing. He knew a fair number of kids from run-ins he had had with them. This group didn't fall into that category. He recognized the Jackson kid he had seen yesterday with his father. Mick tried to give him a nod of recognition but the kid was avoiding his gaze, probably wanted to get the hell out of there, like the rest of them.

Mark Lavelle settled them down, pushing his hands down. "Mr. McKay is here to ask a few questions. Please listen carefully and answer if you can." He stepped aside to let Mick take center court.

"Boys, I asked Mr. Lavelle to bring you down here because I think you could have seen something on one of your runs, something having to do with a robbery. I know it's hard to remember, but this would be about three weeks ago on a Thursday. Mr. Lavelle tells me that you are serious athletes and you have a training routine. First, let me ask how many of you do the run that takes you down Lee Street?"

Fifteen boys raised their hands, like they were getting ready to testify: *raise your right hand.*

"OK, good, good. Now when you do that run, do you usually see anybody? I know it's early, but is there anyone you see regularly on your route?"

One of the boys, with shoulders so wide he looked like he would have trouble getting through doorways, raised his hand. Mick pointed at him and Mr. Lavelle, beside him, said, "Jeff," as if empowering him to speak.

"We usually see a guy in his truck throwing newspapers." The other boys nodded in agreement.

"Good, good, that's just what I'm talking about. Anyone you see on that route?"

Another kid raised his hand. "Chris," Mr. Lavelle said. *Open sesame*, Mick thought.

"We see a couple of ladies doing that walk-run sort of exercise."
Now several hands went up.

"Jake," Mr. Lavelle said, pointing to another.

"There is a lady out on Ninth Street. She waters her garden. I remember because sometimes she puts the sprinkler across the sidewalk and we have to run around it."

"Tim."

"Yeah, that's what I was going to say, too."

"All right, those are the folks you see a lot. Now can you think of seeing anyone new, especially on that Thursday? Anyone who you thought, 'What are they doing up so early?' Or, 'What are they doing out here?'"

The kid, Kevin, called out, "Yeah, Chip, because he sure wasn't running, even with his superfast new shoes." All the boys laughed and Kevin gave Chip a shove: puppies playing.

"What do you mean he wasn't running?" Mick asked.

"That was the day you hurt your ankle, right?" Kevin said.

Mick flicked his eyes toward Chip. "You hurt your ankle that day?"

Chip's reply reminded Mick of a foreign film. He could tell the kid was talking but he couldn't understand what he was saying. Mick thought, *Where were the subtitles?*

"What?" Mick asked moving closer to the bleachers.

"Don't know," Chip mumbled.

Kevin came to his rescue. "Yeah, that was the day. Remember, we had that government test on the fourteenth. I actually studied for it. And you came running in right when the bell rang? I said, 'All better now? I guess you just wanted a little together time with us dragging you.'" The kid looked around like he was expecting a laugh, but the other boys were a little less sure of how to react to the comment, with Mick and, more importantly, the principal, present.

Mick jumped in with, "Thanks, Kevin. That's the sort of thing we need. Does anyone remember anything else from the day Chip fell?"

Kevin couldn't resist being the clown one more time and said, "You have to be more specific. Chip falls down a lot."

Chip did not seem all that amused by his friend's remarks.

One of the other boys decided they had picked on Chip enough. "Oh yeah, well, Kevin, maybe if you had some better shoes you could run with the girls' junior varsity team. I'm pretty sure that's the only way you're ever going to get Jody to go out with you."

A few snickers. It seemed to Mick that the score was settled and he didn't think anyone had anything meaningful to say. He'd let them think and talk among themselves.

"OK, if you think of anything you saw on the day that Chip fell down—sorry, Chip—let me know. And I mean *anything*. I'm going to give you my card. Call me."

Mick pulled his cards out of his pocket. He had them banded together with one of Colly's rubber bands for her hair. He pulled some of them out and passed them along the first row of the bleachers and then reached through to hand them to the boys one row up.

He could hear the rumbling of their feet on the bleachers as they climbed down. It sounded like stampeding elephants. Really, the acoustics in here were terrible. He was glad Colly was getting a chance to sing in some places that were worthy of her voice.

Mick felt like he was spinning his wheels, like the toy cars he and his brother played with when they were kids. You'd rub, rub, rub them and then let them go. Vroom. Only they never really went very far. That was how Mick felt. He just wasn't getting very far.

Walking down the hall to his office, he spotted Rainy. Might as well tell him he hadn't found out anything except that even good athletes sometimes fell down.

"Rainy, wait up."

Rainy turned back and regarded Mick as the bearer of bad news that he was, or maybe he was just being Rainy.

"I didn't get too much at the high school, but there's always a chance that one of those guys will think of something or someone he saw around Colby's house. You know how boys are; something might just occur to them, so we'll see."

Rainy nodded his head. "I hope so, but I think they mostly think about girls."

Watching him walk back to his office Mick thought, *Girls*. He had been playing down the romantic triangle idea, because Sean Spence was on a plane and the gun was stolen.

But Sean wasn't the only one who could be jealous enough to shoot a couple of people. Adam Moore might have had a girlfriend, and she might not have liked him playing around with an older woman or any woman.

Mick pivoted and walked back to his car. He wanted to think without anyone watching him think. As he slammed the door, he felt like he was unlocking a logjam that might make things fall into place. He played the "what-if" game.

What if Adam had a girl? What if Adam and the girl needed a little money and decided to do a few burglaries? Or Adam could have done them himself and just shared the loot with her? And then what if he started stepping out on her? She might have caught him delivering one too many pizzas. Mick liked the idea.

It wasn't perfect, but it did have some elements that made sense to him. First, he always thought the Reluctant Robber was a kid, so that fit. Second, if you were just there for the money, why not make a run for it instead of killing two people? It would make Rainy happy. A lover's quarrel was always preferable to a random crazy person.

Mick decided to check on Adam Moore's romantic interests since he'd already considered Edie's. Adam Moore was a good-looking kid. It was a little hard to see a girl doing these shootings but, hey, look at Amy Fisher. Girls can shoot people, too.

CHAPTER TWENTY-EIGHT

Stephanie awoke before the alarm went off. She was used to waiting quietly for the alarm so she didn't wake Pete up before it sounded. For a split second she remained still. Then she remembered: Peter Popkins was long gone. She could roll around and shout if she wanted to. She didn't.

This was the first time in her entire life when she could do whatever she wanted. She had spent her whole life with a roommate of some sort. She had never imagined herself living alone, never seen that coming. Maybe she should get a cat. Maybe she should get up and do her job instead of lolling around in her loneliness.

Stephanie drove out to National Safety. The azaleas were in bloom along the path she walked on to the door. No appointment, but sometimes that was better. She gave her name to the receptionist, who made her feel old by saying, "Can I help you, ma'am?"

Stephanie asked to see Mr. Jackson and the girl—just barely out of high school, probably—picked up the phone and pressed a button. Soon afterward an older, well-dressed lady appeared. Finally, someone Stephanie could call "ma'am."

"Hi, I'm Grace Saunders, Mr. Jackson's assistant. Can I help you?"

Stephanie explained that she was with the *Bee*, that she just needed fifteen or twenty minutes for a story she was working on, and that she could use Mr. Jackson's help.

Grace said, "One moment" as she turned to head down the hall, and then quickly returned. She pointed down the hall and passed

Stephanie so she could open the next door for her. Mr. Jackson got up and came around his desk, like he'd been waiting just for her.

"Coffee?" he asked, but Stephanie saw Grace glance at her for the answer, so she figured Jackson wasn't going to get it for her but thought he should ask.

"No, no thanks. I don't want to take up too much of your time. I just want to ask you a few questions."

Jackson put his hands in front of him like the statue of the bird girl in the garden, at once offering and showing how little he had to offer.

"Ask away, but I didn't really see anything. I keep going back and forth in my head about if I wish I had gotten there a few minutes earlier and been able to prevent it from happening or if I feel lucky I missed the killer by a couple of minutes because maybe I'd be dead, and my dog, too. It was sort of traumatic. I wish I could have stopped him. I can't say much more than that. I certainly feel terrible for the families. What a tragic loss."

"Yes, it is a tragedy. I can't even imagine how terrible and frightening that must have been for you. But, actually, I'm working on a different story, one I think you can help me with. I'm here to ask you some questions about Harlan Tucker."

Grace came back in with a cup of coffee for Jackson and a bottle of water for Stephanie. She handed Stephanie the water bottle and extended the coffee cup to Jackson. He didn't even reach for it. Apparently Grace had to do everything around here. She walked behind his desk and put it down in front of him.

"Harlan is dead," Jackson said.

So far, not so good, Stephanie thought. "Yes, I know, but the *Bee* is doing a story on him. Did you know he was being considered for a spot on the Chicago Bears football team when he graduated from college?"

"Is that what this story is about? Football? You're writing about football?"

Stephanie shook her head. "Well, it's about football in a way, but it's a little more than that." She wasn't being very clear; no wonder Jackson was staring at her like she had two heads. "Look, let me just tell you the story and then I'll ask for your input. I don't mean to be so vague."

She checked for a nod, but Jackson was still just staring at her. Wow, not like she was in the communication business or anything. People naturally assumed she would be spending all her time on the story of the two brutal murders, not some old sports-related piece. Why was she doing this? It was becoming a good question.

"Harlan Tucker, when he was young, was being considered for a spot on a professional team. Even back in those days there was money and prestige attached to something like that. Not like today, of course, but still, it was a coveted position.

"Anyway, there was a scandal on the Hobart College football team, a gambling scandal. Harlan was accused and the offer was withdrawn. In those days the teams even had chaperones when they traveled. It was just a different time, and a gambling scandal was the kiss of death. So Harlan Tucker missed his turn at the pros and Hobart downplayed his role on the team. However, as far as I can tell, he goes on to have a happy, productive life. And then when he is quite literally on his death bed, he receives a note."

Jackson cleared his throat, "A note?"

He still seemed confused by the direction the interview was going, and who could blame him? He had barely missed witnessing two brutal murders, had shot at a killer, and some crazy lady was here to talk to him, not about any of that, but about his high school football coach.

"Yes, a letter from the person who actually placed the bets. In the letter he asks Harlan to forgive him and acknowledges his guilt. The man, Wendell Connelly, had evidently died before he could send the note, so his son sent it. I guess Harlan was really excited about the letter. Wendell Connelly suggested he could use it to clear his name with National Collegiate Athletic Association. I am going to try and do that now, and I know you were one of his players who stayed in touch with him, so I just wanted to get your thoughts on the story."

Jackson seemed lost in thought, running his hands through his hair, confirming her belief that it was a compelling story. "A letter. A letter. All the years that I knew him, and I didn't know *that* about him. He talked to me about a note the day he died, but I didn't know what he was talking about."

He put his face in his hands. When he looked back up at Stephanie he said, "I'm sorry. I guess I'm still in a little bit of shock over finding those people dead and Harlan dying, everything that happened." He shook his head.

"I know you were friends with Coach Tucker."

"Yeah. You know, his death wasn't unexpected, but I guess you can never prepare for something like that. You know; he'd been in hospice a while, but still . . ."

"Well, I just want to ask you a few questions. One you've already answered. I guess you didn't know about him trying to go pro or the gambling scandal. Did he ever talk about his days at Hobart College? Did he ever mention the name of Wendell Connelly?"

Jackson seemed to be pondering the question, but then he said, "Wait. Are you Roger Gallagher's daughter?"

"Yes. Do you know my father?"

"Sure, sure, we worked on setting aside that land out by the river for a park. Your dad is a real smart guy. That was a great project. Your dad told me you were coming back to Forsyth with your husband—a dentist, right?"

Damn. He was so obviously proud that he had made the connection between her and her father and even remembered about her moving back. She tried to smile back at him, but she was afraid she looked like she was snarling.

"Yes, I moved back, but I am divorced now." She tried to keep the smile on her face, like it was a good idea—maybe even her idea. No luck there, though.

"Oh, I'm so sorry. I hadn't heard that."

Stephanie reached for her water bottle, repositioning herself in her chair as if that would change the course of the conversation. After all, who was interviewing whom here?

"Oh, well," she said as breezily as she could. "So you never knew anything about Coach Tucker's career?"

Jackson picked up his coffee cup and looked into it as if he was surprised by its very existence. "No, I never knew that about the coach, and I think I knew him as well as any of his players."

Stephanie nodded, glad to be back on track again.

"Oh, I know you were a good friend to the coach. His daughters told me how kind you were in helping them find someone to stay with their dad. I know that meant a lot to them, and I'm sure it helped Harlan, too."

"I just wish there was more that I could have done. The coach was a huge influence on my life—well, on the lives of all his players, really. And he was doing me a favor by hiring Rosa. She's married to the head of maintenance here at National, and it's no secret we've had to cut back. People who counted on the overtime are struggling. It was a win-win. Harlan got a housekeeper, and the family got the extra income they needed. I was glad I could facilitate.

"Is there anything else you want to ask me? I guess I haven't been much help with this. I loved the coach; in some ways he was more of a father to me than my own father, but I didn't know anything about the gambling scandal or his earlier life."

He put his hands on top of his head and rocked back in his chair. Stephanie felt like he might be signaling that he was ready to wrap this up. *Not yet*, she thought.

"What kind of coach was he?"

"Hmmm." He seemed to be really considering, lost in thought.

Stephanie had to fight the impulse to reach out and tip him back up straight in his chair. It felt like he was angling away from her.

"He was the kind of coach—and I know this sounds like some kind of cliché—but he was the kind of coach who really cared about his players, on and off the field. Oh sure, he wanted to win, and he made us want to win, too, but it was more than that.

"I remember once, some guy a year or two ahead of me got arrested for some prank. He didn't call a lawyer or his family to help him. No, he called the coach. And the coach got him out. That was how we felt about Coach Tucker. If we were in trouble, we could count on him. I loved him. I don't guess that really contributes to your story, though."

He put his hands on his desk and pushed himself up. Stephanie got the message and decided she had gotten all she could from him.

"If you think of anything else, give me a call at the *Bee*. I enjoyed talking to you. I never met Coach Tucker, but I am coming to respect him, and I can see why you were so fond of him." Stephanie stuck her hand out and Jackson shook it. He had shockingly big hands.

"Thanks," Stephanie said as she left his office.

CHAPTER TWENTY-NINE

She jumped back in her car and rummaged around for a granola bar. She checked her phone and picked up a message from Mick McKay. He wanted to meet her at 10:30 a.m. at Round the Clock. She called and left a message on his machine. She'd be there.

Stephanie got there at 10:25 a.m. She didn't want to be late, but, when she walked in, he was already sitting in a booth with an iced tea in front of him.

He did that little fake stand up, which was kind of awkward in a booth, when she scooted in across from him, polite as always and in his usual blue shirt–khaki pants uniform. She raised her eyebrows and he started in without any of the "how are you?" small talk.

"I want to tell you officially that we got the ballistics test back, and the gun used to kill Edie Spence and Adam Moore was the gun found at the scene. According to its serial number, it is also the gun that was stolen from Martin Colby's home on Lee Street. I wanted you to know first. Rainy'll have a news conference this afternoon."

"Thanks, Mick, I appreciate it. So you think the Reluctant Robber is the killer?"

"I don't know. He could have sold the gun. He could have just tossed it. I know you like the Jean Valjean stealing bread for his family aspect of the story, but I have no leads at this time. So, like they say, all I can give you is the facts. And the facts are that the gun used to kill Edie Spence and Adam Moore was the gun stolen from Martin Colby.

"We recovered six bullets: two from the body of Adam Moore, two from the body of Edie Spence, and two on the ground, fired by the dog walker who discovered the bodies, Jackson . . . you know, the guy who runs National Safety. We were able to get fingerprints from the two bullets on the ground. The partial fingerprints we were able to lift are consistent with those of Mr. Colby."

Stephanie nodded. "So, if you find the Reluctant Robber you find the killer."

Mick took a sip of his tea. "I'm not sure about that. I still don't know if I'm looking for one or two people. Why bring the gun? The robber, who is really a burglar, went places where he knew no one was home. Why did he need a gun? Why kill them? Why shoot two people dead when he could have just run away?"

He was asking, but she couldn't answer. "I know what you mean. It seems incomprehensible that anyone would kill two people over the measly money this guy was pocketing. I just talked to Jackson. He seemed real shook up by what happened."

Mick set his glass down and looked at Stephanie, his interest in her piqued. "You interviewed him about finding the bodies? What did he say? Can I see your notes? C'mon Stephanie, I'm helping you out. Here's your chance to help me. I need to know what he saw or even what he thought he saw. Anything he told you could be important."

Stephanie was shaking her head while he talked.

"C'mon Stephanie. This should be a two-way street!"

"Yeah, I agree. If I had anything I'd give it to you, but I was talking to him about a different story."

Mick's eyebrows shot up. Stephanie could tell he didn't believe her when he said, "Right. A double homicide witness, and you want to talk to him about the state of the economy in Forsyth?"

"Yes, well, not the economy, but I stumbled on this great story about Harlan Tucker. He used to be the football coach at the high school. Anyway, right before he died, he got a note about some old gambling scandal he was supposedly involved in. The letter was exonerating him. I thought it was a great human interest story.

"Jackson not only played on Tucker's team but also stayed close to him after high school. He arranged the housekeeper who stayed with Harlan Tucker, the wife of one of his employees who was having his time cut. I just thought Jackson could give me some background for my story." Stephanie was tempted to add, "Honest!" This guy never believed her.

"OK, if you were talking about football fun, how do you know he was so shook up about the murders?"

"Look, he just mentioned it in passing. You know, as in 'I'm having a hard week; I stumbled on two dead bodies.' He just said was he thinking about it, about if he would have been able to stop the killer if he'd gotten there sooner, or if he'd be dead now, too, along with his dog. That's it. By the way, do you know the last time we had a double homicide in Forsyth?"

Mick thought it over for a second before shaking his head. Evidently he didn't know.

"Never. There's never been a double murder in Forsyth before. Trust me." She hated herself for throwing that in. Trust me? As if that would make him believe what she was about to say. Still, she heard herself saying it again. "Trust me; I know this is a big deal. I am taking this very seriously. I know what you think of the Reluctant Robber stories. But I am not so foolish as to jeopardize your investigation. What useful information would Jackson have?"

Mick took a sip of his tea before answering. It was a little too sweet, even for him. "It's hard to say. I can't be sure if he saw anything. He's being careful. He doesn't want to say anything unless he's sure. And it's pretty hard to be sure about something you just catch a glimpse of while you're discovering dead bodies and trying to keep your dog from eating a pizza. So I'm not sure we'll get much from him," Mick said, although he was pretty sure they would get something from him.

It was better not to let her know that. He wasn't sure if he believed her about the interview with Jackson. It sounded plausible, but it seemed fishy to him that she would happen to come across this other story that involved his only witness to the murders. He looked at Stephanie. Now she was asking about the pizza.

"Did Edie Spence order the pizza?"

"Yeah, we know she ordered it earlier on the day of the murder. And the kid was delivering a pizza. He had it in his hands, and he was at her house. He was delivering it to her. Why do you ask?"

She shrugged. "I guess you're right. It's kind of obvious. Just something the girl at Tony's restaurant said. I guess it's nothing."

Mick knew the pizza order came from the phone at Coad's Funeral Home at the time Edie Spence was there, so that was that.

"So, now you are right to call him a robber. Technically, before, he was a burglar, but not anymore. Now in addition to being a robber, he's a murderer. How's your story about the victims coming?"

She felt the rebuke in the comment but let it go. "It's coming. I feel sorry for Adam Moore. He kept pulling himself out of downward spirals: a bad mother, his accident, trouble at the high school, and now this, the kind of trouble he can't get out of. More in his short life than a person should have to go through."

Mick didn't want to get into a discussion on the unfairness of life. Not much you could do about that. The kid had the right idea: just keep going. If he wanted philosophy Mick would go talk to Billy at the Bait Shop.

"What do you mean, trouble at the high school? I don't have a record of anything."

"Oh, no, it was something minor that Andy told me about Adam and Lacey Thomas, his friend. Some missing cell phone or something. You know that age group, full of drama."

Of course he did know that age group, and the drama.

They chatted a little more about the shock of two murders in Forsyth.

Then Stephanie gathered up her purse and Mick said, "Keep in touch." He half stood up as she scooted out of the booth. He was thinking about Adam Moore and his troubles at the high school, wondering if his troubles had continued after high school, too. He watched Stephanie talking to the cashier for a minute and then returned to his thoughts.

What Stephanie had said about Adam and the phone really struck a chord. He had found out a couple of leads to check. One was Adam Moore and his troubles at the high school, definitely worth checking out.

The other thing that came to him as he watched Stephanie scoot out of the booth was her comment on Harlan Tucker and his caregiver, the caregiver Jackson had helped find. An employee he liked enough to help find his wife a job . . . that was someone he cared about. Someone he might not want to admit to catching a glimpse of in the dark at a murder scene.

He could go talk to Jackson, find out about who the guy was. That would be fairly simple, but the more he thought about it, the more he decided to take a different, less direct approach. He'd talk to the caregiver. Get an idea about what was happening through her. No point in letting Jackson know his strategy. If Jackson didn't want to point a finger and get his friend in trouble, well, Mick could understand that. But if Jackson confronted the guy about the murders, he might run. Or worse, he might kill Jackson.

But first Mick wanted to find out more about Adam and his trouble at school. Stealing a cell phone was an indication that he was not opposed to taking something that didn't belong to him. A kid out stealing was what he had been thinking all along. It fit.

Something else Stephanie said was rattling around in his head. Edie Spence had ordered the pizza. They had checked the phone records. So that was a certainty. But why? Why had she ordered a pizza when she was already making dinner? Mick was no expert in meal planning, but it didn't make sense. Maybe she was planning to freeze the chili from the crockpot?

Maybe he would head back to the Spence house, poke around the kitchen. This was either a new low or he was a genius to investigate Edie Spence's eating habits.

"Thanks, Mick. See ya soon," Stephanie said as she slid out of the booth. The leather, if it was leather, which was unlikely, was creased and cracked in places and she felt the fabric of her skirt catching on it. She gathered the fabric in her hand and pulled at it as she stood.

Mick did his little push up, politely half standing. Whoever invented that rule had not envisioned booths. She freed herself from the booth, waved, and headed to the cash register.

"Hey, how are you?" she said to the woman standing behind a glass counter full of gum and candy. Stephanie had a feeling she should know the woman's name, but if she did, she couldn't remember it now. She did remember she was getting married—or was it her daughter who was getting married?

"So, how's the wedding coming?" she asked. That sounded safe.

"Oh, they got married a couple of weeks ago, and it turned out real nice. Thanks for asking. I just can't believe what's happening in Forsyth. This used to be such a safe place," she said, and Stephanie nodded in agreement.

"Hey, I want to pay for his iced tea, too," Stephanie said, gesturing back toward Mick, presumably the man keeping them all safe— or trying. The woman leaned over the counter to look down the row of booths.

"Oh, don't worry about it. It's always on the house for him."

She handed back her change and Stephanie turned to wave at Mick again, but he was looking down at his glass, deep in thought. She let her hand just hang for a moment and then pushed out into the bright sun.

CHAPTER THIRTY

Stephanie stopped in at the Quick Mart to pick up a Dr. Pepper. She was going to need a little fortification for lunch with her parents before Adam Moore's funeral and Edie's wake. Not that they were ever anything but good to her and her sister, and so supportive of her while she was going through the divorce.

But that was just it. They reminded her of Scrooge's business partner, Jacob Marley, and his ghostly friends who wanted to do good, to help, but they couldn't. Her parents were standing by her, wringing their hands, because really, what could they do? Their daughter was desperately unhappy and maybe throwing her life away. She decided to throw Mark Lavelle's name into the conversation somewhere. That would give them some hope, something to cling to.

"Hey, how's it going?" she said as she pushed open the screen door. First to greet her was Buddy. He came running toward her like she was the last person on earth and he was overjoyed at the sight of her. He pushed his black nose into her hand, his sign for *Pet me! Pet me!*

She ruffled his silky ears and told him, "I should have stuck with dogs. You've always been a faithful friend." He looked at her with adoration. She could use a little of that.

Her mother came out, drying her hands on a dish towel. She did a quick check. Stephanie knew she was looking to see if she looked tired, sad, thin . . . anything that needed fixing.

Stephanie smiled, beat her to the punch. "Wow, Mom, you look great. I like that blouse. What's for lunch?"

Her mother gave her a quick kiss on the cheek and said, "Thanks, I'll call your dad. We're having King Ranch casserole."

Stephanie wondered if there would be a margarita to go along with lunch. Unlikely, but still nice to contemplate.

Her father appeared around the corner and said, "How's my favorite youngest daughter?" Stephanie gave him a big "See? I'm fine" smile. But he still looked at her face more closely than her dermatologist, checking for any sign of unhappiness.

She kept the smile on her face even as she thought about Pete and how she wasn't the only one paying the price for his lies. It would have been nice if her parents had been able to say, "We never liked Peter," or "We didn't trust that guy. We always thought he was going to be trouble. He just didn't fit into our family."

But the truth was, they were as deceived as she was. They embraced him wholeheartedly, treated him like a son, tried to help him when they moved back to Forsyth. Just as deceived meant just as devastated. No one had seen any signs of what was coming. She bent down to pet Buddy again.

"Food in five!" her mother called from the kitchen.

"OK, I'm just going to wash up and I'll be right there." Stephanie ran up to the bathroom at the top of the stairs that she had shared with her sister. Her parents had taken the big daisy wallpaper border down when the girls left home, but she was still flooded with the old feelings of preparing for dates, for life. *Girl reporter getting ready for school*, she thought.

She sighed and here she was, preparing for who knows what. When she and Pete had announced that they were moving back to Forsyth, there had been two standard responses from friends and colleagues. One camp had said things like, how could she stand to live in a place with so little opportunity, no art museums, no operas, and no people worth knowing. They felt sorry for her. The other camp said how lucky they were to be going to a sleepy little town with no demands, no stress. They envied her.

Of course both groups were off. Usually the people who talked about the arts hadn't been to a museum in years, and the fact was, whether you lived in a big city or a small town, you still had to do your job, go to the grocery store, clean out the garage. She dried her hands on the fancy, for-company towel and headed down to try and convince her parents she was over the heartbreak of Pete.

Sitting at the table in her old spot, the chair her sister—and sometimes Pete—sat in, empty, Stephanie sipped her weak sangria. Not a margarita, but still . . .

Her father asked, "So how's the story on the murder victims coming? I think it's a great idea, by the way. I'm tired of the way the media provides so much publicity for these sickos when it's the victims we should be paying attention to. All that hoopla just encourages more deranged people to try and get famous by doing something outrageous."

Stephanie nodded in agreement with her father, but at the same time, she wondered about her Reluctant Robber stories. Did the publicity embolden him, make him feel entitled?

"I know. I worry about my Reluctant Robber story, whether I encouraged someone to commit these murders."

"No, no, that was a simple little petty thievery. No one could predict what was going to happen. Might as well blame the guy whose gun was stolen. It's the fault of whoever pulled the trigger. Besides, the thief probably never even read the paper."

Gee, thanks, thought Stephanie. Her mother looked like she was getting ready to stick a fork in her father's hand. But she was a big girl; she could take the conversation. She knew her father was only trying to be on her side, not make her feel worse.

"Well, actually, he must have read my story, because he returned Martin Colby's driver's license after we published the story about him and the missing license."

Her father took a sip of his sangria and said, "I read the articles you wrote. They didn't encourage him to continue. You were just compassionate."

Time to change the subject, Stephanie thought. "Hey, Dad, I talked to Jack Jackson. He said he worked with you on the River Road park project. He thought you were a really hard worker."

Her father smiled at her, glad to have her help pull him out of the conversational quagmire he had found himself in. "Yeah, that old boy. The wolf's at his door."

"What do you mean the wolf's at his door?" she asked, considering if she should have one of the brownies her mother had just placed on the table.

"Oh, he got into the commodities business, betting big on the price of cotton and I don't know what all. He took a gamble and lost. According to Lonny, he signed personal guarantees. His daddy left him a nice, solid business. I guess he wanted to make his own mark on it. But I don't want to talk about him, I want to talk about my girl. You still thinking you're staying in Forsyth?"

This was a frequent topic. They slid right into it, like rolling to the worn place in a mattress—worn and not all that comfortable. Her parents were worried she was giving up on life by staying here in Forsyth. Even though they lived here, they had somehow fallen into the limited-opportunity camp.

But she had a great job, a nice place to live. She didn't want to pull up stakes and move again. She wasn't sure what to do, so it was easier to do nothing.

"Hey, you and Mom are here. I guess you think Forsyth is a pretty good place to live." Stephanie lobbed the comment that she knew would cheer them. "I saw Mark Lavelle out at the high school. He seems like a nice guy. We went out for coffee."

Her mother stopped in mid-reach for the brownies. Her father beamed at her like she had just told him she was getting a Pulitzer. *Wow, imagine if I'd had a real date with the guy,* she thought.

But when she walked out after a brownie and a cup of coffee, she knew her parents were a little less worried about her. She silently thanked Mark Lavelle for his help. *And who knows, maybe we might go on that real date,* she thought as she waved to her parents standing on the porch, watching her go like she had just picked up her license at the DMV and was heading out on her first solo drive.

CHAPTER THIRTY-ONE

Stephanie walked up the stairs past some young people getting in a last cigarette before the service. Maybe they knew something she didn't; maybe it was going to be a long service. That only seemed fair: short life, long service.

She had been afraid no one would be here for Adam Moore, but she was wrong. The high school soccer team had shown up in force. Even boys who were not boys but grown men now were wearing soccer jerseys over their button-down shirts. The church was packed. She hoped she had contributed to the crowd with Adam's obit. The power of the pen.

The light streaming in from the stained glass windows cast a greenish glaze over the church, making everyone look as if they were slightly seasick. She scanned the crowd, looking for a floozy and wondering if Tiffany had been able to track down her mother after all.

She spotted Mark Lavelle and scooted down the pew to sit next to him. From there she could see Tiffany sitting in the front row, her back straight, facing the front of the church like she was waiting to catch a glimpse of Haley's comet and if she looked away for a minute she might miss it. She was wearing the same dark flowered dress that she wore for Harlan Tucker's funeral.

Then, the minister appeared and the congregation rose. He directed them to open their hymnals and Mark Lavelle leaned over to share his open book with her. The voices of the young people singing "Amazing Grace" sounded pure and sad. Usually at funerals most of the participants are old and gray-haired, remembering anecdotes from a long life. But most of the people filling the church today were young. It made her wince to hear those high, sweet voices.

She listened as the minister talked about God's plan for Adam and forgiveness for the killer.

Stephanie could see the contingent from Antonio's Pizza, the curly-haired girl sobbing into her Kleenex, the boy still not smiling but now, at least, looking more appropriate. She tried to discreetly look around for Adam's mother. She pictured her in a skin-tight leopard-print dress with high spiky heels and beehive hair. She leaned closer to Mark and asked if he'd seen Mrs. Moore. He nodded toward a skinny woman in a white, long-sleeved blouse and a black skirt down to her knees. She looked like she had just stepped out of an Amish buggy.

Mark gave her a nudge and she realized she'd been staring. She was sitting with a man in a suit behind Tiffany, acknowledging that it was Tiffany, not her, who was the chief mourner.

Stephanie could see Mick McKay sitting by himself, which was odd, because about three rows in front of her she had noticed John Mason, also sitting by himself. They must have missed each other in the crowd. She wondered if both men were looking for suspects here.

Of course, criminals sometimes feel compelled to witness the results of their crimes. It sent a shiver down her spine to think about the murderer sitting in this church with her and listening to the minister talk about forgiveness. She wondered how that sounded to Tiffany or, for that matter, to Mick.

After the minister finished he walked in front of the casket and said, "Adam's family wants to invite everyone to lunch in the Memorial Hall."

Stephanie shuffled out of the church with the rest of the funeral goers.

The crowd flowed in to the church hall. It was a huge room with seating for a multitude. Set out on long tables were rows of pizzas. Tony, still in his funeral suit and tie, had thrown on an apron, and he was getting boxes of pizzas out of the giant church ovens. Stephanie thought, *Those are the kind of ovens Hansel and Gretel could have fit in.* Church ladies were helping him set things up. Members of the soccer team were lining up and loading pizza slices onto their paper plates.

Stephanie noticed that the napkins were from Antonio's with the boot-of-Italy logo. Beyond the long, pizza-covered tables there was a card table set up with sheet cakes. She was glad to see they were blank. What would you write on a cake for an occasion like this?

CHAPTER THIRTY-TWO

Mick caught up with Mason outside the church. It always felt wrong to have a funeral on a sunny day. And today was about as sunny as you could get. Mason cocked his head as if he were listening to church bells only he could he hear. Mick knew he was waiting for him to offer some direction.

"We might as well go on down and have a slice of pizza," Mick said, and Mason nodded. They had gone to the funeral to pay their respects to the family—well, to the sister. Mick didn't have any respect to give to the absent mother. But they were also there looking for any kind of suspicious behavior.

As much as he would like to believe that a drifter had been passing through and committed the murders, he knew Martin Colby's gun made that unlikely. Whoever gunned down the nurse and the kid most likely lived right here in Forsyth. He glanced at the crowd pouring out of the church, looking for some telltale sign, but all he saw were the people he saw every day, his Forsyth neighbors.

The hall was full of people and food. He admired Tony for providing the pizza and vowed to make sure he frequented Antonio's. While it was not the traditional funeral lunch fare, it was delicious and, somehow, just right for the occasion.

Now it was time to turn his attention back to the other victim. Mick pushed the doorbell at Edie Spence's house.

He expected the house to be somehow changed, to have a dark cloud over it, but the same bright flowers lined the walk, the same big tree shaded part of the front lawn, the same lawn chairs sat under the tree. All the same, but Mick knew that it would never be the same for the Spences.

Sean Spence opened the door and said, "Come in, come in," like he was actually happy to see him. "Any news?"

Mick understood how the guy must feel. He wanted to know what had happened, who had done this. Maybe even understand why: why *his* wife, out of all the people in the world. Mick winced. He couldn't offer any solace. He was here to get information, not to give it.

"No, nothing new. We do know that the gun was definitely the one that was stolen from Martin Colby. And the lab people are still going over everything. We are also checking pawn shops and known gun sellers to see if we can get a line on anyone who wanted to sell a gun or buy a gun in the last month. Maybe we'll find some kind of connection there."

Sean nodded. Even to Mick it sounded like an excuse. "Meantime, I have a few more things I'd like to talk over with you."

Sean made a sweeping gesture toward some chairs and Mick sat in one and waited for Sean to sit, too. "Something is puzzling me. Your wife was expecting you for a late dinner. She evidently ordered a pizza that night, too, even though she was cooking dinner. Is that something she did often?"

"Well, when our son was home we ordered pizzas a lot more. My daughter's not such a big eater, so the three of us don't usually order pizzas, but it's not unheard of."

Mick was already nodding his head. "OK, I'm just trying to get a better picture of what happened that night. The more I know about what was usual, the easier it will be for me to find the unusual and get some answers. That's all. Would you mind if I took a look around your kitchen? I know the lab people looked at everything, but if you don't mind, I'd like to look, too."

Sean Spence stood and gestured toward the kitchen door. "Of course, I want to help in any way I can. I don't think knowing who did this is going to bring me anything like closure, whatever that is, but I am afraid for my daughter. You can imagine. I worry about her being safe here. I know it was probably a tragic wrong place at the wrong time for both Edie and that kid, but still . . . I want to know what happened."

Mick turned to look back at him as he walked into the kitchen. "Me, too."

"Is there anything I can help you with?"

"No, just give me a few minutes."

Mick pulled out his list of things to look for. They were not the usual things to think about in a murder case. He felt more like Betty Crocker than Columbo, but it was worth a try.

First, he checked the freezer. There was a small container of expensive ice cream, cookie dough. There was a package of frozen southwest-style corn, a package of Brussels sprouts. In the racks there was a box of Popsicles and a cold pack, in case of an emergency. *That's it*, Mick thought. No telltale Tupperware containers, nothing with the date written on it.

He quietly closed the freezer door and opened the refrigerator door. A bag of salad, some sliced turkey, a gallon of skim milk, the usual condiments—salsa, ketchup, mustard. Mick noticed all the Tupperware containers. *Eureka!* This was just what he expected to find. She prepared meals ahead of time and put them in the fridge. That made sense. Order a pizza and eat the chili the next night.

Mick pulled one of the containers out for a closer look. "Alice's chicken and rice casserole with broccoli," the index card taped to the top read. After a quick, disappointing inspection, Mick realized that every one of the dishes had been delivered to the grieving family by neighbors and friends, trying to find some way to help in a situation where no one could help.

Mick let the refrigerator door slowly close on its own, thankful that Sean hadn't seen him looking through his refrigerator. He already felt like he was letting the guy down.

And it did sound crazy, even to him. Some woman decides she wants a pizza. That happened a lot. People ate things they didn't really need. So she wanted a pizza before dinner, and here he was, snooping around her kitchen.

On the other hand, the best thing he could do right now was to keep gathering information. The more he knew, the better the chances of him pulling on the string that would unravel this whole mess, he thought as he slid open a drawer looking for plastic containers.

Finally he walked back to where Sean was sitting. He had the newspaper open, but Mick could tell he wasn't reading it.

"Find anything?"

"No," Mick said as he slumped into the chair facing Sean. "I'm not even sure what I'm looking for, to tell you the truth. I know your wife ordered the pizza. Probably it's just as simple as the Hawaiian Special pizza sounding good to her. Me, I don't think those two places mix, Italy and Hawaii, but what do I know." Mick could feel his discouragement infecting the other man, but he felt powerless to stop the contagion. Chatting about pizza was probably one of the last things you wanted to do after finding out your wife was murdered.

"Yeah, I agree with you. I like mine with nothing fancy on it. What could they put on a pizza to make it Hawaiian, anyway?"

Mick flashed on the pizza box lying in the yard next to the two dead bodies. "Let's see. I know it has pineapple—which should not be on anything but upside-down cake—green peppers, and ham."

"Ham? Are you sure?"

Mick nodded his head, sure.

Sean was leaning forward in his chair and shaking his head. "No. No way would Edie have ordered anything with ham. She didn't eat pork."

Mick had just finished exploring her kitchen. This did not look like the home of a vegetarian. Mick was nodding in a "go on, go on" way, but he was thinking, *maybe she just didn't eat pork with you, buddy*. It made him sad to think it. There were lots of things people kept from each other for lots of reasons.

"So was she a vegetarian or something?"

Sean was still staring at him like he had just uttered a four-letter word in front of a kindergarten Sunday school class. "No, she wasn't a vegetarian, but she never ate pork. Let me explain. When I was in vet school we didn't have any money. We were always looking for things we could do together that were free. I had to take an animal ag class where we watched these movies put out by the USDA.

"I took Edie to some of the films. Not exactly a movie date, but we could sit together and hold hands. Well, I took her to one about hog farms. It showed cute little pink piglets. But then it showed the slaughtering process. You know, pigs are really smart animals and when they scream, they sound almost human. Even for me it was a little hard to watch. Edie, she turned as white as a sheet. I thought she might faint or something, and she was a nursing student, not exactly the fainting type.

"Anyway, I got her outside, sat her down with her head between her knees, and she said, 'I am never going to eat pork again.' She said it very low and serious and, you know what, she never did. She never ate another piece of bacon, never had a ham sandwich, never made a pork roast. Never. Edie would never have ordered a pizza with ham on it. Never."

"It might have been a mistake. She might have ordered a pizza and they delivered the wrong one, or she might not have known that the special for that day had ham on it."

Sean seemed to be thinking this over. A lot of serious thought over something Mick didn't think was all that important.

Mick sighed. "OK, I am going to recheck the ordering process. We'll see if they made some kind of mistake with the order. Thanks for meeting me. I want you to know that we are doing all we can and we won't rest until we have the guy who did this."

Mick stuck out his hand and Sean shook it.

"I'll see you at the wake this evening."

Sean Spence released his hand and repeated, "The wake. Yes, my daughter is taking a nap. She hasn't been sleeping well at night. I promised I would get her up in time to get ready. My son went out to get the car washed. I'm not sure if having a clean car matters but he . . . we need to find useful things to do. I'll see you there."

CHAPTER THIRTY-THREE

Stephanie headed over to Harlan Tucker's house. She wanted to talk to Rosa again about Harlan's last days and his excitement over receiving the note exonerating him. Too bad the old guy who sent it didn't use email. Harlan would have gotten it a lot sooner.

This time when she rang the bell, Rosa answered. The sob sisters must be out. Rosa said they were at the bank but they would be back. She clearly expected Stephanie to receive this news and leave.

"Oh, I want to talk to you," Stephanie said. She said it in English. She could switch later if she needed to. "I wanted to ask you again about people who came to visit Mr. Tucker."

Rosa sighed. She clearly felt she had already gone over this. "No people come. The family is at the wedding of the cousin, the Mister is too sick and sleeping for people."

"Yes, I know you said that, but Mr. Jackson, he came, right?"

"He came, but the Mister is sleeping."

"Hmm. Well, did he just sit with him then, with no talking?"

"Mr. Jackson he says, 'Coach, Coach.' And the Mister is not awake, but he says, 'The letter! The letter!' even though he is sleeping. I think Mr. Jackson, he cries."

Stephanie had some of the coach's last words, at least according to Rosa, and she wasn't wrong about how important that letter had been to him. It was intriguing, but first she wanted to head in and talk to Tom. She needed an anchor right now to keep her from drifting into Harlan Tucker's story and away from the biggest story for Forsyth. She let a relieved Rosa get back to her packing.

Stephanie couldn't explain it even to herself, the pull and

poignancy of Harlan's story. She needed to try and explain it to Tom to clear it up for herself.

Maybe Mick had been right that first night. Maybe she had emboldened the thief with her stories. Maybe she was postponing her stories about Adam Moore and Edie Spence because she felt guilty, like a naughty child who doesn't want to look at the broken cookie jar.

She would have to write the story and say the string of burglaries were connected to the murders. She might even interview Martin Colby again; see if he felt bad about his gun being used. It was too bad she hadn't printed a story about him needing both his driver's license *and* his gun. Then those two people would still be alive. The bigger outlets wouldn't be interested in that little story, but the people of Forsyth would.

This was turning out to be a big week for Stephanie's black suit. When she pulled onto Eighth Street, she became one in a long line of cars snaking up to the funeral home. Coad's was one of those fake Southern mansion buildings with white columns on a wide porch. The scene looked like they were all heading to a party at Tara, only instead of a wide lawn there was a wide parking lot.

The lot was already packed, so Stephanie gave up trying for the lot and pulled off onto Stemmons Street. Other people had the same idea, and so she found herself walking with a group of people not talking much. They walked past the people who were already in line to pay their respects to the family, and then they kept walking. The line to get into the funeral was two blocks long.

She saw Kay Kay and Mary Sue, still holding on to each other. They smiled at her. "We want to pay our respects. Edie was so good to Daddy, you know."

Stephanie nodded, she knew.

"I'm sure the family will appreciate your being here," Stephanie said.

She got to the end and took her turn at the end of the line, but she wasn't last in line for long. People soon lined up behind her. It seemed to her as if the whole town was here. It took an hour and forty minutes to get into the building.

Inside there were pictures of the various periods of Edith Spence's life. In one grouping, she was a baby, then going to kindergarten with her hair in a braid. She got braces, went camping, held her baby brother, and became a Girl Scout. Then, in the next group, she was sitting behind the wheel of a car, posing in a prom dress, standing at a podium for some high school speech, throwing her hat in the air at a graduation ceremony.

Stephanie looked at the pictures and thought, *How did the little girl in these pictures end up being shot in her yard?* She passed pictures of Edie Spence in a wedding dress, in a hospital room with balloons and a tiny blue bundle. The pictures seemed like they were on a conveyor belt, back to babies and braces, this time with Edie as the mother standing next to the smiling graduate. Well, that's the way it works. Stephanie felt sorry for Edie Spence and all that she would miss in what should be the next set of pictures. Edie as the mother of the bride, the grandmother.

But she felt sorry for herself, too. She'd thrown out her wedding pictures, even though they cost as much as a house payment and she had never looked thinner or better. She had no pictures with pink or blue bundles. As she walked toward the Spence family, she thought at least Edie Spence had that. What kind of pictures would they have at her funeral?

Passing out of the overly wallpapered hall, Stephanie noticed that the casket was closed. At least she wouldn't have to repeat any of the inane things people said at a time like this: "She looks so peaceful," or "She looks so natural," even though there was nothing peaceful or natural about not moving, not breathing.

When she reached Sean Spence, she shook his hand and said, "Again, I am so sorry for your loss."

She repeated the statement six more times as she expressed her condolences to the son, the daughter, and Edie's parents and in-laws. It was like running a very sad gauntlet. At the end of the gauntlet there was another room packed with people quietly chatting, catching up with cousins only seen at weddings and funerals.

By the time Stephanie made it into the room, she felt exhausted. She looked around, caught Mick McKay's eye, and waved. She spotted Kay Kay, Mary Sue, and Tiffany Hudson, people from all her recent funerals. She felt caught up in a swirling sadness. The crush of people made her feel dizzy and in danger, like she was at one of those soccer games where people were trampled by the rampaging crowd.

She felt released as she stepped out into the cooler night air. There was still a long line of people waiting outside. She started to walk back toward her car, occasionally stopping to say hello to people. If the Reluctant Robber was still stealing, this would be the perfect time for it; no one was home to stop him.

CHAPTER THIRTY-FOUR

Mick walked back to his car. He could feel Sean Spence's eyes on him, poor guy. He was probably wondering what the hell kind of detective comes over to chat about recipes. Mick turned to wave as he opened his car door, but Sean Spence wasn't standing by the door after all. *Not so good with the instincts,* he thought as he let his hand flop down to his side.

Now his instincts were telling him he should go back and review the pizza delivery information. He nosed his car around and made a U-turn to head back to his office. He called Mason on his cell and told him to meet him in his office with the phone records for Edie Spence.

When he walked through the door, Mason was already sitting at his desk, spreading out the phone records.

"OK, here are the phone records for Edie Spence. I double-checked, and there is a call placed from the funeral home to the pizza place at 4:12 p.m. when she was there. We presume she made the call, because the pizza was delivered to her house. The call lasted twenty-nine seconds. But we knew that. Is there something else we're looking for here?" Mason looked back at the phone records like he was deciphering hieroglyphics.

Since Mason was sitting in his chair, Mick leaned over his desk, but he didn't look at the phone records. Mason waited him out.

Finally Mick said, "Let's do a timeline. Is Austin here? I'd like him to go over what he observed at the wake when he saw our two vics together."

Mason picked up the phone and pushed the button for the front desk. After a brief exchange he turned back to Mick and said, "He's on his way up. He was the escort for the funeral this morning. So, we can ask him if he saw any inappropriate behavior. I sure as hell didn't. All I saw was a bunch of sad people and a life cut short. What'd you think about the forgiveness shit in the sermon, anyway?"

"Oh, yeah, I agree with him." Mason's eyebrows shot up. "I'm planning to forgive that son of a bitch just as soon as he's locked away for good. And I mean for good! Then I'll forgive him."

"Amen to that," Mason agreed.

When Austin got to Mick's office, he was still dressed for the funeral, wearing his boots and his tie, his hat in his hands. He looked a little like he just rolled out of a *CHiPs* episode. "You wanted to see me?"

Mick and Mason both nodded. Mick said, "Yeah, we're running down a timeline, and I want to know if you remember about what time you saw Edie Spence and Adam Moore talking? You know, as exact as you can get."

"Well, actually, I do know almost exactly what time it was. It had to be between a couple of minutes past 4:00 p.m. and 4:15 p.m. I know because I came in at 4:00 p.m. for a bathroom break and a cup of coffee. I was planning to go back out to check the parking lot at 4:15 p.m.

"I was on my way out when I saw the kid and the lady talking. Like I said, she waved me over to ask about the route we were going to take the cemetery. But I got the impression she was asking for him, not for herself. I told her, and she checked with him to make sure he got it, and then I saw Mr. Coad. I walked over and he told me people were having a hard time turning into the parking lot, so I went out to direct traffic. So I was back out a little before 4:15 p.m. Does that help?"

Did it help? "Yeah, definitely, that helps us with the timeline. Tell me again, did you see either of them leaving or see them later in the parking lot?"

"No, by the time I got back out, there was a big line of cars and I was trying to direct traffic into the lot, not out of it. They could have driven by me and I wouldn't have noticed."

Mick stood up to let him know he was finished with him. "Thanks, that'll help us. I'm glad you were so observant."

"OK, what's up with the pizza?" Mason asked as Austin backed out of the room. "I mean, we know she ordered it. We know the kid delivered it. What else is there?"

"Alright, I know, but I think there's something fishy about this."

"Fishy? I'm not getting it. A lady orders a pizza. A delivery boy delivers it. That's it. Right?"

"OK, but it's fishy. First, why did she order a pizza?"

Mason blew out some air in response. "Maybe because she wanted a pizza? That doesn't sound all that fishy to me. Sometimes I want a pizza, too."

Mick frowned. "Yeah, yeah, yeah, but wait; she had dinner already made at home."

"Uh-huh, and she could have forgotten about it. I go to the grocery store all the time and come home with something I already have."

"Just listen to the second point. Sean Spence said his wife hated any kind of pork and would never have ordered a pizza with ham on it." Mick looked at Mason. "How about that?"

"Mick, I'm just not getting this. It's not like we don't know lots of husbands and wives who will swear up and down that their spouse would never do anything like sleep around or drive drunk or cheat on his taxes or, God forbid, have sex with their kid's friends. People don't really know. Maybe once in a while she liked to walk on the wild side and have a pork chop and not tell her husband."

Mick was feeling more exasperated by the minute. This role reversal was wearing him down. Usually he had to keep Mason from going off on a tangent. Why did he feel so sure that Sean Spence was right and Edie would never have ordered a pizza with ham? It wasn't like him to believe something with absolutely no evidence.

"Alright that could be. But how are you going to explain the timeline? By my calculation, she's calling Antonio's pizzeria at almost the exact minute that she's talking to Austin. Now, that is fishy."

Mick looked expectantly at Mason. If he couldn't get him to see what he was getting at, he was sure as hell not going to get Rainy to see it. And maybe he was off.

Mason paged through the papers on Mick's desk. "She talks to

Adam Moore at 4:08 p.m. Maybe she even tells him, 'I want a pizza,' and he says, 'Yeah, well, you have to call; I can't take the order here.' Then she calls Austin over at 4:10 p.m., gets the directions they need. At 4:20 p.m. she calls for a pizza. She goes home. Adam comes over with the pizza, and it's the end of their story. That fits the timeline."

"It makes no sense!" Mick said with exasperation. "She's at a wake for someone she's been taking care of for a couple of years, and she decides to order a pizza? She's standing there talking to Austin and she, according to the timeline, has time to run out and order the pizza. And I do mean run. Let's see if we can see find who else she talked to at the wake. Maybe someone saw her on the phone. Let's at least check."

"Are you still thinking she was ordering more than a pizza? Is that where this leads us?" Mason asked.

Mick slumped down in his chair. He didn't want that to be true. He wanted the Spences to be the nice family that they seemed.

"I've got an idea. How'd you like to have some pizza tonight? Experimental pizza." Mason nodded, but Mick could tell his confidence in him was slipping, a common feeling today. Or was it that his confidence in himself was ebbing?

"Let's re-create what happened that night. We'll get a better idea for our timeline. We can see how long it took for Adam Moore to get the pizza, get in his car, and get to Edie Spence's house. We want to know if he drove there without making any stops. We know that was the only pizza he was delivering, but we don't know if he stopped for gas or to pick up a soda. What if he saw something suspicious on the drive over? What if someone saw him and followed him?"

Mick headed over to Tony's place to explain his timeline plan to Tony. Even in the parking lot in front of Antonio's, the smell of pizza hung in the air like the cigarette smoke that used to cloud every bar.

Tony, the curly-haired girl, and the sullen cook looked up at Mick, their faces filled with expectation. This must be what it's like for doctors walking into a crowded hospital waiting room, everyone checking to see if you are bringing news for them.

And, of course, there was no news. Mick quickly shook his head to let them know that wasn't why he was there. The sullen cook turned back to check his oven, and the curly-haired girl returned to the book she had out on the counter. Tony just sighed and signaled "come on back."

Mick followed Tony into a room stacked with boxes of napkins and red cans of tomato sauce. Tony sat behind a desk so small it made Mick think of playing tea party with Colly when she was little. Mick sat opposite him in a chair that must have been out front once, but it had aged out to the back room.

"We're trying to re-create Adam's movements on Tuesday night. We want to know exactly where he was and when that night. You know, see if he stopped to get gas or needed cash from the ATM. We're just trying to get as much information as possible."

Before he could even get his final words out, Tony was shaking his head, no, no. As soon as Mick finished he added words to his gesture.

"No, Adam wouldn't have stopped anywhere. Listen, he was a good worker. I can't have someone unreliable. The kid came to work with his car gassed up, in his uniform, and if he wanted something to drink, he would have gotten it here, where it's free for employees, not spent his money at the Minute Mart. People want their pizzas hot. He knew that. He wouldn't have stopped."

Now it was Mick's turn to shake his head. "I'm not saying he wasn't a good employee or anything like that. You are probably right. He probably didn't stop, but we want to check his time. We think we know what route he took. We just want to try the whole run. Make sense?" Mick didn't want to let on to Tony that he wasn't sure if it made sense either but what the hell, it was worth a shot.

"Okay," Tony said, "what do you want me to do? How can I help?"

Mick filled him in on the plan. They'd be by at exactly 5:30 p.m. to pick up the pizza, the same pizza that Edie Spence had ordered. Tony agreed to put the order through just the way it had been placed, and they would take it from there.

Mick noticed that the curly-haired girl and the sullen chef didn't bother to look up when he left. He had the feeling they had given up. He couldn't blame them.

Mick wasn't ready to give up for the day, though. He had a few hours left to fill until it was time to play pizza delivery boy. Time to follow up on the other piece of Adam's story that had set off alarm bells in his head: the stolen cell phone at the high school.

CHAPTER THIRTY-FIVE

Stephanie decided to take another trip down memory lane and go back through old issues of the *Flyer*. She was sure there would be lots of material about Harlan Tucker.

The faculty adviser, wearing a blue denim shirt and a tie with Mickey Mouse on it, was sitting at a corner desk reading a current *Flyer* while five or six students stood arguing over a story about the track team's last meet. He directed her to the back issues, way back.

Stephanie couldn't resist a quick look at the papers from when she was the editor. One thing she'd kind of forgotten was how flimsy the paper was, certainly not the *New York Times* she'd remembered it as: just a few pages with small pictures.

She found an old issue with her name on the front: Stephanie Gallagher, editor in chief. She still felt that old surge of pride when she saw it. And why not? She'd spent the last couple of years feeling like a gullible fool, and maybe she had been, but she was other things, too. Here was the proof.

Stephanie turned her attention back to her task. She felt like she was in an old movie where they show the passage of time by flipping the pages of a calendar, only she was going backward, falling through time. And then there he was, Harlan Tucker, surrounded by fresh-faced boys with their shoulders all padded out.

She read through some of the articles. Most were about scores, rivalries, victories, or losses. The coach was leading his team. She didn't see any signs of regret for his lost pro career in the stories. Although, if the coach spent his life wondering what would have happened if the betting scandal had not touched him, on the unfairness of life, it was unlikely to be revealed in the *Forsyth Flyer*.

Still there might have been some kind of hint. It was interesting to note how much of the *Flyer* was devoted to the football team. She came across an article about Jack Jackson, who was part of what was called the triumphant Tripod, the support of the team.

In the photo Jackson was standing next to two boys. The one in the middle had his arm around the other two, staring at the camera while Jackson and the other boy seemed to be looking toward the kid in the middle.

The next paper she picked up had a black border around the edges of it and inside a picture of another smiling football player. *Oh, wait.* She went back to look at the photo of the Tripod. This was one of them. It must be the boy who killed himself, although you wouldn't know it from reading through the *Flyer*. There was no mention of how the kid died, just some information about him. No mention of the coach, either. The kid and the coach just disappeared from the *Flyer*.

She found an article later in the series with the headline introducing the new football coach, nothing about an old football coach. No wonder the old guy was so ecstatic over being cleared in the betting scandal. They sure weren't letting him off the hook here.

Stephanie replaced the papers and got up to walk out, back to where sometimes she wished she could make the calendar pages go faster or, better yet, go backward, but she was stuck in the here and now.

And just to shove her more into the present, as she walked out she noticed Mick McKay pulling into the high school parking lot. If that was supposed to be an unmarked car, it was failing. It screamed "cop car." Mick got out and pivoted in her direction when she called his name.

She remembered when she had written her Reluctant Robber story; Mick had said it was probably just some kid breaking in. She wondered if that was why he was here now.

Mick was surprised to see Stephanie in the school parking lot. He had wanted to get a little information about Adam Moore and the stolen phone. What he didn't want was to admit to Stephanie that he was following up on something she'd said. It was supposed to be the other way around.

"So were you here for the pep rally?" He wanted to deflect the conversation, make a joke, keep it light and focused on her, not on what he was doing.

She laughed and said, "No, those days are over. I was just looking at old school papers for my story about the coach." Her voice rose a little at the end like she wasn't sure he'd remember.

"Oh, yeah, that's going to be an interesting story. Well, I don't want to hold you up. See you later." He pivoted back toward the school.

There, he thought, *I didn't give her time to ask me what I was doing here.* He was proud of himself.

Mark Lavelle looked up at him like *he* was the kid being sent to the principal's office instead of the principal. And, in fact, Mick was planning to give him a bit of a verbal thrashing.

"You told me that Adam Moore was a good student, no problems, but I want to know about any trouble he got into—any trouble."

He watched as Mark tugged his sleeves down in a futile effort to cover his wrists before replying. "I guess you mean about the stolen cell phone," he said with a sigh. "I would have told you about it if I thought there was anything to tell, but there wasn't."

Mick nodded and said, "OK, just tell me. There might be something that doesn't seem important to you that is important to me."

Mark Lavelle gave another big sigh as he launched into his story. "There isn't much to tell. One of the girls accused Adam and Lacey of stealing her phone, or at least losing it, while they were supposed to be watching her backpack. I couldn't prove anything.

"The girl's father came to school screaming about the lack of discipline here and all that. I had Adam and Lacey do detention, just to appease the guy. But I was wrong. It's hard to sort out all the facts, and at first I thought it was possible that they had taken it. But they didn't."

"You know they didn't? How do you know they didn't?" Mick asked.

"Because a couple of days later, Sally Malcolm, the chemistry teacher, came to my office. She'd found a phone in one of the cubbies in her lab. She couldn't tell whose it was. She doesn't allow them in class. So she wanted to hand it in to me, making it difficult for the less-than-avid science student to claim it.

"The thing is, I checked Alyssa's schedule, and she had chemistry right before lunch. She lost it before she ever got down to the cafeteria that day. Did she know she'd lost it and blame them to escape the wrath of her dad? I don't know. But Lacey and Adam had already served their detentions. I couldn't undo that. I figured it wouldn't do anybody any good to bring it up again. So I didn't."

Mick nodded but thought if Adam had had someone in his corner to scream about the injustice of blaming his kid, the situation would have been different.

"What happened to the phone?" he asked.

"I gave it back to Alyssa. Her father had already gotten her a new one."

Mick thanked him for his time. It was hard to be too tough on the guy. After all, Mick wanted to believe the worst about the kid, too. He wanted Adam to be guilty of much worse than winding up with someone else's phone.

CHAPTER THIRTY-SIX

Mick swung by to pick up Mason and maybe Tyler for the timeline drive. The three of them drove through town to Coad's funeral home, where the victims had been paying respects to the dead, not knowing they would soon be dead themselves.

On to Antonio's to pick up the pizza and drive it to Edie Spence's house on Magnolia. They parked in the exact spot where Adam had parked. The three of them got out of the car and Mick, remembering where the bodies had been found, stepped around to the side. Mason and Tyler had no such qualms. They walked over the dead space.

Mick asked himself and the others the question that he had been asking all along. Why was Edie Spence outside? Wouldn't she have waited inside for the pizza delivery?

Did she come home, surprise the thief, and run outside at just the moment Adam Moore got there? Or was she waiting outside for Adam? No answer came to him.

Mick looked at his watch. It was the exact time that some of the neighbors heard what turned out to be shots fired. The three of them got back in the car and drove off at the time of the 911 call. Everything in the timeline fit. No discrepancies.

"We might as well go back and eat the pizza. No point in letting it go to waste."

Back at the office, Mick carried the pizza to the room they called the lunchroom. It was an overly bright room that always made Mick feel like a nurse might open the door and call his name for a doctor's visit.

Mick pulled the pizza out of the container and took a slice. It was still hot. He knew better than most that there were bad people in the world and good people who did bad things. Plus, he was naturally skeptical. In his experience, people had been known to lie. But he just couldn't see Edie Spence taking up with the pizza delivery guy, no matter how good the pizza was.

CHAPTER THIRTY-SEVEN

Mick wanted to check out what Stephanie Gallagher had said about the wife of National's head of maintenance being hired to take care of the old coach, Harlan Tucker.

He was trying to decide who to approach first. He could run it by Jackson, see what he had to say. Or he could start with the woman. If Mick talked to Jackson first, there was a good chance Jackson would say something to his employee. If he talked to the woman first it was a definite she would tell her husband about a visit from the police, but Mick might be able to get a feel for the situation without tipping off the reason for his curiosity. He could ask questions about the coach, not mention the burglaries.

Maybe it wouldn't hurt to give Stephanie a call and see if she had formed an impression about Augustine Morales.

She picked up on the first ring and he suggested meeting at Billy's Bait. They could have a Coke and talk there without anybody seeing them. He didn't want people to get the idea he had something to report and was giving it to Stephanie. And he certainly didn't want people to think he was getting information from a reporter for the *Bee*, even though that was exactly what he was doing. So Billy's Bait was the meeting place.

Mick pulled up about fifteen minutes later. Stephanie Gallagher wasn't there yet. Well, she couldn't speed like he did. She arrived after about five minutes. Mick got out of his car and walked over to her. It was the perfect spring afternoon, and on impulse Mick suggested they go for a walk instead of sit inside the bait shop with the worms. They moved toward the sidewalk path that ran between Billy's and the boat launch.

Mick began, "Your story on the old coach—how's that going?"

If she was surprised by his question she didn't show it. "It's going well. It's an interesting story. I'm planning to do a little research on the man who sent Harlan Tucker the letter. You know, did he atone for his sin, and all that."

Mick nodded. "Atone for his sin, huh? Not easy to do. So you've been out to the Tucker place to talk to Harlan's housekeeper, right?"

"Yes, several times; the housekeeper, his daughters. They're packing up the house. I guess they want to put it on the market."

"What did you think of the housekeeper?" Mick asked—he hoped—nonchalantly.

Stephanie looked up at him. "The housekeeper? She seems competent. I think she's going to miss the job. Why?"

Mick looked down at the path, preparing his answer. He noticed a stick that had fallen across and stepped over it. Stephanie was looking at him, not at the path. Her toe caught the branch and she stumbled, falling forward on her knee.

Damn! Mick thought as he reached for her a fraction of a second too late. He grabbed her arm and pulled her back up. Her knee had little pinpricks of blood from where she had hit the gravel. He reached in his pocket and yanked out a Kleenex, launching his Chapstick down the path at the same time. He bent down and applied the Kleenex to her knee and retrieved his rolling Chapstick.

He stood up, and they both looked at the Kleenex turning red on her knee.

"Are you okay?" he asked.

"Yeah, sorry. I just tripped."

"No, no. It's my fault. This was a bad idea. Can you walk back? I have a first aid kit in the car."

"Yes, I can walk. I just skinned my knee. I'm fine."

Mick took her arm and turned her on the path, like a dance partner. She was limping a little. She steadied herself by grasping his hand. He looked down at their intertwined hands. It somehow felt natural to him, good.

When they left the protection of the pines and entered the open parking lot, he could see Billy look up in surprise from his window.

He gestured to him with his free hand. Come. Billy rolled off his stool, disappeared for a second, and then pushed out the door. Mick opened the passenger door of his car and turned to explain to Billy.

"She fell down."

"You can get into trouble on that path, sure as ice cream melts in August," Billy said.

Mick wasn't sure what that was supposed to mean, but he pointed to Stephanie's leg. All three of them looked at her knee as Mick carefully pulled the red-tinged Kleenex free.

Billy offered to run in for some Band-Aids, explaining he was well prepared because of all the fool fishermen who got hooks stuck in them. But Mick stopped him, reaching around Stephanie for his first aid kit. He suddenly felt shy and self-conscious touching her knee.

When Billy suggested bringing some water out for them, Mick stopped him again, saying he had some ointment. They'd be fine. Like a scared high school boy, he suddenly didn't want to be left alone with Stephanie. He carefully wiped away the dirt, rubbed a little antiseptic over her knee, and put a bandage on. As he pressed it on he looked up to see her watching him. He hoped she hadn't noticed his discomfort, his flushed face.

"There," he said. "OK?"

She reached down and brushed some dirt from her skirt. "Yes, I'm fine. Thanks so much. I promise, I'm not usually so clumsy."

Mick could feel the top of his ears heating up. "No, that path isn't the best."

Billy seemed to be picking up on Mick's neediness. He was just hanging in the background. Stephanie stood up and smoothed her skirt.

"I'm fine, really. Oh no, I got some blood on your shirt," she said, pointing to a red splotch on his blue shirtsleeve.

Mick touched the spot as if he were not sure it was really there. "Oh, don't worry about that," he said.

Mick felt like the interview was over for now. He and Billy both walked her to her car and watched while she swung her bandaged leg in.

"I'll call you later," Mick said as she was closing the door. As soon as the words were out of his mouth, he felt the top of his ears heat up again, like he had something to be ashamed of. Which he didn't.

He and Billy watched her drive out of the parking lot. Billy turned to him when her car was out of sight. Mick was afraid there might be a question in Billy's face so he looked at his car, mumbled a thanks, slammed the back door shut, yanked open his door, and drove away, leaving Billy perplexed in the parking lot.

Stephanie could see the two men standing, staring at her car in the parking lot of Billy's Bait. Her knee felt warm where Mick had applied the bandage. She thought about what Warren had said about touching Mandy's hand and feeling a shock, even through the protective gloves. But maybe what she was feeling was just the tingle from the antiseptic on her skinned knee.

Now she wasn't sure what Mick had wanted to talk to her about. They had only made it through the small talk about her Harlan Tucker story. She fell down before he could bring up what he wanted to discuss about the murders. He would call her later.

She had wanted to ask him why he was at the high school. When she had first reported on the Reluctant Robber, Mick had said it was some kid. But now with a double homicide, he couldn't still think it was a teenage prank. She'd ask him later. She would have to stop at home and change before she headed out to her interview.

When she looked in her rearview mirror, she had an odd feeling that she would see Mick following behind her. He wasn't, of course, but she couldn't shake the feeling.

CHAPTER THIRTY-EIGHT

Hiding her scraped knee in a pair of black pants, Stephanie drove past rows of neat houses with small, well-kept lawns, looking out the passenger side window for number 937. The houses reminded her of perfect square and rectangular packages under a Christmas tree, the gardens out in front like trailing ribbons. It didn't look like anything bad could happen in these houses.

There in the middle of the block, painted light green with dark green shutters, a hose all curled up and hanging neatly on the side of the porch, she found 937. The front door was opening as she walked up the sidewalk. A thin woman wearing jeans and sneakers was holding open the door for her.

"Ms. Atkins?" Stephanie asked walking past her through the open door.

"Oh, call me Donnetta," the woman said.

Once Stephanie was past her she turned and offered iced tea or coffee. Stephanie could see a plate of cookies sitting on the coffee table.

"I would love some tea," Stephanie said and settled down in the big chair Donnetta motioned her to.

While she was getting the tea it occurred to Stephanie that Donnetta was the kind of woman whom you'd expect to see wearing an apron. With her long gray hair streaked with brown pulled back, she looked a little like the women from a polygamy cult or maybe some longsuffering pioneer woman walking beside a wagon train.

Ms. Atkins came and put two glasses of tea on the coffee table next to the plate of cookies. As she sank down on the couch, she gave Stephanie a little nod. Okay, we're set, now what? She seemed like a woman used to waiting, and she sat while Stephanie thought about how to begin.

"Ms. Atkins—Donnetta," she corrected herself before Ms. Atkins had the chance to remind her, "I'm doing a story on Harlan Tucker, and I wanted to talk to you about him." Stephanie scanned the face of the older woman, looking for her reaction to what might be unwelcome words. But her face gave nothing away. It was like paper that had been folded and creased so many times it became soft, the words printed on it unreadable.

Stephanie plunged back in with her request. "I know your son, Charlie, played on the last team Harlan Tucker coached. I just wanted to get your thoughts on the man." Of course what she really wanted to say was, "Do you blame the coach for the death of your son?"

Stephanie waited for a response. She had the feeling that Donnetta needed an apron to wipe her hands on. It seemed like the kind of gesture that would come naturally to her.

Donnetta held up a finger—*wait*—and went into another room. She came back with a couple of photo albums. She opened to a page with the whole team looking earnestly at the camera, never believing they would get old, and, of course, Charlie didn't. Donnetta pointed to him, a handsome boy with brown hair curling over his ears, his football helmet on his knee. She smiled at the picture as she talked to Stephanie.

"Charlie loved football. Oh, and he was good at, good at lots of sports, really. He put his heart into everything he did. I'll tell you, I was always proud of him. And he wasn't like some of the boys, ashamed to show any feelings. No, he'd check the stands to find us before his games, from the time he was little. He'd find us and blow me a kiss! Imagine that. All those cheerleaders and the boys on the other team, he didn't care."

"He must have been a very special boy," Stephanie said.

Next to her Donnetta sighed and leaned over to close the photo album. "Yes, he was, but I don't want to give you the impression he was just a little angel. He was the sweetest boy, but he had lots of fun in him and he had a temper, too.

"One time when he was little, he was out riding his bike with some kids from the neighborhood. Some older boys came by and threw water balloons at the kids. One of the little kids fell off his bike. Charlie leaped off his bike and grabbed the bigger boy's handlebars. Down they both went, skinned knees and a gash requiring stitches on his elbow." Donnetta smiled to herself, and then shook her head. "But you came here to talk about the coach. I guess what you want to know is if we blamed him, blamed him for what happened to Charlie. The truth is I blamed everyone for a while: the coach, the school counselors, the player he fought with, my husband, but mostly I blamed myself. How could I have not known? But that was just it. If I didn't know, didn't see any signs, how could I have expected the coach to know? How could I have expected more from him than from myself?

"He was a good coach. He seemed to be genuinely interested in Charlie and his future, not just what he could do on the football field, but Charlie as a person." Donnetta paused again. "Here, I'll show you Charlie's homecoming picture. He went with Candy Watkins."

Stephanie gazed at the same boy, same hair curling around his ears, a little less solemn in this picture with a blonde girl in a dress with layers of blue netting.

"A cute couple," Stephanie said.

Once again, Donnetta peeled her eyes off the picture to look up at Stephanie. "You know, Candy still comes by to see me when she's in town. Of course she's married now—well, twice, actually. She's got kids older than Charlie was when he died. But I always enjoy seeing her. Some of his other friends stop by, too.

"Jack Johnson, of course; he and Charlie were great friends. Back then it was like he was part of our family. And now, he really is. He came around so much, comforting our daughter Anne after Charlie died. Well, they wound up falling in love and getting married. And Trey Barber, too, such a nice boy he was. He sends me a mum every year on homecoming; imagine that."

"I think that says a lot about Charlie that his friends still come by," Stephanie said. "Did you ever see Harlan Tucker after?"

Donnetta sighed. "He came to the funeral with the team. Those early days we were in shock. We couldn't believe Charlie would do that. Even now with all we know about depression and mental illness, I still find it hard to believe. Back then, it was impossible for us. But even I could tell how bad the coach felt at the funeral.

"You know he never went back to Forsyth High. If I remember right, he didn't even go back to clean out his office. They had to get a substitute teacher for his classes for the rest of the year."

Stephanie heard the whir of a rising garage door from the back of the house and a man called, "Donnetta, Donnetta."

"In here!" she called back to him.

"Hey, Etta, how about a fish dinner tonight?" he said before he rounded the corner. "Oh, sorry. I didn't know you had company." He walked toward Stephanie with his hand held out. "I'm Rusty Atkins, but today you can just call me successful fisherman," he said shaking her hand.

"Stephanie Gallagher. Nice to meet you, successful fisherman. I must admit I don't meet too many of you," she replied. Everybody seemed at ease and almost jolly, not what she had been expecting this interview to be like.

"Stephanie is from the *Bee*. She wanted to ask some questions about Harlan Tucker," Donnetta informed him.

"Hmmm, I saw he died the other day." That did knock a little of the jolliness out of the room. Rusty looked over at his wife, received some kind of signal that Stephanie couldn't get, like a dog whistle, impossible for her to hear. Whatever passed between them, he decided to speak. "We didn't go to the funeral, just because in the years since Charlie died, people would see us together and start gossiping again. It wasn't good for Harlan, and it wasn't good for us.

"But I did see Harlan from time to time through the years. We'd meet for breakfast in Camden. No one knew us there, and we didn't have to worry about the rumor mill. He cared about Charlie, and I think he was really sorry he passed away the way he did.

"I thought Harlan Tucker was a hell of a good coach. Excuse my French, but I thought it before he was Charlie's coach, while he was Charlie's coach, and even after. And he was a good coach off the football field, too." Stephanie raised her eyebrows at him, encouraging him to continue. "Charlie, he had his heart set on being a scientist.

He wanted to go to MIT or CalTech. Not because he wanted to play football there. No, some of the boys, they got all the glory and happiness in their lives on the field, but not Charlie.

"And the coach encouraged him in his academics, set up meetings for him with people he knew who were chemists and some guy down in Houston who worked at NASA. Charlie wanted a life beyond the football field, and Harlan was trying to help him get there. Ironic that, because of Charlie, Harlan gave up football."

Stephanie nodded and asked, "Did you know Harlan Tucker was once considered for a professional team?" Rusty and Donnetta both shook their heads, like those bobble dogs in the back window of people's cars.

"No, I didn't know that, but it doesn't surprise me. He was a natural athlete, and he was one of the best at calling plays. He seemed to know what was going to work by just watching the boys go out on the field. Was he injured in college?"

"No, nothing like that. He was accused of cheating." Next to her she could hear Donnetta make a tsk-tsk sound, so she hurried on. "He was accused and he had no way to clear his name, but the person who actually cheated came forward on his deathbed and cleared Harlan Tucker. So at least he knew he'd been exonerated before he died."

Rusty was still shaking his head. "You know, once when I was talking to him, not about anything special, he told me how he wanted to protect his players from the evil around them. Those were his exact words: 'the evil around them.' Now I wonder if that's what he was alluding to."

"That's very interesting. It does make you wonder. Could I quote you in the paper?"

Another silent message must have passed between them and this time it was Donnetta who spoke. "I don't see how it can hurt us now. We've been trying since Charlie's death to show that we don't blame anyone, especially the coach." She looked over at Rusty, his cue to comment.

"I told him a long time ago we didn't hold him responsible. It wouldn't hurt to see it in writing again," he said.

Stephanie said, "That's very generous of you. I appreciate your kindness. I guess I'd better let you get your fish dinner ready."

As she got her purse and fished for the car keys, Donnetta flipped the photo book on the table open to the last page. There was a note with a green Holiday Inn star on the top. Stephanie bent down to read it.

Coach Tucker,

I am so sorry for letting you down tonight. You have helped me in so many ways and taught me so much in the last four years. I wish I could go back and do the game over again. It kills me to think how disappointed in me you must be. I know there is nothing I can ever do to make this right.

"Don't put this in your article, but that is the one thing that I just never can get over. Charlie wrote the note to the coach and not us. I know that's a silly little thing to fret about with all that happened. I just can't believe he didn't think of us.

"But the counselor we saw afterward said that was just it: he wasn't thinking. It wasn't a thought-out decision. He just felt such despair in that moment that he could never make things right again. Imagine that, about a football game. Sometimes I have conversations with him in my head, with a grown-up Charlie, and he laughs about the game and how upset he was at that moment. And I think yes, that's how it could be if . . . if . . . "

Stephanie noticed the tears trickling down the soft, worn-out wrinkles.

Rusty moved over to hold Donnetta's hand. "You're right. It could have been like that," he said squeezing her hand.

"Well, that's one good thing. Do you know how many couples split up after something like this happens?"

Stephanie demurred, "No."

"It's close to seventy percent. But we hung in there together, and mostly when we think of Charlie, it's the good stuff, right, Etta?" Donnetta smiled back at him through her tears. "Besides, we've had a lot of happy times in our family. Did Donnetta tell you about our grandkids?"

Stephanie, standing at the doorway, fingered her keys. "No, she didn't tell me."

Rusty grabbed a picture from the mantle. "Here they are. Sarah, Hannah, and Charles—although he goes by Chip." Stephanie looked at the photo of the three kids. Donnetta and Rusty beamed at the picture, too. "When Charlie died, the joy just drained right out of our family. We were real worried about our daughter. She adored Charlie, followed him everywhere.

"That was another thing that kept us going. We were worried about her, how she would survive something like that, so we had to survive to take care of her. Jack Jackson, he started coming around, sitting with us, helping her. We were happy she had someone to talk to who loved Charlie, too. Oh, and didn't we think he was being brotherly? But one day they came and told us they were dating, you know? Boyfriend and girlfriend."

"And we were pleased as punch!" Donnetta chimed in. "So he started out as Charlie's friend and wound up as Anne's husband."

Donnetta moved to pick up the empty glasses and Rusty said, "I'll walk you out."

When they were outside Stephanie turned to him and said, "I hope my visit wasn't too upsetting for your wife. I can't imagine all she's been through."

Rusty smoothed back his unruly red hair as if he were preparing to put a cap on. "No, you didn't upset her. Charlie is never far from our thoughts. That's just the way it is. Did you notice Donnetta's hair?"

Stephanie glanced up at him, perplexed. "Very pretty," she said, not quite sure where he was going with this.

"Well, she was supposed to get her hair all done up the day after they went to State. She wanted to be dolled up for the football banquet. Then when Charlie—when everything happened, of course she canceled the appointment. She never made another one. Said she couldn't bear to sit in that chair and think of the way she had imagined everything and then the reality.

"I'd tell her from time to time to go ahead and go. I even bought her a spa package, thinking she could get her hair cut there, but she wouldn't do it. We all have to cope the best we can, and if that helps her, well then I'm for it. Yes, sir, we have to cope as best as we can."

Stephanie felt ashamed of her own coping skills as she waved goodbye to Rusty Atkins.

CHAPTER THIRTY-NINE

Mick checked his list of questions for Jack Jackson. That was another thing he hated about cop shows. Columbo would be leaving and turn and ask the fateful question that would lead to his discovery of the criminal, like he just thought of it. Every good detective comes into an interview more prepared than Barbara Walters.

And he wanted to be prepared for this one. Mick felt that Jackson saw something. He wanted to give Jackson a chance to open up to him. He wanted to reassure him that he was doing the right thing by voicing his suspicions. Mick planned to tell him, "Hell, I know you don't want to get anyone in trouble, but, believe me, we are looking for who did this and one way to find him is to eliminate the people who didn't do it. We don't want to hang this on the wrong guy."

His files were also in front of him. He pored over Stephanie Gallagher's newspaper articles, feeling that odd twinge of guilt again after their incident earlier outside Billy's Bait Shop. He was trying to convince himself that nothing had happened. He was just helping an injured person. He would have done the same for anyone. Of course he'd held her hand; he didn't want her to fall again. He shook his head and shoulders, like he used to call out to Colly at her basketball games. *Shake it off,* he told himself.

He turned his thoughts back to her Reluctant Robber and ran his finger down the list of items taken in the burglaries. At Martin Colby's house, the thief had taken the gun and a wallet. Eighty or so dollars were missing, but there were two twenty-dollar bills sitting there on the table in the hallway when Colby got home. Mick rubbed his chin.

The list from the other places was similar: no big items, a watch, and cash. Mick added up the amount of cash taken and came up with three hundred and twenty dollars. This was not the work of an experienced thief. It was an amateur.

More than that, it struck him as childish. Childish, except for the part where the thief shot two people. And not just shooting wild, either, but deliberately putting a bullet in their heads. Try as hard as he could, Mick couldn't see the same person doing these two crimes.

But how had the first guy gotten the gun to the second guy? It didn't make sense.

One of the reasons he was so annoyed with Stephanie's Reluctant Robber story was the absurdity of the idea this was some grown man trying to feed his family in the face of layoffs at work.

Mick sighed. He'd had a feeling that solving these crimes would lead him to the killer, but what if the kid stealing petty cash, and he believed it was a kid, had just tossed the gun? Mick tried that scenario. The kid walks in, takes some cash, impulsively picks up the gun, and walks out. Later he reads about the old man and his license. He feels guilty, returns the license. He doesn't know what to do with the gun Colby described in the paper, so he tosses it. The gun gets picked up by another thief, who then murders two people. It just seemed like too big of a coincidence.

Mick rubbed his chin again and felt the stubble. He checked his watch. Time to go home. He wasn't getting anywhere with his "kid versus cold-blooded murderer" debate.

CHAPTER FORTY

Mick woke with a start. He wasn't even fully awake and he already felt jittery. He stepped into his garage and crossed another day off the calendar before heading out for a run. He missed Julie and Colly. If they were home he would be spending some of his time thinking about them, talking to them, but now all he had was the murders running through his head while he ran.

Mick arrived at work about an hour later and walked into his office down the hall past the lobby. Tiffany Hudson was waiting for him in a chair outside his office, sitting so straight she made General Patton look like a hunchback. He motioned to her to follow him.

"Any news?" she asked.

One of the many reasons Mick wanted to find the murderer was to make her feel better, to at least give her the comfort of knowing someone would pay for what they did to her brother. He couldn't change what had happened, so this was the only way for him to bring some amount of peace to her.

He gestured to a chair. "No, we don't have anything solid yet. But we will. I need to ask you some more questions about your brother to help us in our investigation."

"But why? Why does any of this matter if he just walked into a robbery? I don't get why knowing about him would help find the person who did this."

"Look, I know what you mean, but we have to look at everything. There's the possibility that the robber killed Adam because he was afraid your brother recognized him or Mrs. Spence. We just want to have as much information as possible. OK?" He smiled to reassure her and she nodded.

"OK."

"Tiffany, I know and you know that Adam had some problems with drugs."

The girl closed down like a garage door sliding shut. She looked at him without expression.

"Look, I'm not here to judge or criticize. My only goal is to find who killed Adam. I think that's what you want, too. Just trust me on this, OK?"

She tilted her head. "Yes, he did get into drugs. I tried to talk to him, but he was so depressed and discouraged about losing his scholarship he couldn't think straight. And let's face it, it's not like he deserved the bad breaks he got."

Mick thought she was right there. Nobody deserved what happened to Adam Moore. "OK, how you can help me is by telling me about some of the people he hung out with, where he liked to go, what kinds of things he did when he wasn't delivering pizzas. Did he have a girlfriend?"

"Adam was going out with Carrie Wasbaugh. I only met her a few times, but I liked her, and she seemed like a nice girl."

"How long had they been going together?" Mick asked.

"Oh, I guess about three months or so. He kind of changed in the last few months, and I think he wanted some new friends. She was one of them."

"What about his old friends? Did he still hang out with them?"

Tiffany was shaking her head. "No, he kind of lost interest or something. He was friends with Lacey Thomas and that crowd, but I haven't seen them in a long time. Once he started delivering pizzas to Mr. Tucker, he was more excited about the future."

"Now don't get mad, I have to ask this. Did you know where Adam got his drugs when he was using?"

Tiffany stiffened. "No, I don't know where he got the stuff. But look, I think you've got the wrong idea about this. Yeah, he ran around and drank and did some drugs, but he wasn't bad. Really, he wasn't. And he wasn't a big-time druggie either. Ask anybody. They'll tell you. We didn't have enough money to buy drugs. We were barely getting by. He was a good kid."

It could be that Carrie liked being able to influence Adam. She wanted to be the one to save him from himself. Another woman in Adam's life might have meant she could feel her control over him slipping away. Or it could mean that Mick was grasping at straws in a sea of uncertainty.

If Dr. Spence had not been on that plane, he would have been the first suspect. Someone very close to the victim is most likely the killer. This time there were two victims. If it wasn't a jealous husband, it could be a jealous girlfriend. Two could play at this game.

Mick turned down Lee Street, organizing his thoughts. He wanted to have a clear picture of the possibilities before he knocked on the girl's door. He wasn't even sure she was really Adam Moore's girlfriend. Tiffany Hudson might have read more into it than was there.

But if Carrie was Adam's girlfriend, she could have been upset about the competition, maybe upset enough to do something crazy like shoot him. There was no telling what a young person in love might do.

Mick had seen a picture of Carrie Wasbaugh. She didn't look like the sort of person who could walk up and deliver two kill shots. But it wasn't always the scary-looking people. A cute girl could kill, too.

He slowed down to check the house numbers. He wished he could surprise Carrie with his questions, catch her off guard. She was over eighteen, but she still lived with her mother. Legally speaking, surprises were not all that easy. She'd probably been expecting a call from Forsyth's finest anyway.

He spotted the address in colorful tiles next to the door. The house was neat and well kept. He could practically smell the starch in the white curtains. Pink flowers spilled out of a pot next to the door, the same kind of flowers that the Spences had. These didn't have any blood on them, though. He rang the doorbell and stood back.

The girl who answered the door had a blonde ponytail and a bright smile. She looked like she just finished doing cartwheels.

Mick stuck his hand in his pocket and showed her his ID. He was looking behind Miss Head Cheerleader to find the parent. And there she was, another blonde ponytail, just a little older version.

As soon as he saw her, he dropped the idea that Carrie Wasbaugh killed her boyfriend and Edie Spence. He knew all the stories about the pedophile turning out to be not the creepy-looking guy in a rain-coat but the guy who looked like he stepped off a tennis court. He'd gone through all the training exercises to make him more aware of biases. But still. He didn't get the feeling this girl was capable of more than occasionally skipping Sunday school. He sat in the chair they offered him, declined a cup of coffee, and tried to keep an open mind.

"How long did you know Adam Moore?"

He noticed the girl didn't glance at her mother before answering. She seemed confident and competent.

"I've known him since fourth grade. We played soccer on the same team. He was a really good player and I loved to play. So we got to be friends. I stopped playing in high school, so we didn't hang out then as much. I ran into him about three months ago and we started talking and then we started dating."

Mick nodded. Nothing he didn't already know, but concise and to the point.

"Where did you run into him again?" he asked.

"Well, right here as a matter of fact. I ordered a pizza and he brought it to the house. I was surprised to see him."

"You didn't know he was working at the pizzeria?"

"No, I was surprised. I mean, when I knew Adam, he was a big deal. I heard about his accident and all, but I just assumed he'd still go away to school. And he was planning to go in the fall. He was working things out." Her eyes filled with unshed tears.

"I guess you really liked him, huh?"

"I liked him and I was happy for him. He had finally gotten his life back on track. He applied to Southern so we could be together." The tears trickled out the corners of her eyes, no containing them now.

Mick nodded. She wasn't coming across as insanely jealous, which is what she needed to be for his theory to fit. Maybe he could stretch it around her with the next few questions.

"Did you know any of his other friends?" Mick asked as a start.

"Yeah, sure. We knew a lot of the same people, from soccer and from school, too."

Now, Mick was ready. "Did you know Lacey Thomas?"

He waited for some flash of jealousy. There was something there when he said the name. He saw the quick glance at her mother, not so self-assured after all.

But she held on to her poise and shook her head, yes. Mick gave her ten seconds to elaborate, and sure enough, the silence was too much for her.

She rushed to fill it. "I knew her, but we didn't hang out in the same groups."

Mick raised his eyebrow and waited to see if he could get her to add something else. This time she was willing to sit out the silence.

"Was she a good friend of Adam's?" He could see the girl wanted to tell him something. He would just have to keep fishing until he got close enough for her to come out with it.

She straightened up in her chair, displaying righteous indignation. "They were good friends, but she wasn't a good friend for him. All she cares about is where the next party's going to be. I know I shouldn't gossip, but you can ask anybody, and they'll tell you the same thing. She wanted to keep him right here, in Forsyth, partying with her. She didn't care if he never went to college or any of that. I'm sorry, but that's just the way she is.

"I didn't want to bring this up now, but you asked. We didn't call the police, we should have but we didn't, and anyway I can't prove it or anything, but someone threw garbage in my yard and wrote dirty words on my mom's car. I'm pretty sure it was Lacey."

Mick was always surprised at what people considered police-calling events in their lives. He was of two minds on the subject. He hated it when someone called because the neighbor ran over their recycling bin or leaves from the neighbor's tree were falling in the yard—actual calls he had received. Was it really his job to sort that kind of stuff out?

On the other hand, unless you are living next door to Mahatma Gandhi, things are bound to escalate. It's better to call before someone keys the car or poisons the dog. Both of which Mick had seen happen over things so trivial he wanted to ask the perpetrators, "Was it worth it?" The dog poisoner wound up spending some time in jail. So sometimes he wanted to get the garbage-in-the-yard and dirty-words-on-mom's-car calls.

The mom broke her silence. "Is this confidential? Because that girl can be mean. I don't want her coming after Carrie. Again."

"Oh yes, this is all confidential. And if anyone threatens you, please call me. We don't tolerate that kind of behavior. Don't worry about that."

Mick felt pleased as he walked toward his car. He'd come to find a jealous girlfriend and he'd found a jealous girlfriend . . . just not the one he anticipated.

CHAPTER FORTY-ONE

Stephanie nosed her car into the parking lot slowly on account of the little kids running around. It seemed like an odd place for a teenage girl to pick for a meeting. Then again, maybe it was perfect if she didn't want to be seen by her friends.

Stephanie got out and scanned the playground. Kids were on swings being pushed by their moms. Another small group of kids were climbing on something that looked like it was made of giant Legos, peeking out holes in the wall while their mothers looked at them and at each other, at them and at each other. It reminded Stephanie of a gazelle grazing on a hill, watching for danger.

She turned and saw a girl sitting on top of one the picnic tables, alone and hunched over. She walked toward her, leaving behind the happy chatter of the playground. The girl stared at her as she approached. She was wearing beat-up jeans and a tank top from which her ample bosom was visible through some kind of tulle wrap. It looked like a tiny ballerina had landed on her shoulders.

"Hi. I'm Stephanie Gallagher. From the *Bee*. Are you Lacey Thomas?" she added, because the girl just looked at her blankly. "Like I said on the phone, I just want to ask you some questions about Adam Moore. You were friends, right?"

The girl nodded and her tutu wrap quivered. "We hung out."

Stephanie had gotten the feeling on the phone that the girl was a little awkward. Now she seemed annoyed.

"How long had you known Adam?" She started with an easy question.

"We both pretty much grew up in this crummy little town, so a long time. But we didn't hang out 'til a couple of years ago."

Stephanie tried to tone down her own perkiness. She couldn't match the sullenness of the girl, though. "Did you like him?"

Lacey looked so bored Stephanie half expected her to yawn. She looked off at the kids on the swings before answering.

"He was just about the only person here that I liked. We had a lot of fun." And then there was just a hint of a smile. Stephanie took that as a sign that she was going in the right direction.

"What kinds of things did you do for fun?" Now Lacey smiled at her for real, a "you poor idiot" smile.

"Not the kind of things you can print in the *Bee*, that's for sure," she said.

Stephanie smiled like she was in on the joke, like she spent her time having the kind of fun you couldn't print in the *Bee*, too.

"I heard Adam was planning to go away to college. Are you planning to go, too?"

The girl rolled her eyes. "Adam and I were going to go out to Los Angeles. He wanted to be a sports announcer and I want to get into fashion design. You don't need college for that. You need talent, and we both have that."

That was interesting. Not the story Stephanie had heard from Tiffany, and it didn't match the college applications she had heard about either. Stephanie felt her natural curiosity get the better of her. She took note of the tutu shoulder wrap and asked, "Did you design what you're wearing?"

Lacey's hand went up to her shoulder, touching the tulle wrap. "Yeah, I did design this. I try to add something of my own to everything I wear. See, I put a little piece of lace on all my designs," she said, fingering a small patch of black lace on the edge of the pink tulle.

Stephanie tried to think of an adjective that would sound like a compliment to the girl. She discarded cute, pretty, and darling. "It's very original and different."

The girl almost smiled. "Yeah, I try to look different."

Time to get back to Adam. "Did Adam like your designs?"

"Adam was great about encouraging me. My mom wants me to

get a job in the hatchery where she works. She doesn't think I'm anything special. So why not be just like her?"

Stephanie tried again to turn back to Adam. "Did your mom like Adam?" she asked.

"My mom couldn't stand Adam. She was afraid I was going to get pregnant. I kept telling her, even if I did, at least I would have made it through high school, which is more than I can say for her."

Now Stephanie felt a little guilty. Poor kid. She really had just lost her best friend. And here Stephanie was pumping her for information, another in a long list of adults who were not interested in her or her dreams. But it was her job.

"You know, I saw Adam's applications for college. I think he really was trying to do better. It must be sad to have a friend leave you behind like that."

Now the girl was staring at the swings again. "I told you, he wasn't going to leave me."

"I heard he had a girlfriend and they were going to go to college together."

Lacey's tutu trembled as she shook her head, no. "You mean Carrie Wasbaugh? That little Goody Two-shoes! Always trying to get him. She pretended to be so sweet and holy and all, but I could see how she was trying to get him, the little slut. He was only trying not to hurt her feelings, that's all," she said, punching her thighs for emphasis. "Adam, he really believed in me. He got me a sewing machine so I could work on my designs. I know Carrie goes around like she was his girlfriend, but she wasn't. He was nice to her. So what? That didn't mean a thing. No big deal."

Stephanie didn't want to disillusion her, but sometimes being nice was a big deal. There was Pete just being nice to poor, skinny Sara. And look what happened there.

"Thanks for talking to me. I can tell you liked Adam a lot and that you were good friends. From everything I'm finding out about him, I think he must have been a special guy. I know you're going to miss him. I hope things work out for you with your designs." Stephanie handed her a business card. "Call me if you want to talk some more about Adam."

Lacey's mouth formed an "O" of surprise, but she took the card. As she walked away Stephanie thought, *Who knows?* Maybe her designs would become all the rage. She certainly had stranger things in her own closet than the tutu wrap.

CHAPTER FORTY-TWO

Mick wanted to check on Lacey Thomas, see if she'd ever been picked up. The name didn't ring a bell, but Forsyth wasn't so small that he would know the name of every teenager who got into trouble. A quick check brought her name up for a couple of speeding tickets and a misdemeanor theft.

Mick put his hands behind his head to think about the implications. Speeding . . . sooner or later, everyone was going to get a speeding ticket. But theft, that was different. He saw the case was dismissed, but that didn't mean there was no theft.

He wanted to run through the possibilities and didn't want to do it alone. He rolled his chair to the door and stuck his head out into the hall. Mason was standing next to their board, writing down the information they had gotten from the neighbors on their timeline.

"Hey, Mason, got a sec?" Mason looked up and headed toward Mick.

"Sure. What's up?"

Mick explained that he had interviewed Adam Moore's girlfriend and come up with some information on the previous girlfriend who was evidently none too happy about being the previous girlfriend.

"In fact, she was so unhappy that she," and here Mick used his fingers to make quotation marks in the air, "'allegedly' threw garbage in the new girlfriend's yard. Plus she was once picked up for theft. So we know she gets mad and she steals. Two things we might be looking for."

Mason shrugged and said, "A girl? I don't see it. Besides, Jackson said he saw a man running away: a man, not a girl."

"I know, I know, but try this for a theory. We know Adam knew at least two of the burglary victims. He delivered pizza to Colby and he knew Edie Spence through his visits with Harlan Tucker. Okay, suppose he is the Reluctant Robber and—"

Mason interrupted, "And he shot himself?"

"OK, no, but just suppose he is."

Mason shrugged.

"But he's not doing it alone. He has a partner, a girl, who is crazy about him. Bonnie and Clyde. He does his thing and she helps. I don't know how, maybe with lookout or a distraction.

"Anyway, he falls for someone else, which makes his partner in crime very unhappy. She knows his routine. Maybe she helped with the planning. He needs her. He can't use his new girlfriend because she's not the criminal type.

"So, they're planning another adventure in theft when the girl realizes that he is serious about the new girl, that he's finished with her. She has a way to get revenge. She knows where he'll be. She has access to the gun because they were in it together. She shows up and waits. Maybe he is expecting her to be there for lookout.

"When naughty Romeo shows up to get a little more cash, she lets him have it. The nurse wasn't supposed to be there, but she is, so she shoots her, too, throws down the gun, and takes off running when she hears Jackson and his dog coming. What do you think?"

Mason checked his nails before answering. "Nice story; nothing holding it together, though."

"But it doesn't sound crazy, does it? And all the pieces fit together. It makes sense. We've always wondered why the shooter didn't just run. Well, this explains it. The shooter's plan was to kill them. Show that boy he couldn't move on so easily."

Mason, getting caught up in the tale, said, "You know, the pizza delivery thing fits, too. A delivery guy could be up on your porch without people being alarmed. Nobody's going to be worried about him stealing stuff. He's bringing something, not taking something. If he gets caught he can always say he got the wrong address. He's driving around town a lot so he knows people's schedules. Plus, it fits with our it-has-to-be-a-kid theory. Have you talked to the girl yet?"

"No, I'm just lining up my questions. I wanted to bounce some ideas around before I see her. I haven't talked to Rainy about it yet either. I think she might be a pretty tough customer."

When he finally sat down with Lacey Thomas, he was the one who felt off balance. He was used to Colly's artistic-type friends, but this girl looked like Miss Havisham in *Great Expectations*. She was wearing a skirt with patches of lace up the sides and a tank top with lace covering her shoulders.

"I know you were friends with Adam Moore and I'm talking to people who knew him, who hung out with him. I want to know as much about him as possible so I can figure out who did this to him."

"Well, I guess that's your job, right?"

Mick sighed. This was not going to be easy. "Yeah, it's my job, but he was your friend, so I imagine you would want to help me do my job."

"I don't know how I can help you. Some crazy person shot Adam because he was at the nurse's house while it was being robbed. What else is there to say? Too bad you didn't catch the man before he killed those people."

Mick felt the heat rising up to his face. If he'd had a tie on he would have loosened it. She was right. He wished he'd caught the thief before the murders, wished he'd taken it all more seriously. She had hit him where it hurts.

"You are right about that. I wish I'd been able to catch him before he did this. But I didn't, so I want to catch him before he does it again." He carefully used only masculine pronouns when he talked. No point in tipping her off about his favorite theory that they were in it together. She certainly seemed hostile to him. He moved on to more neutral territory.

"How long did you know Adam?"

"We knew each other when we were kids, so a long time."

Mick almost smiled but he caught himself. It hadn't been so very long ago when Lacey Thomas was a kid. And of course, he was talking to her because he thought it was possible that she had been on a crime spree, stealing and killing. That sounded pretty grown-up.

188 JENNIFER FARRELL VOSS

"Did you have a lot of the same friends?"

"Yeah, we hung out."

It reminded him of a time he had gone to court to testify. The prosecutor had told him to say as little as possible. He kept his answers to a minimum.

Someone must have given Lacey Thomas the same advice. She was not giving much away. Good for her, bad for him. He had a feeling this interview was going to be a waste of time . . .

CHAPTER FORTY-THREE

Stephanie sat across the cheap desk from Tom.

"Talk journalism to me," he said. "I've been stuck all day trying to get some more advertising. With readership up, I figured I might as well strike while the iron is hot. I know it sounds a little ghoulish, but if they want to find out about things with a local slant, the *Bee* is the place." He sighed.

Stephanie knew it wasn't easy to keep a paper like the *Bee* going, and it certainly wasn't easy to keep it good. She didn't begrudge Tom his attempts to up the ads.

"Nothing new from Forsyth's finest. I've got an interview set up with Martin Colby, the man whose gun was used. He is a good interview. Loves to talk, loves the attention. I'm sure he feels bad about his gun being used for the murders. Who knows, maybe the murderer will read this story, too, take pity on the old guy and turn himself in so he doesn't have to stay up nights worrying about Mr. Colby and his gun."

Tom sighed. "Lightning striking twice. Much as I like to have every one reading the paper, it does sort of give me a funny feeling to know that the killer is a loyal *Bee* reader."

Stephanie shivered and changed the subject. "Hey, my Harlan Tucker story is shaping up. Wendell Connolly's family claims Connolly was a saint. They aren't surprised that he was trying to expiate his sin in the end. I get the feeling that they don't mind talking about it. He was beloved in his little town, a doctor. I guess the family doesn't think a little gambling all those years ago is going to detract from his legacy.

"Who knows though? Maybe I'm off base, focusing on this so

much. Maybe it didn't matter that much to Harlan Tucker either. He had only a couple of days to enjoy the news."

"You know, being cynical is supposed to be my job, not yours," Tom said. "Besides, I have a few more calls to make. Like I said, get 'em while they're hot." He turned back to his phone.

When she came back to Forsyth and got a job at the *Bee*, she thought it would just be temporary. Tom had agreed to pay her as much as he could. It had been fine with her; she was sort of doing it to keep herself busy, to make a living. The move had been for Pete's career. She had planned to work at the *Bee* until Pete's non-compete ran out, and they could get back to their real lives.

When she got divorced, her parents had urged her to move to New York or Washington or Los Angeles, somewhere that would be good for a serious journalist, a Pulitzer Prize–winning journalist. But here she was in Forsyth. Pete's betrayal had stopped her in her tracks.

At first, she didn't have the energy to think of changing anything, as if the change in her marital status had been so momentous that she couldn't bear one more, couldn't even switch cereal brands back to the one she preferred before she married Pete. Where was that perkiness, that optimism about the future, that natural, dogged tenacity that had made her such a good reporter—and a good wife? Did Pete Popkins take that with him, too?

CHAPTER FORTY-FOUR

Mick turned back to his theory of teenage love gone wrong. For one thing he didn't have a whole hell of a lot else to fall back on.

Another misconception about law enforcement was that detectives spent their days out with a magnifying glass like Sherlock Holmes, looking for clues. In reality, the clues usually came to you. Someone called to tell about an ex-boyfriend who bragged about being so tough he killed someone, or someone found a gun. That kind of thing.

He knew, too, the danger of locking onto his theory. When a defendant is proven innocent, the first thing they say is that the police never looked for another suspect. They just tried to mold all the evidence into their case against Mr. Wrongfully Accused. When you think you know who did it, you are unlikely to keep looking, keep considering.

So at this stage Mick felt like he was going through a dating service, trying different scenarios. He didn't want to commit too much to one until he'd had a first date with the others. But when you get one that feels right, it's hard to keep looking. He was still going to date others, but the pizza delivery boy being in on it was very appealing to him.

For one thing, he liked a crime where the victim was also the bad guy. It just made it easier for him. Although a small-time thief didn't deserve what happened to the kid. He hated to think about what it would do to Adam Moore's sister if he turned out to be the thief. But it would make everyone else in town, including Rainy, happy: a nice personal motive, a guy killed while committing a crime. There was some justice in that.

Mick was ready to check up on the dining habits of the Reluctant Robber's victims.

He drove over to Martin Colby's house first, going through the usual canine commotion at the door. Mr. Colby seemed glad to see him; Samantha, on the other hand, looked behind him as if she was expecting to see Mason as well, and then looked at him with sad brown eyes: *only you*.

"Hey, Mr. Colby I wanted to check with you again to see about when you ordered pizza from Antonio's, you know, to be delivered?" He was pulling the picture of Adam Moore out of his pocket. Tony had given Mick the one from when Adam was employee of the month, which wasn't saying much, considering how few employees they had.

Martin Colby took the picture out of Mick's extended hand. He clicked his tongue before answering. Mick braced himself. He knew the old guy liked to talk.

"Well, my son is always trying to get me to eat healthy, but I tell him I made it this long eating what I feel like, so it must be OK. When my wife was alive we had fried chicken and mashed potatoes, the real kind, not like something out of a box. She put a stick of butter in them. We had some kind of cake or pie every night." He sighed, thinking of past meals, and Mick nodded, waiting for him to answer the question.

"Pizza," he prodded.

"Yeah, when my wife got sick, I took over. I wanted to make sure she had what she wanted to eat, and I can follow directions. That's all cooking is, following directions. I used to tell her, 'I've been married for forty-seven years, so you know I'm good at following directions.' I was just teasing her, you know. We used to like to eat out, too. But when she got sick we had to stop going out, so once a week we would order a pizza. She used to say I needed a night off from cooking."

Mick smiled and tried to redirect the conversation again. "And you still order pizzas from Tony's place?"

"When my wife died I just about stopped cooking altogether. To tell you the truth, I was pretty down." The little dog walked over to the old man and put her paws on his knees. He reached down and rubbed the oversized ears. "Things got better for me when my son gave me Samantha for my birthday. Best birthday present I ever got. I tell him that all the time."

Mick nodded again. He was just going to have to wait it out. He couldn't say "pizza" in the middle of a story about heartbreak and redemption. Just when he was starting to think he'd be here till dinnertime, Martin Colby gave him the information he had come for.

"So my son, he tells me to eat healthy. But I'm too old to change. So once a week I still order a pizza. Now that it's just me, I eat one quarter at night and one quarter at lunch the next day, and then on Friday I finish it off. Sometimes I give Sammy a bite, too. Although I don't give her too much people food. It's not good for her."

Mick held out the picture of Adam Moore again, without comment.

"Oh, yeah, he brought our pizza, didn't he, Samantha? She gets excited when anybody comes to the door. When we started out, Tony would come by. Then we had another guy. We had a woman once, too. I think she was related to Tony if I remember right. But this one, he's been coming for a while."

Mick fought the urge to check his watch as he thanked Martin Colby for his time.

Martin apparently wasn't done. "I've been wanting to ask you a question, too, which is funny, because usually you ask the questions, but anyway I got one for you. Do you think I should go to Mrs. Spence's funeral? I don't know if it would upset folks to see me there, because it was my gun that killed them. I want to pay my respects, but I just am not sure what the right thing to do is here. My son said he would go with me if I wanted him to. I just don't know."

Mick thought of a National Rifle Association advertisement he had once seen. "Guns don't kill people. People kill people."

"I think you should go. No one blames you for what happened." He leaned over to pet the dog and shook hands with Martin Colby. "I'll see you at the funeral."

Nobody would accuse him of being oversentimental, but right now, he could relate to Martin Colby's loneliness. He just hoped the other people on his interview list weren't lonely too. At the rate he was going, the killer could die of old age before Mick finished this investigation.

Martin Colby was the only one the thief had returned to the scene of the crime for, but all the other victims had something left behind. Maybe the kid was just trying to make sure they had enough to pay for a pizza.

Mick shook his head as he walked up to the Bentmans' door. Only one way to find out. Well, there was another way, but he didn't want Tony to know he was checking with his customers—yet. He could imagine what someone like Stephanie Gallagher could do with a story like that. "Police investigate victim," which was exactly what he was doing.

He pushed the doorbell of the neat red-brick ranch. He heard movement inside. The door swung open, revealing an oversized boy. He was tall and doughy, with huge Bozo the Clown–sized feet. He took one look at Mick, turned away, and yelled, "Mom! For you!"

Mick waited, and a woman who looked too tiny to have ever given birth to this big galoot came in, drying her hands on a dish towel. The oversized boy sauntered back to his place in front of some video game he was playing with an only-slightly-less-large boy.

"Mick McKay," he said. Mrs. Bentman—Lisa, she told him to call her—led him back to the kitchen, away from the video gamers. She threw the towel over her shoulder and motioned for him to sit at the kitchen table. No one could have been planning to eat there anytime soon, Mick noted, as it was covered with folders and schoolbooks and stacks of old mail.

She offered him a cup of coffee, but he looked around and decided to decline. He liked his cup clean. "No thanks, I'm trying to cut back. I want to ask you a few questions about the burglary at your house." She nodded, ready for anything. "What was taken?"

"Well, forty dollars, some video games, a watch, and a ring."

"Exactly forty dollars?"

"Well, yeah, I have a routine. I put money out in a jar by the door for the boys. It's their lunch money. We all walked down to watch my youngest play in a ball game, and when we got back, I noticed there was only one twenty-dollar bill in the jar. I told my husband, and he thought I'd just made a mistake. But then the boys noticed some of their games were gone, and my husband couldn't find his watch and ring he'd left by the kitchen sink. So we knew someone had gotten in, probably through the garage door.

"We called the police and an officer came and looked around. He asked if one of the boys' friends might not have taken the money. But there was nobody here after I put the money in the jar. He asked me why the thief would leave twenty dollars that he could have grabbed with the rest of the money. I told him I know it sounds crazy, but that's what happened.

"Of course, then I read about the other people getting stuff stolen. I guess he believed me then. When we heard there might be a connection to the murders, you can imagine that put a scare in me! Thank the Lord we stayed down at the park, or that could have happened to us." She shuddered when she said the last sentence.

"I wanted to check to see if there were things you had in common with the other burglary victims. Did y'all ever order pizza from Tony's restaurant?" Mick asked.

"Sure, the boys love pizza. I think Antonio's has the best pizza, but I love the bread sticks they have at Castlebury's, so we get pizza from them sometimes, too."

"When you get pizza, do you have it delivered?" He was reaching into his pocket to get the picture of Adam Moore when she shook her head, no.

"My oldest boy just got his driver's license. He wants to drive everywhere, so he picks up the pizza now."

Maybe she could sense Mick's consternation at her answer. "He's a real good driver. He and his daddy practice all the time, and he is very careful, believe you me!"

Mick regrouped mentally. "That's good to hear. So you never get your pizza delivered?"

196 JENNIFER FARRELL VOSS

She shook her head again. Mick had lost his connection. He was about to get up when she said, "Now, we used to get it delivered, and by that poor boy who wasn't much older than Scotty. But, like I said, as soon as Scotty got his license, he started driving over there. Such a shame about that boy who got shot, though."

Mick felt like someone had tossed him a lifeline. His theory just bobbed back up. What if Adam Moore was using his pizza deliveries as a way to find out who was home when? It fell into place. Now all he had to do was find his partner in crime and he would find the killer. Rainy would love it. The good people of Forsyth would love it.

Mick thanked Mrs. Bentman and stepped over Scotty's big feet and out into the sunshine. He pictured Adam the way he had found him next to that damned open pizza box and felt a wave of sympathy for him. He tried reminding himself the kid was asking for trouble if he was stealing from his customers, but he couldn't squash down the wave of sympathy for the wasted life of Adam Moore.

Guilt in check, Mick looked over his list. Buoyed by the last visit, he was sure he was on the right track.

Back at the office from his final interview, Mick slowed his pace as he approached Mason's desk. He wanted to run in, screaming like a little kid, and tell him about Adam Moore delivering pizzas to the houses that were burglarized.

But he forced himself to take a more nonchalant attitude. He felt like a car salesman getting ready to showcase the features on a car he was trying to sell.

"Hey, Mason, how's it going?"

Mason looked up from the list of stolen items he was reviewing. "Nothing new," he said dispiritedly. "How about you?"

"I'm making progress. I still think there's a possibility that the killings weren't random, that maybe the kid was targeted. Well, I just found out he delivered pizza to all the burglary victims. It looks to me like he knew when they were home, knew about their houses, their habits, and just helped himself to a little cash when he needed it. It all fits. He knew them. I don't know, maybe they gave him good tips, so he didn't want to take too much from them. We thought it was a kid and he is a kid. I think I'm onto something here."

Mick waited for a reaction from Mason. It wasn't easy to tell your boss that he was full of shit, but Mick knew Mason would be honest, bring up the questions that needed to be brought up. He looked at Mason expectantly. He realized he was shaking his leg up and down. He willed himself to be still.

"They got pizza from Antonio's, sure, but do they have anything else in common? Did they have the same maid service? Did they just get some plumbing done, some painting? There could be lots of things besides pizza that they have in common.

"And the kid could have just been delivering his last pie in the wrong place at the wrong time. Do you think Edie Spence caught him trying to get into her house, wrestled the gun from him? I mean, who shot him?"

Mick tried to keep the exasperation out of his voice. "His accomplice. He works with that girl, Lacey. Probably she's the lookout for his thefts. Then one day she doesn't like where things are going and she goes for the if-she-can't-have-him-no-one-can solution." Mick held up his hand to stop Mason's next words before he uttered them. "And the nurse, she was the one who was in the wrong place at the wrong time. The girl probably figured she wouldn't be home yet, so when she sees her, she panics and shoots her, too. Who knows, maybe she thought that her ex and the nurse had something going. The kid was scouting for break-in opportunities when he was dropping off his pizzas." Mick dropped his hand, giving permission to Mason to say what he thought.

"Okay, suppose Adam was the thief and the girl was the accomplice. Aren't you forgetting our eyewitness account? He said he saw a man in a National Safety jacket running away."

Mick had to agree on that one. Maybe it was time to pay another visit to Jack Jackson.

CHAPTER FORTY-FIVE

Mick walked up to National Safety's entrance. He felt the coolness of the air-conditioning when he stepped through the door. He expected that might not be the only coolness he'd be feeling today; Jackson didn't want to talk to Mick without his lawyer. And Mick could understand that. He hoped that it meant Jackson was ready to tell him something substantial, like who he had seen by Adam Moore's and Edie Spence's dead bodies.

Jackson's assistant was waiting for him in the seat belt museum. The receptionist looked up and smiled at him as she answered the phone.

"National Safety. How may I direct your call?" Her eyebrows shot up and she said, "Just a moment, please." She turned to Jackson's assistant and said, "Grace, it's about that shipment from Keller Textile. Should I put it through?"

Grace took a look at Mick and said, "No, I'll take it, if Mr. McKay doesn't mind going on back to the office on his own."

Mick took the cue and said he knew the way. He walked through the glory days of National Safety back to the offices to talk to Jackson and his lawyer. As he walked down the hall, past pictures of ads for seat belt safety, he paused to look at one of a young woman on a stretcher. The caption below read, "Mary didn't want to wear a seat belt and wrinkle her dress." As he read he could hear Jackson's voice and that of a man Mick assumed was his attorney.

The other man sounded exasperated. "For Christ's sake, Jack! Are you crazy? Our best friend died that day! And since then, I've graduated from college and law school, gotten married, had kids! Those are the best days of my life and yours, too, not that tragic day when we were kids. I am sick and tired of talking about something that happened so long ago. I am sick and tired of that tripod bullshit. Just drop it, will you?"

Mick didn't want to eavesdrop in the corridor any longer, so he rapped his knuckles on the door and stuck his head in before Jackson could reply to his lawyer's request about dropping the subject.

"Sorry to interrupt. Mick McKay."

Jackson and his fighting friend were standing in front of one of the framed pictures of the Falcons that Mick had noticed before. He had to know that Mick had heard part of the conversation. His attorney walked toward Mick with his hand outstretched.

"You're not interrupting anything. Trey Barber, I'm Jack's attorney. Nice to see you again, Mr. McKay. I just wish it were under happier circumstances. Jack and I were having an old discussion. We played high school ball together, dated cheerleaders together, and you know how that goes. Old friends, old disagreements. But you're not here to talk football. Have a seat."

Mick noticed Jackson was letting Barber do all the talking. Well, that was what lawyers were for.

"OK, I want to ask some more questions about what Jack saw. I'm sure he told you I'd like to know about employees who had reduced hours, really just general information. We appreciate Mr. Jackson's help with our investigation. I just want to check and see if he remembers any more details, maybe about the jacket."

Barber got out of his chair and walked behind the desk to stand next to Jackson. Mick thought it gave the room a me-against-them feel. Lawyers!

Jackson still had not uttered a word, but Barber said, "What about a jacket? This is the first I've heard about that."

He was asking Mick, but it was Jackson who replied. "It's really nothing. That's why I didn't mention it, Trey. I was confused and upset that night, and I told the police I thought I saw a National logo on the man's jacket as he ran away. I don't want to get anyone in trouble without being certain, and I don't see how I can be certain. I told them everything happened so fast, it's just a blur."

Barber walked back from behind the desk and sat back down in his chair. He turned to Mick. "You want to know who has National Safety jackets? Half the people in town. I have one myself. We can't give you the names of everybody who has one, because we don't know. They give them out along with T-shirts at every company picnic and holiday party."

Mick swiveled in his chair to face Barber. Why pretend he was having a conversation with Jackson? "No, I know there are a lot of those jackets here. But the fact that we found a card calendar at one of the breaks-ins does make it seem like there is a connection to someone here at National. I just want Mr. Jackson to help us by giving me the names of some of the recently laid-off workers."

Jackson rolled forward, ready to jump back in the conversation. It was like they were playing doubles tennis, only Mick was on his own. "We cut hours so we wouldn't have to fire anyone outright. Nobody is being laid off." He looked over at his attorney as if to say, "See, I can talk, too."

Barber took over again. "Look, it's not like we don't want to do everything we can to help. We live here, too. I hate the thought that there's a killer loose in Forsyth, but we don't have anything that can help you. Jack was pretty shook up by what happened. Under the circumstances, I'm not sure he's at his most reliable.

"And I understand the connection between the killings and the Reluctant Robber, but I don't understand why you are so sure it was a National Safety employee. I mean, couldn't it just as easily have been somebody whose hours were cut at Bucko Burgers? When we go through tough times, it affects the entire community."

Mick nodded. "I appreciate that you are trying to help," he said, although he didn't. "We just feel that because of the card calendar and the jacket that we should check it out." He put the "we" in because he was outnumbered. "We aren't asking for anything specific, and you're right, we are talking to everybody, not just Mr. Jackson. In fact, I just talked to your son and some of his friends at the high school, Mr. Jackson," Mick said, turning back to him.

"What were you talking to them about?"

"Oh, we thought some of the athletes might have seen something on their way to school outside of Martin Colby's house. Just routine checking of witnesses. But, like I said, we are talking to everyone. That's the great thing; everyone wants this murder solved. We don't have a bunch of apathetic citizens. Do you know the last time we had a double homicide in Forsyth?"

Here he had them. Both Trey Barber and Jack Jackson were shaking their heads.

"Well, I'll tell you. We have never had a double homicide. Never. We had a murder-suicide about thirty years ago. That's as close as we get. We have never had a double homicide. Look, we are going to solve this. I'm not asking for anything special. Just keep your eyes open, Mr. Jackson, and let me know if anything unusual happens: a guy stops coming to work, someone brags about having more money, a guy seems disturbed, anything. That's all I'm asking. Ask Mr. Barber for his advice before you talk to me. Let's get this killer off the streets."

"We want to cooperate with you any way we can," Jackson said. "I think we can look through and give you the names of employees whose hours have been cut. I'm not sure how helpful that's going to be. It's a long list, starting with me, but we will certainly do whatever we can."

Mick had one more question for him. "You were at Harlan Tucker's wake, right?"

Jackson blinked a couple of times before answering, as if he woke up in a strange bed and wondered how he got there. He looked over at his attorney before answering.

"I've known the coach for a long time. He was our coach and then, of course, we saw each other in the Forsyth business community. So, yeah, I went to his wake, and my son and I went to his funeral. Why? What's that got to with anything?"

"I just wanted to ask if you saw Edie Spence use her phone at the wake."

"What? Her cell phone? No, I only vaguely remember seeing her, and I don't remember anything about her phone. At that point I was thinking of Coach Tucker. Besides, Coad's strictly forbids the use of cell phones."

On the way out, after wringing an agreement for help out of Jackson and his attorney, Mick thought he could understand why Jackson was looking back on his high school days. Nothing like stumbling on a couple of dead bodies to make a man feel his own mortality.

They had promised to give him a list of laid-off employees. Mick already felt like he had an employee to start with, Augustine, the maintenance supervisor whose wife had worked for Harlan Tucker. Jackson had been worried enough about him to secure a job for his wife. Mick checked the address for the guy: 203 Dalhart.

He decided to drive by. He wasn't ready to talk to Augustine, but he wanted to see where the guy lived.

The house was neat, painted a light green color that made Mick think of mint ice cream. In the driveway were various modes of transportation: a pickup truck, not new; a bike with a white basket perched on the handlebars; a skateboard with some decals stuck on; and a stroller with big wheels.

Mick drove around the block and looked at the house again before heading home, his home, where there were no bikes out in front, no slamming doors, no one to say "I'm home!" to. Well, there was some peanut butter. He could go home and have a peanut butter sandwich and a beer. Sounded pretty good.

He parked his car in the garage and looked at the calendar. Still the same number of squares without lines through them as with; still a long time before his wife and daughter came home. His phone rang as he contemplated calling them. He picked it up without looking, just expecting it to be Julie.

But it wasn't. Trey Barber was calling to set up an appointment in his office. Mick understood the need for the neutral territory: not National Safety and not the police station. He hoped he had persuaded Jackson to give him some information about his employees, but he knew it would be a dance. Mick could tell that Barber wasn't going to say much. He'd have to go and dance around, anyway. Any information might help. And tomorrow, after the funeral for Edie Spence, he'd head back out to circle Morales's block again.

CHAPTER FORTY-SIX

Stephanie checked her closet for something to wear to Edie Spence's funeral. Could she just wear what she had worn to Adam Moore's funeral? She was running out of sedate, subdued outfits. She'd write something for the *Bee* about the funeral, but nobody would need to read it. The entire town would be there.

She decided to wear the same dress. It looked good, perfect for a funeral, which maybe said something about her wardrobe and her lifestyle that she should pay attention to. She eased her panty hose over her bandaged knee and thought about seeing Mick McKay at the funeral. She really did need to get out more. She falls down—and not gracefully, either—and the poor guy helps her up and back to the car. He rescues her from her dangerous shoes, and she is casting him in the role of a knight rescuing her from her ruined life.

She had been brought up to be one of those girls who scoff at the fairy tales where the prince rides in and saves the princess. Any princess worth her salt should be capable of saving herself; that also went for cowgirls, movie actresses, astronauts—all jobs she had considered at various times in her life—and even for Pulitzer Prize–winning journalists. Where was her spirit of adventure? But she knew the answer to that, she thought, as she gave up trying to get the nylon over her cut and took off the panty hose. Her sense of adventure was back in Dallas, along with all her hopes and dreams.

She slipped into her shoes. She and her sister drove their parents crazy, asking, "How much longer?" on their trips out to west Texas, and now she was asking herself that question: *How much longer will it take to get over this heartache?* She sighed as she checked to make sure she looked decent. *I don't have time for this sadness. I have a funeral to go to*, she said to herself.

It looked like everybody who had been at the wake the night before had gone home and found three or four friends to bring back for the funeral. Stephanie could see cars parked all the way down both sides of the street, and the church parking lot . . . well, that was overflowing. A policeman in a uniform was waving her on, and really, what choice did she have? She drove about four blocks away and pulled over.

The other people walking back toward the church clustered in pairs or threesomes. She had her satchel so she didn't feel funny going it alone. It was her job. Besides, would she really want to be walking into this church with Pete Popkins? She tried to walk a little taller, but the answer was yes.

Inside the church, folding chairs filled every available spot in the back and up the aisles. She had always heard the expression "packed in like sardines." Even though she had never in her life eaten a sardine or, for that matter, seen one, Stephanie imagined this was what they were talking about.

She headed to a folding chair halfway up the aisle and put her satchel under the chair, out of the way of people moving past her to find their own seat. It was an orderly crowd. This many people usually meant some type of sporting event or a concert. This crowd was quiet and somber. Two pews in the front of the church had been tied off with black ribbon for the family.

Stephanie scanned the room, but she had to nod at so many people she knew that she started to feel whiplash. So instead she looked down at the program the usher had handed her in the vestibule. There was a picture on the front of Edie Spence laughing, with the dates of her birth and death underneath. She thought she recognized the picture from the wake the night before. The program was, like the wake pictures, very well done.

She had spotted Pat, the nurse from hospice, sitting in a pew one up from her folding chair. They had done a great job; they must go to lots of funerals in their line of work. She was thinking of that as a title for piece: "Funeral for Hospice Hero." Not sure about that, though. For the family it might be more important to say "Devoted Mother."

That was the funny thing, she thought. She had always assumed that the challenging part of life would be to get the Pulitzer Prize, to be recognized as a great—well, at least good—journalist. She had just assumed that the wife and mother stuff would be easy, took for granted that it would be part of her life. Never even occurred to her that a Pulitzer might be easier to get than a happy family.

When she looked up again, the church was filling up. People were squeezing themselves into pews like they were squeezing into too-tight jeans. The front pews were still empty, a line between the sad and the devastated.

As the service wrapped up, Stephanie headed outside with the rest of the funeral attendees to get a much-needed breath of fresh air. Standing out of the way of the people exiting the church and heading to the reception, Stephanie saw Mick. He was scanning the crowd, probably looking for suspects or something, but his eyes stopped on her. She waved.

"Hey," Mick said to her as he drew near. "How's your leg?"

Stephanie glanced down at it like she had to check before she could give him an answer.

"Fine," she said, "just fine." She shook it for emphasis. He smiled and the word *divorcée* popped into her head. From an old movie she had seen, the word conjured up a woman on the prowl, up to no good. Still it was what she was: a divorcée.

"I'm working," she said to Mick. People flowed around them as if they were their own little island. She saw Tom and the photographer from the *Bee*, Tiffany, her parents—who just nodded to her, probably concluding she was working, which she was. Talking to the police was part of her job. They all poured past her as if her whole life was passing by. They were heading for their cars and the lunch at the country club that the family had invited everyone to.

Mick seemed to notice the crowd's dispersal, and wordlessly they turned together and walked down the block.

"Are you going on to the lunch?" she asked as they walked in unison.

Mick nodded. "Yes, I'm going. How about you? Need a ride?"

"Oh, no thanks. My car is just a couple of blocks up."

"OK. I'm parked across the street. So, I guess I'll see you there, then."

"OK, see you," she said, and he loped across the street. She realized he was out of uniform; he'd put a navy jacket over his usual blue shirt and khakis.

Mick unlocked his car with the clicker, although, really, who was going to steal something from an obvious cop car? He always locked it, though. He started it up and drove past Stephanie Gallagher, still walking to her car. He wondered if he should have stopped and asked again if she wanted a ride to her car. But he headed past her, thinking about the Spence family.

That's what I'm supposed to be thinking about, he said to himself as he drove on. Sometimes a picture of Edie Spence, her blonde hair streaked with blood, came to him unbidden. He wondered if this is what it was like for soldiers suffering from post-traumatic stress disorder. He didn't want to see Edie that way, but when the vision came to him it made him set his jaw, determined to find the killer.

He drove down River Road and turned toward the River Bend Country Club. Boys in yellow knit shirts and navy pants were out directing people where to park their cars, using big arm swings to move the line forward.

Past the entrance he could see into the dining room with its heavy green curtains tied back with cords and the gold-patterned carpet. Someone had brought the vases of flowers that had been in the front of the church, and they reminded Mick of wedding flowers.

He approached the first knot of mourners, a cluster of women of varying shapes and sizes, and said hello. They introduced themselves as Edie's coworkers. Mick had the uncomfortable feeling of not being a friend of the family and not exactly working either.

He had wanted to come to pay his respects, of course, and to watch the other participants, but somehow he felt like he was caught between those roles, in a no-man's-land. When the ladies widened their circle to allow him in, he felt a sense of relief.

"We were just talking about our action plan for after the funeral," said a short woman with swirly hair that reminded Mick of a doll Colly dragged around when she was little: the brown swirls of hair had been painted on its rubber head.

"After the funeral?" Mick asked, wondering if it was like an after-party for a wedding.

"All the planning and preparation that goes into a funeral can give the family a sense of purpose, but when it's over, they have to face the world without their mom, their wife, their daughter. The reality sinks in.

"Usually, with hospice, we have some time to prepare. But this was so sudden, so violent!" the curly haired woman continued, tears springing to her eyes.

Mick felt it as a reproach. It was, after all, his job to keep everyone safe. And he had failed. His tie felt tight around his neck. He wanted to reassure these women that he was going to get the person who had killed their friend.

"We are going to get the killer," he said, as if that would fix this. The smell of food wafted toward him and he felt an urge to eat something that did not come from McDonald's.

Before he could get in line, Mick noticed Jack Johnson, his head sticking up higher than the rest of the crowd. He was shaking hands with a guy and had his other hand on the guy's shoulder. It seemed like a nice gesture but, to Mick, it looked like he was somehow trying to dominate the other guy.

Mick changed directions and headed back over to say hello to the closest thing to an eyewitness he had. Jackson relinquished his grasp of the other man and turned to Mick. Up close he looked a little off his game, a little tired. Of course this was a funeral for the woman whose dead body he had practically tripped over. That might make a guy look a little less than happy. Mick, himself, felt weighed down by the events of the last few days. And he was a professional.

Mick felt sorry for the guy, but even so, when Jackson reached out to shake his hand, Mick managed to bring his left hand around to clasp the bigger man's arm. He wanted to demonstrate who was in control here, and it wasn't Jackson.

"How are you?" he asked while he shook his hand, his grip just a little firmer than needed.

Jackson dropped his hand and said, "It's a sad day for Forsyth, that's for sure. I've been thinking about what you said and trying to remember more from that night. I want to help." For Mick, it was like running into a girl you had chased after you met someone new. He wasn't all that interested in Jackson and his jacketed employee anymore.

He thought Adam Moore's accomplice in the burglaries—maybe Lacey Thompson—was the one Jackson had seen running away. Now he wanted his witness to say it could have been a girl, but not here.

CHAPTER FORTY-SEVEN

Stephanie walked into the country club dining room. She spotted Donnetta and Rusty with a big group of people standing in front of a dessert-laden table. Donnetta was laughing at something Rusty was saying, throwing back her head. *And here I am thinking of my problems*, Stephanie thought, watching her. She waved from across the room; Donnetta nudged Rusty, he turned, and they both waved.

She saw Mick sitting with Adam Moore's sister, Tiffany, who looked like she was eating, thank God. She saw Harlan Tucker's daughters tearfully talking to one of the hospice nurses. Mark Lavelle was there. Whoever said high school never ends must have had her in mind. People from her past kept bubbling up.

Stephanie made her way over to a table covered with bottles of soft drinks and water. She picked up a water bottle and turned to survey the room. She wanted to find someone interesting to get a quote from.

Her eyes traveled back to the table with Tiffany and Mick McKay. *He would be good for a quote*, she thought, but by the time she made it through the press of people, he was gone. Tiffany was sitting between two men Stephanie didn't know, out-of-town family she surmised. She looked back at Tiffany and realized that one of the men sitting next to her was Martin Colby. She hadn't recognized him in his suit and tie without a dog on his lap. She angled across the room toward him. He would definitely be good for a quote.

She squatted down next to him, putting her fingers on the edge of the table for balance. One of the perks of being an ex-cheerleader; she was flexible. He stood up and offered her his chair, but she found one of the few empty chairs at the next table and dragged it over to squish between Tiffany and Mr. Colby. Even though they were sitting together, they had not made the connection. Stephanie introduced them and took note of Martin Colby's stricken face when he realized she was Adam Moore's sister.

"I am so sorry for your loss," he said. "I feel terrible that it was my gun that was used, just terrible."

Tiffany nodded, said, "Thank you," then looked back at her plate. Stephanie resisted the urge to order her to eat.

Martin Colby leaned forward around Stephanie with his elbows on the table as if he were praying, never at a loss for words, anxious to talk to Tiffany.

"We really liked your brother, Samantha and me. She barked at him a time or two and then she realized he was her friend. I know I shouldn't, but sometimes I give her people food. Heaven knows she makes me happy, so if a few bites of pepperoni make her happy, well, I'm going to give them to her. Of course she knew when your brother came over she would get a treat.

"But that wasn't the only reason she liked him. He was nice to her, always had time to talk to her, and she likes that. You know, sometimes I think she thinks she's human. And she's better than some of the people I know, like whoever did this to your brother. I feel just sick that it was my gun that was used," he repeated. "You know, I showed it to your brother once. I was looking for some money in my hall drawer, that's where I keep—where I kept my gun. I showed it to Adam and told him about how I got it for my wife. I feel just sick that it was that gun," he said for the third time.

"It wasn't your fault," Tiffany said, addressing the mashed potatoes and chicken casserole on her plate.

Stephanie leaned forward slightly, putting herself back in Martin Colby's line of sight and turning away from Tiffany.

"That's interesting that you showed Adam the gun," she said. "What did he say about it?" She was thinking that Adam probably had a hard time getting a word in with Mr. Colby, but it couldn't hurt to ask.

"Well, funny you should ask," he said. "He told me he'd always been a little afraid of guns, but that my gun looked too little to really hurt anyone. I told him a little about gun safety, just like I told my boys when they were growing up. And he minded what I said. I'm sure of that."

Stephanie pictured Adam Moore looking at the gun, the gun that was going to kill him. It made her shiver, like in the movies when you want to scream at the actor, "Don't open that door!" or "Run!" or "Never go back there!" But what good would that have done? Someone else took the gun. Someone else killed Adam Moore and Edie Spence. There was no escape.

She unhooked her bag from the back of her chair, patted Mr. Colby on the hand, touched Tiffany's shoulder, and turned to leave. She kept picturing Adam Moore innocently looking at what was going to turn out to be a murder weapon, his murder. She was sure others would find it compelling, too.

Outside, she climbed into one of the big golf carts that were being used to shuttle guests. The driver headed out to the far end of the lot where Stephanie had parked. She was ready to get back in her car and head to the *Bee* to write her story about the boy looking at the gun that was destined to kill him.

CHAPTER FORTY-EIGHT

Mick opened the door to his garage and walked over to the calendar. He picked up the pen tied to the ribbon and crossed off the day. Still a lot of blank squares to get through but, like ex-drinkers say, one day at a time.

John Mason was standing in the foyer of the station when Mick walked in. When he saw his boss, he held up the newspaper and waved it.

"Did you read the *Bee* today?" he asked. Mick took the paper from him and read the section Mason had folded over. The article by Stephanie Gallagher was about Martin Colby's gun. Mick scanned down and read the quote from Colby about Adam looking at the gun and telling Colby he was afraid of guns.

Mason stood waiting for Mick to finish reading and look up. *Damn, damn, damn*, Mick said to himself. All the questions he'd asked that old guy, and he hadn't asked if Adam knew about the gun. *Damn*.

"Damn," he said to Mason. "Let's go inside."

They walked through the vestibule doors and into Mick's office. Neither one of them sat down.

"Damn, you would think with all the shit that guy told us, he would have mentioned he'd shown the gun to the kid. But no, we've got to read it in the *Bee* for Christ's sake! The *Bee*!" Mick felt his ears grow hot. "It fits with my theory, though. The kid saw the gun. The kid took the gun. I just need a way to prove he had it. I had a gut feeling this was not a random robbery. Adam Moore or his accomplice was getting bored with their little crimes and decided to up the ante by having a gun."

He could tell Mason was coming around to his theory. It only made sense. The kid out delivering pizzas knows who is home, when and where they keep their money, and, in Colby's case, his gun.

Mason was looking at him with an expectant expression.

"Let's go back and show Lacey Thomas's picture along with a few others and see if any of our pizza eaters know her."

Mason stood up and slid his keys across the desk.

Mick considered and then said, "You check in with Stephanie Gallagher at the *Bee* and I'll backtrack with the girl's picture. I've been through it once, so it just makes sense for me to be the one to show up again. Ask if she got anything else out of Colby. Call me and let me know if you find out anything."

Mason dropped the *Bee* on Mick's desk, tossed his car keys in the air and caught them, and headed out. Mick sighed and headed out to go where he had already been.

He retraced his steps and found Mrs. Walker getting ready to leave for work in a shirt with her name embroidered across it. He struck out. She didn't remember seeing Lacey or any of the girls.

He got the same result at Colby's, but with a lot more discussion. For one horrible second, Mick was afraid he was going to show the photos to Sam the dog.

"Do you mean did I ever see them with Adam when he delivered my pizza?" Colby asked.

"No—I mean—yes, if you saw her then or any other time, with or without Adam."

Colby stared at the picture without a spark of recognition.

"No, I don't think I've ever seen any of these girls," he said regretfully with a shake of his head. "I wish I could help."

"Well, you are helping," Mick reassured the old man. He gave the little dog a pat on the head and headed out, trying not to show the discouragement he felt.

He knew if the murders went unsolved, people would attribute it to the size and quality of the police department in Forsyth. They would conclude that such a tiny force was just outsmarted. The reality was, big cities with big departments didn't always have high solve rates either.

Mick straightened up as he walked back to his car. He was onto something and he would find proof that Adam Moore was the intended victim. He just had to place Lacey and Adam together at one of the places that was broken into.

He checked his phone to see if Mason had called. No message. He remembered Stephanie Gallagher writing about Harlan Tucker and his innocence established too late. Adam Moore had spent time there at the Tucker house. No one had reported anything stolen, but that didn't mean nothing was stolen.

Mick picked up his phone to call Mason, who picked up on the first ring.

"Hey, Mick. I just met up with Stephanie Gallagher at the Round the Clock. We're having a cup of coffee."

"Okay, I'll be right there," Mick replied and headed for the coffee shop.

He found Mason and Stephanie sitting at the counter with big, thick white cups of coffee in front of them. He lowered himself onto the stool next to Stephanie. It reminded him of what he and Julie had called Colly when she was little: a Colly sandwich, sitting between Julie and him, their little Colly sandwich. He smiled at Stephanie, thinking about it. She smiled back at him, her happy weather girl smile.

He knew Mason wouldn't ask him in front of Stephanie about what he had found out, so he looked over to see if Mason had any information to share. A tired-looking, up-all-night waitress came over, and he ordered iced tea. When she put it in front of him, he poured some sugar in it and thought about the *Bee* being out front on this investigation from the start.

"I know, wasn't that crazy? That poor kid looking at the gun and even talking about it. It's kind of creepy and sad at the same time," Stephanie was saying.

"So, when did Martin Colby tell you about the gun?" Mick asked, stirring his tea and watching the sugar swirl in the glass.

"That's the funny thing. He didn't mention it until I was sitting with him and Tiffany at the funeral yesterday. I'd interviewed him before. He always had a lot to say and he could be, well, colorful, so he was good for a quote. But he never mentioned any connection between Adam and the gun, not till yesterday. You don't think it means anything, do you?" She looked up and gazed first at Mason and then at Mick. It was her job to gather information, just like it was his job.

"No, we just wanted to get a cup of coffee and check to see if you heard anything else interesting. Hey, how's your leg?" he said.

Mason looked down at Stephanie's leg so she said, "I fell the other day," by way of explanation.

Mick felt awkward for no good reason, so he was appreciative when Stephanie jump-started the conversation and began talking about her article on Harlan Tucker.

"I wish I could have known him. I think he was an interesting man," she said. Mick and Mason agreed.

The mention of Harlan Tucker got Mick thinking. That would have been a very easy place to steal from, especially if you were being invited in to deliver pizza and visit every week. It was time to check and see if the sisters had noticed anything missing.

Maybe Rosa had noticed something. He hadn't talked to her since he stuck her husband on the back burner. Might be time.

He drained his glass and left Mason and Stephanie twisting on their stools. And that reminded him of Colly, too.

Stephanie had been surprised when she got the call from John Mason. She wondered if the lingering awkwardness she felt after quite literally falling into Michael McKay's arms had made Mick decide to send someone else to talk to her.

But the Round the Clock was just a block from the *Bee* office, and the coffee was better there, so she was happy to walk on over and see what the Forsyth police wanted.

John Mason didn't exactly come out and say it, but she got the feeling that he hadn't known that Adam Moore had ever seen the gun. She wasn't sure why Mason would be interested in that. It seemed to her a little tabloid-ish. Oh, she had written the story. Her job was to inform the public, and the dead boy and the gun were the kind of things the public liked to be informed about. But why was Mason interested in the story?

"We thought it was an interesting story, and I wanted to see if maybe Martin Colby had said anything else to you. Or maybe Samantha gave you an interesting story," Mason said as soon as they had their coffee mugs in front of them.

Stephanie laughed. "Martin Colby didn't say too much else. I think he feels sad that it was his gun that was used in the murders. Me? It would be enough to make me submit my resignation to the NRA."

Mason looked up from his coffee. "You're a member of the NRA?" he asked raising his eyebrows.

She smiled. "No, but if I *were* a member, I'd resign."

"So, did you grow up here in Forsyth?" Mason asked.

"Yes, I'm a lifer, here for the duration. How about you?"

"Transplanted convert. I grew up in Marysville, but I love it here."

Stephanie nodded her approval. It drove her crazy when people complained about Forsyth. It was like having someone criticize your family. You could do it, but no one else could.

Mason swiveled his stool around and Stephanie caught sight of Mick McKay striding into the Round the Clock like he was on a mission. And maybe he was.

They exchanged pleasantries. Then he brought up Martin Colby. Colby couldn't possibly be involved in the killings, so why the interest in him? When she told them he hadn't mentioned anything else of interest, she got the feeling that Mick thought she was not telling them something. She changed the subject to Harlan Tucker and her article.

A minute later, Mick must have accomplished what he came for because he drained his iced tea, got up, and left. Mason twirled his stool in little movements like a jittery kid. He put his hand over his coffee cup when the waitress came around with the pot. Stephanie remembered her from high school. She worked here when Stephanie and her friends would come in for Cokes and fries after school. And she was still here. *Well*, Stephanie thought, *so am I.*

She and Mason each left a dollar tip on the counter and turned around on their stools to leave. She was still not sure why Mick had dropped by the diner.

CHAPTER FORTY-NINE

Stephanie walked back to the office. She wanted to leave the murders and sadness behind and work on Harlan Tucker's story for a while.

She ran her finger down the names of the boys who had played on Harlan Tucker's teams. Forsyth was a small town. Lots of the people on the list probably moved away. But she did recognize some names. Trey Barber was one of the attorneys in the same building as her divorce lawyer. That brought her right back.

There were no assets besides Pete's degree. They had been careful about taking out school loans, tried to pay as much as they could, keep their debt down. After all, they had reasoned, they could save later when he started to make money. The idea had been for her to work as much as she could, and then when he got his degree and they had their baby, she would stop working for a while and he would be making enough to support them. Nice plan. Then, by the time it was his turn to contribute, he was contributing to someone else. Pete Popkins did not provide a very good return on her investment.

The lawyer had explained what she could expect in a matter of fact manner. He probably had hysterical women in his office all the time. She noticed the Kleenex boxes all over his office, at the ready for crying women and, she supposed, men, too. She hadn't been hysterical, hadn't cried. She had been the opposite, numb. So the bottom line was she had paid for a great education, just not hers, and Pete could enjoy his new life, new wife, without school loans. Thank you very much, Stephanie.

Stephanie shook her head, trying to clear away these toxic memories blocking her brain. Back to Trey Barber. Hadn't she spent enough time on Pete Popkins already? She picked up the phone to schedule an appointment with Trey Barber, hoping she wouldn't run into her divorce lawyer.

Trey Barber's office was done up to look old, with big red leather chairs and prints of dogs and horses on the wall. *Why so masculine?* Stephanie thought. But when Trey Barber stuck his head out of his door to invite her back, she could see why. Anything else would have looked false.

Trey Barber was one of those big, beefy guys with huge hands and feet. In a more refined setting, he would have looked like a bull in a china shop, like the former football player he was. There was something sweet about him, though. He was like a St. Bernard puppy unaware of its own size. The phrase "he doesn't know his own strength" popped into her head as she shook his hand.

They did the little dance that was required in a place like Forsyth: who do you know, where do you live? He seemed pleased to find out she was born and raised here, too. He knew her parents, and they went through the list of things they liked about Forsyth. When they finished, he asked what she wanted to know about Coach Tucker.

"I'm doing a story on him. As you know, he just passed away and right before he died, he received a letter from a former friend of his. Apparently, this friend had gambled on a game they were playing in, and when it looked as though he might be caught, he diverted suspicion to Harlan. Harlan took the fall. Evidently the former friend felt bad about it for all those years and wanted to apologize and let Harlan clear his name. Had you ever heard of the betting scandal?"

Barber shook his head, which rested on one of those necks that looked like it could support a bowling ball. "No, but the coach was never one to look back. He was always telling us, 'Learn from your mistakes and move on.' He encouraged us to do our best and then forget about it. He knew how to get us to live up to our potential.

"But I don't know that much about his personal life. I guess when he was coaching us, I thought he began and ended on the field. So I don't think I can help you with your story about him."

Stephanie looked at his giant hands resting on his desk. It reminded her of parents and teachers sitting in the little student chairs for conferences, only he was sitting at a giant desk. "Well, you live in town. Did you keep in touch with the coach?" she asked.

He lifted his big hands in a surrender gesture. "No, I suppose I should have, but I didn't. After the last game we played, one of my friends killed himself. At the time, I thought the coach was at least partly to blame. I guess I wanted it to be somebody's fault, anybody's fault but mine.

"I felt guilty that I didn't see how upset my friend was; you know how kids are. I was mad about losing the ball game, mad at him. I still feel guilty about what happened, even now. So, I didn't want to stay in touch with the coach. I didn't want to hang on to that sad part of my life."

Stephanie nodded her head. "I know about your friend. I met the Atkins and they told me about their son. What a tragedy."

Stephanie felt like they were developing a rapport. That was part of her job. She could get people to talk to her, to tell her things, even things she didn't want to know. She probably seemed nonthreatening.

Meanwhile, Barber was shaking his big, handsome head. "I think back to what I should have done, what I could have done to prevent what happened. If there were ever a day I could live over, that would be the day I would pick.

"I thought at the time that there was nothing more important than winning that game, being the state champions. Well, you're from here; you know how football-crazy people can get. Me, Jack Jackson, and Charlie—they called us the tripod, the three of us. We played really well together. When people say stuff about teamwork, we were what they meant.

"And the state championship was our goal. At the time, it seemed like winning that game was the difference between a life of success and happiness and a life of mediocrity and misery. So, when Charlie messed up during the game, I thought he was destroying my chance for a successful life. What happened was, he grabbed one of the players from the other team by the helmet and threw him down. The penalty wound up costing us the game.

"When he came off the field, we all moved away from him, even me. When one kid started yelling at Charlie, we all joined in, venting our frustration. I did it, too, screamed at him. Only he was my friend. I should have stood up for him."

While he talked, Stephanie could imagine him as the over-large boy he had been.

"I guess I have been thinking about it, you know, after finding out the coach died, and all. It just brings back those old feelings I thought I had gotten over. You know when I finally forgave myself?" he asked, but he didn't wait for her to reply. "I forgave myself for what happened when my own son was about the age we were then. I was talking to him about something he had to do for school, and it hit me what a kid he was, how he needed my help, my protection.

"And I thought back to the kid I had been. That was it. I had been a kid. It wasn't my fault, what happened to Charlie. And it wasn't his fault either. I guess I'd been angry at him for what happened. But we were just kids. He was just a kid.

"Charlie was good at school, too. He was smart. I looked up to him, even though we were the same age. So, when he jumped, I took it personally, like he was retaliating against me because I had let him down. It was heartbreaking.

"When it first happened, I thought that someday I would understand, find the answer to what made him do it, but I know now I will never understand. I'll never know." Barber had to pause for a moment. "But you came here to talk about Coach. Charlie's death is so intertwined with how I feel about Coach. You know, he found the note and the body. I guess he was a good coach, and I know in my head that he wasn't responsible for what happened, but in my heart, the sadness of that day overshadows how I feel about him.

"Sorry I couldn't help more with your story. And here I made you listen to me go on and on about some ancient history that I, myself, am always telling people to leave in the past." Barber stood up and Stephanie did the same, thinking, *Everyone has a story to tell; scratch the surface and you'll find it.*

CHAPTER FIFTY

Mick headed over to Harlan Tucker's house. He was pretty sure Harlan's daughters would still be there trying to get everything organized. It had to be a big job.

The women were there, crying over some old, cracked dish, when he knocked on the front door.

"Our father saved this bowl we made him when we were Girl Scouts," one of them explained through her tears. Mick could understand that. He had the snowflake Colly made out of Q-tips hanging from his rearview mirror, one of his most precious possessions.

Right now he wanted to find out if there was something more substantial than a cracked dish missing, something Adam Moore could have taken. But he was keeping an open mind.

The sisters turned their sad eyes on him and asked if he wanted a cookie and some iced tea.

"No thanks. I'm fine. I'm sure you've heard about the burglaries around town, and I wanted to check and see if you noticed anything missing. You've had some time to do a little inventory," he said, gesturing at the dishes stacked on the dining table. The sisters looked down at the things their father had accumulated.

"Our mother's sewing machine," one of them looked around, clearly frustrated. "We can't seem to find that. It wouldn't be worth much, not old enough to be an antique and not new enough to be valuable. We were always trying to get Daddy to get rid of stuff, but he never would. Other than that, it looks like Daddy hasn't gotten rid of anything. We haven't noticed anything missing, but we'll keep checking as we go through more stuff."

Mick felt like he had come full circle on this case. He was back to talking to his eyewitness, Jack Jackson. Now, he wasn't feeling the urgency he had when he first pushed him to tell him what he had seen. Now, he didn't believe it was one of National Safety's workers. Now, he believed Adam Moore had been the target, not just some poor kid in the wrong place at the wrong time. Someone knew he was going to be there and wanted him dead. Edie Spence was the one who was in the wrong place at the wrong time.

So far, he hadn't mentioned his idea to Rainy. No point in getting him all excited until he had more to go on. Which was why he was going to meet with Trey Barber and Jack Jackson again. He didn't want to let anyone know his suspicions. Yet. He had to keep questioning his witness or people would wonder what he was up to. He had to keep up the front while he tried to figure out who Adam Moore's accomplice in the burglaries was.

So, here he was on the way to have a discussion that he had been hot to have a couple days earlier but now had cooled on. Mick couldn't tell Barber that he no longer cared what his client had seen or thought he had seen.

Mick sank into a chair at Trey Barber's office, where everything was oversized, as if it were made for some larger type of beings.

Barber and Jackson had been waiting for him. He knew they expected him to be pushing for information, and he wouldn't disappoint them. He didn't want them to know too much about the shift of his focus from random burglary gone wrong to targeted killing. He started off with the usual questions. "Is there anything else you can recall about that night?"

Jackson glanced at Barber before answering. It was going to be a long interview if each question had to be scrutinized.

"Obviously, I have been thinking about it a lot. I can't sleep. I keep replaying the whole thing over and over again in my head. And the thing is, the more I think about it, the more certain I am that I saw the National Safety jacket. I wish I didn't, but I did."

Mick nodded. "Could it have been a woman you saw running away?"

This time Jackson didn't need to check with Barber. He was shaking his head.

"I don't think so. The shadow seemed too big to be a woman, and, I don't know, the way he was running or something made me think it was a man." Ever the helpful witness, he added without conviction, "I guess I could be wrong."

Mick nodded. That was the problem with an eyewitness. They were like Jackson's Labrador retriever; they wanted to make you happy. Mick didn't think he was going to get anything new. Jackson and Barber might hand over the names of some disgruntled employees, but Mick couldn't shake the idea that this was not a random robbery gone bad. And that was all Jackson could offer him.

He sighed and asked Jackson to go through his story once more, starting earlier in the day, hours before he and his dog wound up witnesses.

At that Jackson looked at Barber. If Mick could have put a word bubble over Jackson's head it would have read, "Aw, do I have to?" Fortunately for him, he didn't have to be the one to tell Jackson, yes he had to. Barber shrugged his shoulders in a "might as well" gesture, and Jackson started in on his story.

Mick knew most of it. Jackson had gone to the wake for his old coach. He had talked to lots of people. He thought he remembered seeing Edie Spence and Adam Moore. He drove home, changed out of his suit, grabbed a leash, and took his dog for a walk.

Mick wanted to say to him, "There now; was that so hard?"

Jackson sighed, finishing up his story. "That's all I remember. That and the fleeting glimpse of the National Safety jacket."

Mick wondered if he had actually seen the jacket. Could Adam Moore's accomplice in the burglaries have worn it? Could she have used it to make herself look bigger? He pictured Lacey Thomas, with her dark ponytail and dramatic lipstick, running away in an old, too-big jacket. He couldn't get the picture to come into focus.

Probably because he couldn't imagine her in shoes she could actually run in. The shoes made him think of Stephanie Gallagher, of catching her on the path. Jackson was still droning on about how he hadn't heard anything because of his music. Catching Stephanie Gallagher made Mick think about what a lonely guy cliché he was becoming. That made him think of Julie and Colly and *that* made him officially tired of this interview.

"We are investigating a new lead now. We think it is possible that the killings were planned and that one of the victims was the target." He wanted to clarify for them why he wasn't more interested in the poor-employee line and then he wanted to get out of there.

He looked at Jackson, who seemed to have not only stopped talking but stopped breathing. "You mean you don't think it was the Reluctant Robber?"

Mick had to draw the line here. He didn't want to tell them everything he was thinking. "We aren't sure about that. We just think that one of the victims might have been the target."

Jackson seemed upset by this news.

Barber noticed it too. "Are you okay, buddy?" he asked his client.

The whole experience had to be upsetting for a guy whose usual stress probably came from losing a round of golf, Mick thought.

"I just can't stand to think that someone set out to kill those people. I guess I've been telling myself it was all a needless tragedy. I hate the idea that someone deliberately killed them. It's another reminder how close I came to being killed myself. Damn. I wish I would have shot at him instead of in the air!"

"Look, we just started this part of the investigation," Mick said, putting his hands on his thighs and leaning forward, getting ready for his departure.

"But the gun, the stolen gun! It had to come from the Reluctant Robber! It has to be the same guy. Otherwise, how would he get the gun?" Jackson asked.

Mick pushed himself to standing. He didn't want to tell them any more about his accomplice theory. "You could be right. It might have been a botched robbery, but we have to examine all the possibilities, and that includes looking at the murders as intentional. I appreciate all the time you've put into trying to remember details and the help with struggling employees, I really do. We'll keep in touch."

As he walked out the door he thought he could hear Jackson saying back to him, "Keep in touch."

But it seemed like a question.

CHAPTER FIFTY-ONE

Stephanie saw Lacey sitting on the picnic table, their meeting spot. Today she was wearing white jeans with bands of black lace on the legs and a black lace tunic over a white tank top. It was kind of cute and sophisticated.

"Nice outfit!" she said as she got closer to the picnic table. "What did you want to talk to me about?" She perched on top of the table next to Lacey, up high, looking out over the playground kingdom.

"You said I should call if I wanted to talk," Lacey said, accusing Stephanie of insincerity with her voice.

"Yeah, I said it, and I meant it. That's why I came here, to talk to you." She hoped she didn't sound petulant. Lacey had enough of that for both of them.

The girl was mollified and looked back out at the swing sets.

"I don't have that many people to talk to. You know, Adam was my friend. We really were like best friends. I could talk to him about anything. And I know, despite what that ex-cheerleader says, I was his best friend, too."

For a second Stephanie thought *she* was the ex-cheerleader, then she realized Lacey was talking about Adam's girlfriend, Carrie.

"I know you two were close, and I'm sure you miss him a lot," Stephanie said.

Lacey hunched her shoulders down, and Stephanie was afraid she was going to start crying, but the next words out of her mouth were defiant.

"And now the police are trying to make it seem like Adam was some badass criminal. I can't stand it!"

This was news to Stephanie. Why would the police care if the crime victim was a choir boy or not? What difference did it make?

"How do you know they're trying to make it seem like he was a criminal? What makes you think that?" she said, dropping the badass part of the comment. She was the adult here.

"I just know. I can tell by all the questions they've been asking me, questions about bullshit things that happened in high school. They are trying to make it sound like Adam stole stuff, like he got what he deserved, or something. I hate them. And I can't tell my mom. She'd just be like, yeah, that's what I figured. You and your friend were big-time losers." Tears rolled down her cheeks.

Stephanie could feel the anguish coming off the girl like heat waves rising off of I-35 on a hundred-degree day. *Poor thing*, she thought, thinking of her own mother saying, *You look like you just lost your best friend.* She reached out and patted the girl on her lace-covered shoulders. There probably wasn't anything here that would add to the story, but sometimes you had to just be a human being.

And she was curious. Why would Mick care about Adam Moore's high school misdeeds?

"Well, the police are probably just trying to find out all they can about Adam."

Lacey shook her head back and forth. "No, no! They asked me questions like he did something wrong, like he was the one stealing from people's house's: you know, like he was the one you wrote about. They don't know who did it, so they want to make it look like it was Adam!

"I know how this works. I've seen it before. In high school, teachers looked down on me, so when something happened, I was the one they blamed first. One time they accused me of stealing some bratty girl's phone, me and Adam. For no reason, they just picked us. Like we needed something like that?"

Stephanie watched the girl and patted her shoulder again. Usually when you heard young people talking about their problems, like not making the cheerleading squad or having your prom date dance with someone else all night, you could smile and say, "It's not as serious as all that" or "You'll grow up and not even remember this little bump in the road."

But looking at Lacey, Stephanie concluded she had real, serious adult problems. Having your friend killed was not the sort of thing you could get over by going out for ice cream.

"Look, I'm sure they are just checking everything they can about Adam. Don't worry. You and I both know he was a good guy. I did all the research on him for the article in the paper, and I can tell I would have liked him. He didn't get very many breaks in life, but he was a good guy. The police are going to find that out, too. So don't worry."

Lacey was shaking her head again. This time Stephanie could see tears being flung into her hair by the motion.

"No, no, no, they think he was bad. You weren't there. You don't get it! You know how I told you about that sewing machine Adam got for me? I got a call about it, asking! They acted like he stole it or something."

Stephanie thought of her latest article about the crimes. Martin Colby showing the gun to Adam Moore, the gun that Adam Moore could have easily stolen. Could that be what the police believed? Adam Moore was her Reluctant Robber?

It was true: with all the research she had done on him, she had come to like Adam. He was the kind of person who wouldn't take more than he needed. But was he the kind of person who would take anything? And if he was the Robber, how did he end up dead?

She realized she was still patting Lacey on the shoulder: a small betrayal, because the idea that maybe the police were right about Adam was seeping into Stephanie's thoughts.

"But you know for a fact that he didn't steal the sewing machine, right?" Stephanie could tell Lacey didn't like the question at the end of that statement.

"Yeah, I know he didn't steal the sewing machine. He wouldn't do that. He really liked that old guy. He would not have stolen from him or anyone else. Adam saw the machine at his house, and he talked about me, and Mr. Tucker told him to take it. No one else was going to use it. Really, what was an old guy like that going to do with a sewing machine?"

Stephanie wasn't sure what any of this meant. But she was, after all, an investigative reporter. She would investigate.

"Look, Lacey, I'm sure you're just being overly sensitive to the questions the police asked you." She could sense Lacey beside her, getting ready to cry or contradict her, so she hurried on. "It's only natural for you to be sensitive. Adam was your friend. But I will check around. I promise."

Lacey looked at her like she had just thrown her a life preserver in choppy seas, this poor kid with no one to turn to. It made Stephanie think about her parents and her sister and all the support they had heaped on her over the last year.

Lacey was lowering herself off the picnic table, and Stephanie thought briefly about giving her a reassuring hug, but it seemed wrong, like trying to pet a wild animal, so she stood and plastered her best smile on her face.

She was about to tell Lacey she would call her if she found out anything, but Lacey, distrustful by nature, beat her to it.

"I'll call you," she said to Stephanie, who could imagine all the people in Lacey's little life who had said they would do something and then not done it.

Stephanie watched her go. As she herself was turning to leave, she caught sight of someone waving at her from the playground.

"Stephanie, hi! It's me, Lori! Lori Gilbert."

Stephanie had barely recognized her in her stylish workout clothes pushing a baby in one of those fancy strollers. "Lori, hey, it's great to see you!"

"Andy told me he ran into you at the high school. So sad about that young man and Edie Spence."

Stephanie nodded. Very sad.

"Andy really appreciated your articles about Adam, all the nice things you wrote. We'd love to see you sometime, when you're not so busy with all the reporting about the . . . the murders. Actually, we're having our monthly barbecue this Saturday. You should come!"

Stephanie was about to protest, but what did she have to lose? "OK, that sounds great." She smiled at Lori. "Let me know if there's anything I can bring." *As long as it's microwaveable*, she thought.

"Sure, I'll text you. See you, Stephanie!" With that, Lori jogged away, pushing the stroller in front of her.

CHAPTER FIFTY-TWO

Mick sat at his desk picking at a peanut butter sandwich. With regret, he had accepted the fact that Adam Moore might somehow be involved in the burglaries. Mick had felt from the first that the thefts were perpetrated by a kid. The act of leaving some money was, well, juvenile. Did Adam Moore see Edie Spence at Coad's and decide she would be there long enough for him to go to her house and rob it?

But how had Adam known she was going to order a pizza? Mick remembered Spence talking about his wife and her ham aversion. Then an idea hit him. What if the kid ordered the pizza? Suppose he called in an order, picked up the pizza at Tony's place, drove it to a house he thought would be unoccupied, walked in, and took the cash? If anyone saw him, he had a perfectly good reason to be there. He could shake his head and say Jessica must have gotten the order wrong if he encountered trouble.

Dr. Spence was right. Edie hadn't ordered ham on her pizza; Adam Moore had. With that, Mick sped up, deciding he needed to go back to Antonio's Pizza.

Before he could make it to his car, a call flashed across his screen: Stephanie. Thank goodness for caller ID. He had time to mentally prepare before answering.

Caller ID! Jessica would have known it was Adam Moore calling. She would have seen it on caller ID. He wrote "caller ID" on the pad of paper in front of him. Another thing to check out.

"Hi there, Stephanie. What can I do for you?" Mick was brisk.

232 JENNIFER FARRELL VOSS

"Hey, Mick. I just talked to Lacey and she seems to think you are getting ready to accuse Adam Moore of some crime. I told her you were just doing your job and investigating his life."

"You told her right. We are investigating every avenue."

"But you are not investigating Adam as a criminal, are you? He was a victim for heaven's sake!"

Mick answered carefully. "We are looking at every possibility. That is how this works."

"On the record, Mick, do you think it is possible that this was not a random crime?"

"On the record, Stephanie, we are looking at every possibility. Look, I've got to run."

"A development in the case?"

"We are heading to Tony's place to check on Edie's pizza order." Why had he answered that? Still, it didn't matter. Stephanie knew about Sean Spence's story about Edie not eating ham. He wasn't giving her anything new.

"You know the last time I ate a Twinkie?"

Mick tried not to sound surprised by the change in topic. "No, when?" he asked.

"When I was six years old. One of my friends told me that people would spit into the whipped cream when they were making the Twinkies. Of course I've known for years that people are not spitting into the whipped cream at the Hostess factory, but you know, to this day I can't bring myself to eat a Twinkie. So I guess I believe Sean Spence when he says his wife would never have ordered that pizza."

"He could be right," was all Mick said.

"OK. Well, thanks, Mick." She sounded subdued. Mick had the feeling that he had just escaped a close call. What the hell was the matter with him? You'd think that woman was a powerful magnet, able to pull information out of him.

Mick hung up and looked at the words on his yellow legal pad: "caller ID." He tore the page off the pad, folded it, and pushed it into his pants pocket.

He saw Mason across the station's parking lot and called, "Pizza for lunch. I'm buying." Mason gave him a thumbs-up.

When Mick got to the pizzeria, only the sullen pizza baker was there. He ordered two large pizzas, one mushroom and one sausage. He didn't want to think about the Hawaiian pizza.

He asked the kid when Jessica would be in, but he just shrugged. Mick was guessing that the kid was related to Tony when Jessica breezed in the door, her curly hair bouncing. She stopped when she saw him. He got it. No one wants to see a police officer, except when they need him.

"Hey, Jessica. I came by to pick up some pizza for lunch." She moved again at that. "But I was wondering if I could ask you something, something about the call the night Adam was shot?"

She came over and sat at the table with him. "When I saw you, I thought maybe you were coming to tell me you caught the guy who did this."

It was a statement, not an accusation, but Mick felt the sting.

"No, but trust me, we are working very hard on it."

He felt the folded paper in his pocket. "We are going to find the person who killed your friend," he said, but even to himself he sounded like a little boy whistling in the dark. "That's why I'm here today. We are looking at every tiny bit of evidence we have. And I want to check with you about how you get your delivery orders. I especially want to know if Adam's caller ID ever came up on the orders. Like, did he ever order a pizza for Mr. Tucker, for example?"

Jessica's forehead wrinkled, perplexed. "No . . . why would Adam order a pizza? If he wanted one, he would just tell me or Brad. And he wouldn't order a pizza for anyone else."

"OK, good," Mick said, nodding like he had gotten some good news. "I know you get lots of orders."

And, as if on cue, the phone rang. Brad scowled out at Jessica before picking up the phone. Something about his attitude made Mick want to jump over the counter and punch him. He wanted to grab him by his apron and yell, "We are trying to solve a murder, you little prick!"

He felt the heat rise in his face as he continued with his questions for Jessica.

"With all the orders you get, I'm wondering if you remember

the caller ID on that last delivery that Adam made." He watched as the girl cringed and pulled a napkin out of the shiny silver holder. He could see her brush her eyes with the tip of Italy printed on the napkin.

Mick was cursing himself for the way he had approached this interview. It should have been easy and here he was saying things like "the last delivery" that were guaranteed to make her cry. Nothing he could do now but pat her hand.

The girl pushed the bottom of the boot of Italy into her eyes and, without looking at him, said, "I do remember. I keep thinking about it, like it was some kind of sign, you know? I mean it scares me."

"What scares you, Jessica? You know I can help, right?"

She nodded, with Italy still covering her eyes. "It was creepy, that's all . . . creepy how the call came from the funeral home. I told Brad, 'I guess even dead people like my uncle's pizza.' And then Adam died that night. It was like getting a call from the future or something."

It sounded to Mick as though Jessica was reading too much sci-fi or fantasy fiction. "You remember what the caller ID said?" he asked.

Italy slid sideways down her face and she said, "Coad's Funeral Home."

The sullen boy slapped two pizza boxes on the counter and looked his way.

Mick patted Jessica's hand again and said, "Thanks, Jessica. I'll be in touch." He paid for his pizza, grabbed a handful of napkins, and looked at the map of Italy like he was headed there and needed to know how to get from Forsyth to Rome.

The pizza was still hot when he brought it into the lunchroom for all the staff. They grabbed some Styrofoam plates, and it occurred to Mick that this was the best and most balanced meal he had eaten in a while.

When it was just Mason and him left in the room, he told Mason what he had found out and that he wanted to head over to Coad's and see if anyone remembered Adam Moore making a phone call.

"If the kid made the call, we're done. We'll know he had to be the Reluctant Robber and the shooter had to be his accomplice."

Mick was in a hurry. He wanted to get to the funeral home, have his suspicions confirmed, and put that piece of the puzzle into place. He would still have to prove that Lacey was the shooter, but once he had Adam Moore as the thief, the other pieces would fall into place. He was sure of that.

When they pulled into the parking lot of the funeral home, there were just a few cars, in contrast to the last couple of times he had been here, when it had been jammed. Mason parked next to the hearse. *Fitting,* Mick thought, *for this investigation.*

Once inside they found the more-jovial–than-you-would-expect Mr. Coad. His office was cozy, with a big desk and a couple of comfortable-looking chairs covered in yellow flowered fabric.

Mick and Mason sank into the chairs, the way he imagined countless grievers had. He felt like it was slightly obscene to be so ready for the interview that he expected would put the nail in Adam Moore's coffin, so to speak.

Lem Coad was wearing a suit and tie. Apparently he worked in the one profession that had not gone business casual. When he had settled into his chair facing the two police officers, he asked, "What can I do for you?"

"We want to find out who had access to your phones at Harlan Tucker's wake and to see if you gave permission for someone to use your phone or noticed anyone using it. Is this the only phone?" Mick asked glancing at the phone sitting on the desk.

"No. There is another phone upstairs and one in the prep room. But no one would have access to those except people who work here. The phone in this office would be pretty much available to anyone who was attending the wake. We have had so many problems with people using their cell phones here. You can't imagine how many people will take a call in the middle of a prayer service! And it's not just kids, either.

"We had this one incident where the deceased's sister made an appointment to get her hair done during a very solemn moment in the service. We all had to listen to her telling her stylist that she had to cancel her regular appointment because her sister died.

"But the worst one was some lady who set her purse down next to the casket and forgot it. During a moment of silent prayer her cell phone started ringing. It sounded like it was coming from the deceased. It was distressing, to say the least. After that I went right out and had these signs made." He pointed to a sign over the door that said, "No Cell Phones, Please."

"We do ask our guests who we see using a cell phone to refrain, and we direct them in here, to use our phone. It cuts down on the problems we have maintaining decorum."

Mick looked at him and realized that did solve the mystery of why Edie Spence or Adam Moore had not used a cell phone to order the pizza. Edie would have been an old hand at funerals because of her hospice work. She would have been aware of the cell phone rule, and Adam would have seen the signs, too.

"You mean anyone can just wander into your office at any time?"

Coad was shaking his head, no. But he was saying, "Yes. I mean this isn't really my office. It's more like a meeting room. I don't keep any files or paperwork here."

Mick looked back at the desk with just a lamp on it, no stacks of papers, no envelopes, no computer.

"So anyone could just walk in here?"

"Well, yes, they could. As I said, we direct callers in here, and sometimes if people need a private moment they might step in here. We encourage them to use the room if they need a little space in a troubled time. It happens. Occasionally, there are family problems, and we like to keep the groups separated. It can be a stressful time for families, losing a loved one, and it can bring issues to the surface."

Mick understood there might be a need for a room such as this. But was it good news or bad news for his theory? Adam Moore could have come in and made the phone call, but so could have Edie Spence—or anyone else at the wake.

"Mr. Coad, did you happen to see Adam Moore in here using the phone at Harlan Tucker's wake?"

Coad paused to think about it. After a few seconds he said, "No. I didn't see him in here. I do recall seeing him in the Sunset Room. That's our biggest room, and we had a crowd that day. "

"Well, how about Edie Spence? Did you see her in the office on the phone?"

This time there was no hesitation in Coad's answer. "No. I sure didn't. I did see her at the wake. In fact, I saw them together. I remember because I was a little worried when I saw her wave over the policeman who was directing traffic that day. I thought maybe there was a problem in the parking lot or that they had a complaint.

"But one of Harlan's daughters wanted to ask me something about the guestbook, and by the time I went to check to see if there really was a problem, the officer was back outside, so I figured it was okay."

There was no way to tell who had made the call. That was the news he was getting from Lem Coad. They knew someone had ordered a pizza to be delivered to Edie Spence's house. But he couldn't shake the idea that it was someone other than Edie Spence.

CHAPTER FIFTY-THREE

Mick was going to have to talk to Rainy and get a search warrant for Adam Moore's house. He was trying to think of a way to make it easier for Tiffany to bear. He didn't want to add to the poor kid's troubles, but that was what he was going to do.

Mick headed back to the office. Once there he picked up a folder containing a list of the stolen items and headed down to Rainy's office. He didn't really need the folder; it was more for armor, just to have something with him to hold when he asked Rainy to do the things that Rainy would not want to do.

He knew how Rainy thought. He was still wishing the murderer was a transient passing through Forsyth on his way to anywhere but here. Asking him for a search warrant for Adam Moore's home would be like reporting that there was a crime spree going on right here in Forsyth. And the sad thing was that he would be right.

Mick walked in, slapping the manila folder against his leg.

"We need to get a search warrant to check Adam Moore's home. If he was the Reluctant Robber and he kept the gun, there might be other stolen bits that he had squirreled away at his house."

Rainy was sadly shaking his head. "Let's be sure before we do this, Mick. The town just got used to Adam Moore as a brave victim. For Christ's sake, Stephanie Gallagher has been writing articles about the poor bastard and his struggles. Forsyth is going to get whiplashed by this if it turns out he was somehow involved."

Mick watched as Rainy got sadder.

"Yes, but we want to solve the crime. I think the people of Forsyth want that, no matter what." And, really, Mick was thinking, he shouldn't even have to say such a thing.

"OK, OK. I'm not saying we won't get a search warrant. I'm just saying let's make damn sure we really need one before we do it. We are both trying to do the same thing here, protect and serve the people. But let's not do something we'll regret, like drag this kid's name through the mud, until we're sure he was involved."

"That's just it, Rainy, we need the search warrant to find out," Mick said slapping the folder against his thigh for emphasis.

"Just let me think about it, OK?"

Mick was tempted to slap the folder on top of Rainy's head, but the DA was right. He himself had been reluctant to besmirch Adam Moore. And if Stephanie wrote the article in the *Bee* that he thought she would, maybe something would shake loose without a search of Adam's place.

Back at the station, he tossed the folder on his desk and sat down with his hands behind his head. He could wait out Rainy and his search warrant decision. Then Mick had a thought, one for which no search warrant was required. He checked his watch and realized he could pick up a pizza at the same time, a good investigation. He had been eating a lot of pizza lately.

He got in his car and headed out to Antonio's. When he got there he went through the same drill, ordering a pizza from the sullen kid, asking for Tony, going back to his office–storage room. But Mick had remembered a block of lockers on the wall. He wouldn't need a search warrant to look in Adam's locker. All he would need would be permission from Tony. It was his property. Mick found himself standing in front of the metal locker that had been Adam's just days before.

"I wasn't sure what I should do with his stuff. I never even looked to see what was in there. I guess I thought I would wait and then pack it up for his sister. This is all so overwhelming for me. I just kinda didn't get around to doing anything yet."

Mick nodded. Of course there wasn't a handbook for what to do if an employee gets murdered on the job.

"I don't think there is going to be anything in there about the murder, though," Tony continued.

Mick didn't want to tell him, but he had his doubts, too. Still, it was worth checking. It was possible the kid kept his loot in his locker so his sister wouldn't find it.

He glanced at Tony who looked at him expectantly. He gave the locker a tug and beheld its contents.

Not much. A couple of old T-shirts wadded together, a sweatshirt, a *Sports Illustrated* magazine—not the one with the girl in the swimsuit, though—and a Rangers baseball cap. Mick picked up the cap and found a letter tucked inside. *Hidden,* he thought, *hidden inside.*

The thick envelope had been ripped open and the contents stuffed back inside. It was addressed to Adam Moore from Southern. Mick was unsure about looking at the mail without a warrant, but he tried not to show any emotion as he tugged one of the pages free from the envelope. It was a letter dated two days before the murders. "We are pleased to inform you that you have been accepted to the business school at Southern."

Mick pushed the page back with the other pages. The kid must have just heard. Great day in his life. It would have been better if it hadn't been the last day.

CHAPTER FIFTY-FOUR

Stephanie finished her article, hinting that the random killings might not be so random. She walked it down to Tom. They went over exactly what Mick had said and how she had translated it into the article. Tom was dubious.

"I just can't believe someone would kill either of those two on purpose. That means you did a good job, Stephanie. I feel like I know them. There must be something there, though, or Forsyth's finest wouldn't want to see it in the *Bee*. I wonder what they found."

"I don't see how Mick McKay could have been any more vague about the information he gave me. To tell you the truth, I had the feeling he just wanted to rile up the investigation. Oh, and did I tell you about meeting Lacey Thomas?"

Tom looked at her blankly.

"She hung out with Adam Moore. Anyway, she had the idea that the police thought Adam was involved in the Reluctant Robberies. When I talked to Mick about it, he didn't exactly bend over backward denying it. The thing is, the article is true to what Mick said, so I don't think we'll have any legal issues. We aren't even saying which victim was the intended. I think we're OK with it."

She waited for Tom to agree with her. From her perspective it had already been a great conversation. Tom telling her he felt like he knew her subjects? Well, that was high praise, and she was pleased to get it.

"I think you're right. I don't see any problems with the article. I think you're right about it stirring things up, too."

She went back to her office and pushed "submit." If it did stir things up, they'd find out soon.

Later that evening, after a dinner of scrambled eggs, Stephanie swung by the office to see the morning edition which featured her article about the nonrandom nature of the killings. It still gave her a little bit of a thrill to see her byline, a sense of accomplishment. Yes, she was living alone now, but for some strange reason she was feeling hopeful about her future, a feeling she hadn't felt for a long time.

The next day, still feeling that tiny bud of hope, Stephanie walked into the office after an interview with yet another of Coach Harlan Tucker's former players. Usually when she was doing a story and wanted a little background filler, she set up appointments with more sources than she could possibly use. Some would decide against it. Where criminal activity was involved, some might be in jail. Some would just flake out on her. So, she always set up more appointments than she actually needed.

This time, though, every one of the boys who were now men wanted to talk about the glory days of playing high school football in a small Texas town. If she was looking for color, she had the entire spectrum of the rainbow by now. Between those interviews and the crossover article she had done on Harlan Tucker as the man who brought them together—complete with his picture centered between photographs of Edie Spence and Adam Moore—she had spent a lot of time getting to know old Harlan.

She paused at the front desk to check in with the *Bee*'s reception-ist, Joan, but before she got the chance, the door pushed open and Jack Jackson walked in.

"Hi, Stephanie. Hello, Ms. Joan." Stephanie thought that if he had a hat on he would have tipped it at them, but of course he didn't. "I just wanted to drop off this check for the Cotton Parade ad spon-sored by us at National," he said, taking a check out of a bank pouch and handing it to Joan.

"And hey, Stephanie, I wanted to ask you something, something about your article in the paper today."

"Oh, sure, what is it?"

Jackson hesitated, looked around, and Stephanie picked up the clue.

"Come on back to my office." It wasn't really an office, but oh, well.

She turned without setting down her purse and looked at him. She didn't ask him to sit, because she couldn't imagine anything about the article taking more than a second to answer. She arched her eyebrows.

"It's no big deal or anything. I just wondered what you meant about the police looking into whether those poor people were really targeted."

Stephanie prided herself on her journalistic skills. But she couldn't grasp where this conversation was headed. Maybe because he had been the closest thing to a witness there was, it worried him to know someone was out there stalking.

"Well, I can't tell you too much more than was in the article. The police are working on the idea that it wasn't random. I don't know too much more than that."

"Oh, yeah, it was just such a shocking thing to see. I guess I am having a hard time not thinking about it. Now when I close my eyes, I can see the back of that National Safety jacket as clear as I'm seeing you. It's just hard, you know." He tapped his fingers impatiently on the back of the chair. "Well, I'm glad I ran into you. I'll see you at the parade, right?" he said with a forced brightness.

"Wouldn't miss it!" she replied. And she wouldn't. Last year she had gone with Pete. It was right before she found out about him and Sara.

Ordinarily, when she thought about Peter, darkness came over her, like the sun going behind a cloud, but today she didn't feel it. The sun stayed out. The parade was a fun part of her past, and she was going to have fun at it in the future. And really, who could be bothered with Pete at a time like this? Stephanie needed to finish her piece on Harlan Tucker.

"I'm glad I ran into you. See you later," Jackson said, heading out of her cubicle masquerading as an office. She waved, recalling her riding-on-the-float technique.

"Joan, what's the theme for the Cotton Parade this year? Do you know? Jack Jackson got me thinking about it."

"Hmm, let's see. It's Colorful Cotton; not sure how that's going to translate to floats. What did Jackson want to see you about, anyway?"

"Want to see me? I don't think he wanted to see me. I think he just wanted to ask about the story since he was here. Probably showing interest because of his involvement, is all."

Joan tilted her head to the side like the RCA dog. "I know I'm not an investigative journalist, but that man was waiting for you. I saw him out in back when I took my break. He walked by a couple of times before you pulled in and then waltzed in as soon as you got here. He was looking for *you*; that's what I wanted to tell you when you came in. And in all the time that National Safety has run advertisements, he has never once personally brought the check over."

Stephanie wasn't sure why Jackson would want to talk to her that much. She could understand his need to talk about the crime, but if he really was concerned about the case, the Forsyth police would have more information than she did.

But she just said, "You're probably right. He did want to ask me about the story in the *Bee* today, one of a lot of people who are going to have a hard time believing that poor Edie Spence or unlucky Adam Moore was being targeted. It's kind of unbelievable to me, too. Thanks, Joan."

Stephanie headed back to her cubicle. Joan always smelled a little too fresh and minty, probably trying to get rid of the smoky smell that clung to her like dandruff on a black sweater.

Poor Jackson. Not surprising he was having a hard time with the murders. And then to add insult to injury, to think it was someone working at your company, someone you saw every day. It would spook anybody. That was for sure. But as they say, "In other news . . ." And she was in the news business.

CHAPTER FIFTY-FIVE

Mick started off his day by happily crossing off another day on the calendar, bringing his girls closer to home. He had been concentrating on how much he missed them, and of course he knew they missed him, too, but the two of them were together. They had each other.

He decided to take a trip through the drive-through at McDonald's for a large coffee. Usually he paid, especially in the drive-through. It wasn't like they could see he was a policeman. But today, the manager recognized him. Like Edie Spence and Adam Moore, his picture had been in the paper, too, and not just the *Bee*. So today his coffee was free.

He had the paper with Stephanie Gallagher's headline on the seat next to him. She had written an approximation of what he would have wanted. He just hoped Lacey Thomas would pick up on the news. The headline said, "Police Investigate Victims as Targets." As he walked into his office his phone was ringing, and he raced the last few steps to catch it, balancing his coffee. He grabbed his desk phone and splashed coffee on the sleeve of his white shirt at the same time.

"Mr. McKay?"

"Speaking." He recognized Sean Spence's voice and belatedly realized he should have told him about the article, given him a heads-up.

"I saw the *Bee* today. Is it true that you think someone wanted to kill Edie or Adam Moore?"

"We do think that might be a possibility. And as I told you, we are committed to looking at everything we can to find out who did this to your wife."

"I get that, but I want to reiterate that Edie didn't have an enemy in the world. There was no jealous boyfriend or girlfriend, no unhappy patient. We didn't have that dramatic of a life. I don't want to see the police wasting their time pursuing something that is so obviously wrong. I want the person who did this found more than I can say, but there's no way this could have been intentional. No way. My kids read that article and, of course, it has them worried and confused. I told them that it was not true that their mother was a target."

Mick was kicking himself for not calling. "I know what you are saying, and I know about what kind of person your wife was from all the people we've talked to about the case. Keep in mind, two people were killed. We are looking into a possible motive for killing Adam Moore. But it's just one theory. We have to follow every lead. Try not to let these kind of news stories get to you."

He looked at the coffee stain on his cuff and rolled it up. Time to do laundry. A white shirt meant that he had gone through all of his blue shirts. If he didn't do something soon, he'd have to wear the Hawaiian shirt Julie had gotten him on their honeymoon.

Mason stopped by Mick's desk with the paper in his hand. "Did you see the article in the *Bee* today? The one that makes it sound like this was some kind of planned murder?"

Mick took a big gulp of his coffee before answering. How did they manage to keep the stuff so hot?

"I saw it. I think it might put the fear of God into Adam Moore's accomplice. Maybe make her nervous enough to decide the jig is up, and she better come in and confess to the all-knowing, all-powerful Forsyth Police. Think it will work?"

Mason scrunched up his face to show his doubt. "For this to work, you have to be right about everything. The Reluctant Robber has to be a kid, he has to have someone working with him, he has to have a disagreement with that someone, and that someone has to plan to kill him and maybe Edie Spence. Oh, and the Robber has to be Adam Moore. That's a lot of rights."

Mick closed his eyes for a second and took a deep breath. He remembered a conversation about being surrounded by yes-men. At this moment, it sounded good to him.

"I know might isn't right, but, I might be right about all of it. Anyway, the story says we are pursuing all leads. Can't hurt, might help."

But he wasn't so sure. Maybe the story would hurt. Mick had already heard from Sean Spence. If wispy Tiffany read the story, she too might call him, outraged. At that very second his desk phone rang, and he picked it up, prepared to hear the outrage in Tiffany's Hudson's small voice.

But it wasn't her. Mason waved and walked out. Mick heard Trey Barber say that he and Jackson wanted him to come to National Safety's office. They needed to show him something. He didn't want to say anything else over the phone.

This was not Communist Russia. Who did Barber think was going to be listening in? At heart, lawyers were showmen, but this seemed a little overdramatic.

He took another swig of his coffee, wishing he hadn't spilled on his shirt. He didn't relish going in to talk to a couple of well-dressed guys with a stain on his sleeve, but he couldn't go home and change. Besides, there were no clean blue shirts hanging in his closet.

Mick arrived at the National Safety office building, expecting to have the receptionist buzz Jackson while he took yet another look at the seat belt museum. But Jack Jackson and Trey Barber were standing out front when he got there, waiting for him.

Barber looked like he could go play eighteen holes of golf, but Jackson looked like he needed some time at the nineteenth hole. Mick reminded himself that it had to have been very hard to find two dead people, shoot a gun in the air, and wind up as the sole witness to the worst crime in Forsyth history. That could wear on a guy.

The pair retained an air of mystery as they led him deeper into the building. He followed them down the hall, but instead of stopping at Jackson's office, they continued down the corridor to a locked steel door. Jackson unlocked it and reached his arm around to switch on the lights. Bright fluorescence poured down on them.

There were shelves neatly stacked with boxes of paper towels, enough Windex to shine up the Hall of Mirrors at Versailles, white plastic tubs that reminded Mick of the ones he saw the fishermen down by Billy's using, royal blue National Safety jackets, wrapped in plastic and stacked by size.

At first Mick thought maybe they had brought him here to avoid the surveillance that seemed to be making Barber too nervous to talk on the phone. But then he realized they were parting the paper towels to show him something, like when he was a kid and his dad had lifted up the branches to show him the baby bunnies he had found when he was mowing the yard.

But when Mick peered into the space what he saw was not as cute as baby bunnies. He knew without even touching anything what it was he was looking at. After all, he had gone over and over the list. On top was a wallet, Martin Colby's, and inside he knew would be his credit cards and a picture of Samantha with bows in her hair but no driver's license. He also saw the missing watch and a small wad of cash.

He pulled his gaze away from the paper towel tunnel and looked at the men.

"Did you touch anything?" He would have to go to his car and get his gloves.

"Yeah, sorry, but I just found this stuff and I wasn't sure what it was at first. Then when I looked in the wallet I saw a credit card with Martin Colby's name on it and I realized it was the stolen property. I called Trey, and we called you. I didn't touch anything else," Jackson said.

"OK. That's good. Who has access to this room?" Mick was looking around, judging the size of the room.

"Well, it is the storage room for the cleaning staff, so Augustine has the key. I don't know if he allows anyone else on his staff to have one. I don't micromanage. It's his area. I just happen to have the master key."

Barber nodded as his client and friend talked, as if reassuring him. And he probably needed the reassurance.

Mick said a silent sorry to Adam Moore and Lacey Thomas. He had been wrong about them. His theory blew away like a feather in a windstorm. He thought about his trip around the block with

Augustine's house on it, the nice family in front—the nice family of a murderer. Like reshuffling cards, Mick put the pieces together: the work slowdowns, the National Safety jacket sighting, the pocket calendar, the reluctance of the thief to take everything. It all fit.

Why kill Adam Moore? He might have recognized him from Harlan Tucker's house. Sure, that works: at some point imagine the pizza delivery boy and the husband picking up his wife arriving at Harlan's at the same time. Augustine would have known Adam could identify him. He panics, shoots him, and then sees he has to shoot Edie Spence because she's a witness. It was pure luck that Rex the dog wanted a slice of pizza. That probably gave him enough time to start running before Jackson saw him. No wonder Jackson was shaken. He had been seconds from getting killed himself.

"Who knows that you found this stuff?" Mick asked.

"No one but us. I didn't tell anyone else here. I didn't even tell my wife. I didn't want to worry her."

"Alright, let's go back to your office."

They left the storage room and Mick turned back to watch Jackson flick the light switch and pull the door closed. One thing sure to attract attention was the president of the company, a lawyer, and a police detective talking in the closet. Nobody was in the hall when they walked out.

Mick waited till he got to Jackson's office to call for the county tech team. He kept the office door ajar and faced the hall. He wanted to make sure no one went into the storage room while he waited. Barber and Jackson eyed him. They had handed over the reins and now they were just along for the ride. It made Mick feel even jumpier. He paced the room.

"How often do you go into the storage room?" he asked Jackson.

"Oh, maybe once a month or so. It depends."

"Well, why did you go in today?"

"I spilled some coffee and I needed to grab some paper towels. Then, when I was getting the paper towels, I found the stuff I showed you. I don't go in there that often, like I said. Usually, if I need something, I ask Augustine. I think of the room as his space. He keeps track of what's in there, reorders supplies, everything."

Mick nodded, keeping his gaze on the hall. "No one else uses the room on a regular basis?"

Here Jackson looked mournful. That was all the answer Mick needed. The funny thing was, now that he had his first real hard evidence, he wasn't feeling that rush you get when the last pieces of the puzzle fall into place.

CHAPTER FIFTY-SIX

Stephanie showed up at Andy and Lori Gilbert's house for the promised get-together. There were glasses on the kitchen counter and white wine in an ice bucket. She poured herself a glass of wine and turned to face the group.

She felt a shock of surprise when she noticed Mark Lavelle there. Then again, maybe it wasn't so strange, considering he was Andy's boss. He looked a little awkward and out of place.

Suddenly she had an *aha!* moment. They had invited him for her. Come to dinner and we'll not only give you an entrée but a man too! A feeling of annoyance came over her as she turned back to the wine and splashed a little more into her glass to give her a second to decide how to proceed.

She took a deep breath and another sip of wine, and the feeling of annoyance drained out of her. Why be mad at people who were trying to help her? She slapped on a smile and approached the high school principal. She shifted her wine glass to her left hand and stuck out her right.

"Hey, Mark, I didn't know you were coming to dinner!"

He shook her hand and held onto it just one beat too long. "Hey, I didn't know you were coming either! This is a great surprise! Andy had called to say he needed one more to round out the table, and I couldn't say no."

Stephanie realized that he, too, hadn't known in advance that he was being set up.

She had the sense that all the people in the room were looking at them to see how they were going to get along. Well, she'd show them. She reached out her right hand and touched Mark's sleeve.

"That's nice of you. Do you help your friends move, too, or is that where you draw the line?" she asked.

She was settling into her flirting groove when she felt her phone go off. "Sorry, I have to check this," she said, turning away from Mark.

She walked back to the hall and heard Tom say, "Something is up at National Safety. Better get over there and find out what."

She turned and walked back in looking for Lori. She felt a tinge of regret that she had to leave, but she never considered not leaving. She made her excuses and expressed the desire to come to another dinner. Right now, she couldn't miss any developments on her stories.

CHAPTER FIFTY-SEVEN

The evidence team finally got to National Safety after forty-five minutes of tense waiting. Mick led them down to the storage room feeling like he was drifting down a river with crocodiles on the banks watching him. Virtually the entire office staff were trying to catch a glimpse of the team. The pretty receptionist in the front office had been so flustered she forgot to point out items of interest in the museum.

Mick stood by the door while the photo guy took pictures of paper towel rolls and stacks and stacks of stuff. He photographed the floor, the ceiling, and the walls as if Spiderman might have been the perpetrator. Getting the items out and sealing them in bags strengthened Mick's impression of the team as bomb squad detonators. They worked carefully and methodically, photographing each item before carefully placing it in a bag. Watching them take out the stolen items reminded Mick of watching a team of doctors carrying a newborn to the NICU.

When they were finished, Mick looked around the room. Every flat surface now had a film of white dust: the shelves, the walls, even the floors. Every place a finger could have touched or a foot could have walked had been checked. It looked like the home of Charlie Brown's friend Pig Pen from *Peanuts*. They put some yellow tape over the door (not dusty like the roll in Mick's trunk had been) and watched as Jackson locked the door.

Mick walked out with the team, then made his way back into the building to talk to his most important witness times two. Jackson was standing in the hall with Barber, whose expression was serious. Jackson's was somber. They both turned into Jackson's office.

"My client feels like he might have some additional information," Barber said, prodding Jackson like a parent encouraging their child to say thank you for a candy.

"I guess I didn't want to believe it. I didn't want to think that Augustine was capable of doing something like this. He's been with me for twelve years. I know his family. When I saw the man running away, I thought there was something familiar about him. I just couldn't bring myself to admit it might have been Augustine I saw running away that night. I was going to tell you even before I found the stolen things."

Barber added, "My client wanted time to think about what he saw, to be absolutely certain before he made a statement."

"And you are sure that the man you saw running away from Edie Spence's house was Augustine Morales?" Mick asked.

Jackson looked at Barber again, who did what he was there for, counseled. "Jack, you have to tell him everything you know. There is no protection you can give to this guy. This is as serious as a heart attack. Tell him what you saw."

Jackson nodded and straightened. "I think it was Augustine Morales I saw running away that night. No, I can go farther. I am positive it was Augustine Morales running away that night."

"Do you know where Mr. Morales is right now? Is he here at National?" Mick asked.

"No, I checked. His truck isn't in the parking lot."

The three of them turned to look out the window. The happy, primary-colored crime van was parked there. Stephanie Gallagher was leaning against her car. How'd she already get tipped off? John Mason was pulling in to the space vacated by the van. A few other cars were in the lot. What was not there was Augustine's blue truck.

Mick headed out to the parking lot to intercept Mason and fill him in on the treasure in the paper towels.

Stephanie was still smiling when she pulled into the National Safety parking lot. The van they used for anti-crime events was driving out. She had seen it before when she had done an article on child safety.

It could be they were doing an event here, a place where they make seat belts.

But she could tell by the people hurriedly exiting the building, looking back at it as if it might be following them, that something else was going on. She saw the young girl who always called her "ma'am." The girl would be unlikely to tell her anything, but if she thought Stephanie was already in the know she might want to talk about it.

"Wow. I can't believe what just happened. Can you?"

"I know. All this time the stuff was hidden *here*. It's unbelievable. What do you think it means?"

Hidden stuff. *They must have found the Reluctant Robber's stash,* Stephanie said to herself.

"I guess it means there is a murderer working at National Safety," Stephanie said, and this time she wasn't trying to lure the girl into saying something; she was saying what she was thinking. The girl's face froze like she was holding a note in church.

"I just want to get out of here. I can't believe it. You know, there aren't that many people who have a key to the storage room, and I know them all. I just can't believe it. Anyway, the office is closed, so you can't go in now," she said as she clicked her car door open.

"Yeah, thanks," Stephanie said and moved out of the way so the receptionist could pull out and get away from the place.

She noticed Mick's car in the lot on the other side of the van. She could have been drinking a glass of wine and flirting with Mark Lavelle instead of leaning against her car in a parking lot.

After fifteen minutes or so, she saw Mick come out with a team that looked like the bomb squad—if Forsyth had a bomb squad. They were wearing blue booties over their shoes, but they didn't stop to pull them off. They proceeded to the van, carrying packages in front of them like they contained nitroglycerin. It took the three people and their packages another ten minutes to load up and drive away.

John Mason arrived in a squad car and Mick walked toward him. She walked between Mick and the car.

"Were you having a crime prevention lecture here at National, or is something going on?" she asked him.

Mick waited till he was close enough to whisper to her before he replied.

"So far, what we are saying"—by which he meant, "what you can print"—"is that we have discovered some items that may have been from the recent burglaries."

"Oh my God! So Jack Jackson was right. He did see someone running away in a National Safety jacket."

Mick was shaking his head at her like she was a kid reaching for a cookie he didn't want her to have. "No, we can't be certain about the things we found until we have time to examine them."

"You found them, the Forsyth police found them?" she asked.

"No, the discovery was made by someone who works at National Safety. I didn't find them. They were found in the building."

Good thing she wasn't playing hide-and-go-seek with him. She'd never be able to find anything with the clues he was giving. But it did not take an investigative reporter or a detective to reach the conclusion that she had been right all along. The Reluctant Robber was someone who was being laid off at National Safety. She thought about the relief that was going to bring to Lacey Thomas. Her friend Adam Moore was a victim, nothing more.

"That's good news for Lacey. She was worried you were going to hurt Adam Moore's reputation or, worse, try to pin this on him."

Mick looked at her and then at the car. She had the feeling he was thinking, *How do I get from here to there?*

"Stephanie, the investigation isn't over yet. Like I said from the beginning, we are going to look at everything, leave no stone unturned. Speaking of which, I'd better get going to see what *has* turned up. If I find anything, I'll call you; you know, local press first, and all."

"OK, thanks. I guess I'll be talking to you later, then. See ya."

Released, he turned and got in the car.

Stephanie was about to do the same when she saw Jack Jackson and Trey Barber striding out of the building. They were both big men, but now Jackson seemed somehow smaller, diminished, even from across the parking lot. This had taken a toll on him: finding the bodies, suspecting it was someone he worked with, the investigation. Barber still looked like he could rip off his suit and tie and live in the mountains, but Jackson, he didn't look like the big football hero he had been—or even the president of the company.

"Mr. Jackson, Mr. Barber! Can I talk to you?" Stephanie called.

Both men looked up, startled. She used their slight pause to walk quickly up to them.

"We were just leaving," Barber said, stating the obvious.

Jackson was quiet, not his usual jovial self. Understandable.

"Oh, I see that, but could I just ask a couple of quick questions?"

Barber seemed to consider before replying, cocking his head at an angle on his giant neck.

"We don't have too much to say. You should check with the Forsyth police. They are handling the investigation."

Stephanie fell in step with them. "Oh, I know. I saw Michael McKay a minute ago. But I wanted to see how Mr. Jackson felt, finding the stolen items here. I guess you were right about seeing that jacket."

"We don't want to say anything that might jeopardize the investigation," Barber said, trying to get away from her.

"I feel terrible, rotten. I didn't want to believe it could be somebody from here, but when I found those things, I knew. This is like a nightmare I can't wake up from," Jackson said, rubbing the top of his head like he was surprised to find his hair there. He did look distraught. Still, she had the sense that he wanted to talk as much as Barber didn't want him to.

Stephanie reached out and put her hand on his arm. "This must be so terrible for you. I can't even imagine."

He stopped to look at her. She almost blurted out the question that sprang to mind when she looked at him: "Have you been crying?" He seemed crushed by his circumstances. So much for nothing ever happening in Forsyth.

She felt a wave of pity for him, but not so much that she was going to get in her car and let him go without any comments.

"I know you are exhausted, so I will keep this real short. Better to talk to me now than have reporters hounding you later." His hair was pointing in all directions from the rubbing it had taken. It made her realize that she had never seen him, well, disheveled.

"What is it you want to know? There isn't much I can tell you, not because I am trying to keep stuff from you. I'd rather talk to someone from the *Bee*, that's for sure. It's just that I don't really know anything."

Trey Barber was trying to move Jackson along with him. It made Stephanie feel like she was back at Camp Longhorn, playing tug-of-war—a game she never lost.

"Okay, I just need some easy stuff. Who found the stolen items?" She waited while he remembered he was paying Trey Barber and glanced at him before answering. Barber seemed annoyed but was pretty good at hiding it. It just so happened she was better at detecting feelings than he was at hiding them.

And she had already won the tug-of-war. Jackson had come to a complete stop in the parking lot. She didn't even offer a hint of a smile, though; she kept a look of concern on her face.

"The stolen items?" Jackson repeated. She nodded. "The stolen items? I found them. I wasn't sure what it was at first, but I remembered your story about the guy who had his license returned, and I recognized his name on a credit card in the wallet. I called the police, and they came and checked out everything. I'm just glad they are going to catch the guy. I hate that he works here, but at least now we know, and there won't be a killer on the loose."

Trey Barber put his arm over Jackson's shoulder and directed him toward his car.

Having gotten at least part of what she wanted, she could afford to be gracious. "Thanks, I hope you can get some rest, now. I know you are right. It will be easier for every one when the killer is caught."

Trey Barber gave her a salute, maybe acknowledging her tiny parking lot victory, and she returned the gesture before turning back to get into her own car.

CHAPTER FIFTY-EIGHT

Mick filled in Mason, radioed Austin, and told him their destination. Then he told Mason to put on the lights and the siren. He wanted to get there fast. There was that. But it was a race for justice, too. It seemed like the least he could do for Edie Spence and Adam Moore.

He touched his holster. Driving with the siren and lights was rare. Pulling his gun was like a leprechaun sighting. He could count on his hand the number of times he'd had to use it. Maybe today would add to that count.

Mick and Mason turned down Live Oak Street. They could hear the wail of Tyler Austin's sirens in the distance like a wounded animal responding to their own wails. Mick felt a little adrenaline rush, a powerful mixture of excitement and fear. He was on his way to bringing a stone-cold killer to justice.

When he pulled up in front of the Morales house, the stone-cold killer was out in front, attaching training wheels to a pink bike so tiny its rider must have just hopped off a tricycle. A little girl with a ponytail was solemnly offering a screwdriver and a wrench. She looked up wide-eyed as they pulled up, sirens sounding.

Mick and Mason got out of the car and walked toward the surprised-looking duo. Before anyone could utter a word, Austin came to a screeching halt in front of the house. All four of them turned to watch this new development. And they were not alone. A few people had come out of their houses to see what was happening. The door of the Morales house also popped open, spilling out a couple of boys.

Mick leaned over and looked at the upside-down bike, stuck on its back like an immobilized turtle.

"Hey, how's it going? Nice bike," Mick said to the little girl. "We need to talk to you, Mr. Morales."

Mick could see the surprise in the guy's eyes. "Is something wrong?" he asked.

Mick wanted to get him out of there, away from the little girl and the other spectators. "We just have a few questions for you. Would you come with us?"

Everybody knew this was a formality. He was going to go with them.

"Sure, sure, OK. Nita, you go inside with your brothers. Papa will fix the bike later."

The girl did not move until he gave her a little nudge. Then, momentum carried her up to her equally scared brothers. And they were right to be afraid. Mick was here to change their lives, and not for the better.

Once in the car, Mick read Morales his rights.

"But what is this about? I haven't done anything."

"Well, there's no problem, then. We'll just ask you our questions and get everything straightened out," Mick said. For Mick it could have not gone better. The guy was even wearing a National Safety jacket.

Augustine Morales did not seem to believe that was what was going to happen any more than Mick did, but they drove the rest of the way in silence, participating in the fairy tale that all would be well.

At the station it was lights, camera, action time. Despite the popular idea that lots of criminals get away because of some technical police mistake, that was a rare occurrence. The fact that it did happen at all made it vitally important to have everything on video.

Once they settled into a small interview room for the video recording, Mick backtracked and asked Morales if he had understood his rights. Did he want an attorney, an interpreter, a butcher, a baker, a candlestick maker? It could have been a party, but Morales said no, no attorney, no interpreter. Mick was hoping for the grand prize, a confession, with details only the killer would know.

Morales voiced his confusion as if he were reading from the interview script. "I don't understand. There must be some mistake. I have done nothing."

"Well then, you don't have anything to worry about." Mick replied.

Mason's first comment seemed to startle them both. "You're lying, Mr. Morales," he said.

There was a reason people used the good cop, bad cop method of interrogation: it worked. All of life was driven by the carrot and the stick.

This was the same. They wanted him to be afraid of Mason and want to help Mick. It required finesse to be the good cop. It went against nature. You had a guy sitting in front of you who you knew had done something horrible, like this guy killing two people. You wanted to pound him. That was instinct. Being good to someone who could commit an act like that went against the grain.

"We want to talk to you about some recent thefts. Just tell us what you know about them, and we can clear things up and send you home to finish with that bike," Mick said.

"But I don't know about that. I didn't steal anything. You can ask Mr. Jackson, I work for him for a long time. Ask him. He'll tell you. I don't steal."

Mick was not surprised to hear him say this. He wanted to hit him with stealing first and then move to the murders. The guy might give in and admit to the thefts to show how he was playing along, but continue to deny the killings. Mason reached into a thick manila folder and pulled out a photograph of the stolen items.

"Ever seen these things before?" he asked.

Augustine obligingly looked at the photo. Looked back at them and said, "No."

"No? Well, they were found where you hid them."

Mick's turn. "Look, we know you did this. We have the evidence." He patted the folder in front of Mason. "Now, I can help you. I can say you cooperated. I can say you were under stress. I can say you never meant to shoot anybody. But if you don't cooperate I can't help you. This is Texas, and I don't need to tell you what can happen to you here. You know. Save your family the pain and tell us what happened."

Augustine exclaimed something in Spanish so Mick asked him again, "Do you want an interpreter?"

"No. I don't know why you are asking me this. I don't know anything about who killed those people."

"OK, OK. Can you tell us where you were on that night? We can clear this up."

Now the guy looked determined. Answer this question correctly and he could go home. He put his head down, concentrating. He used his fingers to count something out. Mick watched him. Who felt more desperate here? It was a toss-up.

"Thursday, I think it is on Thursday that I drove after work to pick something up. I had to go to a place and wait for a man to bring some new supplies. I think that was on that day. Maybe Mr. Jackson will know. You can call him."

Mick suspected that the fact that Jackson hadn't said he saw Morales running from the scene might have given him the idea that he was being protected. He might believe that Jackson would lie for him. Unfortunately for him, finding the stolen items had been enough for Jackson to see things clearly. There would be no more protection.

"Well, see, that's all we need. You tell us the name of the man you met, and we'll talk to him, and then we're done with you. All we need is his confirmation that he met you at that time."

Mick smiled as he said it, but Morales was already shaking his head. *Got you now*, Mick thought.

"No. I went there but the man, he did not come. I waited, but he did not come, so I went home."

Mason's turn. "Oh, so you want us to believe that you went to meet someone, but he wasn't there. We should just take your word for it? Was there somebody else there? Did someone else see you? If they didn't, that's not a very good alibi, friend."

"No, I was there. I went to the address. I waited. Yes."

Mick shook his head sadly at this news. "That's a problem. We don't know where you were the night of the murders, and we found things stolen from other homes in your possession. It makes it look like you were there. I want to help you, but it really is better if you tell us what happened.

"I personally don't think you meant to kill anyone. I think you panicked when the pizza delivery kid showed up. They saw you and you reacted without thinking. You were never planning on killing anyone. It just happened. I understand how things happen when you are under pressure, a mistake. I'll help you explain how it was."

Mason turned to Mick and said, "We don't have to help him. All the tests that we've been running are going to prove he was there. I don't want to help him. Let's wait and get the proof to nail him. I think that's what he deserves."

Mick waited for Morales to realize the trap he was in and start talking, but he wouldn't budge. He was supposed to be picking something up that night, and he had never seen the loot found in the midst of his supplies. Mr. Jackson would help him. Those were the three things he repeated, no matter what they said. They could not knock him off his story. They were just going to have to wait him out.

As soon as he could, Mick looked over the items that had been found in the cleaning closet. He wore his gloves, even though contamination at this point was irrelevant. Everything had already been checked. No mistakes.

He knew the list of items by heart now. He had only seen them listed on a piece of paper. The reality of the items made him feel like he had found some old friend that he had thought was gone.

He opened the baggie with a wallet in it, Martin Colby's wallet he knew from the description. He spread the wallet, opened like a frog to dissect in a biology class. He found what he knew would be there: two credit cards; an old, yellow picture of two smiling boys; a brand-new, bright picture of Samantha; and a card with the date for his next eye doctor appointment on it. And, of course, he found what was not here; the slot for his driver's license was bare, having been returned by the remorseful Reluctant Robber. There was a receipt wadded up and stuck where there would have been cash.

But something about the receipt didn't seem right to Mick. He thought back to his interviews with Colby at his house. It hadn't been the tidiest house he'd ever seen, but he couldn't imagine the old man balling up a receipt and jamming it into his wallet.

He smoothed it out on his desk and studied it. It was from a store in an outlet mall about thirty miles away, in Camden. He made a copy of the receipt, grabbed a National Safety brochure, and picked up his keys.

He called out to Mason, showed him what he had found, and they both took off at a trot for the car. Let the evidence techs look for evidence. He was going to go ID the thief and, more importantly, the murderer.

In the car, Mick's earlier ambivalence gave way to the euphoria of being close to solving the case.

"I guess that calendar was his calling card, almost as if he wanted to get caught or something," Mason said as Mick drove, eager to get there, eager to finish this.

Mick appreciated John Mason not mentioning the obvious, that Mick had given up on the National employee in favor of some love-lorn teenagers on a crime spree. He wasn't one of those guys who wanted all the credit for solving it. The end result was the important thing.

"Yeah. It's too bad Jackson seemed so shaky in his identification. He was so damned unsure that it was hard to have any faith in what he saw. And who knows about the calendar? That could have been dropped at any time. It still might turn out not to be related to the murders.

"You know, I've been meaning to come over here to the mall and pick up some new shirts. If we find the guy, and I'm pretty positive we will, I'm coming back down here and buying a dozen of them!" He felt happy and relieved. Case almost closed. No need to go to Tiffany Hudson and tell her her brother was a criminal.

Then he thought about the bikes in the driveway at the Morales house, the woman and the little girl waiting on the porch. It would be hard for them. He knew that. The murdered people would not be the only victims here. The murderer's family would pay a high price, too. And for what? All in all, the money stolen and the items taken were not worth more than seven or eight hundred dollars—and that was being generous.

He conjured up the faces of the people who would find some relief in the arrest. Tiffany Hudson and Sean Spence, old Mr. Colby . . . and Jackson, of course, he could rest easier knowing that the man who came inches from killing him was gone.

CHAPTER FIFTY-NINE

Mick and Mason strode into the sporting goods store like racewalkers, badges at the ready. They passed by barrels of basketballs and shelves of baseball caps, headed for the manager's office.

The manager looked like he had just left a college campus or maybe even high school. He was wearing khaki pants and flip-flops, bouncing to music from his earphones while he scanned a computer. They were in a hurry and he was not.

His face registered surprise and alarm when Mick tapped him on the shoulder and showed him his badge. "Sorry, dude, I didn't hear you. What's up? Somebody steal something?"

Mick was pulling the receipt out of his jacket pocket, carefully, like it was nitroglycerin. The kid stood up, pulling the plugs from his ears. Mick handed him the receipt, safe and secure in its plastic bag.

The kid looked at it and looked back at Mick with questioning eyes.

He handed it back and asked, "What can I do for you, sir?"

Mick was pleased to be elevated from "dude" to "sir." He wanted this mini-manager to take this seriously. Because it was serious.

"Well, for a start, you can tell me what the item purchased is, exactly."

The kid nodded and took another look at the paper resting on Mick's palm.

"It's for Nike Five Hundreds. They are our biggest-selling shoes right now. We sell so many we can hardly keep them in stock."

"Shoes," repeated Mick. "Can you tell me who bought them?"

"No sir. Not on a cash sale like this. Sometimes the customer will give us his email so we can let him know about upcoming events, but this one didn't."

Mick pulled out his National Safety Brochure. "Do you see the person who bought the shoes in this brochure?" he asked pointing to the National Safety brochure.

The kid shook his head. "Dude, we get like lots of people in here. I don't pay that much attention. That guy could have been in here. I'm not saying he wasn't, all I'm saying is I wouldn't remember him. Sir."

They could get a search warrant and check out Augustine's house for the shoes. But they were in a hurry. Mick had jumped out of the car with victory in sight and he didn't want to get back in and go through the red tape of another search warrant.

Then it popped into his head. This was no time to be in a rush, no matter how compelling it seemed. *Think carefully*, he reminded himself.

"Do you have surveillance cameras?"

He felt a wave of disappointment as the kid shook his head.

"We don't have them in the store. Anyway, most of the crime we get around here is car break-ins. You know, people put their bags in the car and go into another store. We were having a lot of those kind of break-ins. They put the signs in the parking lot when they put up the cameras out there."

Mick was already backing out of the office, carefully replacing the receipt in his jacket pocket. They racewalked over to the mall manager's office, which consisted of two cubby holes with desks down a long gray hall past the family and handicapped restroom.

The manager had on a polo shirt stretched to the limit over his belly and tucked into pants that had nothing to do with his natural waist. It was as if he had been waiting for the opportunity to be helpful to law enforcement personnel. Mick was afraid he was going to salute them when they showed him their badges and asked about parking lot security.

"I can set you up right here. Just give me the time you want to see, and we can look at the camera closest to the sporting goods store. Now, the perp might have parked in a different lot. All our lots are numbered. Just let me know what you need to see and I can show you."

Mick and Mason exchanged a glance when he said "perp," but the man was helpful enough.

Within minutes Mick was sitting in the chair staring at a screen with Mason hanging over his shoulder. The images on the screen were jerky, like the notebook cartoon Mick and his brother had made when they were kids. The people hung for a fraction of a second before moving on to the next frame.

Mick was waiting to spot Augustine's truck pulling in. He could see the time stamp getting closer and closer to the time of purchase. No truck. No Morales. Someone caught his eye, though. He thought he recognized one of the people in the parking lot.

"Look," he pointed, but Mason didn't catch it. They rewound and went back in time and watched people they had just seen exiting their cars going in reverse, walking backward to their cars and climbing back in.

"The kid?" Mason asked. "I don't recognize him."

"I do. I saw him at the high school. That's Jackson's kid. I'm pretty sure anyway."

They watched as he went forward again into the sporting goods store. They went through the next half hour watching for him to exit the store and when he did he was carrying a shoebox.

Mick looked at Mason. "Are you thinking what I'm thinking?"

Mason replied, "If you are thinking this kid would have access to the hiding place in the cleaning supply closet, then yeah, I am thinking what you are thinking."

Mick added up the facts: the National Safety jacket, the calendar, the idea that these crimes seemed to be the work of a young person.

"Christ! The little bastard was running down Martin Colby's street right before he got his license back. I remember now. One of the other guys said this guy fell, but really he was kneeling down to slip the license under the newspaper. When one of the boys notices him down on the ground, he pretends to be hurt. It makes sense."

"Yeah, it makes sense, except why would a little rich kid like that be out stealing? His daddy could buy him shoes any day of the week. He didn't need to steal to get them."

"Maybe it was the thrill of getting away with something. I don't know. All I do know is that this receipt ties him to the Reluctant Robber's stash. I'm not sure if Jackson saw him or not. Let's see if he's still got the shoes. We'll have to check his age. Jackson will be screaming at us and at Rainy if we question him and he's underage. Trey Barber is going to earn his money this month, that's for sure."

In the car driving back to Forsyth, the reality of what they had found hit Mick. If the Jackson kid was the Reluctant Robber, then he had to be the murderer, too.

Mick thought about the kid hanging back behind his father when he'd run into them at the school. It was hard to imagine that quiet kid taking down two people with such lethal accuracy. On the way to the outlet mall, he had felt jubilant, but now he felt weighed down by the certain sadness that was coming closer to him with every mile he drove.

He called Rainy to fill him in on the afternoon. Rainy, too, seemed even sadder than usual. If only it could have been a love triangle, or a drug deal gone bad . . . even a cult murder was better than what was going to descend on Forsyth if what they suspected was proven true. A rich, privileged kid out on a stealing spree.

He thought about the shock for Jackson and his family, the pain they would go through. It crossed his mind that Jackson might have recognized the shooter as his son, but he dismissed the thought. If Jackson had any suspicions about his kid's involvement he would never have showed them the Reluctant Robber's stash of stolen items.

When they pulled into the parking lot, Rainy was waiting for them with the warrant. He was somber.

"You're sure? There isn't some other way this could be explained? We don't want to make a mistake that could ruin this kid's life unless we are really sure."

Mick didn't bother to answer. He wanted there to be an alternate answer just as much as Rainy did. But there was no other explanation. This time he knew. They had found the Reluctant Robber.

They drove to Jackson's house. And what a house it was, bigger than anything else in town. It really was the house on the hill, gleaming in the sunshine like nothing bad could ever happen there. But Mick knew he was about to change all that.

CHAPTER SIXTY

Mick rang the doorbell at the Jackson's house. It was the kind of place where you wouldn't be shocked to have a butler answer the door. Instead, they could hear an excited *woof, woof* and the sound of paws hitting the door.

Jackson answered the door, pulling back on the big black Lab's collar. "Come on in. Let me get him settled. Come on, Rex. Be a good boy!"

The dog sauntered off to a big round pillow in the corner but kept his eyes on the visitors in case they wanted to play. Jackson looked at them with the same expectancy.

"So, I guess this means you made an arrest," he said.

Mick met his gaze but it wasn't easy.

"No sir. We haven't made an arrest yet. Is your son at home?"

"My son? What's he got to do with anything? He didn't see anything. Why do you want to talk to him?"

"I am sorry to inform you that we are here to take Charles Boylan Jackson into custody. We are charging him with theft of property."

Mick really was sorry to have to deliver such devastating news, and he could tell Jackson wasn't taking it well. Who would? It occurred to him that they might have a problem with Jackson. Taking the kid out was going to be traumatic enough, but taking him out under duress with screaming and fighting would be worse.

He wanted to convey that to Jackson before things got out of hand. Jackson was holding up his hands to stop them from moving further into the house.

"You're wrong. There must be some mistake! Augustine stole those things. My son doesn't know anything about it! You're making a mistake. Please!"

Rex the dog got up and barked at the strangers he had been happy to see only seconds ago. Now he sensed they were not friends at all, and he paced in front of them, barking.

The commotion brought out Mrs. Jackson. She looked confused at the melee in her hall. Mick wanted to defuse the situation as much as possible. This was one of those times when he could say, "Things can go easy or they can go hard. Your choice." He wanted to let the parents know that this was going to happen. There was nothing they could do but make it worse.

"We are going to take Charles into custody. He is leaving with us. If there is a mistake, he'll be back home. Soon."

Just then the kid came loping down the stairs, pulling out earplugs to better hear what was going on. He stopped when he saw Mick. You didn't need a degree in psychology to read the guilt on his face. If Mick had a sliver of a doubt, the look on Chip Jackson's face swept it away. There was a second of silence when all the adults standing below him in the hall looked at him on the stairs. It was as if they had all read the same sign. His mother gasped. "No, No!"

Mick was worried about her, but the old man was taking it worse. He pressed against the wall and just went down with his feet straight out in front of him. The dog came over, puzzled by what looked like playful behavior, but even he could pick up the switch in the room. Jackson tried to push the dog away.

Mick nodded to Mason. He did not want to take his eyes off the kid on the stairs. He was why they were here. Mason leaned down and tried to pull the big man up but he outweighed Mason by about fifty pounds, and he was dead weight at this point.

Mick motioned the kid down the last couple of stairs. Coming down, Chip reminded Mick of the scarecrow in the *Wizard of Oz*. His legs were giving way, but he made it. Mick did what he had to do.

"Charles Boylan Jackson, you are under arrest for theft of property. You have the right to remain silent . . ."

While he was getting the rest of his statement out, the kid started crying.

"I didn't kill those people. I would never hurt anyone. I did steal stuff, but I never hurt anyone. I made sure of that. I took some stuff, but I didn't take everything. I was trying to be fair. And I never would have hurt anyone. I don't know how it happened. Honest, I don't!"

Mick had finished reading the kid his rights and asked, "Do you understand?"

"Yes, yes, I understand. But you've got to believe me, I didn't kill anyone. I don't know how the gun got out of the cleaning closet. I don't know!"

The kid turned to his parents. His father was on the floor, with Mason trying to pull him up. Chip turned to his mother. "Mom! I didn't do it!"

It sounded to Mick like Colly saying she didn't leave her bike out in the rain.

Mason was still pulling on Jackson, trying to get him to his feet, but Mrs. Jackson sprang into action.

"Honey, don't say anything else. They can't make you say anything. Don't talk till we get in touch with Trey. He'll straighten this all out. Don't worry." She glanced at her husband on the floor. "Jackie, Jackie, get up. We need to call Trey right away." She turned back to Mick. "Mr. McKay, I know that you have to take Chip to clear this up, but can I go with him? He's just a kid."

Mick was shaking his head. "No, I'm sorry. He has to come with us alone, but you can probably see him in a while. Come on, son. Let's go."

Once Mick had had to rescue a cat from a tree. It happens; every cop and fireman has done it. When Mick got his hands on the high climber, he thought it would scratch him, but the poor thing was just shaking. Mick handed the trembling kitten back to its owner, and yes, it was an old lady with a hairnet, to complete the cliché. That was how it felt now when he put his hand on Chip Jackson's arm to steer him out the door. Only this time he wasn't doing a kindness. The sight of his son being propelled toward the door roused Jackson. He threw Mason's hands off of him and stood up.

"I saw him! I saw Augustine that night. That's why I didn't try and shoot him. I could tell it was Augustine. Charlie wasn't there. He doesn't have anything to do with this. You are confusing him, scaring him. That's why he said those things. Just leave him alone."

Mrs. Jackson moved to his side. Mick understood their panic. The best that could happen to Chip Jackson would be life without the possibility of parole. Both the parents had started to cry, but the kid was silent, now in wide-eyed shock.

The father was still insisting they should take Augustine instead, like they were boarding lifeboats on the *Titanic*. Women and children should stay here safe, and they should drag Augustine's ass off to jail. The kid was going to have to pay for what he had done. And in the state of Texas, he was a man, not a kid.

The wife followed them out onto the front porch, which looked like a *Southern Living* magazine cover. She was crying into her phone as they secured the kid in the back of the squad car.

Mason rode shotgun with Austin, and Mick got back in his car to drive to the courthouse. Mrs. Jackson ran down the driveway after the car carrying her son to justice and uncertainty. Mick had to pass her on the long drive. He was afraid he was going to have to drive over some the flowers lining the way to avoid hitting her, but she stopped to let him pass. This could be the worst day of her life, Mick thought, watching her in the rearview mirror.

It had not been the great day he was anticipating when he had found that receipt either. He had just taken in the person responsible for the brutal deaths of two people. Why did he feel like he was the bad guy in this scenario? At least the little girl with the pink bike would be OK. One family safe, one family devastated.

He took some small comfort in the fact that the rest of the day would be easier, at least for him. Now it would all be strictly by the book. They would go through the procedure, step by emotionless step. Mick was confident that Trey Barber would be there when they got there, but he would know the steps, too. He would follow procedure, step-by-step.

There would not be the devastating turmoil like what he had experienced at the house that was disappearing behind him. They would never return to normal, but for Mick, the return to normal was only possible by apprehending the killer. He had done that now.

CHAPTER SIXTY-ONE

Stephanie watched Trey Barber jump out of his car and run to the courthouse. He was a big man and she would have bet he would be a slow, lumbering runner. But she would have bet wrong. He sprinted past her with a speed she would not have imagined such a big man was capable of. She fell in behind him, anxious to see what the hurry was. She was on the same team as Trey Barber, although he didn't know it yet.

With the arrest of the maintenance man at the plant, she would dust off her Reluctant Robber stories. She was already planning what she would say about the poor guy, driven to desperation by economic conditions he could not control, turning to robbery only after exhausting all his other options, committing a horrible crime because he was pushed to it—but pushed to murder? It would drive Mick crazy, and she had to concede he'd have a point. It was hard to see how any economic straits justified the taking of two innocent lives.

At least it looked like Trey Barber was taking it very seriously. Good for Jack Jackson. He was going to provide for his employee's defense, at least initially. She was hurrying to catch up with Barber, but to no avail. He took the courthouse steps two at a time and was through the doors before she made it to the steps.

Once inside she saw Rainy hurrying down the hallway. Trey Barber running was unusual. Rainy running seemed impossible. He was the slowest, most measured man she could think of. It had to be something big to get him to run. Of course the arrest of the only double murder suspect in Forsyth history might just do it. And so far, she was the only press person. She knew they wouldn't give a statement until Rainy was ready. She tucked herself into a corner, texted Tom, and waited.

Mick started on the processing, fingerprinting, paperwork. Watching the kid get his picture taken for the mugshot made Mick think these pictures were a poor substitute for the prom pictures that would have been taken just a few weeks from now. The kid still had a dazed look on his face, as if he couldn't believe what was happening.

Mick could hear Trey Barber trying to wrangle the kid's parents in the other room. He said a silent prayer that they would pay attention to their lawyer and let the process continue. Rainy was calling to make sure they would have a courtroom available. So far, they were only charging him with the burglaries, but Mick was waiting for Rainy to make the decision about the rest of the charges. They would probably not file until tomorrow, just to make sure they had everything lined up.

No matter what they filed initially, Mick knew the press would put together the entire picture. The Forsyth police department would be in the news in a positive way. They had found the killer of two innocent people, the thief who had been sneaking into their homes and stealing from them.

The arrest had not brought him the feeling of elation he had thought it would. He felt drained, waiting now for the kid to clear through processing and for the other shoe to drop with the murder charges being filed. He was waiting through what he thought would be a long day. Little did he know it was just beginning.

Stephanie was in her hall corner, waiting for Rainy to come out and tell the press what was happening. So far the press was just her and a KLIF radio station reporter, a guy in his seventies who was becoming even more obsolete than the *Bee*.

When she saw him straighten up and push away from the wall, she knew he could see Rainy coming down the hall with his statement. The elderly reporter was pulling out his microphone, so she powered up her laptop: dueling media.

When Rainy came into view, she was surprised at how dour he looked. From the expression on his face, she wouldn't have been shocked to hear him say an asteroid was crashing into Earth and they all had only moments to live. She thought he might have been more triumphant about catching the killer. When he started to speak, she understood.

"We have arrested Charles Boylan Jackson, eighteen, in connection with the burglaries at"—and here he listed the addresses, one after the other, including the address of Martin Colby. "Mr. Jackson is being processed, and we are continuing our investigation at this time."

Stephanie raised her hand to ask about murder charges being filed, but Rainey's only reply was, "No questions at this time."

Rainy was already fast-walking down the hall before she could get out the last words. She turned, stunned, to the KLIF reporter. He was looking at his microphone as if it had morphed into a snake in his hands. How could that be?

He turned and hurried out, and she called Tom to tell him there was going to be a big story for the *Bee*.

He was as shocked as she was when she related what had happened.

"You mean the kid did it? Holy shit! Stay down there. Send me what you've got. They won't have to charge him with the murders to hold him, but I'm sure they will do it soon. They won't want to leave that hanging. Man, that kid had everything going for him. Why the hell did he do it? Thrills? He couldn't have needed the money."

Stephanie had no answers; she was just as mystified. She thought back to what her father had said about the wolf being at Jackson's door. Maybe the kid had felt it breathing down his neck.

"Yeah, I'll hang tight and see what else we come up with."

"Okay, keep me posted. I'll be ready to run whatever you give me."

She had a feeling that she would not be tucked in her corner all alone for long, and she was right about that. She started hearing the helicopters overhead about a half hour later. This was going to be a big story: "Son of big business owner charged with theft and murder." Forsyth was about to erupt like a volcano. Life can turn on a dime, her father used to say.

This time it was a very bad turn for the Jackson family. She thought about her interview with the grandparents, Rusty and Donnetta. For them, this would surely be a reminder of their earlier tragedy. Their son lost at such a young age and in such a senseless way, and now their grandson, named for his uncle, involved in an equally senseless tragedy. She hoped Mick knew the kid's background. Suicides did sometimes run in families: look at the Hemingways.

She thought about her alma mater's motto, "Ye shall know the truth and the truth shall set ye free." Either way, the truth of this story was not going to provide freedom for anyone, and she doubted that even all the Jackson's money could help their boy now. The town would not forgive a young man who was rich and privileged.

If Adam Moore had been the perpetrator instead of the victim, the town consensus might have been that he was a poor boy who had been neglected. Maybe if they had acted on his behalf, this crime might have been prevented. But for the scion of one of the wealthiest Forsyth families, there would be no pity.

Did she pity young Chip Jackson? Was that going to be the story angle for her? What Mick McKay had said about her was true; she had been rooting for the Reluctant Robber and sorry he had been pushed to do what he had done. But no one was pushing this rich kid. The entire thing made no sense, and she imagined people shaking their heads saying just that: "senseless crime."

Feeling restless, Stephanie decided to go find a better spot to pick up on what was happening. The courthouse complex also contained the police department offices. She could walk around the building and check out what was happening there. She could always scurry back to her place if she heard anything about Rainy making another statement.

She walked through the side parking lot to the police station entrance. Inside she could see a young policeman sitting behind the glass partition. He did not look bored. He looked like he was on high alert, waiting for an intruder, an invasion, some kind of trouble. And trouble was coming, but not from her side of the partition. She could hear someone shouting down the hall. She recognized the voice as Trey Barber's. Two surprises from him in one day: first his running speed, and now the power of his voice.

"For heaven's sake! Just shut up! You are making things worse, can't you see that? You screaming you did it is the same as announcing that you are so convinced your kid is guilty that the only way to save him is to confess yourself. Just shut up and let me handle this. For once in your life, do what someone else tells you to do. I am trying to get better legal counsel for Chip, but I can't do a damn thing until you settle down and shut up. Please, Jack, listen to me. Let me do my job. I want to help Chip, and what you are doing is not helping!"

Stephanie could only imagine what Jackson was going through. She quickly stepped back outside and around to the seldom-used side door. She had a hunch that Barber would use it today to avoid the press and the curious.

So she was standing there when Barber did indeed push through the door. He did not look happy to see her. "Hey, Stephanie, I'm kind of in a hurry here. I think you can appreciate that if you were here for Rainy's statement."

"Hello, Mr. Barber. Yes, I heard the statement, but I also heard you talking to your client. I gather he wants to confess to the murders?" she asked it as a question, but she knew he would know that she had heard the discussion.

"Well, as you know, anything I was discussing with my client is privileged information. But besides that, I am sure you would not want to take advantage of a distraught parent."

Stephanie knew that there were lots of news stories that could hurt someone, and as for the privilege, in this case it didn't exist. You cannot shout in the hall of a public building and call the shout privileged. Barber was trying to bluff. She didn't call him on it.

"OK, what *can* you tell me? Who are you getting to represent Charles Jackson? What are they charging him with? Do you expect him to get out on bail?" She waited to see which question he would answer.

"I don't know who we are going to get to represent him. That's why I'm in such a hurry. So far, they have charged him with theft of property, so I would expect him to get bail after his hearing. I think they will hold him for the whole forty-eight hours. I am not sure if there will be additional charges. Stephanie, he is just a kid, a confused kid. Remember that when you write about him, will you? I don't have to tell you about the power of the press; just have some compassion for a kid who may have made a big mistake. I have to go. I'll see you later."

With that, he took off running toward the parking lot.

CHAPTER SIXTY-TWO

Mick walked into the interview room where Chip Jackson sat. It was a couple of clicks bigger than a closet. There were three office chairs and a small table. Chip was slumped down in one of the chairs like a melting snowman; another twenty minutes and all that would be left would be a puddle on the floor.

"Hey, Chip. Need anything? Something to drink? Something to eat?" The kid barely looked at him before he shook his head.

"Can I see my parents?"

Mick could hear the sob that was right behind the request. Now it was his turn to shake his head. "You can see them in a little while. First we want to ask you some questions."

The kid straightened slightly in his chair and said, "I can't say anything till I talk to my lawyer. I'm sorry."

Mick was sorry, too, but not surprised. The kid had obviously been keeping some very big secrets. He wasn't going to stop now.

He winced a little as they could hear his old man down the hall, yelling. Mick didn't want to tell him that disappointing his father was now the least of his worries. Where he was going, his father would only get to express his disappointment through a glass window, twice a month.

"OK, I'll check back in a minute," Mick said. He wanted to go down the hall and pound the shit out of Jackson. He could understand emotions running high and all that. This was going to be one of the worst days of his life, but the man needed to calm down and pull himself together, at least for his kid and wife.

Trey Barber was out getting someone to represent young Jackson. Mick had no idea what Rainy was doing—probably wishing for that elusive vagrant who could have been the murderer. Rainy could wish all he wanted, there was no changing the fact that Chip Jackson was a thief and a murderer. Rainy knew it. Jack Jackson knew it, and Mick knew it. Pretty soon all of Forsyth would know it, too.

Trey Barber was true to his word, as a good attorney should be, and Charles Jackson had his representative at the courthouse in a record forty-nine minutes.

The guy looked like he had rolled out of bed and into the courthouse. "Sir, I am Sam Wily. I represent Charles B. Jackson, and I would like to see my client, please."

Mick shook his hand and pointed him to the room holding Charles B. Jackson. "He's in there, Mr. Wily. Let me know if you need anything. Coffee?"

Sam Wily shook his head. Mick knew it was going to be a long day, and old Sam here might need the caffeine. You could only lead the horse to water, you couldn't make it drink the coffee.

So, Mick watched him go into the room. The kid looked up, but his eyes were dull, like those of a fish caught two hours ago. Mick could see Barber striding toward him, his head almost touching the ceiling in this part of the building. He needed to be in the courthouse, with its high ceilings.

"Detective McKay, would you speak to Chip's parents? They are distraught, of course. Jack, he just wants to talk to you. I know Chip is eighteen, and you are not obliged to speak with them, but if you could . . . Jack has some idea of confessing to the crimes himself. I've told him that is not what Chip needs now. I think I've convinced him to drop that line. But, he wants to talk to you. I'd sure appreciate it."

There was nothing to do now but wait: wait for the lawyer to allow him to talk to the kid, wait for Rainy to decide to drop the big bomb and charge the kid with the murders. Wait. So while he was waiting, he could talk to the parents, even if it was only to explain the process to them, give them an idea of what to expect. Maybe he could even persuade them to go home. They could not help anyone here.

He and Trey walked down the hall to the conference room they were using to contain the parents. He tapped on the door before he opened it, as if they had a choice as to whom to let in. Mrs. Jackson was sitting at the table, staring at her hands. Jackson was pacing and running his hands through his hair as if he could rub out his problems. Unlike his son, when Jack saw the door open, he was animated.

"Please, I need to talk to you."

Mick said, "OK, talk."

Jackson seemed exasperated by the comment. "No, no. I need to talk to you alone. I don't want to upset my wife."

It was a little late for that. She looked like the calm before the storm. Mick could feel her trying to hold herself together. If she stopped pressing her hands on the table they might just fly up and destroy things, maybe destroy her.

Also, they were running out of rooms. This was not the Hilton.

"Mrs. Jackson, would you like to go to the lunchroom and get some coffee, or a soda?"

She stared at him blankly, and he thought she didn't understand what he was saying. Before he could repeat himself, she gathered herself together and stood up. She held her hands together in front of her, and it reminded Mick of someone praying. Maybe that was what she was doing.

Jackson stepped forward and patted her on the arm. "I am so sorry, so sorry," he said to his departing wife.

If she wondered what he had to be sorry for in all this mess, she didn't show it.

As soon as the door closed behind her, Jackson turned to Mick. "I did it. I killed those people."

Beside him, Trey Barber threw his hands up in the air. "Jack, please! This does not help your son. You are wasting time. The police are not incompetent. They aren't going to say, 'Oh, well, that guy confessed, so he must have done it.' They are not idiots." Here, Barber glanced at him, and Mick nodded. *Thanks for the vote of confidence, although "not idiots" seemed a bit of a low bar.* "The police have evidence, evidence against Chip. If they didn't, they would not have charged him. They'll look at the evidence, and they will know it wasn't you. Let's do what we need to do now and concentrate on helping Chip in a positive way. OK?"

There was a knock on the door. Everyone was being polite tonight. It was Mason.

"Hey, Mick, could I see you for a minute?"

Mick said, "Excuse me." As he started out of the room, Jackson came with him. Barber made a grab for him, but Jackson shook him off. Barber tried a little harder to get a grip on Jackson's arm and they had a little pushing-pulling thing going on.

Now, normally, Mick liked a good fight as much as the next guy. Sometimes they served their purpose and cleared the air. This was not one of those times. A fight in a police station was like fighting in the bullring dressed in red. Mick and Mason each grabbed one of the offenders and held them apart.

"Come on, guys. You don't want to do this. This is no place for shenanigans." Mick released Jackson and he took off out the door.

Barber was calling him. "Wait here, Jack! Wait up and I'll drive you home, you and Anne. I'm sorry, I know how upset you are. Wait!"

But Jackson did not wait up. Mick watched him walk out the side door. He remembered the call he had gotten from Stephanie reminding him about Chip Jackson's uncle killing himself. At this moment Jack Jackson seemed more likely to solve his problems that way than Chip.

Barber came out of the room with his jacket and car keys in hand. Chasing his client around the parking lot would have looked unseemly, so he stood in the hall. Mick motioned to Mason to head back into the room so they could talk.

"I wanted to tell you the kid's lawyer wants to talk to you. What do you make of old man Jackson putting up such a fuss?"

"Well, if I were a betting man, I'd say he was trying to set us up for a fall. At the trial the kid's attorney can claim we never investigated anyone else, we rushed to judgment. They can ask if anyone else confessed, if we investigated that person. It'll put a dusty layer of doubt all over our actions. I kind of don't blame him. I'd try anything to save my kid, too."

Mason nodded, and Mick wandered down the hall to check on the kid, his prisoner.

CHAPTER SIXTY-THREE

Stephanie was still standing next to the side exit when Jack Jackson came down the few stairs that led to the door. If she stayed here long enough she could probably meet every important character in the case.

Stephanie was gearing up to try and get Jackson to talk to her, but when he saw her he acted like she was just the person he was looking for. Before she could utter the words "Can I talk to you?" Jackson was saying them to her.

"Stephanie. Hey, could I talk to you? I need to tell someone about what's happening. They won't listen to me in there," he said, jerking his thumb back to the building.

"Sure, we can talk." Stephanie said and leaned back against the wall.

"No, not here. Come on." He started walking, walking too fast for her to keep up, so he turned around and waited. He was running his hands through his hair, seemingly undecided about what to do next.

"Let's go to your car," he said. It seemed odd to her, but if the father of the boy accused of the only double homicide in Forsyth history had something to say to her, she was going to listen.

"OK. I'm parked in the back lot." They walked to her car, and he waited while she threw all the items that had been accumulating in the front onto the backseat and then climbed in.

He rubbed his hands through his hair and began to talk. "Please let me just tell you what happened. Just listen before you say anything."

She nodded and sat back to listen. She was good at that.

"You would think that, after keeping this secret for all these years, it would be a relief to finally tell someone the truth. But it doesn't feel like that at all. Let me start from the beginning. Let me see if I can make you understand.

"Football is important in this town now, and maybe even more so when I played in high school. You grew up here, you understand. Charlie, Trey, and I we were great together; there was no stopping us. They used to call us the Tripod. Did you know that? The three of us, we held up the team. And I loved those guys.

"Back then anything was possible for Charlie and Trey. Charlie had a scholarship to MIT. Trey was trying to figure out what he wanted to do with his life. He had a lot of choices. Me, I could look down the road and see everything that was going to happen to me. I knew playing football here was going to be the best thing. After that, college, then right back here to National Safety. I was already working there in the summers.

"A lot of the kids I went to school with, well, they envied me. The kid with the rich old man, the kid who was going to run his own company. To them it looked like I had it made. But Charlie and Trey, they understood. They knew how trapped I felt sometimes. But when I played football, I felt like people saw me, saw that I could accomplish something that didn't have anything to do with National or my dad. And we were good.

"Coach Tucker, he was a great coach. He could pull something out of you that you didn't even know was there. He made me want to play my heart out, because I knew he cared about me. And it wasn't just me; for all the guys on the team it was the same. We played hard to show him: not to win his approval, but because we couldn't stand to let him down. And he made us feel like a team, so we didn't want to let each other down either.

"That last game? I can't even tell you how charged up we all were. Four years of practices to get to the state championship game. Four years of almost passing out in one-hundred-plus-degree weather. Four years of aching muscles. It all came down to this one game. Only for me, it wasn't a game. I knew I would be spending the rest of my life in Forsyth. I had something to prove. I wanted to bring that state championship trophy home. I wanted to be on the team that won state. We all wanted that, of course, but it was something different for me, something essential. And it wasn't a crazy, unrealistic dream either. Hell, we were almost there.

"That last game, when we ran through that paper banner out on the field, I felt like I was a god or something. People were cheering and clapping for us. There were reporters and news cameras. People in the stands were taking our pictures. Flashes everywhere. Man, we were stars, and we knew that when we won it would only be bigger. Our whole senior year would be one big happy event. We played like a team. That's how we got to finals. We understood each other, knew each other's strengths and weaknesses.

"We all knew about Charlie's temper. It was two sides of the same coin. His fire and anger made him a great player. He could push through a brick wall when he was fired up.

"But he made mistakes, too. One time, sophomore year, he was tackled by this big guy, one of those cocky kind of guys who just can't help themselves from doing that little prancing-around shit. Charlie jumped up. It almost looked like he was on a string and someone pulled him up. He just came straight up and charged the guy. I can still see the expression of surprise on the guy's face and the look of fury on Charlie's. It was a damned miracle we went on to win that game. Or maybe it was just a testament to how good we really were. Coach had a big talk with Charlie.

"Even so, at the end of the game some old fat-ass fan from the other team came up to us while we were walking toward the locker room and said, 'Hey, buddy, you were one of our best players! Thanks!' It took me and Trey and about three other guys to hold Charlie back. And this was right after he fucked up on the field. No remorse when he lost his temper. That was Charlie.

"So we knew it was his weakness, but for Christ's sake, we had been working on it for four years! Four years! I spent I don't know how many hours working on my running, just trying to get faster, more agile. That was my weakness and I worked on it. Hard.

"Late in the game, when we were about to score what could have been the winning touchdown, Charlie grabbed some kid by his face mask and shook him like a rag doll. It was like they say about dying, how you see your whole life flash before your eyes? Me, I saw my future, slogging along at National. No spotlight; no starring moment. One minute we were seconds away from a victory that was going to bring me everything I ever wanted, and the next Charlie is shaking some kid around by his face mask and everything that was possible, everything that was so nearly mine, was gone.

"We couldn't recover from the penalty, and we all knew it. Oh sure, we still went on playing our hearts out, but we knew. On the sideline when Charlie came off, there was a parting like the Red Sea. He stood alone. No one wanted anything to do with Charlie, not even me and Trey. I just stared at that scoreboard as the seconds ran out. I always thought they should have put an asterisk after the state championship game that year. With something like 'Forsyth won except for one crazy mistake.' Coach Tucker was disappointed, too.

"We were all walking off the field with our heads hung so low it looked like we were searching in the blades of grass for the answer to how we could have lost like that. I swear, if the other team had been better than us I could have taken it, I would have accepted that. But they weren't. We were the best, and still we lost. Coach yelled at Charlie, but not about the game. He said, 'Charles, that temper of yours is going to cost you big one of these days if you can't get it under control. You head up to my room, so we can talk about it.'

"I still remember thinking; cost you big one of these days? One of these days? His temper had just cost us the state championship. Back then I thought that the coach was planning to rip into him in private. But now I think he was protecting Charlie from our wrath. Oddly, though, the team spirit took over and everyone was saying shit like 'good game, man' or the juniors were saying 'next year.' But, for me, there was no next year. It wasn't a good game.

"After quick showers, we were heading back to the hotel. We had a team bus, and if I hadn't been so dejected I would have ridden on it, still following rules, but Charlie asked me to go up to see the coach with him. We had a friend who had played with us the year before who gave us a ride to the hotel. So that was how we wound up in Coach Tucker's room that night.

"I wasn't mad at Charlie. Well, I was, but that wasn't what I was feeling the most. I felt numb, like someone who is suffering from amnesia. I just had this feeling like, did that really happen? Did we just lose the state championship?

"The door to Coach's room was unlocked, so we went on in, and Charlie sat down at the desk and picked up the pad with 'Holiday Inn' written across the top. Some holiday. He wanted to write a note to the coach. He said something about how sorry he was he had screwed up the game, but how he would come back from MIT or wherever he was going and tell the next team about the lessons he had learned by losing the championship for us, something like that. He wrote so big he had to use two of pieces of paper from the pad.

"I watched him write the note, and then when he looked up at me and said, 'Sorry,' I just got up and shoved the chair with him in it. He got up and shoved me back. He was saying something like, 'Hey, man, take it easy' or something.

"We kept shoving each other and then we were on the balcony. I can remember the silky curtain brushing my wrist when I pushed him. I just wanted to scare him, to get him to see how serious what he had done was. I pushed him against the balcony rail. It was like a joke. I was going to hold him over for a second until he said he was sorry or said he gave up or something.

"He was holding on to the rail on the outside and I was just trying to shake his hands loose. That's all, just shaking him. I couldn't pull him up the way he was holding on. But then he let go of the rail and made a grab for my hands and I just fell backward and lost my grip on him. I leaned back over to try and grab him again but I wasn't fast enough. I watched as he fell, all the way down, four floors.

"After it happened, I went into shock. Before Charlie even hit the ground I knew that my life was over. All the things that I'd felt so ambivalent about, National, Forsyth, even Anne, I realized how much I wanted that life when it literally slipped from my hands.

"Coach came in and saw me staring over the balcony. He realized what had happened, and I don't know, maybe he thought I would jump off, too. Who knows? But he stepped in front of me like Superman in the movies stepping in front of a speeding train, only that train wreck, it didn't leave him unharmed, it damaged him. He paid a price for saving me that day.

"And he did. He saved my life. To this day I can't remember if I asked him to save me or if he just came up with the idea on his own. Now I think maybe he felt guilty about what happened to Charlie, too. I think he sent him up to his room to protect him and, ultimately, he didn't. I'm not sure. We're not talking a lot of time here. All of this took place in a matter of minutes.

"I do remember crying and showing him the note Charlie had written. He looked at it a while and, I swear to God, if we discussed what we were about to do I don't remember that either. Suddenly there was a plan. That's all I know.

"Coach called the police and people from outside started screaming. I wanted to go back out on the balcony and look down to see, if maybe by some miracle Charlie was alive. But the coach held me back. When the police got there Coach told them we just walked into the room, found the note, and then heard the screams from below. He showed them the note and I think they put it in a plastic bag.

"At that point, I was so scared I could hardly breathe. I felt like those rioters that they shot the fire hoses at; I just couldn't get up, couldn't catch my breath. Coach asked the policeman if I could go, because this was such a shock for a young person, and just like that, they let me go. Everyone thought Charlie committed suicide. They had the note that the coach gave them and it was in Charlie's handwriting. So, that's what people believed.

"The bus ride back to Forsyth was surreal. No one noticed anything about me being upset and agitated because we were all like that. The next weeks were agony for me, partly because of what I had done, but mostly because I lost Charlie. Coach never, ever mentioned what happened. Never. Maybe he thought he hadn't protected Charlie, but he could protect me.

"Anyway, it got so that I believed the story, too. One time about a month after it happened, I was playing some pickup basketball with a bunch of the guys who had been on the team, and we started talking. They were all saying how shocked they were and all that, and Trey said maybe he had seen some signs and how he wished he had paid more attention to them.

"He said Charlie once told him he couldn't imagine how his life was going to turn out and maybe what he was trying to say was that he didn't think he was going to live a whole life. I remember agreeing with him, saying I'd heard him talk like that before, too, and looking back, maybe he was trying to tell us something. Something we missed. I stood out on that basketball court, trying to remember signs. And I knew. I knew! I knew he hadn't killed himself. I knew, but somehow I let go of that reality. I just let go and, I know this sounds strange, but I believed what everyone around me believed. Charlie threw himself off that balcony.

"The coach, he never talked about what had happened. Maybe he started to believe Charlie had jumped, too. I don't know. People in town were mad, mad at Coach. They said stuff like he pushed us too hard and made us all afraid of letting him down. They said what happened to Charlie was his fault. I tried to stand up for him, of course. A lot of the other guys did, too. But he lost his job, stopped coaching.

"You know most of the rest of the story. He went into business and did OK for himself. I never asked him exactly, but I believe he was happy. And I tried to be, too. I got married, had kids, and ran the business. Everything I was supposed to do.

"I kept in touch with Coach, and when he got old and sick, I tried to help him. I found him a housekeeper. I visited him. I tried to redeem myself. Coach—he never let me down, and I owed him the same. Every once in a while he would call out in his sleep. Called to me and Charlie. He called me John, and Charlie, he called him Charles. He'd call like he was trying to call us back off that balcony.

"But then he started talking about the letter that could prove he wasn't a bad guy, how he wanted to show people before he died, to get the truth out. I thought he was going to show the second page of the note Charlie wrote, the one that said see you next year and all. If he showed that, questions would be asked. It would have come out about what I had done. I just couldn't have that happen.

"You remember when you came to interview me about him? I was shocked to find out he wasn't talking about Charlie's note at all. He was talking about something completely different—that letter about him cheating or something. But I didn't know that until you told me that day.

"When the Coach died, I thought I was still safe. Rosa's English wasn't good enough for her to understand. She told me his daughters hadn't been there for a few days, so they didn't know. No one in his family would know.

"The only two people who knew were the two people he saw on a regular basis, his hospice nurse and the kid who brought him his pizza. If he told them, what was I going to do? That was the dilemma. If they saw the note, even if they didn't know what it meant, they might talk to someone about it. It would come out. And it wouldn't be just me that would be hurt by the revelation that I had killed Charlie. I had my wife to think of—my kids, my business even. It would destroy so many lives, not only mine.

"I went back to my office to think things over, to try and come up with a plan. I thought about running away, just leaving, going to Mexico. But I couldn't leave my family. I locked myself in the janitorial storage room, to think. I got so frustrated and so angry with myself that I knocked something off the shelves, throwing things around, like a kid throwing a temper tantrum.

"I heard this thunk when something hit the floor. At first I felt bad. Here I was making things worse by breaking stuff in the storage room. But when I leaned over to see what had fallen, I saw the gun. I looked behind the paper towels and I found wallets, money, and a few pieces of jewelry. And I knew. I knew I was looking at what the Reluctant Robber had stolen. Your Reluctant Robber, Stephanie.

"I thought it must have been Augustine. I knew he was desperate for money. He had a relative in Mexico who was sick. I had helped his wife get the job with Harlan Tucker. And then it hit me. It was like a sign, like it was meant to be. This was the answer."

Stephanie felt the hairs on the back of her neck stand up. She looked around the parking lot. There were lots of people going toward the building or to their cars. Still, she felt very vulnerable. She surreptitiously checked the door locks to make sure they were open, to make sure she could jump out if she needed to because she had an idea where this story was going.

Jackson seemed to notice her nervousness and he took a deep breath.

CHAPTER SIXTY-FOUR

The lawyer was with the kid. It was a waiting game for all of them now. Mick was waiting for Rainy to make his decision; the young attorney was waiting to see how best to advise his client; and Chip Jackson was waiting to find out when he could go home. That was not going to happen.

Mick poked his head into their room to ask if they needed anything, as if they were houseguests he was checking on. The young attorney asked if the kid could talk to his parents. He had gotten his lawyer. He was over eighteen and this was not a social gathering.

But Mick told them, "I'll check. Maybe in a little while. Want anything to eat or drink?" They didn't. The kid looked miserable.

Rainy came and stood beside his desk. He waited, presumably collecting his thoughts before he spoke to Mick. It reminded him of the Justice statue with the scales. Rainy was even now weighing what to say.

"I looked over everything, and I think we have enough to charge him with the murders. I know we have him on the break-ins. Good work on that, Mick. We can hold him on those, so I am going to announce the other charges tomorrow. Who knows? Maybe we'll have a confession by then. Just wanted to let you know what was going on."

Mick didn't have to ask why the delay. He knew at this point they didn't have to rush, plus for Rainy there would potentially be a bigger audience for his news conference tomorrow rather than tonight. Prime time. He'd get a chance to put on his best suit. It all made sense to Mick.

"So, I want you to tell the press that we are holding him on the burglary charges, put him in the lock up, and we'll pick up in the morning. We can take him straight to the courtroom in the morning. I can tell you—this is not how I saw this case turning out."

With that, he walked back down the hall, leaving Mick to figuratively and literally turn out the lights and lock the door.

Stephanie could tell where Jackson's story was heading, but she knew there was no escaping the end of the story. She nodded at Jackson to continue. He did.

"Don't you see? The gun was like the answer to a prayer, something so unexpected as to be almost unbelievable. Of course, I would only act if I absolutely had to. I didn't want to hurt anybody. I would never do that unless there was no other way. But I knew the gun could never be traced to me. A stolen gun, untraceable. It was like a gift, like it was being put in my hand to save my family. I had no idea my son had taken it.

"National Safety . . . as you know, we are having problems, financial problems. I told my son that when we were laying off people it didn't look right for him to be going around spending money, and the truth is, there just wasn't much money left after the financial guarantees I gave the bank. Virtually my entire net worth is tied up at National. So, while we weren't going to be broke, it was time to cut back everywhere we could. I should have known how upsetting it would be to him, but I had to stay focused on the business, just to keep it going."

Stephanie knew he was telling the truth. It was an unbelievable story, unbelievable but true. She decided to let him finish. She wasn't sure she could stop him even if she wanted to. The floodgates had opened, and his story was pouring out. She wanted to get Mick or John Mason or Rainy or her father, anyone, to listen along with her, but at this point she couldn't stop either.

"I never would have done anything. Never. Unless I was threatened, that was the only way I would do something. If I was threatened, I would save myself and my family. You understand that, right?"

Stephanie was too numbed to even nod, but evidently it didn't matter, because Jackson kept talking.

"I went to Harlan's wake. I had the plan, but I didn't think I'd have to use it. That changed when I got there. I saw Edie Spence talking to Adam Moore, and they were looking at me. Then they went over and talked to the policeman who was working at Coad's. I overheard them make arrangements to meet the next day. That's when I knew I had to use the gun that had been provided for me. It was the only way.

"I knew immediately what I had to do. I went into the office there at the funeral home and called Antonio's. I ordered a pizza to be delivered to Edie Spence's house.

"I went home, changed clothes, got my dog, and walked down to the Spence's house. I walked back and forth down the street. Nobody pays any attention to a guy out walking his dog. When Mrs. Spence pulled up, I asked her about her garden, just chatting to keep her outside. They needed to both be in the yard.

When the kid pulled up, I shot him in the chest and he fell down. Mrs. Spence turned, and I shot her in the chest, too. I walked over and shot the kid in the head, and then I turned and shot the woman in the head. I shot twice in the air. That was it.

"I walked to the front yard and called 911. Even after the investigation turned from a random shooting by a thief to a possible targeted killing, I knew I had my ace in the hole. If anybody got too close, all I had to do was turn over Augustine. Give the police his stolen items. No one would ever believe he wasn't the killer once they knew he was your Reluctant Robber. I felt bad doing that to him, but what choice did I have? And he was a thief.

"But then . . . then it wasn't him after all. Now I have to save my son. That's why I did all this in the first place, to protect my family. They won't listen to me inside. Even Trey Barber, who knows me as well as anyone; he thinks I'm making this up. But you know I'm not. Don't you?"

"Yes, I know that you are not making this up," she said. She wanted to sound firm, but to her ears she sounded only sad.

"Stephanie, I just want to close my eyes for a minute. I am more tired than I have ever been. Can I rest in your car? Just for a little while? You'll be able to tell them I am not lying and after that I don't know when I'll have another chance to rest. Not for a long while, I guess."

296 JENNIFER FARRELL VOSS

When Mick walked toward the front of the building, all the reporters stood up and looked at him expectantly like people in the hospital waiting room, waiting for news about a loved one's surgery. The only difference being that these people would welcome bad news. The news he was planning to give them was really no news, and that surely would not make them happy.

They looked up at him expectantly and he said, "Charles Jackson is being held on suspicion of burglary. No other developments tonight."

He watched their faces fall altogether, as if he had just announced to a bunch of kindergarteners that there was no Santa Claus. He heard a few shouted questions: "Will he be charged with the murders? Where is he now?" Just routine stuff.

Out of the corner of his eye he saw Stephanie Gallagher. She wasn't shouting a question at him, but she gestured for him to come, bending her arm and motioning. He thought back to the night of the murders, how she had folded her hands together, pleading with him to talk to her. This time she seemed to be ordering him to talk to her. It caught him off guard, but there was something so intent about the gesture, like his mother telling him and his brother to come a running, that he couldn't resist.

He edged around the dispersing crowd. Nothing to see here folks, move along. And that is what they were doing: going home disappointed, like empty-handed shoppers.

Stephanie closed her car door softly, knowing Jack Jackson was probably right. He would need his rest for the future awaiting him.

She walked into the courthouse, filling up with press, just in time to hear Mick say they were only charging Chip Jackson with the burglaries. He had no idea how close he had come to indicting the wrong man. He was going to look brilliant when this story came out.

She gestured for Mick to come and talk to her. With the killer—and that was what Jackson was—napping in her car, this was not a time for dilly-dallying. Mick must have sensed her mood because he made a beeline toward her through the dispersing crowd of press people. *Have I got a story for you!* She would have liked to tell them, and she would, but not yet. Mick was already giving her his "I don't believe a word you say look."

"Mick, I need to talk to you. Now."

"Okay, as you heard, there isn't anything new. I don't have some kind of scoop for you."

"I know. I have one for you, though. Jack Jackson killed Edie Spence and Adam Moore."

At that he turned around again. He didn't believe her. "No Stephanie, he didn't. He wants you to believe that, and maybe he even wants you to print that to help his son. But Stephanie, I know. I know that the kid is the Reluctant Robber. Obviously, I can't tell you all I know yet, but the kid did it. I feel bad for Jackson, too. I'd be trying everything if it were my kid. But the kid did it, no doubt."

Mick started to walk away from her. He thought the conversation was finished. She grabbed his hand and held on to him.

"Mick, you are not listening to me. I know you are right about the kid being the Reluctant Robber. But he didn't kill Edie and Adam. It is a long story, but it has something to do with a boy who died a long time ago, a high school friend of Jack Jackson: Chip's uncle, the one he is named after.

"Jackson and Harlan Tucker let everybody think it was a suicide. But it wasn't. Jackson killed Charlie, not on purpose, but he killed him. Remember that story in the *Bee* about Harlan Tucker being cleared of some old gambling charge by a letter someone sent him?"

Mick was shaking his head. It was exasperating. She wanted to tell him he should be reading the *Bee* more carefully.

"OK, anyway, that is what happened, only Jackson thought the letter Harlan was talking about had something to do with the death of his high school friend. He found the gun and he killed the only two people Harlan had talked to. Well, except for the housekeeper. He didn't think she would be able to understand what Coach Tucker was telling her.

"He killed them, Mick. He killed them to save his reputation, his family, his business. He married his dead friend's sister. Holy smokes, Mick! Think about it! Does that scared little kid in there seem like he could shoot a couple of people in the head? Listen to Jackson's story. He is not making it up."

She watched as Mick chewed on his lip. She could tell he still didn't believe her.

"Stephanie, you know who called to tell us about the stolen items? It was Jackson. Why would he do that if the evidence was going to point to him? That makes no sense."

"Yes, yes it does. He actually thought the thief was the maintenance manager. Jackson knew Augustine was desperate to earn some extra money. He'd already helped him find work for his wife. He knew that the police would believe that the robber and the murderer had to be the same person, and he was right. That is what you believe.

"But what if someone found the gun and used it? Don't you see? That is exactly what happened. He found the things, thought they were stolen by Augustine, took the gun, and planned to blame him for the killings as well as the burglaries. He never dreamed it was his son he was setting up. At least listen to the guy. Mick, I'm asking you."

She put her hand on his arm, imploring him, and felt a little current of electricity crackle through. Maybe he felt it, too, because he changed course and asked where Jackson was.

"He's sleeping in my car, at least he was when I came back into the courthouse." She wanted him to feel the same sense of urgency she felt.

"Stephanie, you know if we investigate anyone else for the murders, the defense team will make a big deal of it. They'll try to cast doubt on our case by saying we had different suspects, that we were unsure. That is reasonable doubt right there. I want you to understand that a killer could go free if we do the wrong thing here. This isn't an academic exercise. This is just what I said, life and death. So you have to be sure about what you are asking."

Her mood was solemn, too. She felt like she was making a commitment, almost like a vow, when she said, "I am. I am sure."

CHAPTER SIXTY-FIVE

When Mick saw Jackson sleeping with his head against the window of Stephanie Gallagher's little car, he had his doubts. He had seen the video of Chip Jackson buying the shoes. He was certain the kid had returned the driver's license to Martin Colby when he was running by the house. There would be additional evidence found on the items from the cleaning closet. He knew he could convict the kid. Stephanie's story was far-fetched. She had grabbed his arm and here he was in the parking lot.

He tapped on the window and Jackson jolted awake. He turned his head, surveying his surroundings, a "where the hell am I?" look on his face. He looked crestfallen when he recognized Mick on the other side of the window, almost as if he thought he might be having a nightmare and then realized this is reality. Mick motioned him out of the car and he got out, looking like he had been living in the car for weeks instead of an hour.

"Mr. Jackson, what we are doing is as serious as a heart attack. I want you to know that if you are purposely trying to mislead a police investigation, there will be consequences, not only for you but for your son as well. So, I want you to think about that on the way in. Do not do anything that will place your family in greater jeopardy. Do you understand me? And remember, in the great state of Texas, it is impossible to convict on a confession alone. There must be evidence. It's the law, and it's what Mr. Barber would tell you, too."

Jackson nodded his assent but, for the hell of it and for a little extra emphasis, Mick said, "OK. I am going to read you your rights."

And he did, watching Jackson take in words he had probably heard many times but never expected to hear directed to him. At the end he said he understood his rights and did not wish to have an attorney present.

"Are you sure you don't want me to get Trey Barber? I saw him a few minutes ago. We could wait a few minutes for him. I know that is what he would advise you."

But Jackson declined the offer. Stephanie Gallagher was watching Mick for signs that he was really going to do what he said and listen to this guy tell him some story. He had thought he'd be able to shake Jackson off like a bad mood once he started on the heavy stuff, but so far he was holding.

Mick put Jackson in a room, closed the door, and went to tell Rainy the latest. Mason was in the hall outside the room where Chip Jackson was conferring with his attorney.

"Hey, Mason, why don't you take Stephanie down to the vending machine for a Coke or something? I am going to talk to Jack Jackson for a minute. He's been talking to Ms. Gallagher and she wants me to hear what he has to say."

If John Mason was surprised by what he heard he gave no indication. He reached into his pockets and pulled out some coins.

"Cokes on me," he said. And off they went. Mick thought for a second about just forgetting that Jackson was in the room. But he had told Stephanie he would listen to the guy, and he would.

He rapped on Rainy's door. The DA was sitting at his desk, looking forlorn as usual.

"This is going to be the trial of the century for Forsyth," he said, and Mick could not tell if that was good news or bad news according to Rainy. It might be his ticket to a judgeship, but if anything went wrong, the world—or at least the part of it that mattered—would be watching, and that could be bad for Rainy.

"Listen Rainy, I am going to question Jack Jackson. He told some crazy story to Stephanie Gallagher and she is convinced that there might be something to it. I read him his rights and the riot act, and he still insists he wants to talk, so I am going to hear him out."

He expected Rainy to put up a fight, but he told Mick to go ahead and do what he thought was best, probably planning to blame

Mick if something went wrong. It was OK with him; that was part of his job, providing cover for Rainy if needed.

Mick sighed. "I'll let you know if I get anything."

Mick headed back down the hall and into the tiny room with Jackson. He made one more attempt to get Jackson to see reason. "Look, I know Mr. Barber would tell you not to be saying anything. I just want to urge you, man to man, to talk to him."

Jackson nodded his head. So if he wanted to be a criminal, Mick would treat him like one. Let him get the full treatment.

"I am going to turn on the camera for this interview. Will you state for the record that I have read you your rights and that you do not want an attorney present for this interview?"

They went through the responses, and then Mick sat back in his office chair.

"So, let's hear your story."

Jackson rubbed his head a few times.

"I shot those people," he said.

Mick was not having it. "Look, I know your kid is the Reluctant Robber. Hell, he has confessed to being the Robber. And the other thing I know is that the Robber stole Martin Colby's gun and used it to murder two people. Tell me something I don't know."

Jackson looked down at his hands. "I found the gun with the other things. I used it to shoot those people because I knew the Robber would be the only suspect. I thought the Robber was Augustine. I thought he had stolen those things and that everyone would think he had to be the killer, too."

"OK, well, how do I know you are the killer and not your son? How can you convince me that he didn't steal those things, take the gun along, and then kill Edie Spence and Adam Moore?"

Looking at Jackson Mick was reminded of stories he had heard about people whose hair turned white overnight. He was watching him change before his eyes, watching him shrink down from his robust self to a shell, both aging and regressing at the same time. Glad-handing gone. Whatever the man had to say it was taking a toll on him. That was clear.

"I ordered the pizza from Coad's office. Did you know that?" Jackson asked.

Now he had Mick's attention. He could not have known that detail, could not have known unless he really was the one who called or he knew who did. It was possible he had seen his son make the call, put things together from that. He would have known something was up with that and could have put it together afterward.

Mick sighed. "We tested your clothes. There was no blood on them. If you had shot two people at close range, you would have had blood on you."

"I wore a plastic poncho to cover my clothes. I took it off before I called 911."

"Oh, you took it off? I was there, remember? You didn't have time to hide a blood-spattered poncho. We went over that area so close we looked behind every blade of grass. There was no poncho, so what happened to it?"

"I took it off and put it in the sack I was carrying for my dog. I didn't think anyone would check that bag, and I was right. I threw it away in front of the police station."

Mick thought back to John Mason getting out of his car on the night of the murders and holding his nose. He had watched Jackson throw the sack away, watched unquestioningly as evidence disappeared right before his eyes. *Jesus! This guy might be telling the truth.*

His mind kept turning, and Mick remembered the interview he had done with one of the Spences' neighbors: the frazzled Mom with her two little children. She'd as good as told him that Jackson's story made no sense, she just didn't know she had. The shots happening all together, seeing Jackson on the street with the dog as early as 6:30 p.m. He'd been waiting, not walking. Mick could see why Stephanie had been so adamant. This story seemed plausible.

Mick had moved to the edge of his chair without being aware of it. Now, he realized he would have to be more careful in this interview. First, he checked to make sure he could see the little red light that meant the recorder was working. He could see the light— good. Next, he opened the door and shouted for Mason. He wanted backup, another officer to be paying attention to the story with him.

He sat back in his chair and waited the long twenty seconds it took Mason to jog down the hall.

Mick looked over at Jackson and told him, "Wait a minute. We'll have John Mason in here, too." Jackson's body put Mick in mind of those sponge creatures Colly used to have. You'd put them in water and they would expand to be a seahorse or a pony. And when they dried out, they shrunk back to their tiny size again. Jackson was like the dried-out version.

Mason's eyebrows went up like question marks when he came in and sat down across from his boss. Mick reminded Jackson that he was being recorded and that he had been read his rights, and then he asked him to go through his story again for Mason.

He listened carefully as Jackson went through the details again of finding the stolen items, calling the pizzeria, shooting Adam Moore and Edie Spence, firing the gun into the air, stuffing the plastic poncho in the dog poop sack, and calling 911. Mick was listening for any deviation in the story, something added or left out, something to confirm whether Jackson was lying or telling the truth.

The one thing that was true about all the police shows he had ever seen was that a good detective noticed things. He always prided himself on being that guy. Although he had seen Jackson tossing the sack in the trash, he hadn't paid any attention to it. He looked over at Mason to see what he was noticing. Mason could have been a professional poker player for all the emotion he was giving away on his face. It wasn't that he was stone-faced, just impossible to read.

"Why, why would you kill those two people? What possible reason could you have for doing it?" Mason asked, including Mick in the question.

"It was because of what I thought they knew, something Coach Tucker told them about me." Jackson was telling the story to Mason now.

And Mick watched. He was the observer, now. That was why they taught you in police techniques to have two people in the interview room. Mason was still showing nothing, which seemed to make Jackson more emotional, more determined to make him understand, to feel the desperation that possessed him the moment he thought his true self would be discovered.

"I was involved in an accident when I was in high school. I didn't want people to know about it. I just couldn't have that happen." Then Jackson went back though the "accident" for Mason's benefit.

"But even if he had shown them the note and they put everything together, it would have been nearly impossible to prove that a crime had been committed. In all probability nothing would have happened to you," said Mason, his impassive expression not giving anything away.

Mick watched to see if Jackson had a reply. Mick knew the answer, knew what Jackson had lost already. He could never again be the nicest guy in the room, the guy who put his hand on your shoulder when you shook hands with him. That was over. He could never be the guy Forsyth thought he was, or the guy he thought he was.

There was a sharp rap on the door. Mick stuck his head out, expecting Rainy, but it was Trey Barber with a determined look on his face. The problem with a small town setup like the one they were functioning in was that it was small. It wasn't difficult for Barber to see which room they were in and just knock on the door. They had a metal detector that they had gotten with Homeland Security money, but that didn't prevent Barber from coming down the hall to find his client.

"He has relinquished his right to counsel," Mick told Barber.

"OK, OK. I just want to talk to him for a few seconds. In your presence," he threw in, trying to get into the room.

Mick opened the door and let him in. Barber sat down and looked over at the shrunken Jackson, maybe thinking that Forsyth's finest were berating him into submission.

"I have a new attorney with Chip. He's going to get the help he needs. Your wife is looking for you. We all want the same thing now, to help Chip. You confessing to something you didn't do is not going to help him."

Jackson's voice was getting smaller, too. When he replied there was none of his former heartiness in it. "I did do it, Trey. I'm not lying now. For the first time in a very long time, I'm not lying. I killed them because I thought they found out something about me, something they were going to tell."

"That makes no sense! What could they have found out that would be so bad you had to kill them?"

"I thought they found out that I killed Charlie Atkins."

"What the hell are you talking about? That was nobody's fault. We couldn't have known what he was thinking. Even today I can hardly believe it. How could anyone have thought what happened was your fault!"

"It was my fault. I killed him. It was an accident, yes, but I killed him. We were horsing around. I was mad at him about losing his temper at the game and I—we—were pushing each other. I was sort of holding him over the balcony. I didn't mean to hurt him, just to get his attention. But then things went wrong. I dropped him."

Mick and Mason listened to the story again. Mick could see that Mason had become a believer, too. They had both had their road-to-Damascus moment. They believed that what Jackson was saying was the truth. He was the killer. Barber wasn't that far down the road yet.

"No, that can't be, he left a note. He left a note for the coach. I saw the note! I know he wrote it!"

"Yeah, he wrote the note. But that was only half the note. Do you remember what it said? Because I do. I remember every word.

Coach Tucker,

I am so sorry for letting you down tonight. You have helped me in so many ways and taught me so much in the last four years. I wish that I could go back and do the game over again. It kills me to know how disappointed you must be. I know there is nothing I can ever do to make this right.

Jackson paused and looked at his lawyer. "But there was another page. The rest of it said:

I promise I will learn from this and if you ever want someone to come back and talk about making stupid mistakes, I will come back to talk to every one of your teams. I'll have to take what the Forsyth fans dish out and I'll remember what you told us about being proud of how far we made it. I know I couldn't have gotten here without a great coach like you. I hope you can come see me play next year. Sorry.

Charles

Jackson repeated it as if he were reading it from a paper right in front of him. "The coach, he tried to help me. He let people believe that it was a suicide, to spare me. Even though it meant he was hated as the coach who pushed his player to kill himself. You hated him after that. A lot of people did, but he was protecting me. And he would have, forever.

"But then, before he died, he was in and out of his head. He was talking about the note that could prove he hadn't done anything wrong. I thought it was the other half of Charlie's note. I didn't want my family to know—Anne and the rest. I didn't want anybody to know what had really happened."

Trey Barber was a big man, but he shot straight into the air like he was in the ejector seat in a jet and lunged for Jackson. He grabbed him by the shirt and hauled him up before Mick had a chance to move. Mick thought of himself as fast, but not like this. He and Mason pulled Barber off Jackson and held him. Mick had seen some bad attorney-client interactions, but nothing quite like this. He felt like he was on the *Jerry Springer Show.*

"How could you? How could you let us all believe that Charlie had killed himself? His family? Me? How could you? You know that changed my life. You know how terrible we all felt about not being there for Charlie. How could you do that to us, to his family, to your wife? You bastard!" Jackson went limp like a naughty toddler finding a way to slip out of his mother's grasp. He slumped back into his chair.

When Mick had first heard Jackson tell why he had murdered two people, he had been in disbelief. A ruined reputation was worth the lives of two people? Come on. Jackson had been convinced that he was trying to protect his son, because no one would commit murder to keep people from finding out that you had an accident when you were in high school.

Now, after this outburst, he could see why Jackson had felt compelled to protect himself by committing murder. Jackson would be hated. Mick understood, and he believed.

Stephanie was pacing the hall in the courthouse. She was not alone. Camera crews were standing by for the next juicy tidbit. What could be juicier than the well-to-do son of a prominent citizen robbing homes and killing people? She was alone in that she was the only one who knew how juicy the story really was. Prominent citizen and well-to-do son out on a crime spree. She felt like a high school girl with a juicy secret. "And then he said . . . "

Tom had told her to start the story, but they wouldn't run it in the *Bee* until they had some indication that the Forsyth police actually believed Jackson.

"He is telling the truth," Stephanie had told Tom. He trusted her, and she could hear his intake of breath as he processed the information.

She was writing the story in her head, weaving in the characters. She had a working title for her article: "The Sins of the Father." She would unearth a picture of Jackson at the age he was when he dropped his friend off the balcony and run it next to a picture of his son. That was how she began her story.

EPILOGUE

When the Forsyth police announced that they were arresting Jack Jackson for murder, Forsyth became a boomtown. Helicopters circled overhead, reporters and photographers surged into town, all looking for the nugget that would make the story interesting to the people who would shake their heads and say, "What is this world coming to?" They were prospectors, certain to strike gold with a story of colossal misfortune and sadness.

And it had been a lucky strike for some in Forsyth. There was no denying that. Lawsuits went a-flying. Augustine Morales had won an undisclosed amount of money (which everyone took to mean a lot of money) from the Jackson family. And rightly so; he had almost gone to prison for crimes he did not commit. So he deserved his money. Even the lawyers on the losing end, like Trey Barber, came out ahead.

Long after the news trucks had packed up their wires and unplugged their cords, and the reporters and photographers and the rest of the world had moved on to the next tragic story, long after that, Forsyth was still riveted by the news about the lawsuits. There were competing theories on what had really happened. Harlan Tucker's daughters disputed Jackson's claim about Charlie Atkins's death. Where was the proof? No second page of the note was ever found. And many people still believed that the father was protecting his son. For a while there, at every barbecue, book club, and church picnic people discussed whether Jack Jackson or his son was guilty.

Readership at the *Bee* had gone way up. Everybody wanted to know who was going to get money and how everyone was coping with the tragedies. Stephanie's old colleagues, who had thought she was crazy for going off to the backwater of Texas with her dentist husband, began to think she was not so crazy after all. And she agreed with them, except for the dentist husband part. That had been crazy. Just the other day she had gotten a piece of mail addressed to Stephanie Popkins. For a split second, she had wondered, *Who is Stephanie Popkins?* In that instant she realized that the pain and bitterness of Pete's betrayal and the divorce was all behind her. Now it felt like it had happened to someone else.

In that same batch of mail, she had gotten a brochure from Lacey Thomas. She had gotten a job as a seamstress at a bridal shop in Dallas. Her love of lace had paid off for her. She was in demand, because all the brides had confidence in her ability to alter a dress to perfection. And she still sewed on the side. She didn't come back to Forsyth very often, but Stephanie had seen her when Lacey was altering the short, lacy dress that Stephanie had chosen for her second wedding.

Tiffany Hudson had been a participant in the many lawsuits swirling around the case. Her mother, true to character, tried to get all the money from the wrongful death suit turned over to her instead of split between the two of them. Happily, she did not win, and Tiffany wound up paying for nursing school with some of her money. Lacey had a picture of them together and Stephanie had commented on how good Tiffany looked. She had grown out her wispy hair and looked healthy and happy. Extensions, Lacey had explained.

And she wasn't the only one with a new hairdo. Stephanie had been surprised to see a totally different Donnetta when she ran into her at Round the Clock. Donnetta's hair had been cut in a cute new style, looking more like her old self from the pictures printed of her at the time of her son's death. Stephanie complimented her and delighted in her reply.

"I guess it was time. I'd spent so much time worrying about where I had gone wrong as a parent, even though I know you shouldn't blame yourself. Ever. Now that I know Charlie wanted to come home to us, well, that just means so much to us. I'll always miss him, but in a strange way I feel like I got some part of him back. My Charlie, he died in an accident, and I do believe it was an accident. I feel like I can resurrect all those happy memories of him.

"For a long time I felt as though I couldn't have known my son as well as I thought I did, couldn't have known his essential self, but I did know him. It's like recovering from amnesia; I can reclaim all my happy memories of my son without the tinge of sadness that was clouding them over. I'm glad I finally know what happened, and I think I could have forgiven Jack back then for the accident. It's harder to forgive him now for what he put us through all those years.

"And, Coach, I'm not sure why he did what he did. I guess he was trying to help Jack, but he hurt us in the process. But I don't know why you're letting me go on and on about this. I heard about your big news! Congratulations! Your picture in the *Bee* was stunning, just stunning, not to mention that handsome man you got. You make a cute couple." She winked at Stephanie, her smile bright amid the wrinkles.

For her part, Stephanie agreed they did make a cute couple. She didn't ask Donnetta, because for once it wasn't any of her business, but Forsyth was a small town and she had heard the rumors about Donnetta's daughter, Anne Jackson, and Sean Spence.

In some ways it made perfect sense. Anne and Sean had both been devastated by the murders. They had both been forced to start over making new lives. After sitting through the trials together, it was only natural that they might come together. It was also natural there would be some gossip. Forsyth was a small town. But most of the people wished them well. After all that had happened they deserved to find some peace and happiness.

Mick still tossed and turned occasionally, wondering if he could have prevented the murders by catching Chip Jackson earlier. Julie had told him, "You know you aren't God." He thought about the victims, and there were plenty of them, when he drove around town. Just the other day he had been driving by Burns Park and noticed the new sign, "Adam Moore Soccer Field." It was a good way to remember him.

Even old Martin Colby had been affected. He had felt so bad about his gun being used, but at the funeral he had met the hospice group, and now he took Samantha on visits to hospice patients. Mick imagined it gave him someone to talk to. He had heard that Tiffany

Hudson was going to school with the settlement money. He hoped it turned out OK for her.

The Spences, they had each other to lean on, and he had heard that Doc Spence was keeping company with Anne Jackson. What had happened to their families was a tragedy, but the victim he worried the most about was Tiffany, out there all alone in the world. He knew how hard it had been for him during the weeks that Julie and Colly were away. He hoped that she would meet somebody nice and have her own family.

He couldn't help but think of Chip Jackson as a victim, too. In the interviews with him, he had sounded childish, talking about why he started stealing. He had grown up one of the richest kids in town, and when he felt that his father was arbitrarily taking that away from him, he decided to steal. He would be out of jail in two years, a young man able to start over. Mick knew he was taking college classes while he was in jail.

But what a shambles he had made of his life. He would have to spend the rest of his days knowing that the events he set in motion had led to the deaths of two people, the destruction of his family, and a forever altered life for him. And there were people in town who thought he was the real murderer, that he had gotten away with it. He had no future in Forsyth; that was for sure.

His father, thanks to the wishes of the victims' families, had gotten life without the possibility of parole. Jack Jackson had joined the prison football team, maybe trying to return to his glory days. They played flag football, probably because of what might happen if all those violent types started tackling each other. After all, this was not one of those white-collar country club prisons. He had, by all accounts, adjusted and settled into prison life.

Now, though, Jackson was going to get the justice that the State of Texas did not give him. He had been diagnosed with pancreatic cancer. Mick could not help but wish, with everyone else, that the cancer had come a little earlier and spared them all the tragedy. Even Jackson could have died with his family beside him, his reputation intact. He was going to die this year, and that was not the worst thing that had happened to him.

Mick liked to listen to everybody talk about the case. It seemed to him almost like the whole thing had happened while he was feverish. He certainly had worked feverishly on the case. And now that it was over, his fever had broken. Life went back to normal. The case was closed.

Stephanie looked around the table. It was hard to believe it was over. Twenty-eight months, two trials, two incarcerations, more articles than she could count, and now it was coming to an end. It reminded her of the way she felt when she walked off the court after cheering at her last basketball game. She could almost hear the book slamming shut. Or when she signed the divorce papers, that "well, that's over" feeling. She had to smile as she passed the pitcher of beer to Mick McKay. It was over but in a good way, a very good way.

"Hey, Mick, want some more beer?"

Mick took the pitcher from her and said, "I guess I better, since I seem to be the only one drinking here."

Julie McKay held up her glass. "Not so fast, there, I'm drinking, too. And I think it is very sweet of John to give up drinking with Steph, very sweet. I think it indicates that he is going to be a great father!" She held up her newly filled glass as if in a toast.

Stephanie agreed with her, it was very sweet. But then their entire romance had been sweet—as Mick said, so sweet he felt like he had to brush his teeth after hanging out with her and Mason. John said he knew the first time they swiveled on their stools at the Round the Clock, but she counted their first date right after the arrests, when she had been exhausted, with dirty hair and rumpled clothes. She was, after all, a print journalist. It wasn't supposed to matter what she looked like.

And when he suggested driving her to breakfast after that long night, she had said yes. So while the Jackson family was falling apart, Stephanie and John were coming together, constructing their own happy family. She had never felt better, except for the afternoon naps and the swollen ankles.

They got together often, the four of them, sometimes adding in Rainy or Tom, and talked endlessly about how crazy all that had happened was. The pieces falling into place like some elaborate domino design, one tile falling and setting off a chain of others till it was hard to see where they started and stopped. They talked about the roles they had played in solving the crime, even Mick, the most modest and taciturn of men, added to the conversations.

They had all attended the trials, including Julie, when she could get a seat. Sometimes they would shake their heads in amazement at how much their lives had changed. Forsyth itself seemed changed: somehow more grown up, less innocent. National Safety was hanging on. At first, everyone had feared the worst. Without Jackson, the plant would surely be closed or relocated.

But Rusty and Donnetta didn't raise any fools. Their daughter walked in and kept the company going. Turns out she was not a betting woman, and that is just what National needed She came to her son's trial, sat behind him, occasionally crying, like when her son talked about trying to keep up with the other kids in his social circle. She did not attend her husband's trial; by then she had obtained a divorce. That had made Stephanie sad.

"I feel sorry for him, for Jackson. He lost everything he was so desperate to hold onto: his family, his standing in the community, his freedom. The last thing I heard was that his wife—ex-wife—was going out with Sean Spence." They had all hashed and rehashed this conversation, so she knew what John's response would be.

"How can you feel sorry for someone who killed three people? One accidentally, and two intentionally? And don't forget what he was willing to do to Augustine Morales. That guy could have found himself dead or in jail for life! I know it worked out OK, but it could have been bad."

Mick looked around the table and thought about endings and beginnings. He had gotten a call from one of his buddies about a new program for Sky Marshals. It was his dream job, combining his love of flying and his experience with law enforcement. He was glad to

314 JENNIFER FARRELL VOSS

have the trials ended, the guilty verdicts adding up to Jackson never getting out.

Too bad the cancer hadn't gotten him before he killed. Mick had heard that he was using his illness as an excuse for what he had done. The cancer had made him act in ways that he wouldn't have otherwise, still trying to salvage his ruined reputation, an affront to cancer sufferers. He had listened to the arguments about Jackson's degree of evil many of times without adding his own thoughts. Now he did.

"No, it wasn't three people, it was four. Once Harlan Tucker started talking about the note, Jackson knew his secret wasn't safe. The housekeeper had told him that Tucker was calling out about the letter. He was desperate to keep the truth about Charlie from coming out. In his mind, Tucker had already potentially talked to two people. Jackson had to stop him before there were more. Easiest thing in the world, to hold a pillow over the old man's face. No one would question the death of someone in hospice. In fact, no one did.

"It'd be impossible to prove, but I know he did it. He killed the man who had helped him and protected him all those years. And now he has pancreatic cancer. So yeah, I feel sorry for him, too. He'll have to live the rest of his limited life with those four people on his conscience. And he'll have to answer for what he did in the next world."

ACKNOWLEDGMENTS

I am deeply grateful to Barb Zerby, the volunteer coordinator at St. Thomas Hospice, for taking a chance on the idea of pet therapy for her patients. The dedication of the nurses and staff at St. Thomas Hospice inspired me to write *The Reluctant Robber.*

I would like to thank Kelsey Grode, an excellent editor, who encouraged me to tell my story by saying more with fewer words. Her enthusiasm for the project never wavered. My heartfelt thanks to Clint Greenleaf for his knowledgeable guidance and to Sheila Parr for her amazing design work.

I am forever grateful to my children, Anna Lee Wahls and Mitchell Voss, for becoming my cheerleaders and, in a reversal of roles, encouraging me to pursue my dream. My husband, Bill Voss, was not only my first reader but also my biggest fan. I hope it will always be so!